ISLE OF CHAOS

GOLDEN AGE TALES

SOPHIE & CHRIS BROUSSEAU

Published by Maple Lion Fiction
Unit 64956, PO Box 6945,
London, W1A 6US

Print edition ISBN 978-1-8384372-0-6
E-book ISBN 978-1-8384372-1-3

Edited & Typeset by: Claire Jennison

Cover image & chapter headings designed & created by: Sara Oliver
Designs

Super special thanks to Andrew Symons for his invaluable feedback and
direction.

A CIP catalogue record for this title is available from the British Library.

Visit us online at www.maplelionfiction.com

CONTENTS

ABOUT THE BOOK

Isle of Chaos was originally released as a five-part novella serial (Pirates of Nassau), but it was always our intention to release it as a full novel.

The story is set in the city of Nassau during the early 1700s and follows the lives of six colorful characters, during a time when pirates greatly outnumbered the local residents on this once tranquil isle.

Whilst set in the Golden Age of Piracy the language we have chosen to use is modernized. Inspired by the complex morally gray characters of The Sopranos, the adventure and fun of Pirates of the Caribbean and the story structure of a good Seinfeld episode (where a characters seemingly arbitrary actions create a chain reaction for the other cast members). **Isle of Chaos** combines our love of storytelling in all its different formats be it TV, video games, movies or books.

Warning! This book contains both violent scenes and explicit language. It is intended for mature audiences only.

To each other and for each other – always.

POOR OR RICH, DEATH MAKES US ALL EQUAL.

German Proverb

ISAAC CARVER

It was a bad day to lose a friend. Isaac panicked. His eyes searched the bloodthirsty crowd for Popino. A glimpse of his tanned cheeky face or frilly white shirt was all he needed to reassure himself he was still alive, but it was impossible to see anything through the hordes of eager spectators. A ravenous appetite for destruction hung in the air as the crowd swarmed the wooden platform in Nassau's center square. Townsfolk pushed one another out the way, desperate to score a front row view of the morning's events. Isaac copped a shove to the back and tumbled to the ground. Why had they tried to steal from a pirate captain today of all days? Isaac scrambled to his feet and brushed the dirt from his hands. There was still no sign of Popino.

He ducked and weaved his way forward and caught sight of the condemned Captain Kidd, slumped on the gallows with a tight noose around his neck. Next to him, Isaac spied a tall frightening figure who he assumed to be the executioner. His hooded, faceless black robes sent a chill down Isaac's spine. Another much smaller, round, balding man stood by them clutching a scroll. Isaac recognized him from the tavern. He was the town chaplain and a drunk.

"For we must all appear before the judgment seat of Christ!" the chaplain shouted in his stern and righteous tone.

Isaac was now wedged in to the thick of the crowd. He couldn't move a muscle. He needed to find Popino but his chances of that grew slimmer by the second. His eyes cast to the platform above.

The captain appeared to be irritated by the chaplain's words. "You'll never find it all!" Captain Kidd shouted through labored breaths. His eyes were shut. His body visibly thin and weakened. "You may have found some, but there are still thirty-thousand doubloons buried that'll never see the light of day!"

The crowd gasped and chatter spread like wildfire. "Thirty thousand?" everyone uttered at once.

Isaac stared ahead without blinking. For a moment he forgot about his friend. That was more doubloons than anyone in Nassau could ever dream of, and they were buried somewhere, just waiting to be found.

"Quiet down!" the chaplain ordered. The crowd edged closer and closer to the platform. A wash of panic spread across the chaplain's face.

Kidd cackled. "Have fun with them!" He spat at the chaplain.

"Now!" the balding chaplain commanded and brought down his hand with vigour. He rocked forward a little as he did.

The executioner pulled the lever and the floor beneath Kidd disappeared.

The crowd gasped.

Isaac couldn't look away. The noose tightened around Kidd's neck. The gallows creaked as his scrawny body swung back and forth. Kidd kicked and wiggled his legs. Isaac held his breath as he watched what bit of color the captain had left in his face slip away. He waited for the chaplain's final word. It would be any moment now. Instead, Kidd's body hit the deck. He rolled from side to side and laughed hysterically. The well-used rope had snapped.

"It's a sign from God!" someone in the crowd yelled.

"Nonsense! Nonsense," the chaplain cried as the hubbub of chatter in the crowd grew deafening.

"You'll never find it!" Kidd screamed.

The crowd edged closer as the executioner stepped in, scooped Kidd up and hurled him back onto the platform. The captain, too weak to put up a fight, lay awaiting his fate as the executioner held him under one arm and tied a fresh noose around his neck. He wasn't taking any chances this time and stood over Kidd as he shoved him down the hole again. This time, the rope took. Kidd convulsed for a few moments, until his lifeless body hung still.

"That's it everyone, you may all return to your lives knowing we are safe once more," the chaplain said with his nose in the air.

Isaac stood dumbfounded. Townsfolk bustled past. "Thirty thousand doubloons," he said under his breath.

As the square emptied out, talk of the buried treasure was on everyone's lips and it would be the only thing anyone spoke of for weeks to come.

"Isaac!" Popino ran toward him. His white shirt was dirtied and torn.

"You're not dead!" Isaac grinned at his best friend. "Did you see it? The rope snapped!"

"I missed it but..." Popino looked over his shoulder. "We scored big!" He waved a metal seamed, tan colored cloth pouch at Isaac. The contents jangled. "Hold this, I've just got to fix myself up. I saw a pretty girl over there."

Isaac rolled his eyes and took the pouch. Popino was only two years older than Isaac but already the girls wanted him. Isaac brushed his hand over the metal seams and gave the weighty pouch a shake.

Popino dusted off his shirt and tightened his ponytail of dark brown hair. "How do I look?"

"Never mind that!" Isaac lowered his voice to a whisper. "Was that a captain we stole from? This pouch is heavy!"

Popino pressed his lips together and nodded. "Something else fell in too—a piece of paper."

"Then let's go to the coop and look at it! Forget about the girl!" Isaac tugged on Popino's arm.

"Okay, but just this once and just because that pouch is very heavy." Popino rubbed his hands together and grinned.

Isaac and Popino made their way back to the tavern where Isaac spent most of his time. Unbeknownst to Popino, the tavern (or rather the tavern's chicken coop) was where Isaac lived and had been living for the past five years. He brought Popino here often but made out as if it were just a hiding spot for them.

"Let's see what we got." Popino clapped his hands together. The boys made their way into the chicken coop and found a spot to perch whilst they divvied up their finds. Popino held his breath in anticipation as Isaac opened the bag and dumped the contents onto the hay covered floor. Isaac counted the coins, splitting the nine reale evenly enough; five for Pino and four for himself. He held up a thick golden coin in the air and stared at its magnificence.

"I've never held a doubloon before. Have you?" Isaac said and rubbed his thumb over the coin.

"Yes, my parents have some. I don't have any of my own though."

Isaac scrunched his face up as he contemplated their predicament. Truth be told he wanted to keep the doubloon for himself, but he knew they had both worked equally hard for it.

"How do you want to split it?"

Popino smiled. "Why don't you keep this one, and I'll get the next one."

"No, I can't... we both earned this one." Isaac shook his head and held out the coin to Popino.

"Yeah, but I think you can make better use of it. I'll probably try to buy myself a whore!" Popino winked and pushed his friend's hand away.

"You're obsessed!" Isaac laughed. He knew Popino only said this to make him feel better. Humbled, Isaac accepted the coin and tucked the glinting beauty away into his pocket for safe keeping. "Thanks, Pino." Isaac nudged his friend with affection and grinned from ear to ear. "Now let's look at whatever this is." He reached into the pouch and pulled out the folded paper, placing it on the ground. He unfolded the corners one by one, trying not to tear any of the edges. Etched in black was a map which showed the islands all around Nassau with Xs marked over half of them. Isaac pointed to an almost illegible scribble in the corner of the map. "What does that say?"

Popino picked up the tattered paper with care and held it to his face, squinting to decipher the terrible writing. Isaac admired Popino's ability to read, a luxury few could afford. "It's not very clear but I think it says: *C. Kidd treasure not found.*" Popino turned to Isaac. "What does that mean?"

"Kidd? Treasure not found?" Isaac's eyes grew wide.

Popino stayed silent, mouthing the words.

"Pino, that's who was on the gallows!" Isaac sprang to his feet. The chickens flapped and fled at the sudden movement.

"Was it? But it says treasure not found so it can't be his." Popino rubbed at his chin.

After a few moments, Isaac blurted out the only explanation that made sense to him. "Maybe the Xs aren't marking the treasure, they're marking where he's already searched! Not Kidd... the captain we stole from!" Isaac jumped on the spot and clapped his hands. "Pino, I think I'm right about this. This map has to be a record of where that captain's already searched. He must have known about Kidd's treasure already." Isaac's heart soared with excitement.

"You think?" Popino scratched the back of his head.

"It's the only thing that makes sense to me. I can't believe this. We should keep this safe." Isaac spoke at a rate of knots as he folded the paper and placed it in his back pocket. "I'm going to start marking the places that others have searched. I hear all kinds of stories in the tavern, I'm sure some of them will talk about where they've explored."

"Okay. Excellent plan." Popino beamed as he gathered his coins and tossed them in his metal seamed pouch. "I've got to go home for dinner, but let's meet up tomorrow." He moved a chicken to one side. "We're going to be rich! I can feel it!"

He scurried out of the coop and gave Isaac a wave.

"Bye, Pino." Isaac took a seat on the dirty hay covered floor. He crossed his legs and propped his head up with his hands. He wished he had a home to have dinner in. He pulled out the doubloon and traced his fingers over it. He closed his eyes and dreamed of finding thirty-thousand more. Pino's right! We will be rich, he thought. He imagined all the things he would buy with the treasure. Fine clothes, feather pillows and a bed, plus there would be food on the table every night. All he needed to do was listen to people's stories in the tavern. Might as well make a start now, Isaac thought.

He dusted off his hay covered pants and scuttled out the coop without looking up, bumping headfirst into someone. "Sorry!" Startled, he shoved the coin back in his pocket.

Isaac looked up to see his father standing before him, notably drunk and swaying. For a moment, it was as if he didn't recognize him. "Son! There you are." His eyes were near shut and his breath stank of liquor. Isaac wondered if he could get drunk off the fumes. His father scowled as he rocked back and forth.

Isaac sensed he was moments away from a beating but had something that might brighten his father's mood. He reached into his pocket and produced the coin. "Dad! Look what I found!" He held up the glinting gold beauty and beamed, eager for approval. "This can help us," Isaac said and waited for a smile.

"A doubloon! Where'd ya find this?" Isaac's father picked him up. "You did good, boy." His eyes lit up as he admired the thick golden coin, and for a brief moment he seemed happy.

"We can get somewhere to stay?" Isaac said.

His father's face dropped. "You were planning on

keeping this for yourself, weren't ya?" He snatched the coin and dropped Isaac to the ground.

"No!" Isaac's heart sank as his father's usual sullen, mean spirited demeanor returned. Why did he never believe good of him?

His father's eyes narrowed and his lip curled. "Son, you owe me. What are you good for in this world? Nothing!"

His words cut through Isaac like a knife.

Isaac's father fixated on the coin. He tucked it away and turned his attention to his son.

Isaac's heartbeat pounded in his chest. Tears welled in his eyes. He wanted his lip to stop trembling but it wouldn't.

Isaac's father grabbed him by the scruff of the neck. "It's because of you that I'm alone. I don't know why I chose you over your mother, but I did, and I was wrong!" He pushed Isaac into the coop and smashed the makeshift door shut. "I won't make the same mistake twice."

Isaac scrambled in the dark. Outside he heard his father dragging something in front of the door. "Dad? Please! Please let me out!" he pleaded in between sobs. He tried the door but something blocked the way.

"You're dead to me, boy! The way it should have been."

Isaac hammered his fists on the door and tears poured from his eyes. He slumped down on the ground. The sound of his father's stumbling footsteps faded. Isaac squeezed his eyes tight and covered his ears to shut out the world.

Hours passed before the tavern keeper found him, huddled alone in the chicken coop, his dirty face stained with tears and just nine reale and a map to his name.

POPINO BELTRAME

10 YEARS LATER

"Papa, when will Mama come back?" little Rose Beltrame asked. Popino's heart sank. He had tried his best to explain what happened, but at five years old, her young mind still struggled to grasp the finality of death. Popino held her tight, the thought of Rose being a part of Elizabeth brought him comfort.

"Rose, I already told you, Mama isn't going to come back. Remember? Now, why don't you go and clean your room, get everything ready for tonight."

"Alright, Papa." Rose kissed her father on the cheek and ran off to her bedroom.

Popino stood in their dining room and admired the hand-crafted furniture which filled it. He brushed his hand along the solid mahogany dining table and remembered the day he bought it from one of the most famous carpenters in Nassau. It had been a surprise for Elizabeth. They were newlyweds then and life was good. His gaze shifted to the charming brick fireplace where a family portrait hung; Elizabeth's smile was so filled with love. He let out a loud sigh. Sickening guilt and sadness filled his heart every time he thought of her. "I'll make it up to you," he said to no one. "I'll raise our daughter right. Make you proud."

"Sir, I'm here."

Popino, still lost in the painting, jumped at the sound of the voice. His face flushed as he attempted to compose himself.

"Clara, please come in."

"Was I disturbing you? I'm sorry, sir. I—"

"No not at all, please come in," Popino rushed his words out. "I'll be late for work if I don't leave now." The thought of escaping to the docks came as a welcome relief. "The devil makes work for idle hands, Clara!" Popino let out an awkward laugh as he walked to the dining room cabinet. "Let me get you your advance for the week."

The cabinet was an entertainer's dream, overflowing with plates and glassware. He shook his head at the thought of all the coin spent on filling it, and whilst it seemed useless to Popino, he couldn't bear to part with it. He opened the bottom cupboard and pulled out an embossed golden coffer which he used to store his coins. The key sat in his pocket with a small stone attached for safe keeping.

He unlocked the heavy gold box and tallied the contents—thirty-five doubloons and two-hundred reale. He grabbed five reale for Clara, and ten for the trip to work. "Here you go." The coins clinked as he dropped them into her outstretched palm. He locked the coffer and sat it back in the cupboard.

"Thank you, sir. Have a good day at work." Clara gave a polite nod as she pocketed her weekly payment. She didn't smile much but Popino understood why. Her life was hard and the only thing that hadn't been taken from her was her son, Lucas. Popino recalled the gruesome story of her journey to Nassau on a slave ship. The Spaniards often brought in slaves from West Africa and many, like Clara, worked for the wealthy of Nassau in the hope of earning their freedom. Clara had not yet earned hers, but Popino always did what he could to help with that.

"I'm off. Have a good day, Rose."

"Bye, Papa!" she shouted from her bedroom.

Popino closed the door behind him and stepped out onto the roughly paved street. He raised his eyebrows and gave a small nod of his head to acknowledge the street guard as he strolled past. Few streets in Nassau had their own set of guards but as the number of pirates grew, the rich insisted.

He made his usual detour and stopped by a tall building just streets away from his house. It had been a pretty family home once upon a time but now an air of sadness surrounded it. The paint peeled from every surface and the window shutters hung off, rotten from the salty air and lack of care.

Popino approached the weather-beaten wooden door with caution. He gave his usual soft knock but no one answered. He pushed a little and the door creaked open. Coming here was always a risk but that was part of the fun. He checked around to make sure nobody was watching when, to his left, he spotted an old, bearded man with an eye-patch crouched next to a handful of paintings, staring straight at him.

Popino twinged with annoyance. He just wanted to go inside but prying eyes around here were never good. He swaggered over to the odd old man. If he played it cool, maybe he'd get a better price. "How much is it going to cost for you to go somewhere else?" he asked and stroked his chin.

"Why would I leave? This is where I make the most coin." The old man glared and spat in a small jar beside him.

"I haven't seen you here before." Popino narrowed his eyes in suspicion. The street was not typically busy but then again those that did pass by were exceedingly wealthy.

The old man shrugged. "Maybe you haven't looked."

"Yes, yes. How much then?" Popino asked and tapped his foot.

"Well, let's see. I've only got these four paintings left to sell. Why don't you just buy all of them? Then I won't have any reason to stay." The old man grinned.

"Just name your price." Popino's frustrations mounted. He just wanted to go inside but couldn't afford to be seen.

"Twenty reale."

"Twenty! I only have ten on me, will you take that much and stay away for the entire week?"

"Deal." The old man jumped up, grabbed the reale and ran.

Popino gathered the paintings but couldn't shake the nagging feeling that he had just been ripped off. He swung around, eager to finally venture into the house, only to find himself face to face with a well-dressed, ruddy cheeked gentleman. Popino tried to step around him but the flustered gentleman blocked his way.

"Excuse me, sir, but what are you doing with my paintings?" he asked as he tried to catch his breath. He stuck his hands on his hips and glared at Popino.

"Your paintings? I just bought them from some old man." Popino realised he'd been had and shook his head.

"Yes! These are my paintings!" the gentleman snapped as he snatched them from Popino's arms. "I ought to have you both hanged!"

Popino released his grip on the paintings and threw up his hands. "I didn't know, did I?"

"I truly do not care! These belong to me!" The gentleman tucked the artworks under his arm and marched away.

A rather unfortunate start to the day, Popino thought to himself. Time to change that. He rubbed his hands together and made a dash for the door. He ran up the stairs taking two at a time. "Darling, I'm home!" He stood in the bedroom doorway with his chest puffed out.

"Do come in." Eva beckoned to her lover and reclined on the bed. She pulled a thin sheet over her soft, silky skin. Popino could see her nipples pointing through it and it drove him wild. The front of his pants tightened. He pulled his shirt over his head and tossed it aside. Eva stared at him and bit her lip. "What took you so long? You knew I'd be waiting." She pouted and threw off the sheet, exposing what Popino loved most about her.

"Oh, I'm sorry, darling." Popino kicked off his boots and tore off his pants. "I'm sure I can make it up to you." He dove onto the bed and kissed her thigh. "Is he gone for the day?"

"He is, mon cher, we have all the time in the world," Eva said in her charming French accent.

She had travelled to Nassau long ago with her husband Lucien, whose reputation for brutality preceded him. Popino recalled the story of the dismembered man found just last month. Apparently, he had borrowed money from Lucien and fallen behind on his payments. His wife found her husband's body later that day, laid out in pieces on the bed. The story around town was that Lucien and his men tore the man limb from limb. Now is not the time to think of such things, Popino told himself and pushed the ghastly story to the back of his mind as he pulled Eva in close. Their lips locked and the fire between them sparked as they rolled around on the bed, lost in lust.

Popino lay next to Eva, out of breath, his face flushed. He gazed over at her with fondness. His time with her was one of the best parts of his day, aside from seeing his daughter. "That was everything I wanted and more, my darling." Popino sat up in bed and slapped Eva on the thigh.

"You were magnifique, as always, mon cher." Eva rolled toward him and ran her hand down his back. "Maybe we could—"

"Shh." Popino held his finger to his lips. "What was that?" His eyes grew wide. Outside the bedroom door the floorboards creaked. He looked at Eva. The colour drained from her face and her hands shook as she clutched the sheet and sunk behind it. The bedroom door flew open with such force that it smashed back into the wall and broke the hinge.

"What the hell is going on here?" A stocky mean-faced man stood in the doorway, his face red with fury. His hands were wrapped around the biggest, shiniest sword Popino had ever seen. "How could you! With him!" the stocky man yelled. Spit sprayed from his mouth and the veins in his face bulged.

Popino sprang to his feet. "I'm sorry, friend, you know how it is. When you ignore a woman, she'll find a better man." Popino rushed to button his pants, fumbling more than his mouth made out. He made a dash for the window and smacked the dusty curtains aside. He tapped his hand along the base of the sill until it struck the familiar blade he had hidden there long ago, in the event that Lucien ever showed up.

"Just how long have you been sleeping with him?" Lucien demanded as he stomped toward the bedside opposite Popino. He towered over Eva, every inch of him shaking.

Before she could open her mouth to answer, Popino held up his blade, shaking and pointing it in Lucien's direction. "Honestly, it wasn't very hard to best you considering what I've heard about the size of your cock." An arrogant smirk spread across Popino's face. He stood there shirtless flexing his bronzed, rippling muscles.

Eva clutched at the sheets, covering her naked body, her mouth agape in horror.

"You whore!" Lucien screamed in Eva's face and smashed his sword into her thigh with such force that it pierced the mattress beneath her. She howled in agony. "You're worthless to me now," he bellowed as he yanked his blade out and attempted to strike her again.

Without further ado, Popino burst into action, blocking Lucien's blade. "You coward! You should never lay a finger on a woman." He leapt onto the bed and punched Lucien in the face, who stumbled backwards with the blow. Popino jumped down. His eyes met with Eva's. They were dizzy with pain. Blood poured from her thigh, saturating the bed sheets.

Popino panicked. If Eva died and Lucien lived, Popino would be painted as her murderer. Lucien would make sure he hanged for it. Afterall, Lucien was in bed with some very powerful men and Popino, on the other hand, was only in bed with their women.

Lucien recovered and lunged at Popino across the bed. His huge blade nearly reached him but not quite. Popino pressed his back into the wall and looked for an exit.

"Please, get help!" Eva cried.

"Shut it! Whore!" Lucien yelled. He ran around to Popino. "You're a dead man!" He rushed at Popino with his blade, hacking and slashing toward him. Popino dodged and blocked each blow. He leapt onto the bed and Lucien followed.

"There's not enough room for all of us!" Popino kicked at Lucien's legs and gave him a shove. The pair both lost their balance and tumbled to the floor. Popino wasted no time. He pushed himself up and ran back to the other side of the bed. His eyes connected with Eva's. The blood drenched mattress suggested she didn't have long.

Lucien hauled himself back to standing. He brought his sword up over his head and swiped it across the top of the nearby dresser. Trinkets and vases shattered into smithereens. He scowled at Popino and his breath grew heavy.

"You look a little tired, friend, you know... if you were to lay with your wife a bit more, maybe you could last longer in a fight." Popino couldn't help himself. "And from what I've heard you could stand to last a little longer in bed too."

Popino stood beside Eva, the bed separating them from her raging husband.

A furious Lucien threw down his sword. "Fight me like a man then! C'mon! Weapons down!" Lucien bobbed from one foot to another.

"You'll have to catch me first!" Popino said and lured

him over to the window. Its dusty, green curtains now pushed aside, allowing the searing sunlight to stream in. Popino nicked the fabric loops with his blade and the heavy cloth tumbled down around Lucien. Popino backed away toward the bed. He had to kill this man. There was no other choice. Lucien huffed and puffed his way out of the heavy dusty fabric. Popino knew exactly what to do. He scrambled onto the bed next to Eva. Lucien hurled himself toward them. Popino took his blade and placed it into Eva's hands. He grabbed her wrists and squeezed them together to hold it. Lucien leapt open armed onto the guilty lovers and, as he did, Popino thrust the blade into his stomach, slitting it wide open over Eva. Blood gushed out and Eva recoiled in horror as the crushing weight of her husband fell upon her.

"I can't believe... how could you..." Eva lay still, bleeding out as her husband faded away into the afterlife.

Popino stood at the foot of the bed, His mind raced through every eventuality, but it all came back to Rose. He couldn't leave her an orphan and if anyone suspected him of this that is exactly what she'd be. Even if he was to try and save Eva, one of them would be blamed for Lucien's murder but if he walked away now, no-one would be the wiser. They'd just assume it was a violent dispute between husband and wife that got a little out of hand. He considered the plausibility of the latter as he scanned the carnage in the room.

"Please mon cher... please help me," Eva whispered as the crushing weight of Lucien's body smothered her. Tears ran down her face and rolled off her beautiful, pouty lips that had pleasured Popino countless times.

"I'm sorry, my dear, I never meant for any of this." Popino rubbed his palms over his face. The choice was clear. He walked over to where Eva lay. "Maybe your spirit will return to God." He grabbed Lucien's hand and closed it tight around the blade. "I did love you, I hope you know that," he whispered into her ear as he thrust the blade deep into her neck, killing her instantly.

Popino squeezed his eyes shut. He felt sick to his stomach. What had he done? He forced himself to look. Eva and Lucien's bodies lay in a heap. Blood-drenched and limp. He wiped his face with his shirt and tried to compose himself. Every inch of the room was splattered in blood. He crept over the upturned furniture to check no trace of himself was left behind when a knock on the door stopped him in his tracks. Popino froze.

CAPTAIN CROW

"What do you mean, they don't trust us?" Crow snapped as he paced the room.

"The men, sir... they're starting to think you can't deliver. It's been six full months since they've seen any pay, and from what I hear trouble's a-brewing," Nelson explained in his matter of fact tone with a hint of apprehension. He was a ruddy faced pudgy fellow, tall as he was round with a sharp mind and a loyal heart. His ever-logical thought process was indispensable to Crow, and not only had it kept them out of a lot of trouble but it had helped them to score many riches along the way.

Crow paced faster and muttered under his breath. His weathered, black, captain's jacket swayed with each stride and caused the nearby lantern to flicker. He thought his men appreciated the riches he'd already made them. He paused and scratched at his chin through his thick graying beard. Greed breeds greed, he brooded. "Any idea what we should do?"

"Well, I've been doing a lot of thinking, sir, and I figure the best way to appease them would be to find some coin and pay them. Just a bit, but enough to restore their faith in you." Nelson stood with his hands on his hips and nodded. "Once they have a taste of that reale again, they'll stick with us."

Crow stroked his beard as he considered Nelson's proposition. To the public eye the captain was an angry, unpredictable man to be feared but to Nelson, his long time friend and loyal quartermaster, he was both a kind and generous man. They stood within a weathered shack, just outside the hustle of Nassau's center. It had been thrown together long ago with off cuts of ship wood. Nothing fancy but it was home, at least on land anyway.

"And where do we intend to get this here reale?" Crow crossed his arms and stared at the floor. Burning hot anger bubbled up within him. "If only we still had the map! That stupid boy!" He slammed his hands down on the small cedar wood table which sat in the middle of the room. His eyes blazed with rage, fists now clenched and shaking.

Nelson sighed. "You mean Popino, sir?"

"Of course I mean Popino. If it weren't for that weasel, we'd be waist deep in Captain Kidd's doubloons by now. The men would be rich, we'd be rich, everyone would be happy." Crow stomped his foot.

Every time they walked by the square he remembered that wretched day. It was bad enough they'd got Kidd but then that stupid boy bumped into him. He had relentlessly pursued every avenue to find out the boy's identity, or rather Nelson had. It had taken years to find him and by the time they did Popino had grown up, married and become rather wealthy. Not the type to go missing without a trace as had been the plan. They'd even ransacked his fancy house but to no avail. There was no trace of that map anywhere.

"Nelson, what happened to all the doubloons from that job? The big one."

"You mean the Thiggins heist, sir?"

"Yes exactly!" Crow's eyes lit up. "We scored big on that one, didn't we?"

"We did, sir, but that was about three years ago now and all that coin has gone."

"Right. Well, what about..." Crow stroked his beard. "That other one, the one we did for Vella." He patted his forefinger on his lips as he considered how long it had been. "That can't have been more than a year ago?" Crow shook his head as he recalled their escapades. "Remember there was that man, with that ridiculous green wig!" His eyes crinkled at the thought.

"Oh yes, sir, that was quite something. Vella ended up taking most of those coins though."

"Oh, blast and dammit, Nelson!" Crow clenched his fists and punched the air. "We wouldn't have had to keep doing all these stupid jobs if we had just held on to that map!"

Nelson cocked his head and sighed.

"I can't stand this. I need a drink, maybe we'll get an idea at the tavern. Maybe I can whore myself," Crow said.

"I'd buy you, sir."

Crow grumbled and scrunched up his face. The corners of his mouth turned down as he let out an exasperated sigh.

"Come on, to the tavern we go!" Nelson said and jigged his arm.

It was hard to believe it was still morning as patrons spilled out onto the street outside The Rusty Trombone. The tavern's reputation for debauchery and the most potent bumbo in town meant that it was full to bursting most days.

Crow and Nelson strode through the door and were greeted by a sea of inebriated men who stumbled around spilling booze onto the sticky stone floor as busty corseted waitresses moved from table to table, serving up drinks. Crow's eyes shot to their corner table where a rather sloshed and scrawny weakling of a man sat in his seat.

"Move, you're in our spot." Crow placed both hands on the table and tapped his index fingers with impatience. The scrawny drunk leaned his head back and peered through bloodshot eyes. Crow let out an infuriated sigh. "What's your name, boy?"

"Luc," the man slurred, as he swayed back and forth in his seat. He struggled to sit, let alone stand up to move from Crow's seat.

"Well Luc, nice to meet you, but you're in my seat." Crow glared.

"Oh, okay." Luc hiccupped and held his hand over his mouth. His eyes shut. His chest heaved.

"Move!" Crow snapped.

Luc hiccupped once again and erupted like a volcano, spewing out waves of vomit all over the table. The foul smelling, brown liquid dripped down onto Crow's favorite seat and pooled on the surrounding floor. "It's all yours, sir," Luc said. Vomit dripped from his chin.

The tavern fell silent. Crow had a reputation for being unpredictable and prone to violence. For these reasons, people respected him and knew better than to test his patience. Only one person would come off worse and it would never be him.

He scanned the tavern for his men who were now standing up, waiting to see what he would do next. All eyes were on him and the question on everyone's faces was clear. Would he continue to uphold his reputation—a man to be feared—or were the rumors true? Was he getting soft in his old age? Crow knew what needed to happen, but this was the part of the job he hated. He was never cruel out of desire; it was simply expected of a captain. His father's words rang in his ears, 'To be a pirate captain one must command respect and to be respected one must be feared." Crow had dreamed of becoming a renowned pirate for as long as he could remember and whilst he'd made it to captain, he'd never gained the sort of notoriety that someone like Kidd had.

"Sir, people are staring at us," Nelson whispered. Crow snapped out of his thoughts. All eyes were fixed on him, eager for the morning's entertainment to begin.

Luc stumbled to his feet and swayed next to the vomit drenched seat with a gormless grin spread across his face, oblivious to the scene unfolding.

Crow grabbed him by the throat and thrust him up off the ground. His legs dangled in the air as his breath grew short. At six foot four without his boots, Crow towered over most men and Luc was no exception.

As Luc struggled for air Crow released his grip, allowing him to draw a single breath. Then he tightened it again and shoved him into the wall. Vomit dripped down onto Crow's hand. The overpowering stench made his stomach churn though he dared not show weakness to the bloodthirsty crowd.

"How dare you!" Crow shouted, loud enough for

everyone to hear. He needed to put on a show for his men, now more than ever.

Luc tried to speak, and Crow released his grip enough for him to splutter, "I'm sorry." Chunks flew from his mouth as he spoke.

"I don't care how sorry you are. Nobody sits at my table except me. It's reserved." Crow pointed with his other hand to the table, where a now vomit covered rough carving of a black crow was whittled in the wooden top.

"Everyone knows it, I'm sure you were warned." Crow smashed Luc's frail frame into the wall. "No excuses."

Nelson stepped over to Crow and spoke in a low voice. "You'll have to kill him, sir, to show the men you haven't faltered." Nelson handed Crow his blade and gave him a nod. It was a custom-made dagger, with a crow on the handle. The very sight of it evoked vivid childhood memories for Crow. Growing up, he had loved nothing more than sitting outside watching the birds all day long. Crows had always been his favorite. He admired their intelligence, the way they sought vengeance and how they never forgot a face.

Crow brought his lips to Luc's ear. "I'm sorry, Luc, but I have to do this." He thrust the blade into his chest. Blood gushed from the wound and spilled onto the tavern floor. Crow stabbed again, this time aiming a little lower. Blood and guts spilled out onto the floor. The tavern remained silent as Crow dropped Luc's body like a sack of potatoes. He made a fist and cracked his knuckles, then handed the dagger back to Nelson and stood by his table, his head held high.

The busty waitresses rushed over to clean up the mess, which was commonplace in the tavern. Nassau had grown a reputation for violence and bloodshed over the years and most of it happened under the roof of The Rusty Trombone. The volume of chatter rose once again as the thirsty patrons continued about their business.

Crow ordered two glasses of rum as Nelson sunk into the seat across from him. Bumbo wasn't going to cut it today.

"Sir, are you okay?"

Crow swallowed his rum and nodded.

"That might have just bought you a few votes." Nelson tried to catch his gaze.

"You said trust was being questioned not that we're heading into a vote. Ugh, this is bad."

"Yes, I believe in a week's time they would like to call for a vote."

"And who's my opposition?"

"I believe it's Johnny Ives, one of our best swordsmen."

"Ives. Pfft. He's been around just a few years. I trained him, taught him how to fight properly. Guess this is the thanks I get."

"You know how these men are, sir, they win a few fights and think they have what it takes to be captain. Unfortunately, though, it's maybe looking like he might win." Nelson fumbled over his words. "He has more than half of the votes from what I've gathered."

"How are we going to fix this, Nelson? Don't our men know how rich they'll be if they stick with us?" Crow slammed his fist on the table.

"They do, or at least they know what you tell them, sir, but it's been six months with nothing. And Johnny... well, he's been starting rumors." Nelson hesitated. "He says you're past it, sir, might die at any moment."

"Me? I'm as healthy as a clam." Crow took a sip of his drink and looked down at his bloodstained hands. Sure, he was getting older, but not weaker. He cast his eyes over Nelson, who had been with him since the beginning, even before he had gotten his first ship. His hair was gray and thinning, and his pudgy face crinkled.

"We are getting old, aren't we Nelson?"

"We are, but as you have just demonstrated, sir, we are not weak." Nelson took a gulp of rum as he leaned on the table and put his hand to his chin. "It's hard to believe we don't have any coin left at all. We just need a bit for the men."

"How much?"

"Maybe forty doubloons, total?"

"Forty doubloons? That's a lot, Nelson. I don't have it. You know I put everything I get back into the crew."

"Of course, sir. It's just, I think if we paid some of them, we'd have their vote. We don't have to pay everyone right now but say Victor? He'd be able to get us about ten votes out of the total eighty. I'd say you have about fifteen right now, so that would bring you to twenty-five."

"Is there anyone else we can pay?"

"Richard's group has about five men, and to win their votes all they would need is a few nights down the whore house."

Crow shook his head and placed his finger and thumb on his eyelids, pushing them in. "Yep, so we're not just talking about a few reale are we. Where are we going to get it?" He was beyond frustrated and hated the thought of his men distrusting him. At the same time, he couldn't blame them. He would feel the same way in their shoes.

Crow's train of thought was interrupted as the tavern door burst open, and an inebriated man staggered through it. He wore a blue leather captain's jacket and looked like he hadn't washed all year, though his ruggedly handsome face certainly distracted from that. Crow didn't recognize the man, so he must not have been a reputable captain, if he even was one at all.

The drunk stumbled over his own feet into the bar, jumped onto the first table he saw, and shouted, "Good morning, everyone!"

Crow peered down at his near empty glass. It was still just morning and he'd already murdered someone. Not the start to the day he had hoped for.

"Cheers! To good times, good friends and good—" The man fell backwards and hit the ground hard. He lay there stunned for a few seconds before getting back up.

"Nelson, who is that drunken idiot?"

"Him? That's Isaac Carver."

"Is he a captain?"

"No! Look at the state of him, just dreams of being one. He's an orphan boy that likes the rum a little too much. Grew up in this here drinking house."

Crow observed the man as he wandered from table to table, cracking jokes and attempting to make friends. He appeared to be enjoying himself at least. Isaac eventually made his way over to their table. Crow sighed; he had hoped to avoid another scene today.

"Well, hullo there," Isaac slurred, his breath rancid. He stumbled a little and plonked himself down next to Crow, across from Nelson. "Do you know..." Isaac trailed off and stared at the wall, for what felt like an eternity to Crow.

"Do I know what?" Crow asked with impatience, confused as to what this boy was doing or wanted from them.

"Wait, why is there sick everywhere? Did you throw up?"

Crow glared.

27

"Anyway, do you know... that I could be rich?" Isaac shut his eyes for a moment. "I'm so close." Isaac patted at his pocket and seemed relieved. "Whew, it's still there."

Crow struggled to make sense of what he was talking about.

Isaac clambered to his feet and stuck his hand out. "My name is Isaac Carver, it's a pleasure to meet you, sir." Crow shook his hand in return and nodded.

"I'm having dinner with my friend tonight. He's rich, you know. My friend the bastard. Well, he's not actually a bastard, his parents were married and such, but me, I'm a bastard. In both senses of the word. I'm a bastard because I'm a bastard child, but I'm also a bastard because of what I do."

"Who's your friend?" Nelson enquired in his unassuming manner. Crow often let him do the talking, as he was much more articulate and friendly than him. He was everything Crow couldn't be.

"You know, the rich guy. He had a wife, but she died. Has the child still though." Isaac continued to talk. He was very drunk, and Nelson looked uncomfortable. "His name is Popino. I mean, Popino! What a weird name. I think it's weird." Isaac trailed off and began to stumble away, tripping over the bench and almost falling to the floor again. "Farewell friends, pleasure to meet you both." He walked to another table, looking for a new group of men to torture with his incoherent chatter and his horrible breath.

Nelson's eyes grew bright, and a huge smile spread across his face. He glanced over his shoulder and turned back to Crow. "Sir, did you hear what he said? Popino! He's friends with Popino!" Nelson kept his head low as he spoke.

"So?" Crow said, wiping Isaac's spittle from his face.

"Think about it! He's rich, we need coin and now we have an in."

"That drunken idiot?"

Nelson rolled his eyes. "Trust me on this."

"I bet that weasels still got the map!" Crow balled his fists and squeezed them so tight that they shook.

Nelson sighed. "We don't know that, just forget about the map! What's important is he has coin, sir and now we have access!" Nelson rubbed his hands together.

"You think?" Crow stroked at his beard.

Nelson nodded.

"Looks like we'll avoid a mutiny after all." Crow grinned widely, showing every one of his yellowed front teeth.

"Well, you won't be guaranteed a win, but you'll be closer than you are now." Nelson pushed himself out from the table. "I'll be right back."

Nelson jumped up and walked over to Isaac. He placed his arm on his back as he guided him to a table where they could speak alone.

Crow eyeballed the two of them standing there talking. He drummed his fingers on the table and watched their mouths as they spoke. Isaac seemed to be buying whatever it was Nelson was selling, nodding drunkenly and smirking like a fool. Nelson took out a stick of graphite from his coat pocket and lent on a nearby table. He etched a couple of words, handed Isaac a small piece of paper, shook his hand, and walked back to Crow.

"And?" Crow asked, impatient as ever.

"He said he'll complete our mission and we just have to give him some information in return. I've set up a meeting for when he's a bit more sober."

"What kind of information?"

"I'm not exactly sure, he rambled a lot, but I told him we'd find out whatever it is he needs."

"And he'll steal from his friend?" Crow pressed.

"Well, I didn't actually specify. I set up the meeting and said we'll work it out then. I mentioned a coffer, but just not who it belonged too." Nelson looked away.

"Doesn't matter. Fine work, Nelson! You always come up with a plan. Did you ask him about the map?"

"That falls into the find out later category too, I didn't want to say too much. Anyway, the doubloons are our priority for now, sir."

Nelson's words faded into the background as Crow watched Isaac stagger out the back door of the tavern, singing to himself. He wondered where he was going, but not enough to follow him.

The captain and his quartermaster finished their drinks and headed out the tavern door.

"Where to now, Nelson?"

"We've some business to attend to before we meet with Isaac again. We need to see Vella."

"Oh? I wasn't aware." Crow grew hot under the collar. It had been a while since he had seen Vella, and for good reason.

"It will be fine, sir, it's been a long time."

Crow considered it for a moment. "Yeah, you're right, it has been a while."

Vella's house sat on the outskirts of Nassau. It was quite the trek, but they were spurred on by the prospect of regaining the respect of their men.

They made their way to the dirt road leading out of the city, it was rough underfoot but snaked through beautiful forests of palm trees, making it somewhat more pleasant.

Crow's mind raced. He'd rather die than see Ives take his captaincy. He wasn't captain material.

Click.

"Don't move."

Crow recognized that familiar sound, the sound of a flintlock locking into place, ready to shoot. He did not however recognize that voice.

MOLLY WEAVER

"Get off her immediately." Molly spat her words with venom as she yanked the rampant pig off Sophia by his half-undone pants.

"What the hell? You old cow! I was about to have some fun with this one." The half-naked man leered at Sophia as he licked his lips, face red from excitement.

"Sophia, are you okay?" Molly reached out to help her up.

"I am now, thank you." Her voice was soft.

"I just said I wasn't done yet!" The half-naked man glared at Molly and reached for Sophia's arm.

Molly had met his sort a thousand times before. She blocked the advance and stepped toward him. She was taller than almost every man in Nassau and stronger than most too. "And I told you, get your disgusting hands off her."

He threw a right hook hoping to take Molly by surprise. She shook her head as she blocked the attempted blow and caught his hand with hers, gripping it tight.

"Right, that's it," Molly snapped, her jaw clenched with

rage as she tightened her iron grip on his hand and marched him toward the bedroom door. He struggled, thrashing his arm up and down as he tried to free his limp fingers from her grip.

"Sophia, I'm sorry about all this, I'll be right back."

Molly pushed him through the door and out into the hallway where lustful moans and raucous laughter filled the air. He stumbled forward. "You're a lonely old cow!" he said as he steadied his footing.

Molly cracked her neck to the left, then to the right as anger surged through every inch of her body.

"You're just fucking jealous. No one would want to fuck you!" He glared back at Molly.

The words rang in her ears as she blinked her eyes and stared through him. She needed to snap out of it, but it was too late. She snatched his arm and twisted it with both hands until it snapped.

He fell to the ground clutching his shattered limb. "What the fuck! You fucking monster!" the man cried out.

She stood over him. "You won't be coming back here again, nor will you be pleasuring yourself for a long time, you disgusting, ungrateful pig!"

She knew she had already done enough damage, but she couldn't stop herself. Her temper knew no bounds. She brought her leg down with full force into his side. He wailed in agony and writhed on the ground in pain. She grabbed hold of his long, ratty hair and dragged him toward the well-worn stairs which she planned to kick him down. His body grew limp as it scraped down the hallway. She knew her temper would one day be her undoing. She needed to calm down immediately or she'd kill him and that wasn't good for business.

A moment of clarity came over her. She breathed

deeply and counted in her head. One... two... three. Her thumping heartbeat slowed. She released her grip and discarded the clump of hair gathered in her hand. The broken, battered man squirmed on the ground in agony, yelling obscenities. She distracted herself with thoughts of Daniel and a wind of calm swept over her. She scooped up the angry, floppy armed man and proceeded to walk down the brothel stairs.

The Milky Way was dark and dank, dimly lit by flickering oil lamps. The well-trodden, green painted stairs creaked with every step and led down to the reception area where Molly and others manned the front desk. She had worked in the brothel for what felt like an eternity and over the years the girls had come to see her like a mother.

As she walked down the stairs, incoming patrons gawked at the wailing man in her arms, eager to see who was foolish enough to cause trouble in Vella's place. The regulars all knew so long as they behaved, they would get their pick. Besides, no one wanted to face the wrath of whoever manned the desk that day.

Molly reached the front door and kicked it open revealing the beaming morning sun. The half-naked man now lay still in her arms, limp and pale. As she tossed him out the door into the dirt, sand scattered, creating little clouds of dust. "Leave and don't come back." She wiped her hands clean with her handkerchief and let out a loud sigh as she slammed the door closed.

Molly walked back behind the brothel counter and shook her head. She looked as old as she felt but despite her years she was still as strong as ten men.

She gave a wry smile as she thought of Fugra's words: 'Do what you need to survive in this brutal man's world, rule with fury and trust no one, for even the devil himself was once an angel.' Fugra had been tough on her but she had taken Molly in when she had nothing and no one. There weren't many people Molly cared for in this lifetime, but Fugra had been one.

"Time's nearly up, Molly," Grieves announced as he strode through the brothel door. He was one of few men in Nassau tall enough to look Molly in the eye and wide enough to challenge her. Grieves and Molly had tested their strength many times before, but he was no match for her. She came out on top every time.

"Busy day?" Grieves enquired in his jovial manner as he joined Molly behind the counter.

"Oh, you know, the usual."

"You responsible for that mess outside?" He pointed toward the door. "I saw a lad crawling away from here. Figured that was your work."

"Oh yes. Well, you know how I get sometimes." Molly grew angry again at the very mention of what had happened.

"He's foolish that one, Jacky Boy," Grieves remarked.

"His name's Jacky Boy?" Molly scoffed. That's far too sweet of a name for that disgusting pig, she thought.

"Heh, you're more brutal than I am. I'm surprised these punters still push their luck when you're here. You have a reputation around these parts y'know."

"Good," Molly replied.

The last hour of work flew by and before Molly knew it, she was out the door. She hated being late and walked with haste as she made her way up the road toward The Rusty Trombone. The tavern's back alley wasn't the most pleasant place to meet but it served its purpose and that was to be discreet. The stench of vomit filled her nostrils and as she drew closer she could almost taste it. She rolled her eyes with displeasure as she navigated the piles of rotten waste and empty rum bottles. In amongst the debris, two bearded oafs lay slumped against the tavern wall, still clinging to their bottles of rum. "Disgusting." Molly hovered a finger over their mouths; a short burst of hot air came from each. "Dangerous game resting out here," she remarked to the comatose drunks.

"That's her, that's the one," a somewhat familiar voice came from behind Molly.

She turned around only to be met with a forceful smack to the head. Molly stumbled backwards and her surroundings blurred. She tried to fixate on an object and widened her eyes. She made out the shape of a man standing before her, hunched over and holding one arm, his head thrown back with laughter.

"This time I brought friends, let's see how tough you are now you old cow."

Before Molly had time to think, an incoming punch struck the side of her head. She put her arms up to shield herself and crouched low to the ground. The incoming blows kept coming but Molly didn't falter. Her vision returned to normal, and she narrowed her eyes to identify the figure standing before her.

"You again! I thought you'd learned your lesson, Jacky Boy." Molly rose from the ground with regained strength. She grabbed the two punching assailants by their throats, lifted them off the ground, and tossed them onto the piles of discarded rum bottles. "You're going to regret this." Molly towered over Jacky Boy and looked down to meet his eyes.

"Oh shit." His laughter turned to fear as Molly's eyes blazed with rage. He winced in anticipation of the pain that was about to flood his body as she swept his legs from underneath him. With only one arm to brace his fall his head hit the ground with a thud. Blood poured out as he lay dead-eyed, impaled on shards of broken glass.

"Didn't see this coming did you, bitch?" One of the punching assailants had recovered and found himself a rusty cutlass which he wielded at Molly.

She lifted her arm to take the impact of the blade. She'd rather lose an arm than her life. Molly closed her eyes and braced.

"What the hell do you think you're doing, fool?"

Molly recognized the man's voice. She opened her eyes with relief and saw Johnny Ives standing next to her, his arm extended with his sword in hand, blocking the incoming blade.

"You stupid fucker." Johnny scoffed as he rolled his eyes and pushed Molly's cutlass wielding assailant to the ground. Johnny was a well-built muscular man, tall with a chiseled jaw and a tiny, thin mustache. He wore a pale yellow, long sleeved shirt, with the arms rolled up. It was tight in all the right places and showed off every bulging muscle in his body. "Do you even know who Molly works for?" He peered down at the cutlass wielding man before thrusting his sword into his throat. Blood gushed out as the man clutched at the wound, choking and gurgling to death. "Fools, the lot of them, Molly."

Johnny swung around to face the other two fallen men. Jacky Boy hadn't moved. He lay twitching, making occasional attempts to roll himself off the shards of glass, a difficult task with a broken arm. However, the other was making his way to Johnny. "What the fuck is wrong with you lot, rocks for brains?" Johnny shook his head. "Who are these idiots, Molly? Been making new friends again?"

Molly dusted herself off. "Put your blade away, Johnny." Her eyes intensified and burned into the approaching attacker.

"Heh. Anything you say." Johnny placed his blade back in his leather baldric which draped across his chest then backed away. He knew what was to come.

Molly's strength was unrivaled in Nassau. She picked up the man standing before her by the arms and brought him up to her eye level. "Seems you've made a big mistake today. You see, I don't like using weapons, far too messy. But you'll have wished I did because dying by the hand of a blade is much quicker than what I'm about to do to you." She threw him against the wall of The Rusty Trombone, and he landed amongst the piles of rotten waste. Molly strode over to where he lay and bent down.

"What the fuck! You giant old cow, what are you doing?"

Molly wrapped one hand over the top of his head and punched him in the face over and over until his eyes swelled shut.

"I wouldn't speak to her like that," Johnny chimed in, laughing in the background.

Molly walked toward Johnny. She motioned for him to move out of the way as she grabbed Jacky Boy by the face. His eyes were wide with terror as silent tears streamed down his cheeks. "I don't know what you were hoping to do today but you got these two killed, didn't you? Did you think you could take me on? Wasn't a very smart move, was it now?"

He stared blankly to the side. "Fuck... you... you're an

ugly old cow..." He whimpered under his breath as snot and tears ran down his face.

Molly scoffed as she stood up. "Not even an ounce of remorse. Men like you deserve to suffer." She grabbed his boot then jolted his leg until she heard it snap. He let out a scream so deafening it could have woken the dead. "Seems cruel to leave you to hop about," Molly joked then lifted her foot and stamped it down on his other ankle bone. "Don't worry, I'm not going to kill you, Jacky Boy," she mocked as she rolled him to the side and left him alive to suffer.

"Feel better, love?" Johnny asked, laughing and looking around at all the bodies in the alleyway. "You could've picked a better place to meet though."

Molly mopped the sweat from her brow then wiped the blood from her hands with her handkerchief. "Yes probably, but we do need to be discreet." She was still sweating but could feel her heartbeat returning to normal as she busied herself with the business at hand.

"Well then." Johnny smiled and got closer to her. "Shall we begin?"

"Yes, let's." Molly pulled out a brown leather satchel from behind a wooden crate. She had hidden it there a few days prior. "This should do the trick." Molly retrieved a thick brown glass bottle from the satchel and held it up for Johnny to eye.

"If you light this wick on fire and toss it, it will explode similar to a cannonball. Not only will it knock men to the ground, but this has a little something extra." Molly's eyes glimmered with excitement. "It holds heat too and spreads fire to all it touches."

"Wow." Johnny nodded his head in awe of Molly's expertise.

Molly had dabbled in apothecary from a young age. She loved to make perfumes for the girls, and deadly concoctions for the boys. Word had spread throughout Nassau of Molly's abilities and it was a reputation she was proud of though not everyone approved.

"Excellent." Johnny took the bottle and smiled at the prospect of the havoc he could wreak. "Looks like I can execute my plan now, will you help me?" He leaned in close to Molly.

"With Crow?" Molly re-packed her satchel and waved a piece of woven fabric at Johnny, motioning for him to wrap the bottle up.

"Ah yes, of course, I should be careful with this one." Johnny nodded as he wrapped the bottle with care. "Now Crow… I have to show the others how weak he's become. He's too old to lead."

An inebriated man stumbled out the door, slurring words to himself and chuckling. "Ooh. Well, if it isn't Molly the Mountain."

"Hello, Isaac," Molly said and laughed.

"Who's…" Isaac hiccupped mid-sentence. "Who's this guy? He looks strong." Isaac sized Johnny up.

"I'm Johnny Ives. Who the hell are you? Molly, is he troubling you?"

"No, no." Molly put her hand on Johnny's chest to hold him back. "Isaac's a good friend."

Molly had grown somewhat fond of Isaac over the years. They were cut from the same cloth.

"Well, nice to meet you, Isaac. I'm Johnny… I mean you're Johnny. I'm Isaac." Isaac shook his head, trying to snap out of his intoxicated stupor. "Hold on. What are you doing back here?"

"What are *you* doing back here?" Molly asked in return.

"Oh, I just had an interesting conversation... with..." Isaac stared down at his hands. "With..." Isaac looked up at Molly again. "Crow? Yes, Captain Crow and that strange little man of his, Nellie."

"Nelson," Johnny interjected.

"Yes, of course. Nelson, that's the one. Good man. I think. I don't really know. I don't know them well."

"Wait." Molly grabbed Isaac and brought him in closer. "You spoke to Crow and Nelson? Why?"

"Oh, you know, they..." Isaac gazed around again, confused. "Why are there so many bodies?"

Johnny got closer to Isaac and gave him a light tap on the face. "Snap out of it, man, what did they want?"

Isaac shook his head again. "Oh, they set up a meeting... with me!" Isaac pointed to himself.

Molly and Johnny exchanged glances, their eyes wide with excitement at the potential advantage they were about to gain.

"Interesting." Molly put her arm around Isaac. "Can we come? Just to keep an eye on you whilst you have your meeting?"

"Sure!" Isaac said without hesitation and waved the note under her nose.

"Excellent, we'll see you there," Molly said.

"You're a good man, Isaac." Johnny put his arm around him too. "Here's some coin, go on in and get yourself another drink." He gave Isaac five reale and pushed him off back toward the door.

"Damn. Thanks, fella." Isaac walked back into the bar and out of sight.

"Well, that was rather convenient." Johnny smiled as he walked away. "Thanks, Molly. A pleasure doing business as always."

He gave a cheeky salute as he headed down the alley, back out onto the main street.

Molly leaned against the tavern wall and closed her eyes for a moment. She felt numb. When the rage took over it consumed every fiber of her being, but once the surges of adrenaline left her body she felt empty and ashamed of what she had become. She let out a sigh and opened her eyes.

At the entrance to the alley she spied something moving in the sparse hedge of Ficuses which grew wildly throughout the island. More trouble? Surely not. She'd had enough for today. Molly tried to be discreet which wasn't always easy with her towering stature. She narrowed her eyes to a squint. She recognized the figure. It couldn't be... "Daniel?"

JOY LAFITTE

Joy cringed as she watched Isaac stagger about the tavern playing the fool. He pranced from table to table, spilling liquor everywhere and slurring bad jokes. It was a recipe for disaster if ever she saw one. How were they once together? "Such an idiot," she said to herself and shook her head at the thought.

The years had been tough and Joy had changed, but her former lover clearly hadn't. She had responsibilities now, a purpose, and the once wild, worry-free girl she'd been with him had had to grow up fast. "He's... infuriating," the words escaped her mouth before she could catch them. "He's so brazen, especially with Captain Crow sitting right there." She threw her hands up in the air out of exasperation.

Despite her frustrations, Joy loved the tavern. The constant stream of drunken punters made for interesting entertainment and provided a much-needed escape before hitting up a mark.

She sat alone in a back nook of the tavern, picking the dirt off her black pointed boots with a stick. Her green eyes sparkled as she narrowed her gaze and focused on the task at hand.

"Why, hullo there, pretty lady. Can I help you clean your boots?" An inebriated, loutish man poked his head around the nook and leered at Joy. He tugged at his shirt in an attempt to conceal his fat, hairy stomach which poked out from underneath it and flashed Joy a devious, toothless grin.

Joy was no stranger to this kind of attention but raised her eyebrows to feign surprise as she leaned over, allowing her cleavage to spill out from her jacket, and continued with the task at hand. She learned from a young age that the men in Nassau wanted one thing, and she made sure to use her feminine charms to her advantage.

"Nice jacket you got there." The lout stumbled closer to Joy, bringing his crotch to her eye level. She sported her form fitting, hand-made leather jacket, which she had designed herself. The jacket wasn't just for show. It was a uniform. Its hidden pockets concealed her varying knives and flintlocks, plus she had requested a few extra spots be sewn into the sleeves for her signature poisoned blades. The plume of feathers on her striking, black, tricorn hat brushed at the man's crotch as she again sat upright.

"You know what, hun?" She cocked her head to one side, giving him a coy look, then grabbed him by the shirt and pulled him down into her bust. From the bulge in his pants, she knew her routine was working.

"Wh... what?" the lout spluttered as he licked his lips with anticipation.

"Go to hell." She jabbed a small blade into his neck, stood up and made for the exit, scanning the room for prying eyes as she went. Gets them every time, Joy thought to herself. A loud thud came from behind as the drunken lout hit the deck. As she walked away, she wrapped the small blade back in its cloth and shoved it into her jacket pocket. It had been laced with a unique and deadly paralyzing toxin. It would take a few minutes before he bled out and that was long enough for her to be gone. For now, he just looked like another passed out drunk.

As she made her exit, she spotted Nelson, Crow's right-hand man, talking to Isaac. From memory, she didn't recall them being acquainted. She considered for a moment what they might be discussing. That's one to remember for later, Joy thought as she stepped out the tavern doors and onto the dusty road. Joy had a remarkable memory. She remembered every face, every mark, and every detail; a distinct advantage around these parts.

She let out a sigh and half-hearted laugh as she strode through town. Good job people walk around with their eyes shut, she thought as she snaked her way through traders and townsfolk gathered on the street.

A few men seemingly deep in conversation stopped talking as she skipped past. "Fancy a good time, darling?" one of them piped up.

"Beautiful day, fellas." Joy stuck her chest out and gave an exaggerated wink as she went on her way. Once upon a time she would have torn strips off them for such a comment, but it wasn't worth the effort nowadays.

She arrived at her destination, a rundown wooden house, which appeared uninhabited. Overgrown bushes lined the front and planks of wood sat piled up at the front door. It was situated in a notoriously bad part of town but it was the part Joy loved the most; it was home. She jogged toward the street facing open window, grabbed onto the ledge, and flung herself through the window legs first.

"Joy!" a petite girl cried out and ran over to her.

"Raven! How are you?"

Joy's younger sister hugged her tight.

"Yeah, okay thanks. How was your day?" Raven asked, tucking her wild, long, brown hair behind her ears. She wore a tattered cloth skirt, with an oversized plain beige shirt tucked in. Her clothes all dwarfed her petite frame, something Joy had made sure of. She didn't want her attracting attention of any kind after what had happened.

"Oh, you know, same old. What on earth are you making? Smells great."

"Chicken! Do you have time for some, or have you somewhere else to be?"

"Sorry, sis, I've gotta go get something. Save me some though, okay?" Joy smiled and tried to catch Raven's eye.

"Sure, but only if you promise me you'll fix the door. I hate using the window."

"Fine, I'll sort it out. Promise!" Joy said and kissed her sister on the forehead then jumped back out through the window, laughing.

She liked to check in on her sister throughout the day, in between jobs. Maybe it was a little much, but she couldn't be too careful after what happened. It was her responsibility to keep Raven safe, and she was going to do everything in her power to do so.

Out on the street Joy made a right and headed for the bounty office, which rather conveniently wasn't too far from home. At the crossroads up ahead she spied a familiar figure, jogging and skipping down the street. Typical Isaac, she thought. Though she hated to admit it, her heart still fluttered a little whenever she saw him.

They had been together for over a year, which was the longest either of them had been with anyone. It was fun whilst it lasted but when everything happened with Raven, Joy withdrew. Rage and revenge consumed her, and Isaac didn't know how to cope. The pair grew distant and Isaac leaned into the bottle for comfort, more than ever. Since then they had only seen each other in passing, keeping things short and simple, never talking for too long to avoid fighting. He looks pretty happy with himself, the talk with Nelson must have gone well, Joy pondered as she walked along, though she was still puzzled by what they would have been speaking about.

Joy knocked on the office door: three short quick knocks, followed by a pause for three seconds, rounded off with one final hard knock. She listened for the shuffling of feet. The door swung open and there stood the smallest man Joy had ever known.

"Ah Joy, welcome, please come in." The small man pushed the door aside with his full body weight and waved his arms toward a chair. "Please, go on in, have a seat. I'll be with you shortly." Joy walked through the door and felt his eyes follow her.

"How's it going, Roy?" she asked, as she plonked herself down in her favorite hole-filled chair. The stuffing spilled out and it smelt a little, but Joy didn't own anything half as comfy.

"Better now you're here. I just heard about your latest and greatest. Very well done," Roy praised with a smile in his eyes.

Clouds of stale pipe smoke hung in the air of the dimly lit windowless office. Two lanterns flickered in the corners of the room as Roy made his way to a large counter which concealed the safe. Joy sat back in her chair and craned her neck to get a better view of what Roy was up to, but she saw nothing.

"Aha!" She heard Roy exclaim from behind the counter. He shuffled back to her carrying two items. A pouch of what Joy assumed was her twenty-five reale for the completed job, and another package: a small binder with parchment papers inside.

"Here's your cut," Roy announced with an over-the-top grin. "If only they all made it as easy for me as you do."

Joy's method was simple. Kill them. No matter who. No matter what. She may get less money for not bringing them in alive, but it kept things simple and that meant she could move onto the next one quicker.

Roy was a fan of this arrangement as his payment remained the same regardless. Less work, same money, it was ideal. "So, how'd it go? Burly lout that one," he enquired while fiddling with his shirt. Roy was always busy fixing his clothes, pulling them down, adjusting them. She wondered if he was forced to buy children's clothes, but always kept these thoughts to herself. She didn't want to embarrass him.

"He was drunk and easily seduced by these." Joy smirked and pushed her breasts together. Roy didn't know where to look. He fumbled with his shirt and shifted awkwardly in his seat. "Anyway... he walked over, I stabbed him in the neck with the poisoned blade, and he's likely dead by now." Joy cackled as she relaxed back in the chair.

"He certainly is dead. Word spread quick. They blamed some Isaac fellow." Roy raised his eyebrows and chuckled. "The thought of that boy being blamed for the murder does make me laugh."

"Ha!" Joy laughed a little herself as she sat nodding, her lips pressed together. Must have been why he left the tavern, Joy considered, though it doesn't explain why he appeared to be so happy. What a drunken idiot. Why did he have to be so handsome though? Joy daydreamed for a moment before snapping herself out of it. "Fool," Joy muttered under her breath.

"Who?" Roy asked.

"Oh, ignore me! Sorry, Roy. So, do you have anything else for me?" Joy leaned forward and rested her arm on one knee.

"Yes actually. This one, might be a little more difficult though."

"How so?"

"Well, hmm. How much more do you need for what's his name? That man, you know who I'm talking about."

"Grimm? He wants thirty doubloons. Won't talk for anything less."

"And how many are you at right now?" Roy asked. He always seemed to be invested in Joy's quest.

"Ten doubloons."

"Excellent!" Roy's face lit up like a candle. "Then this one is exactly what you need." He tore the binder seal, pulled out the papers and thrust them across the table in Joy's direction.

"What's this?" Joy scrunched up her face.

"A fifteen doubloon kill." Roy clapped his hands and rubbed them together.

"What?" Joy didn't know what to say, a mark this big was a rare find. The paper read twenty doubloons alive, fifteen dead. It was always easier to kill them but if she could bring this one in alive, that would be it! She could pay off Grimm and be one step closer to revenge.

Joy dreamed of the day she could lay her hands on the wretched soul who had stolen Raven from her for so long. She had heard stories of him around town. How more children were being kidnapped and enslaved by him or sold off to the highest bidder for who knows what? Why Grimm knew his identity Joy didn't know or care. All she knew was that she felt sick to her stomach knowing that this monster was still breathing and would not rest until he was gone.

"So this should do it then, right?" Roy said and nodded with excitement.

"Yes!" Joy couldn't believe it.

Roy stood on his chair, jumped onto the table and launched himself at Joy, wrapping his arms around her tightly.

For a few moments Joy felt a wave of relief wash over her. She hugged Roy back then placed him on the ground. "Wait, why does this one fetch so much? Who is it?"

"Well..." Roy picked up the paper which fell on the floor during their brief celebration. "Do you know who Jane is?"

"Jane? I know lots of Janes."

"Do you know the Jane that lives in that giant mansion with her army of mercenaries?"

"Hatch?"

"Yes... Jane Hatch, it's her." Roy stared at the floor as his smile turned to a frown and his brow crumpled.

Joy sunk back into the chair and tipped her head back. "Give me a moment. She runs the camp, right?"

"Yes."

Joy closed her eyes. She wondered if it would even be worth trying to get close to Jane to bring her in alive. Her 'kill them and flee' method might be a better option. Sure, she was a good fighter but bringing them to Roy still breathing required great skill and came with a lot of risk.

She sat upright and grabbed the paper once more,

scanning the details. Whoever ordered the kill wanted Jane gone, one way or another. Twenty doubloons would buy her the information she needed. But if she did have to kill her, then fifteen doubloons would still bring her close to her target. Those extra doubloons would take her months to make at her normal pace though. And she was growing impatient. "Any ideas, Roy?"

"Yes, one, but it's a timely investment. More of a long-term game but it could just work."

"Alright, let's hear it." Joy leaned in closer. "I'm all ears."

"Well, she runs a pretty tight ship, people in her camp respect her, they love her."

"Right." Joy nodded.

"So, I was thinking that you could join her mercenary crew. I mean, you're a fighter so it shouldn't be a problem for you. That way, you could get in close with her, gain her trust and then strike when her guard's down."

Joy considered Roy's proposal. It wasn't a terrible plan, but Jane was most probably heavily guarded at all times. Then again, twenty doubloons in one shot would be amazing and quite possibly worth the risk. She took off her hat, letting her wavy, long, brown hair flow free. She tugged her hands through it and ruffled the hair on her scalp.

"It's possible, I guess. Do you know anyone that could help me get in?" She often relied on Roy's knowledge and connections to execute her plans of attack. Roy knew a lot of people and they liked him enough to always offer to help him out. She hoped he could pull in a favor for her on this one.

"I do, but you'll have to go through the trial like everyone else."

"A trial? That shouldn't be a problem, or at least I don't

think so anyway." Joy winked as she put her hat back on and tucked her hair in.

"No, not for you it shouldn't. I can't promise you'll get in, though, I can only promise you the trial."

"Fair enough. Just tell me where to go and when."

"Can do. I'll let you know when I know." Roy stood up and extended his hand out to Joy. She shook it with both hands and gave him a nod.

"I really appreciate this, Roy."

"I know." He walked over to the door and let her out. Joy bent over and kissed him on the cheek, her bosoms smothered his face. "Thank you."

"Oh, don't thank me yet." Roy let out a nervous laugh as he waved her on her way.

Joy headed up the dusty path toward home. Her mind bounced from one thought to another. She wondered when Roy would call on her. She had a feeling it would be soon, and she knew she had to be ready.

She peered down at her pouch of reale and imagined it chock full of doubloons. "Closer by the day," she said with pride as she ducked through a backstreet toward home.

She slid in quietly through the window and crept toward her bedroom, hoping not to disturb Raven. It was a simple home, just two bedrooms and a kitchen, if you could even call it a kitchen. Once in her room, Joy took out her coffer from under the floorboards, a treasure she had stolen from a mark long ago. Nobody knew where she hid her coffer, not even Raven. In fact, Raven had no idea what Joy did during the day. She often lied and told her sister that she worked on the docks, but that the pay was terrible.

She added in twenty reale, put the coffer back in its hiding place and came out of her room to give Raven the remaining five. Joy always made out this was the pay for the week when she handed it over to her little sister to manage. It alleviated some of the guilt from lying and besides, Raven was a much better housekeeper than Joy.

"Raven, I've got something for you," Joy said, waiting for Raven to run out from her room like she usually did. Nothing. It was silent. "Raven?" Joy opened the door to her room. She was nowhere to be found. If she wasn't in the kitchen or her room, there wasn't really anywhere else she could be. This wasn't like her, she never just took off like this. What if she had been kidnapped again, what if she was dead? Joy panicked. "Fuck!"

Without taking a breath, she hurled herself back out of the window and raced down the main street. Up ahead in the distance someone crouched over a motionless body on the ground. "Raven!" Joy cried as she ran toward the body. As she grew closer, her heart sank.

ISAAC CARVER

The familiar head throb set in as the rum haze wore off. With every step Isaac's legs grew heavy but he had to keep going. He paused to catch his breath. A wave of nausea washed over him. "Today was going so well."

"Stop him!" a voice came from behind.

What did I do this time? Isaac wracked his brains for a hint, but every thought drew a blank. He glanced over his shoulder only to see three angry men, donned in long navy jackets. Guards. "Shit." Isaac picked up his pace and ran in the direction of the center square; his go-to escape. He'd be sure to lose them there.

The streets were teeming with people and he was doing his best to dodge them, but some didn't budge. "Sorry! Emergency!" Isaac apologized as he shoved townsfolk out of his way.

"Isaac, what did you do this time?" a shopkeeper yelled from the side street and tossed him a small rock.

"Not sure, Alden, I'll fill you in later." Isaac caught the rock and hurled it in the direction of the guards, but it did nothing to slow them down.

"Damn!" Isaac bolted down the side street to the right. His eyes searched for an object which might help. Nothing. He ran back out into the crowded square. No guards in sight.

"Got ya!" A guard jumped from within the crowd and tackled Isaac to the ground.

"Bastard!" Isaac landed face down and copped a mouth full of dirt as the guard pushed his head into the dusty earth. He kicked his legs in all directions trying to wriggle free.

"Stop moving. You are under arrest."

"For what?"

A crowd formed around them. "Hey, that's Isaac," he heard a voice cry.

"Leave him alone!" a nearby merchant said and pelted the guard with a stone.

Isaac continued to wriggle about but the heavy knee in his back made this difficult.

"He's a good man!" another voice chimed in. "Yeah, well, sometimes anyways." Laughter spread through the crowd. "When he's not drunk!"

"Oi! I've got him," the guard yelled and smashed his fist into Isaac's face.

Isaac peeled open his eyes and braced for another thump to the head, but instead the weight of the guard vanished from his body. He pushed himself up and turned to see a burly brute of a man pinning the guard to the ground. Fists flew from every direction, pummeling the guard as he tried to crawl away.

Isaac sprang to his feet and dusted himself off. "Hey fella, where's the other two?" He grabbed a plain looking man with a brown shirt by the shoulders.

"Close, you'd best get out of here." He motioned with

his eyes toward one of the fruit stalls. "The crowd's trying to hold 'em."

"Right. Thank you, friends." Isaac gave a salute and sped off. He made a sharp left and headed for a gap between a vase emporium and an inn.

He swiped a vase from the table outside displaying the store's many wares and sandwiched himself in the gap. Cobwebs strung across the entrance and broken bottles crunched underfoot. He looked up to see a short figure standing at the entrance, his hands on his hips.

"Not so fast, Mr. Carver." The short, old, mustached man beckoned with his finger for Isaac to come out.

Isaac shook his head and held his finger to his lips. "Shh!"

"Don't shush me. This is not happening again."

"I know, I'm sorry, but I really need this right now Mr. Van Deem. Please be quiet. Please." Isaac made his way out.

"I told you to stay out of trouble." Mr. Van Deem wagged his finger at Isaac and snatched the vase back.

The guards turned the corner "You there, old man!" They pointed to Mr. Van Deem. "Don't let him go!"

"Oh, now I see." Mr. Van Deem nodded.

Isaac's heart raced, so much so that he thought it might explode. He still had no clue as to what he'd done. The guards never listened to reason. He'd be hanged within a week.

"You!" The guards stopped. They wagged their fingers as they caught their breath after being given the run around. "Isaac Carver, you are under arrest."

"For what?" Isaac stomped his foot in frustration.

From out of nowhere, two heavy clay vases smashed over the heads of the guards, knocking them to the ground. Mr. Van Deem's two sons stepped into the light and grinned at Isaac.

"Thank you. Thank you. Thank you." Isaac clasped his hands together. "I owe you. I can't..." Isaac's pounding heart flooded with relief.

The guards moaned in pain and confusion.

"Don't tell anyone about this." He looked back at Mr. Van Deem as he clocked the guards over the head with the hilt of one of their swords and proceeded to empty their pockets.

"Ten reale do?" He dropped the coins into Mr. Van Deem's outstretched hands and pocketed two for himself. Mr. Van Deem's face lit up.

"Thanks again!" Isaac turned on his heel and made his way back onto the main street.

He ran until the guards were no longer in sight. He paused for a moment and took in his surrounds only to be met with a heavy blow to the skull. Isaac put his hand to his head and stumbled to the ground. "What the...?" He groaned as he lay still for a moment then opened one eye and tried to focus but the world around him was spinning. The throbbing in his head deafened him. He tapped at his pocket and fumbled around. His hand struck the sand-filled pouch, and he dug his fingers in, scooped up a good amount and threw it in the eyes of whoever just hit him. The sand contained a potent mix of spices which temporarily blinded whoever it hit.

"My eyes! What's wrong with you?" Isaac heard a figure cry as he blinked over and over in a hope to regain his own vision.

"What's wrong with *you*?" Isaac yelled as he clambered to standing, his pounding head and nausea overwhelming.

He stumbled over to the small figure and continued to

blink as his vision restored. He had assumed it was another guard. It wasn't. His heart sank as he saw a little boy, no more than nine years old, writhing on the ground in agony.

"It burns!" The boy rolled around clutching at his eyes. "Please help!"

"Yeah, bit tricky. I'm so sorry." Isaac scratched his head. He felt terrible. "It'll stop hurting in about an hour."

The small boy sobbed and rubbed at his eyes. A shovel lay beside him which Isaac assumed was the object used to hit him over the head.

"Why did you bloody hit me with that?" Isaac asked, confused.

"I was just walking by!" The boy cried out in agony, his eyes swollen and red.

Isaac wiped the sweat from his brow and shook his flask. "Empty. I could really use a drink right now." He shook his head and sighed.

"You! What did you do to my boy?" An angry giant of a man ran toward them, his fists clenched tight. Isaac could see the veins pulsating in his neck and rippling through his monstrous muscular arms.

"Oh no, is he your son?" Isaac cringed and reached into his sand filled pouch again. He threw a scoop into the angry man's eyes.

"I'm going to pretend this day didn't happen and I suggest you two do the same."

"My eyes! You bastard!" The big man dropped to his knees, clutching his face in pain. Isaac had created the concoction many years ago and it often came in handy but today was not one of those times.

"So sorry to both of you, truly I am. It was an honest mistake." Isaac took the two reale he had stolen from the guard and threw the coins at them. "Hope this helps." He sprinted up the street until they vanished into the distance.

Once he reached far enough away, he relaxed for a moment. He found himself a few streets away from the center in a raucous part of town. It was quiet now but once the sun set, men would be stumbling about looking for their favorite whores to satiate their needs, Isaac included. He smiled as he thought back to the tavern. It had started out as such a good day. He'd spoken to... someone. He always spoke to someone. Today had been different though.

"Who was it?" He patted down his jacket pockets hoping for a clue. "Hmm." He reached into the inside pockets and pulled out a small dagger, a tattered cloth and a few small balls covered in spikes. "There must be something." He checked his pants "Ooh, hello, what's this?" He retrieved a small piece of paper and unfolded it. The words written meant nothing to him. "Uh!" He had never learned to read and couldn't remember for the life of him what it was even about. Isaac stood perplexed for a few moments.

"Nellie!" he yelled out to no one. His eyes widened and his heart fluttered with excitement as vague memories from the tavern came flooding back. "Nellie, what did Nellie say?" He scrunched his eyes shut to help him think. Did we speak about the map? He wanted me to do something, and he'd give me the last location in return? Wait, how would he know what locations were left? How would he know about the map? Oh, I can't remember! He smacked his palm on his forehead in annoyance.

"You there!" a voice yelled, interrupting Isaac's thoughts. He turned to see two guards running toward him.

"That's him!" the taller guard yelled and hurtled toward him.

"Oh boy." Isaac took off down the alleyway which snaked off into many smaller alleys. It was like a rabbit warren, and he knew it like the back of his hand.

"Oi!" the tall guard shouted from behind him.

Isaac ran as fast as his legs would carry him. He zigged and zagged through the different alleys until the guards disappeared from sight. The muscles in his legs twitched and his head throbbed. He couldn't run forever, at least not without a top up. He spotted a door down one of the lanes propped open just a tiny crack. He bolted for it, opened the door and closed it behind him. Tired, he leaned into the wooden frame and caught his breath as his eyes adjusted to the darkness of the room.

"Welcome." An old woman with a thick silver nose ring appeared from the darkness and eyed Isaac up and down.

"Shh. Please." Isaac put a finger to his lips and leaned his ear against the door. The old woman joined him and leaned her ear against the door too, her face facing his.

"Shh," she mimicked Isaac and gave him a wink.

Isaac heard the guards running past the door and held his breath. The crunching of the sand and heavy footsteps faded into the distance. "Thank God."

"Don't thank him. You can thank me." She laughed and coughed as she motioned for Isaac to take a seat at a small table.

"Thank you, Mrs... I should probably head off." Isaac looked around the dark room. A candle flickered on the table next to a stack of cards.

"Nonsense. Come sit." She took her seat at the table and began to shuffle the cards.

"What's your name?" Isaac asked as he stepped toward

the table and brushed a red drape aside. Strings of beads and cloth hung from the walls and ceiling of the small candlelit room. The smell of musk and smoke filled the air.

"Ah, I thought you'd never ask!" The old woman tapped the table. "Sit first, then I'll tell you."

A seat would be a welcome rest but something told him it might not be a good idea. "Okay, but I can't stay long." His heavy legs gave in and he plonked himself down. The old woman reached over and squeezed his arm.

"Such a strong young man." She rubbed her finger across her lips. "My name is Pont Neuf." She traced a half circle with her hands over Isaac's face and shuffled the cards once more. "You are rugged yet alluring."

"Um, thank you?" Isaac shifted uncomfortably in his seat. "Are you from around here?" Isaac didn't know what else to say. He found the whole situation beyond strange, and he desperately needed a drink.

"No!" She laughed. "I am Parisian." She placed her hand on her heart with pride and gave a small bow.

"Parisian? From the desert?" Isaac asked.

"Ah, not quite. You have a lot to learn." Pont licked her lips and leaned in close. She placed the deck of cards in front of Isaac. "Cut the deck, mon cher," she said with a smile, her thin lips lost amid the wrinkles on her face.

"Um, I'm sorry Mrs. Neuf or is it Pont? I'm quite confused. Look, I really do appreciate you helping me, but I really must go." Isaac wasn't sure what he had walked into, he'd never seen anything like this in Nassau.

"Stay." Pont put her wrinkled hands on top of his and held him down with more strength than he expected. "Cut... the deck." She lowered her head, looked him square in the eyes and smiled.

"Fine." Isaac sighed under his breath and cut it at the top third.

"Excellent." Pont rubbed her hands together and closed her eyes as she took the top three cards from where he had cut it. She flipped the cards over in turn. Each one had a detailed drawing depicting strange demonic-like scenes.

"What's this one?" He pointed to a card with a crow feeding off a dead body.

"Oh, this one. Hmm." Pont peered into Isaac's eyes.

"There's a lot to tell. Stay a little while. Let me tell you your fortune, dear boy."

"Oh. I thought this was some fun game." Isaac got to his feet, this time avoiding the woman's grasp. "I can't afford it anyway. I really must go."

"This one is free, mon cher." Pont looked him up and down.

"For a fine specimen like you. It'll always be free."

"I really have to go." Isaac made for the door.

"Oh, my dear boy, you'll want to hear this." Pont pouted at Isaac's haste to leave.

"I really don't..." Isaac spied a bottle of rum beside her chair. He took out his empty flask. "May I bother you for a top up before I leave?"

"Of course!" She clapped her hands with delight.

"You have a seat and I'll tell you what's to come." Pont heaved the large bottle of rum which sat at her feet and placed it on the table next to the cards. "You can help yourself."

"Everyone's a winner," Isaac said nervously as he unscrewed the lid of his flask and poured in the sweet brown liquor.

"Excellent. I'll be quick." She tapped on the card which depicted a crow feasting on the dead. "Death. It surrounds you." She handed the card to Isaac. "Keep these, so you remember." She put her finger on her lip and smiled as she tapped at the second card, a snake biting at a man's neck. "An old love will cause you great harm." Pont Neuf stared Isaac in the eyes. "Maybe even death. It's unclear."

Isaac raised his brows and grabbed the card, half ignoring the mad woman, half concentrating on drinking the precious liquor from his flask.

"Go on..." Isaac wanted to get this whole day over with.

"Ah yes, yes..." She showed Isaac the third card, a coyote missing a leg, digging in the earth. "Trust. Be very careful with it. The coyote can turn at any moment." She rose to her feet and shimmied around the table to him. "You're so very handsome, my dear." She smacked the card into his chest and rubbed her body against his. Her perfume was strong and intoxicating.

"Well, thank you for that. I needed it." He tucked the cards in his pocket with his treasure map.

"The rum or the reading? I'd say both." She walked her fingers up his chest.

He nodded toward her. "I'll be off then. Have a good day."

"Oh, I will. I just wish I could say the same to you." She tossed her head back and gave a wild laugh.

He licked the rum on his lips and made for the door. Out on the street he checked the coast was clear and made for his favorite whorehouse. He shook his head at the day's events. A visit with his beautiful Sophia was sure to take his mind off things.

The rum kicked in to full effect. He felt warm and relaxed as he strode up the street. The Milky Way was in sight. "What a day," he laughed to himself as he opened the door with glee. It was much darker than usual. No flickering candlelight, no bevy of naked women waiting for his coin. "Ladies?"

He trod lightly as he stepped through the door. His foot slipped in something. The floor was wet. He tried to make out what it was as his eyes adjusted to the darkness.

"What..." He looked up in horror and stepped back out onto the street. The blood drained from his face as he took in what he'd seen.

"Finally!" a voice from behind him snapped him out of his shock.

"Wait, no!"

"Isaac Carver, you're under arrest." His legs were swept from beneath him and his face hit the ground. His chin scraped against the floor and a knee dug in his back as a rough rope was wound around his wrists.

"We finally got him," another voice said. A big black boot pressed against his ear and forced his cheek into the ground.

"Ignore me!" he screamed. "Look in the bloody brothel!"

"Shut it!" The guard increased the pressure on his head and searched his pockets.

"Well, what have we got here?"

Isaac's heart sank as the contents of his jacket pockets were emptied out.

"Looks like we got ourselves a map."

"A map? Lucky us." The trio laughed and tossed the three cards on the ground in front of Isaac as the tallest of the guards pocketed the map.

"We'll be keeping this."

POPINO BELTRAME

"Hello, anyone home?" an unfamiliar voice came from downstairs.

Popino's pulse raced. Whoever was at the door was sure to find him, along with Eva and Lucien's lifeless bodies. He scanned the room desperate for an escape route.

"What do I do?" Popino panicked and shut his eyes tight in the hope that a miraculous answer would come to him. Maybe he could hide? Forever? Probably not. Maybe he could kill whoever was at the door? But he wasn't really a killer, at least not intentionally anyway. He needed to escape. It was the only plausible solution.

"Hello?" The weather-beaten front door creaked open.

"Yep, window it is." Popino squeezed out of the small second floor window and stepped onto the rotten wooden sill. It crumbled with each step. What was I thinking? He looked to the rooftop above which was out of reach.

The street below was quiet but quite the drop. He contemplated leaping on to a nearby tree but decided he'd never make it.

"Not one of my brightest ideas," Popino uttered to himself as he made his way back inside.

"Eva? Are you here? I'm ready, darling," the voice called out, followed by the rattle of boot buckles slowly treading up the stairs.

Ready for what? Popino scrunched his face, puzzled. Then it dawned on him. This was another suitor, another man coming for pleasure. How many had she been seeing this whole time? We must have all been on some sort of schedule, Popino huffed to himself.

He caught sight of Eva's blood drenched body. It didn't seem real. His insides churned. It didn't matter how many men she was seeing, she never deserved this. "I'm sorry," he mouthed to her. He had loved her... in his own way. He loved all of his ladies.

The footsteps reached the bedroom door.

"Oh fuck!" Popino gnawed at the knuckle of his forefinger. There wasn't anywhere to go. He couldn't escape through the window without breaking a leg. But he couldn't face the gentleman caller. He'd be on the gallows before sunrise. Why hadn't he made a run for it?

He questioned his poor decisions as he weighed up a hiding spot in the room. He dropped to the ground and tucked himself under the bed. Better than a broken leg, Popino reassured himself as he lay on his back, barely daring to breathe.

The gentleman caller strode into the room. Popino turned his head in an attempt to identify the man but from under the bed he couldn't make out much. He tried his best to silence his breath and lay motionless as his heartbeat echoed in his ears.

Silence filled the air. Why wasn't he saying anything? Or moving? Maybe he was so horrified by what he saw that he was speechless? Popino's thoughts raced as he braced for the worst.

"Ha! Good!" the gentleman caller finally remarked as he circled the lifeless bodies. The man continued to speak as he walked back and forth around the bed. Popino winced at every step.

"Someone told me another man was in here, said he'd seen him here a lot! Goes by the name of Popino or something like that. I thought I was your 'cher' but when I heard another man was here at this hour I knew precisely what was going on, you stupid whore!"

Popino's eyes went wide with fear at the mention of his name. The gentleman caller stopped pacing and stepped toward the bed. His polished black cavalier boots came into sight. Popino scrunched his arm in tight to avoid it being grazed by the toe of the man's boots.

"Ha! If it isn't the Boucher of Bayonne himself. Guess your husband dearest finally found out what you were up to, you disgusting whore!" The boots moved away from the bed, toward the window. "That filthy rat Popino must still be out there."

Popino shook his head in dismay. Why did he have to know his name? It wasn't exactly common around Nassau. They only had to check down at the docks to find out that he'd never made it in that morning. He'd be strung up. Hanged in the center square by the so-called governor and his band of brutes. His heart filled with dread as he thought of his sweet Rose, orphaned and alone.

Popino pulled himself to the other side of the bed, rolled out and scrambled to his feet, dishevelled and soaked in blood.

"If by 'out there' you mean in here then yes, I am... but

it's not what you think." Popino put his hands in the air to signify surrender.

"You bastard!" A pompous, slender man stood before Popino with his chest puffed out and lips pursed. His right hand was bloodied and bandaged. His sword hand, however, was fully operational and holding a striking stout blade with an ornate brass covering at the hilt.

"Let's all calm down here." Popino nodded his head as he made eye contact with the sword wielding suitor in a bid to gain his trust.

"Oh, I'm calm, but you on the other hand shouldn't be. Look at what you did!"

"Clearly it wasn't me. I found them like this," Popino lied. He pointed to the sword placed in Lucien's hand. "Look, you can tell that monster of a man stabbed poor Eva."

Popino's heart beat faster and faster as the suitor eyed the bodies with suspicion.

"Well, why are you here then?" The suitor pointed his blade at Popino.

"Why are *you* here?" Popino fired back.

"It doesn't matter. What matters is that I found you here with two dead bodies, and that is all people will need to hear for you to hang." The disgruntled suitor turned on his heel and stormed out of the door.

Popino panicked. That couldn't happen. He'd gone this far. He wasn't going to leave Rose now. Everything he did was for her. He'd made a promise and come hell or high water he was going to stick to it. He grabbed his bloodied blade from Eva's hand and ran out of the room toward the staircase in pursuit of the suitor.

"Just one question?" Popino did his best to calm his tone.

As the puzzled suitor turned back to face Popino he was met with a blade, which Popino thrust deep into his stomach.

"You bastard," the suitor cried as he gripped at his gaping wound.

Popino acted fast. As the injured man fell backwards, he grabbed him by the scruff of the neck and dragged him back up the few stairs he'd climbed down. "I'm sorry but I can't take the blame on this one," Popino said as he sliced the suitor's throat. His body slumped to the ground.

Popino blinked in shock as he took in the surrounding carnage. He had been fighting for as long as he could remember and was used to a bit of blood, but this scene turned his stomach. He crouched down and put his head in his hands. Why couldn't he just keep his cock in his pants? He blinked back tears and took a deep breath.

"Now is not the time for reflection," he said with sorrow and rubbed at his face with his palms, as if to erase the images from his mind.

He rose to his feet and dragged the gentleman suitor closer to the bedroom door. He had to make it appear as if Lucien had caught the pair in bed and the suitor had fought off the deranged 'Boucher' as best he could, before making a run for the door. However, he never made it and Eva avenged her lover's death by killing her husband.

He pulled off the suitor's bloodstained cavalier boots, followed by his belt and pants, then flung them around the bedroom. He placed his blade back in Eva's hand. "Wrong place, wrong time... for all of us." He shook his head in shame as he cleaned himself up at the washstand, then grabbed two fresh shirts from the bedroom dresser. He threw one on and used the other to hold his bloodied items. He scanned the room, making sure all other traces of his presence were gone. This day would not weigh lightly on Popino. He was not a brutal man at heart and certainly no cold-blooded killer.

Lucien's oversized shirt billowed out around Popino as he ran down the stairs. He paused at the front door and questioned if anyone would notice that it didn't belong to him. He tucked the linen deep into his pants. "What's wrong with me?" He smacked his head with his palm at his own stupidity. An oversized shirt would be the least of his worries if he were to walk straight out the front door and risk being seen. He ran to the kitchen and peered through the only window big enough for him to fit through. From memory, the side street which it overlooked was mostly empty throughout the day. Popino slithered out, one leg at a time, and made for the docks. Judging by the position of the sun, he should have been there a few hours ago.

Once he reached far enough away, he hurled the soiled shirt in a nearby bush. The sun was bright and hot as he jogged toward the harbor down the cobblestone street. He needed to think of an excuse as to why he was late. Everyone would ask, they might even be worried as he was rarely tardy. He ran through the potential excuses in his head. "Well, I was visiting one of my numerous lovers and then ended up killing her and two others," he muttered under his breath and choked back the welling lump in his throat.

The salty sea air hit Popino as he drew closer to the docks. He stopped jogging and slowed to a walk as he passed by the merchants lining the main path. He gave a nod and a wave here and there, as he tried his best to evade unnecessary attention. Just a regular morning, he told himself in a bid to calm his nerves.

The dock was one of the best places to work in Nassau. It was surrounded by crystal clear waters and white sandy beaches, and lined with palm trees whose gentle sway in the warm breeze was undeniably soothing. Not only was it beautiful but a hive of activity. Working there meant you were privy to who had arrived, what had arrived and what was going to be done with it. Popino had seen everything, from prized elephant tusks and rare animal hides through to entire ships filled with enough gunpowder to blow up the whole of Nassau.

"Popino! Where 'ave you been?" a heavyset dock worker yelled over to him as he heaved a crate onto shore. The sweat-drenched workers had five ships queued up, filled with wares and loot waiting to be unloaded.

Popino hadn't come up with a reason yet. He couldn't get the blood drenched images out of his mind. He had to say something quick or else it would seem like a lie. "Sorry Jo, Rose was taken ill overnight so I had to stay back with her until she felt well enough for me to leave her with Clara."

Was that too much detail? Popino wondered, fraught with nerves.

"That's too bad, you missed a busy morning." Jonas dried his wet hands on his pants.

"Yeah, I can't remember the last time we had five dock at once." Popino let out an awkward laugh in an attempt to sound jovial.

"Don't worry, there's still lots to do." Jonas put his arm around Popino and led him toward a ship docked at the end of the pier. "First though, you should see what we found in one of the crates."

"What is it?" Popino asked, his mind swimming with guilt.

"Come 'ave a look." Jo ran down the long dock with excitement and stopped at a crate near the end. Four men were gathered around it, all peering inside.

Popino was still trying to process the morning's events and became distracted by the other ships docked. He stopped and stared. They were grand vessels. He recognized two. He'd unloaded them before.

"Quick, Pino, come see!" Jonas hollered and waved his arms, motioning for Popino to join them.

Popino, though reluctant, ran down. He didn't want to appear out of character but by the same token he really didn't want any more surprises after the morning he'd had. He peered inside. "That's disturbing... who does that belong to?"

"Ha! Did belong to." Jonas elbowed Popino and winked.

JOY LAFITTE

"Raven?" Joy struggled to see as tears filled her eyes. The lump in her throat made it hard to breathe.

She kept running and as her sister came in sight a wave of relief washed over her. It was Raven, but she wasn't the one lying on the ground. She was knelt with her back toward Joy, cloth in hand, tending to a young boy.

"What happened? I thought it was..." Tears spilled from Joy's eyes at the sight of her little sister's face. She caught her breath and steadied her shaking hands.

"I'm not sure, I just found him like this." Raven crouched over a young boy who couldn't have been more than nine.

He rolled from side to side, clutching his head in pain.

A few paces ahead lay an older man swearing in a frenzy of anger and pain.

"What happened? What hurts?" Joy asked the injured pair, confused by the whole situation. She wiped her tears away with her sleeve.

"My eyes!" the young boy screamed and rubbed at them.

"I'll go get some water. I'll be right back." Joy ran to the nearby inn and pinched a bucket from out the front.

The pair continued to writhe on the ground in agony, gripping at their red faces.

"That fucker! I'll kill him," the older man yelled with rage.

Joy sprinted back and doused the pair. They yelped with shock.

"Why do people keep throwing things at us?" the older man shouted.

"We're trying to help," Joy said and rolled her eyes in frustration.

"It burns so much." The young boy sobbed as Raven continued to dab at his eyes.

After a few minutes and what felt like an eternity to Joy, the wounded pair calmed and sat up, blinking. Her mind was swimming with possibilities and preparations for the trial. Becoming part of Jane Hatch's crew of mercenaries would be no easy feat. She needed time to prepare, but she couldn't just leave these people to suffer.

"Let's bring them home, take care of them for a bit and find out what happened," Raven said and looked to Joy for approval.

"Good idea." Joy grabbed the older man's monstrous arm and helped him to his feet whilst Raven took care of the young boy.

"I'm surprised anyone would mess with you," Joy joked. The older man was built like a battleship.

"He'll live to regret it," the older man said through gritted teeth.

Joy and Raven walked the pair to their home.

"Ah yes, slight issue... we can't really open the door," Joy said.

Raven looked at the floor, her head hung in shame.

"But never you worry, I'll sort it." Joy climbed in through the window and retrieved the only two chairs they owned. Rickety old things they'd found in the dumps one day. She passed them out the window to Raven whose cheeks had flushed with embarrassment.

Joy often thought about using her hard-earned coin on making their home proper, but when she thought of what her sister had gone through it just didn't seem right. She had to take care of business first and make sure Raven would be safe for good.

The wounded pair sat recovering, their clothes covered in a mix of sand and dust from the path.

"What are your names?" Joy asked.

"Tom and this is my boy, Jim," the older man answered and looked to his son. "You? Miss?"

"I'm Joy, that's Raven." She motioned towards her little sister who had ducked inside. Raven handed two mugs of tea-water to Joy through the open window. She climbed back out of the house with a clean cloth wedged under her arm. Joy admired her sister's warm nature. Despite what she had been through, she still wanted to care for others.

"Thank you." Tom grabbed both mugs and passed one to his son.

Raven smiled. "You're welcome."

"So, what happened to you two?" Joy asked.

Jim rubbed at his eyes. "I don't know, I was on my way to meet my friend, just walking. We were gonna dig a hole, so I had my shovel in my hand, then some man came from nowhere and threw sand in my eyes."

"Then I ran over to see what my boy was doing rolling on the floor and some fella was stood there gawping, so I asked what he'd done to my boy and he sure as hell showed me." Tom shook his head with disappointment.

"Sand you say?" Joy cocked her head to the side trying to work out what sort of sand would inflict such pain. Tom and Jim's eyes were swollen and glowing red like embers in a fire. Joy finally clued in. She knew exactly who was responsible for this. That fucking idiot Isaac.

She shook her head. "Why?"

"I don't know." Jim shrugged. "Sorry, Dad."

"You've got nothing to be sorry for, boy. It was all that fucker." Tom's neck veins throbbed with rage.

Joy kept quiet. Though it pained her, she couldn't help but hold a soft spot for Isaac.

"Well, thank you both so much for the hospitality but we'd best be on our way," Tom announced as he stood up and signalled to Jim. "I'll come by and fix that door for you at some point."

"That would be great," Joy said and elbowed Raven.

"That would be really great." Raven beamed.

"Come, Jim, let's be on our way. Say thank you to Raven and Joy."

"Thank you, Raven and Miss Joy." Jim waved as the two proceeded down the dusty path, back toward town.

Raven climbed through the kitchen window and helped Joy bring the chairs back inside.

"Now that they're on their way, I need to talk to you about something."

"Am I in trouble?" Raven asked, her mouth turned down at the corners.

Joy couldn't help but smile. "No, sit down you fool."

Raven sat across from Joy, her eyes filled with worry. Joy leaned forward and put her hands on her little sister's knees to reassure her.

"Raven," Joy started, "I have to go away for a bit. It could be a few days or it could be a few weeks."

"What? Why?!" Raven chewed her lip.

Pangs of guilt struck Joy. She always lied to her little sister about her line of work and lying to those she loved didn't sit well with her, but she dared not tell Raven the truth. She wouldn't understand.

"You know how I've been working here and there, whenever I could?"

"Yeah." Raven nodded.

"Well, there's this job, and they want to pay me two doubloons for it. Only problem is I don't know how long it's going to take." Joy leaned back in her chair and stuck her hand in her pockets. She retrieved ten reale and put it into a pouch.

"You can use this to feed yourself while I'm gone. It's more than enough to last you two, even three weeks if you use it right."

She handed the reale-filled pouch to Raven. It had metal seams around the edges, just like Isaac had taught her. That reminded her... Isaac. She had to find him before Roy called on her to leave. Her stint at the mercenary camp meant she would be tied up for a while and there was no way she would let him get off scot-free after what he did.

Raven's bottom lip quivered as her eyes brimmed with tears. Joy placed her hand on her chin and lifted it. "You're stronger than you think, sis."

It was rare for them to be separated from one another nowadays, but it had to happen.

"What sort of job?" Raven asked, her voice soft and her brow furrowed.

"It sounds pretty boring actually. Some crates need

delivering. It's far."

Raven shut her eyes tight and nodded.

"Anyway, never you worry. It'll be okay, sis. I won't be long."

Joy stood up, gathered her things and made her way to the window. "Love you."

Raven ran to Joy and hugged her tight. "I'll miss you. You be safe, promise?"

"Of course! Start planning my welcome home dinner, okay? I'll be hungry."

"Love you too." Raven choked back sobs.

Joy turned and climbed out the window, blowing a kiss as she went.

She threw on her hat and checked her jacket for blades.

"Right," she declared to herself. "Time to find that fucker." She laughed.

It wouldn't be hard to find Isaac. If he were being blamed for murder, and had attacked an innocent father and son, he would be feeling terrible. There was only one place he would go for a little cheering up—The Milky Way. And lucky for Joy, it was just down the road.

ISAAC CARVER

A dusty boot pressed into Isaac's head as his wrists were bound tight. The rough rope burnt his skin.

"Look inside!" he cried, hoping to distract the guards. He couldn't believe they had his map. He had been working on it for so many years and it had been snatched away in the blink of an eye.

"Should we give it to the boss?" The guard ignored Isaac and tried to read what was written on it. "*C. Kidd... Treasure not found.*" The guard paused for a moment. "C. Kidd. Do you think it's—"

"Oh no, not that stupid map again." Isaac heard a woman's voice, a familiar voice, one that excited him but also scared him.

The big black boot pressing into his head vanished. Blood splattered on the ground before him, just missing the old woman's cards. A blade grazed his wrists and cut the rope which bound them. He propped himself up and saw that beautiful familiar face he missed so much. "Joy!" He looked around and saw three motionless guards, slumped on the ground, their throats slit.

Isaac scooped up the cards and shoved them in his top pocket. Joy held out the map toward him.

"You dropped this." She had that beautiful goofy smile he so enjoyed, but sadly missed now that they weren't together.

"Oh my goodness." Isaac stood with his eyes closed, shaking his head in grateful disbelief. "I can't thank you enough."

"It's true you can't. You look rough."

Isaac took the map and tucked it in his pocket. "Yes, well, it's been a rather long day so far."

"I know the feeling." Joy raised her eyebrows.

"I owe you."

"You do." Joy smiled and pushed her way past Isaac. "What happened here anyways?"

"Joy, I wouldn't go in there," Isaac warned.

"Yeah, yeah." She stepped over the guards and opened the brothel door. "Oh my..."

"I know." Isaac followed her in.

His stomach churned as his mind tried to make sense of what he was looking at. The hairs on the back of his neck prickled and sent a shiver down his spine. Mounds of brutally severed heads were strewn about the brothel's reception area. Some had been carefully placed on the front desk, their eyes staring vacantly at whomever entered. Isaac's chest grew tight. He'd witnessed some grisly goings-on throughout his life. Hell, he'd been part of some, but nothing like this.

His boots squelched as he stepped through the pools of blood and guts which lined the floor. To the right of the desk, naked bodies of men and women were piled high with a severed head sat atop.

"This is fucked up." Joy's face grew pale. "Isaac. Why were the guards arresting you here?"

"I genuinely don't know." He held his hands up and shrugged.

"Nothing to do with this, was it?"

"No, of course not. You know I'm not capable of something like this. Surely."

Joy nodded and crept forward. "Are they all..."

"I think so."

"Who would..."

"I don't know, I'd just got here." Isaac slumped in a chair behind the reception desk. He let out a deep breath and rummaged in his top pocket for his flask. The fortune teller's stiff cards brushed his hand. 'An old love will cause you great harm.' The old lady's words echoed in his ears. He looked to Joy who joined him behind the counter. She was wild but then again so was that old woman.

"Flask!" she said and reached out for it. She knew Isaac well. He handed it over and she took a gulp.

"Look at these poor fuckers. Lost and soulless in this dark bloody hole." She shook her head and handed the flask back to Isaac.

"And that is exactly why we should probably get going." He tipped the remainder of the rum into his mouth and shook the empty flask. "Remind you of old times?" He shot Joy a wink.

"Ew, no." Joy nudged him with her shoulder.

Isaac saw the way she looked at him. She used to look at him like that a lot. In the early days anyways. "We should get out of here, whoever did this is clearly very angry and very brutal." Isaac dusted off his jacket and scraped his blood-soaked boots against a brush behind the counter. "Sophia!" Isaac caught sight of her severed head.

Her lifeless eyes stared back at him. "You were my favorite."

"Mmm we all remember her, don't we?" Joy said with disapproval.

"Yes, well, made that a bit awkward, didn't I? Sorry."

"Ancient history." Joy shrugged. "We should find out who did this."

"I dunno, Joy, I'd rather stay out of it. Just close the door and pretend I never saw anything."

"I'm going upstairs." Joy nodded and made for the blood splattered stairs.

"Joy, don't. Please..." Isaac wondered if he would ever shake his feelings for her. He missed her, he missed them, but he didn't miss her ridiculously stubborn outbursts. "Gah, Joy!" He clenched his teeth together in frustration and stomped after her. At the top of the stairs, he caught her arm. "So, what's your plan then?"

"Look around for clues. Check the rooms. See if anyone's left." She shrugged.

"Fine. Guess I'll go first then." Isaac opened the bedroom door closest to the stairway. "Empty."

"Empty." Joy replied as she gripped her blade and opened the second door, ready to spring into action.

Isaac couldn't shake the sinking feeling in the pit of his stomach. Everything told him this was a terrible idea, but he knew Joy wouldn't stop until she checked every door. "Joy, let's just go. Please."

"Shut up, check the other doors."

The worn floorboards creaked as they crept down the hallway.

"There's nobody left, Joy. This is pointless."

She turned to Isaac and looked him square in the eyes. "What if there is? What if that was you! You'd want someone to come looking." She wagged her finger in anger. "Quit your whining. You're either with me or..." They both froze at the sound of voices coming from downstairs.

Joy and Isaac put their backs to the wall. Their fingers were almost touching. Isaac could feel the spark between them. Joy smacked his hand away and sidestepped down the hallway toward the stairs. She crouched and peered through the wooden banister which overlooked the reception and beckoned for Isaac to join her. Isaac shook his head, but Joy gave him a look which said it all. He reluctantly joined her, and they peered through the banister together.

Downstairs, three well-built sweaty men stood with their hands on their hips, their foreheads still wet with sweat from the slaughter they had no doubt just finished. The tallest and meanest looking member of the trio wore a red bandana and a permanent snarl. He towered over the other two goons who stood either side of him.

"Boss, why'd we have to come back? Doesn't seem like a good idea," the smallest of the three asked. He wore a black bandana and a gormless toothless grin.

"I already told ya, we need to get that coin." The tall one adjusted his red bandana and took out a blade. It was curved and broadened at the point with a handle big enough to fit both of his ginormous hands.

"Thad's gonna be pissed if we get caught," the toothless goon muttered as he crept across the slippery floor.

"He's gonna be more pissed if we come back without it! So shut your mouth and get looking!"

"Sorry, boss." He put his hands up apologetically.

"Look at them. All naked, massive knockers," the other goon piped up as he grabbed a handful of a dead girl's breast. "Such a waste of good flesh." He pulled at his thick black beard and licked his lips.

"We have to kill them," Joy whispered to Isaac.

"Are you kidding me?" He kept his voice low and his face so close to Joy's that he could almost kiss her. "We should hide, let them do whatever they're going to do, then get out of here. Do you even know who Thad is?" Isaac had never laid eyes on him, but he'd heard. There was always talk at the tavern of his merciless thirst for brutality.

"Thad? Who cares? He's just a man," Joy huffed.

"No, I don't think you understand. Look at what three of his men did, probably on their own." Isaac pointed down to the pile of bodies. "I don't want to end up on the pile." Isaac shook his head.

Downstairs the trio ransacked the room.

"It's not here." The toothless goon shook his head.

"Search the bodies, tear 'em apart! We have to find it!" the boss growled.

"This is messed up. I can't watch this." Isaac tiptoed into the closest bedroom and beckoned for Joy to join him. He wasn't going to risk his life for this.

Joy ran to the top of the stairs and stood tall. "You!" She pointed her blade down at the three men.

"Oh fuck!" Isaac hit his head against the wall in frustration. He couldn't let Joy do this alone. Could he? "Are you mad?" Isaac whispered from the bedroom.

"Why did you do this?" Joy shouted, ignoring Isaac. "You're fucking sick!" She trod slowly down the blood-smeared stairs, wielding her blade.

"Joy, no, no, no." Isaac muttered to himself and crept out of the room to the banister. He crouched low and kept out of sight, then watched on as Joy bravely trod down the stairs. Isaac had forgotten about her perilous pursuit of justice and how it inevitably landed them both in trouble whenever they were together.

"It looks like we forgot one of them, boys." The red bandana wearing brute looked up at Joy and rubbed his hands with glee. "Don't you see what we're doing here, sweetheart? Are you that stupid?"

"There's only one person around here who's stupid and it ain't me." She held her blade out and pointed it at the giant brute. "Make that three actually." Joy stepped down the rest of the stairs.

"I don't need to answer to you!" The brute was enraged by Joy's insolence. "Add her to the pile boys!"

The two goons charged at Joy, wielding their blades, whilst their boss folded his arms and watched. "Have some fun with this one, she's pissing me off."

Isaac peered through the wooden rail. The toothless goon charged at Joy, slashing in a haphazard manner at her side. These were no skilled fighters. They had brawn on their side but nothing more. Joy was quick. She blocked the incoming blade with hers and kicked the goon in the face, knocking him to the ground. Isaac heard a loud thud as if someone's head hit something hard.

Joy stepped back up the stairs with care as the bearded goon lurched at her. "C'mon, darling, give me a taste." Sweat dripped from his brow and judging by the surrounding carnage he was already pretty exhausted. He lunged again and his sword met hers. Each strike was blocked as Joy slowly made her way up the stairway back to Isaac.

Maybe I should jump in now, Isaac thought as he rose to his feet and checked his pockets for something to break up the duelling swords.

"This is too easy!" Joy taunted as she kicked the bearded one down the stairs. He tumbled, coating himself in blood as he went.

Joy ran down the hallway toward the farthest bedroom and motioned for Isaac to stay put. He tucked himself in the corner with his back to the wall. His eyes darted between the stairway and the far bedroom.

The toothless goon had recovered and jumped up the stairs two at a time. "Fucking whore!" He sprinted down the hallway screaming.

Joy rolled into the bedroom, slammed the door shut and hit the latch, locking herself inside. Isaac watched as the goon pounded his fists on the door.

"Where is she?" The bearded goon had recovered from his fall and came stomping up the stairs to join his friend. The pair hammered on the door with their fists but it was solid timber, probably with the added extra of Joy's entire weight pressed against it, Isaac assumed.

Heavy footsteps filled the air as the burly leader stomped up the stairs. "Bash that fucking door down would ya!"

"Surprise!" Isaac leapt from behind the stair rail and launched himself at the giant brute of a man. The pair tumbled down the stairs, their limbs flailing and clattering into one another. Isaac was first to his feet and scrambled to the reception counter through the slippery blood pools. He climbed up on it as the giant brute recovered from the tumble and stormed over to Isaac, his red bandana displaced.

"Looking a little worse for wear, fella," Isaac mocked.

The brute erupted in rage and brought his blade down into the counter, missing Isaac by an inch. Isaac kicked him in the face and as he turned, leapt onto his back. The brute dropped his blade as he stumbled about trying to pull Isaac off of him.

From upstairs came a loud crash and the clattering of swords.

"Cyrus! You killed Cyrus!"

"Yeah well, you killed everyone." Isaac heard Joy fire back followed by more clicks and clangs of blades.

Isaac didn't let up. He clung to the brute, his arms wrapped around his neck and his heels dug into his thighs. There was no shaking him. The brute struggled to breathe under Isaac's iron grip and stumbled out the front door. The pair toppled over the guards' bodies and landed face down on the dusty path.

Isaac jumped to his feet and ran ahead.

"You're dead." The big man clambered to standing and stomped toward him.

"I'm dead?" Isaac said as he reached into his pocket. He pointed to himself, smirking. "I don't feel very dead." He poked himself in the ribs. "In fact, I feel very much alive. Unlike you, big fella. Catch!" Isaac tossed a smoking pouch.

"Wha..." The burly brute caught the pouch and peered inside, his red bandana hanging down across his face. The pouch sizzled before exploding, knocking him to the ground. A wave of fire spread across his entire body. He writhed on the floor in agony as flames lashed at his flesh and engulfed him.

"There you go," Isaac said, impressed. "Thanks, Molly."

Screams came from the brothel doorway. "You're crazy!" the bearded goon shouted as he came hurtling out of the door. He scrambled over the guards' bodies and sped off down the road.

Joy stood in the doorway wiping her blades clean and shaking her head.

"Good job, nice of you to finally join in," she said as she strode over and joined Isaac. "You always were a late comer." She smiled and raised her eyebrows.

"Haha very funny." Isaac rolled his eyes. "You going to let him get away?"

"He'll be dead in a few hours." Joy held out a small blade and tucked it back in her jacket. "Poison."

"What if he..." Isaac checked around for onlookers. "Tells Thad about us within that time?"

"Good." She smirked. "How?" Joy pointed to the flaming body.

"I know. Pretty great, isn't it? I've been saving that for the right occasion."

"Wow."

"Seriously though, Joy, let's hope Thad doesn't find out about this."

"Who cares? Thad can go to hell." Joy threw her hand up, dismissing Isaac's concerns. "I'm surprised you even helped out in there. You don't normally do anything unless there's something in it for you."

"That's a bit unfair, I'm not that bad. I just try to stay out of trouble."

"Ha! Please. Anyway, the reason I came to find you..."

"Yes, good point. Why did you actually come here?" Isaac gazed at The Milky Way hoping to forget the atrocities that had occurred. It had long been one of his favorite pleasure dens and it was rather tainted now. He would miss Sophia, but he was sure there would be many other Sophia's in his lifetime. He tuned back into what Joy was saying.

"Did you blind a young boy and his father with that dust of yours?" Joy asked with scorn.

"What? After all this? That's all you wanted to know?" Isaac threw his head back and groaned.

"Well, did you?" Joy pressed, stepping in closer to Isaac.

"There you are!" A man with a wooden eye came shuffling around the corner. "I just went by your house. Little girl said you'd already left. Didn't expect to find you here though." He grew distracted by the flaming body. "What's been going on? How'd that happen?"

"Never you mind. Though you can join him if you'd like?" Isaac readied his fists for a fight.

Joy burst into laughter. "Don't worry, Isaac. I know this man."

"Excellent, I'll be off then." Isaac started to back away, taking the opportunity to escape Joy's questioning.

"Not so fast." She grabbed Isaac by the collar and turned to the wooden eyed man. "Yes, what is it?"

"Roy sent me, Miss Joy. Said it's time to be heading to the camp for the trial." His gaze on the flaming body didn't falter. "I'll uh... I'll be discreet with what I've seen."

"That would be appreciated. Thank you." She nodded as he backed away, almost bumping into a wall. "Now you!" She turned her attention back to Isaac. "Little boy and his father, you blind them?"

"I've got to go see Pino." Isaac slipped out of her grasp and jogged backwards in the direction of the docks. "And yes, I did!" he shouted once out of reach. Isaac could see Joy standing in the middle of the road alone, hands on her hips, shaking her head in disapproval.

"You better make it up to them, Isaac!" she shouted. "Or I'll make you regret it."

"I might." He gave her a wave and sped off.

JANE HATCH

"Miss, they're here," Jane's right hand and confidant, Margaret announced as she bounded into the room. She paused and bowed her head to Jane.

"Margaret! I told you not to bow to me. You of all people don't have to," Jane said in a hushed tone and rolled her eyes.

"The men love it! Plus, it makes you look even more important." Margaret grinned.

"But it's just you and me in here?" Jane shook her head. "Never mind, just show them in." She sat at her desk and fixed her cropped, dark blond hair. The light caught her piercing hazel eyes and high cheekbones.

She stood up to welcome her three male guests. Men were always enchanted by her, but truth be told she couldn't care less. None were a match for her. They were either too stupid, power hungry or sexually ravenous to serve any real purpose in her life.

The guests stood in the doorway waiting for her signal. This was the best part of it all—the power which she wielded over others and the respect they had for her.

It had taken years to amass but their reactions made it all worthwhile. She recognized the look on their faces. As soon as they stepped into the room, they shrank back into themselves, struck by the room's enormity and the treasures it held. Jane liked to host all of her meetings in her armory. It was strategic. It showed not only her wealth but her power too. The walls were lined with row upon row of flintlock pistols and muskets. Well-polished swords and daggers waited to be selected for the next job.

"Are you just going to stand there and gawk?" Jane started strong. If they were to negotiate well today, she needed to assert her authority early.

"I'm so sorry, ma'am." He wore a crimson bandana and matching sash.

Jane liked to home in on every detail: clothing, hair, how people carried themselves. It all spoke volumes to her. He was clearly the leader of the group as he had stepped forward and spoken up. And he was also the only one wearing anything half decent.

"I'd like to pay for your services," he continued, whilst trying to maintain eye contact and seem confident, though the sweat brimming at his temples told a different story.

Jane looked to Maddy and Leon, her two guards hovering in the doorway, and signaled for them to stand down.

"Why are you so nervous?" Jane walked up to him and put her finger against the exposed part of his chest. She traced her finger across his shoulder as she circled him. She stood behind him and tapped her finger in the middle of his back, knowing this would intimidate him. "You know my usual rates, don't you?" The other two scruffy fellows stared straight ahead, not daring to catch her gaze.

Flustered, the leader turned around to face her. "Umm, yes, what was it? Four doubloons?"

"Well, that depends on what you want."

"I just need four men, no guns."

"Then that'll be six doubloons."

"Six? Last time it was four."

"Come sit." She beckoned the trio to be seated.

Jane continued to stand, knowing the advantage in height would increase her chances of getting two extra doubloons from this bumbling idiot.

"Rates have gone up since last time."

"But it's only been a week."

"Yep, and we've been very busy. As I'm sure you know, it's all about supply and demand."

The trio looked disgruntled. They couldn't argue with that logic and Jane knew they weren't smart enough to negotiate with anything other than their fists.

"Well, we don't have it. Four is steep compared to others and that's what we came with."

Jane walked over to her window and gazed out. "You came to me because you know I'm the best." She turned to face her captive audience. "No one's forcing your hand in this. So, you either go elsewhere knowing to never come begging at my door again, or pay the extra coin as requested."

"We're not begging!" The outraged leader stood up.

"I didn't say you were, but you might be soon enough." Jane took out a small dagger and readied it at her side. "So, what's it going to be?" She asked, grazing the blade down her palm.

"Fine. We'll pay up. Sorry for the trouble." The man tossed his coins into the coffer which sat on Jane's desk. "But I want my pick!"

"Of course," Jane agreed and took a seat at her desk. "Now, four men you said?"

"That's right."

"Ah ha. I'll put that down as four mercs and you can let me know which men or women you would like." Jane noted the transaction in her ledger.

The trio walked out, empty pocketed and angry, but it didn't worry Jane. She had every faith in the quality of her mercenaries. They were well paid, well fed and well trained, which Jane found to be a winning combination. She stuck her head out of the solid oak double doors. "Maddy, Leon, you're both dismissed for lunch."

"Thank you, ma'am," they said in unison and tagged the hands of the new guards who sauntered down the corridor for duty.

Jane walked back and stood in position. "Alright, who's next?" She motioned for the new guards to open the door to the next eager person waiting to present their case to her.

A short and bony man with deep, dark bags under his eyes walked in. He looked like he hadn't slept or eaten a proper meal in years.

"Not again, Slim." Jane put her hand to her brow and sighed. "What is it now?"

The man came shuffling in at a pace which drove Jane to distraction.

"Hello, Jane."

Even his soft voice irritated her. Something about him just always seemed a little off. He was always polite, so it wasn't that. He did leer at her, but then again, most men did.

She pushed it to the back of her mind and concentrated on what was coming out of his mouth.

"I'd like to join a crew heading to Devil's Cay. Do you know anyone going?"

"I believe we've had this conversation before, haven't we? Nobody goes there, Slim, not yet anyway, it's too dangerous. We haven't been to that island in years."

"But ma'am!" He raised his fist in the air. "You know I've gone before, many times! It's not dangerous for me to go." His eyes widened and his smile grew. "Only three people in all of Nassau have ever gone and come back alive, and I am one of them."

"Yes, I do know, Slim. You tell me this every week."

"But I must go back, ma'am! My brother, he's still on that island."

"I'm sorry, Slim." Jane pressed her fingers into her eyes. "There's no reason for me to go there at the moment and I can't justify sending a crew out just to save your brother."

"I understand, ma'am." Slim bowed his head. "Please, let me know if anyone does want to go. I can show them the way." He shuffled toward the door, dragging one leg behind as if it were injured. "I'll see you next week."

"Sure." Jane shook her head.

"Miss!" Margaret knocked on the door and rushed in, her short round body shaking.

"What's wrong?" Jane ran over to her. "What happened?"

Margaret reached into her satchel attached at the hip, uncorked a bottle and downed the contents. "For my nerves."

"Of course, what is it? What's happened," Jane pressed.

"Miss Maddy." The colour drained from Margaret's face. "She's dead!"

"What?" Jane was taken aback as Margaret collapsed in a heap on the floor.

"Margaret? Can you hear me?" Jane dropped to her knees and shook her friend's shoulders but received no response. She leapt up and ran to the door. "Search the halls! Look for anyone acting suspiciously," Jane yelled out to the new guards.

She returned to Margaret's side. Sweat poured down her forehead, her eyes shut. Jane put her ear to Margaret's mouth and watched the rise and fall of her chest. Shock, she must be in shock, Jane reassured herself and ran out into the hallway.

"Leon!" she shouted and sprinted to where Maddy lay cold, blood pooled around her.

Leon came running, a piece of bread stuck on his hook where his hand used to be. "What happened? What happened to Maddy?"

"I don't know! Go tend to Margaret! She's in shock, in my room." He sprinted down the hall.

"Did anyone see who did this?" Jane yelled to her mercenaries who were appearing from the downstairs rooms in droves. Why didn't I hear anything? Jane questioned herself. It didn't make sense.

"I saw those men leave, they were pretty angry," a slight, well-groomed man piped up.

"Probably couldn't stand a woman having power over them," Anna added. She was the newest of Jane's recruits. An act-first-think-later, skilled and merciless killer.

"Right!" Jane sped down stair after stair and paused at the mezzanine which overlooked the grand circular foyer. She clapped her hands above her head to get everyone's attention. "Anna, Jose, you're coming with me!"

Anna sprinted down the stairs. A grin spread across her thin, weathered face. She secured her dirty, blond hair and grabbed her partner in crime. Jose almost jumped for joy at being called up by their leader. He tied his black headband and winked at Anna. The pair were bloodthirsty and increasingly inseparable.

Jane observed them flirting—a lot—but it really wasn't any of her business, so long as the work got done to her standard she couldn't care less about their sexual escapades.

She marched through the marble floored foyer, seething with rage. Anna and Jose followed close behind, their eyes thirsty for action. Jane stormed through the thick double doors out onto the rough gravel path which crunched underfoot. The path purposely snaked around in a loop, slowing down visitors' entries and exits. A patch of tall grass sat in the middle which made for the perfect cut through to the main gate.

The trio ran through the grass until the wanted men came in sight. They sat in the back of a wagon, jiggling to and fro with each bump in the path. Jane ran to the driver and stepped in front. The driver knew better than to continue. He bowed his head in respect... and fear of what was to come.

"We don't want no trouble. We paid up, didn't we?" the leader said as Anna and Jose joined him in the back of the wagon.

"Well, that's some horseshit! Why'd you kill my girl then?" Jane stormed around to where the trio sat in the back of the wagon. She clutched a dagger in one hand and a flintlock in the other.

"Who?" one of the scruffy runts piped up.

Jane eyed his behavior. He spoke with newly found confidence.

"My guard, you saw her. I dismissed her shortly after you left," Jane pressed, raising her pistol.

"I didn't do it! We didn't do it!" The leader sat stiff with fear, shaking his head from side to side. "I promise. I wouldn't. We were annoyed about the money but that's just 'cos the boss will be."

Jane watched as he talked. He didn't move his hands, his eyes didn't grow wide, and his voice didn't falter. Everything checked out; it seemed as if he were telling the truth. "Okay, I belie—"

"You liar!" Anna stuck a knife in the leader's throat. "I hope you rot in hell!" She spat in his face as the life drained from his eyes. Jose grabbed the scruffy runt closest to him as if inspired by Anna's outburst, and stabbed him in the chest, looking to Anna for approval. Then he moved the knife down to the stomach and kept going.

Jane was horrified. She'd hired these two because they were brutal but seeing their sick, sexually charged, murderous game churned her stomach. She wasn't driven by a lust for blood. There was no element of desire in what she did. It was simply business.

"Stop!" Jane shouted as the wagon filled with blood. "He wasn't lying," she said, holding her thumb and forefinger to her eyes. "Everyone off the wagon!" she ordered.

The remaining scruffy runt sat frozen with fear. "You too, what's your name?" She pointed her dagger in his face and eyeballed him. "What's your name?" she yelled.

"They were… my friends…" he stammered, paralyzed with fear.

"Yeah, well, Maddy was ours. Eye for an eye." Jose lifted his hand to strike him, but Jane interjected.

"You both need to calm the fuck down." She eyed Jose and Anna.

She looked back at the man in the cart. "Who do you

work for?" Jane asked, grabbing his arm and tugging him down from the wagon.

"What?" The man's lips were quivering, his legs weak.

He stumbled down to the ground and crouched, using his hands to steady himself.

"I said who do you work for?" Jane grabbed his chin and burrowed her eyes into his.

"Thad Horn."

Jane nodded, her face tensed. "He can never find out about this."

The scruffy runt nodded frantically. "Yep, yes, I understand, ma'am."

"I'm sorry you got caught up in this mess." She grabbed him by the hair and slit his throat. Better to die by my hand than Thad's, she thought as she tapped on the wagon, signaling for it to leave. She turned to face her new recruits.

"You realize they were telling the truth, right?" Jane stepped closer to them. "They weren't lying and now you've cost me business," she shouted.

Anna and Jose stood smirking, arms folded, heads cocked to the side. "Sorry, ma'am, but we don't know they didn't do it for sure," Anna said.

"Are you doubting my judgment?"

"No, ma'am"

"Do you even know who Thad is?"

Jose lifted his hands and shrugged. "Should we?"

"You see that big old castle up there?" Jane shook her finger toward the tallest point in Nassau where the grand residence stood, surrounded by thick brick walls.

"Yeah," Jose said, squinting his almost black eyes.

"Well, that's where Thad lives. Know how he got so rich?"

"No."

"Neither do I, but I once met a man who got into a brawl with one of Thad's men at the tavern. He came to me for protection. Ended up buying thirty of my men, of which twenty-nine died. Do you know who was left?"

Neither of the bloodthirsty duo batted an eyelid. "Who?" Jose said, unimpressed by the threatening story.

"Todd. You remember him, right? He's at our place right now."

"You mean like short Todd? No legs Todd? That Todd?" Jose said, holding in a laugh.

"Yep. You should ask what Thad did to him and those twenty-nine other men because that's what he's going to do to you or worse... That was a while back though, maybe he's developed new techniques now." Jane lowered her voice. "You're mercenaries, not savages. Pull this sort of thing again and I'll kill you both myself." She turned on her heel and headed back through the grass.

It was rare she had a moment to herself, but she needed to simmer down before facing her crew. She felt proud of what lay before her. The merc mansion housed fifty residents at any one time. It stood on a steep hill, giving it a great vantage point over Nassau. It was a bloody business, but it provided people with a home. They had companionship, hot food at every meal, and all the liquor they desired.

The black and white flag flapped in the breeze and she gave a nod to the white fox painted on it as she approached the house. She glanced back down the hill at Anna and Jose before heading inside. They seemed to be cleaning up their mess at least and so long as the driver did as he was paid to and didn't breathe a word of this to anyone, everything should be fine, she thought.

The mansion doors slammed open and a frantic, blood covered Leon stood panting.

"Ma'am, you have to..." He caught his breath. "Up to your room." He doubled over, hand and hook on his knees, trying to slow his breathing.

"Leon, what is it?"

"Margaret!"

Jane noticed Leon's blood covered hook. She sprinted up the stairs, taking two at a time. He struggled to keep up and followed as close behind as he could. Jane reached the armory and stormed in, smashing the doors open, searching for Margaret. Papers from her desk had been thrown to the ground. Her books and ledger gone from sight.

"Leon! Where is she?"

"Behind... behind the desk," he blurted as he slid down the wall and sat with his head hung low, in between his knees.

Jane peered around the desk, fearful of what she was about to see. "Margaret!" Jane grew cold as she knelt down next to Margaret's bloodied body. She had been slit from her throat to her stomach.

"How did this happen? She was fine when I left, shocked but not..." Jane stifled a sob as a tear escaped from her eye.

"Leon, what exactly happened here? Didn't you stay with her the whole time?" Her eyes burned into him.

"She came round but she was muttering." He stared at his feet. "I thought she could do with a wet cloth and something to drink... When I came back, I couldn't see her anymore..."

"How long were you gone?"

"It felt like five minutes, must've been closer to ten. She

was talking so I thought she was okay. Safe at least." He didn't move.

Jane forced herself to look at Margaret's blood splattered face, her eyes had bulged out of her skull in fear. "Who would do this to you of all people?" Jane blinked back tears and wiped her eyes when she noticed something wedged in Margaret's mouth. It looked like a crumpled piece of paper. She stuck her fingers in to fish it out then closed Margaret's eyes and walked to the window. She needed air.

"Leon, cover her will you. I can't bear it."

She focused on the note and tried to steady her hands.

Dear Jane Hatch...

CAPTAIN CROW

"Don't move!" the voice behind Crow repeated. As the gun's cold barrel pressed into the back of his neck, Crow struggled to remember a day when he wasn't involved in an altercation of some kind. Every day he woke up he was surprised he'd made another, and after all these years, being threatened at gunpoint was commonplace.

He looked over at Nelson whose usually ruddy face had lost all of its colour.

"What do you want with us, miss?" Crow asked in a measured tone. Out the corner of his eye he spied the flintlock held at the back of Nelson's head. It was positioned at an angle, suggesting both weapons were being brandished by the same source.

"If... if it's coin, then... umm... unfortunately we're both in the same situation," Nelson stammered.

Without any warning, Crow dropped to the ground, propped himself up with his hands and kicked out his back legs as hard as he could, like a bucking donkey.

The flintlock wielding miss was caught off guard and fell to the ground, winded. Crow flipped around and whacked her over the head with his pistol, knocking her out cold.

"And that's how you do it." Crow dusted off his hands. She looked vaguely familiar to him. Long, matted, dreadlocked hair, burgundy shirt belted at the waist. "Looks like one of Vella's girls." He collected the flintlocks and handed them to Nelson.

"Hmm, could be." Nelson bagged the pistols and bent down to inspect for clues, his shirt soaked in sweat from the action. He peeled back the front left-hand side of her jacket which revealed a white circle with a V stamped inside. "Yep, that's Vella's mark."

"Shit. This isn't going to help us with our meeting, is it?" Crow rubbed the back of his neck. He was already filled with dread at the prospect of seeing his former lover and this whole situation would only add to the can of worms.

"Well, we can just hide her in the woods and not mention this whole thing." Nelson shrugged. "We'll have our coin by the time she wakes up."

"Yep, that works." Crow dragged their unconscious assailant by her legs into the undergrowth. "Great plan, Nelson."

"Sir, it was all you. We should head off though, we're going to be late."

Crow groaned. Vella would never let them hear the end of it if they were. She was a stickler for punctuality. They slowed their pace to clean up as Vella's house drew into sight. The royal blue paint finish on the doors and windows sills looked fresh and perfectly contrasted the sandy-beige stone. Crow had stayed here on and off for almost a year when they were together. It was comfortable but it had never felt like home. Life on land never did.

Nelson knocked on the door and nodded to Crow. "Be nice. We don't want a repeat of last time."

"Too hard. I'll be quiet instead," Crow grumbled.

A young girl with brown dreaded hair pulled the door open. "Hello, how can I help?" The thick hoop which pierced her lip gave her a lisp.

"Yes, we have an appointment with Vella. Nelson and the captain." He gave a polite nod which turned into more of a bow.

Crow gave him an elbow. "Don't overdo it," he muttered.

The girl stepped aside and showed them in. "Take a seat and I'll let her know you're here." She gestured to two well-worn upholstered armchairs.

Crow perched on the edge of the chair. "This place..." Not much had changed. The same naval paintings hung on the beige walls and heavy, navy drapes sheltered them from the beaming sunlight.

"It's classy," Nelson said under his breath. Crow curled his lip and huffed. It was nice enough, but too nice. Everything had a place. It felt forced, and soulless.

The lip-ringed door greeter re-appeared out of a far room, a book tucked under her arm. "She's ready, if you'd like to follow me." She jogged up a flight of stairs and walked them to the last room in the corridor. Crow knew where to go, but he didn't let on.

"Thank you." Nelson smiled both to the girl and to Crow for behaving.

Inside the room, stacks of books and papers were piled high. Ripped maps and shipping schedules pinned to the wall. Crow never understood the way Vella worked. She assured him there was a method to the madness, that everything had its place, but to him it looked a mess. Crow recalled how Vella would pore over texts for hours, absorbing everything there was to know about Nassau and the surrounding waters. He always thought she was a bit mad, but it had been part of the appeal. She wasn't like anyone else.

Nelson cleared his throat. Vella froze for a second then looked up from her desk.

"Nelson, Crow, it's been a while." She stood up and stuck out her hand.

It took Crow every fiber of his being not to make a snide remark—that it wasn't long enough—but as her small, smooth hand touched his, memories of happier times came flooding back, and he softened.

"Yes, thank you for meeting with us, Vella." Nelson squeezed himself into an armchair as Crow hovered on the edge of another.

Vella sank back in hers, hands clasped together. Her wild, dreaded hair flowed over the chair. She raised an eyebrow as she spoke. "So, what brings you two here?"

Crow couldn't help but stare. She had added in burgundy wraps around sections of her hair. Her face didn't look any different, but the slits shaved into her eyebrows had gotten bigger and moved as she spoke. He had always found it distracting but now they seemed more prominent than ever.

Nelson leaned forward. "Well, we'd like to borrow a little bit of coin from you. The plan is to get it back to you as soon as we can... We're just in a bit of a bind right now." He clasped his hands together and looked at Vella with pleading eyes. "You know we're good for it."

"What's wrong, Crow? Can't keep your men in order?" Vella smirked.

Crow's eye twitched in anger. He hated being made out

105

to be bad at what he did, and Vella knew it. "Nope, just a little snag, you know how it is." Crow scratched at his beard and moved to sit back in his chair, trying his best to stay calm.

"Actually, I don't know how it is, but I'll take your word for it." She chuckled under her breath.

Crow clenched his fists in his lap. He felt like a coiled spring, ready to unravel at any moment.

Vella searched her desk for her ledger. "Got it. This was a fascinating read by the way." She tapped the book. "This man wants to make paper money, would you believe? Ha!" She tossed the book in question to the floor. "So, how much do you need?"

Nelson's eyes widened. "Ten doubloons should do it."

Vella snapped the ledger shut. "Ten doubloons? Are you crazy? Do you know how hard it is to make that?"

"Well, yes. That's why we're here," Nelson said. He rubbed at his thighs and shifted in his seat.

Crow rolled his eyes. He had expected this kind of behavior. She loved toying with people.

"I'm sorry but I can't afford that."

"I knew this was a waste of time, Nelson, let's go." Crow stood up. He knew her tactics and what was coming next.

"Sir, we need this money, it's the only way." Nelson pleaded and remained seated.

"There is something you can do for me, if you'd like?" Vella leaned on her desk, her eyes mischievous like a cat playing with a mouse.

"What is it?" Crow snapped.

"Well, if you'd like to sit back down and show me some respect, I will discuss it with you."

Crow's simmering temper was close to boiling point.

He hated her having the upper hand. It was just like old times. "Fine." He plonked himself down and sighed.

"Go on." Nelson, eager to hear Vella's request, smiled and nodded.

"You know there's a war brewing between Jane, Thad and myself. We're all in the same business, we all do the same things. Only a matter of time, I guess."

"Right." Nelson looked uncomfortable at the very mention of their names.

Impatiently, Crow tapped his forefinger on one of his crossed arms. He was tired of hearing about this. It was all people in Nassau talked about these days.

"So... if you can help me take out either one of them, then those doubloons are yours."

Nelson nodded in agreement and looked at Crow. "Well, that sounds gr—"

Crow cut Nelson off with laughter. "Kill one of those two? Are you kidding me? You'd have to pay me a thousand doubloons to agree to that. What kind of fools do you think we are!" Crow slapped his thigh and shook his head. "They're the most dangerous people in Nassau."

Crow's words seemed to have stung Vella. She folded her arms and sat back in her chair. "Do I look like I'm kidding? Maybe you should be flattered I'd even ask such a thing of you." Vella poked her cheek with her tongue.

"He just meant you're different to them, Vella. You actually care for your crew. Right, sir?"

"Yeah, exactly. You take 'em all in. Lot of these girls would be otherwise dead." Crow agreed.

"Well, you may be right." Vella tipped her head back and stared at the ceiling. "Those two would be worth a lot more money anyway."

Crow was taken aback, she never agreed with anything he said.

"So, is there anything else we can do?" Nelson enquired with hope.

"I'll loan you the coin, but I want it paid within a year. Twice over. Plus, I get to call on you for a favor at any point in time." She snapped back to sitting upright and re-opened the ledger.

"May I have a few moments to speak with the captain in private?"

"Sure." Vella went to the far most corner of the room and busied herself with a book from the closest stack.

Nelson and Crow leaned into one another and hushed their voices to a whisper. "What do you think, sir?"

"I think it's fair, so long as the favor isn't to kill that pair. Worst case scenario, we could always refuse. Also..." Crow looked to where Vella stood, immersed in a book. "We should go soon, the girl might be awake. It would blow this entire deal."

"Yes, understood," Nelson whispered back to Crow. "We have a deal!" Nelson clapped and stood up.

Vella walked over to the two men and shook their hands.

"Great! Pleasure doing business." Vella grabbed a pouch and filled it with the ten golden coins. She handed it to Nelson who secured it to his belt.

"Thank you so much. We knew we could count on you." He beamed.

The door burst open, and the lip-ringed girl stormed in. "What is it?" Vella did not seem to appreciate being interrupted.

"Miss V, I have to tell you something." She hurried over and whispered in Vella's ear.

"What do you mean she's dead?" Vella's face changed from one of smug satisfaction to anger.

Crow and Nelson looked at each other.

"You'll have to excuse me, I have something to deal with. I'll let you know when I need that favor." Vella rushed out of her office and disappeared from sight.

Nelson and Crow remained silent as they made their way out of the house.

"Might not be who we're thinking, sir."

"Can't be, she was breathing."

They made their way down the main path back to town. Up ahead a group of women with dreaded hair and burgundy shirts stood in the undergrowth, tending to a body on the ground.

"Keep going," Crow whispered out the corner of his mouth to Nelson, as they snuck past.

"Sir, it can't be."

"Of course not, well, maybe. Regardless, we don't want to be explaining ourselves to them."

ISAAC CARVER

The breeze picked up as Isaac neared the harbor. He flipped his prized silver coin in the air and guessed the outcome. "Ship! Again." He threw his head back and let out a laugh. Over the years Isaac had developed a knack for forgetting terrible situations, he learned fast that it was the only way to survive in Nassau.

He clutched the coin tight and distracted himself with thoughts of Kidd's treasure and all the things he might buy. He envisaged the moment he would find it and imagined digging his hands into wooden chests chock full of jewels and doubloons.

Isaac jolted back to reality at the sight of his favorite merchant and tucked the coin away. "Daniel, how are you?" He gave a cheeky salute and watched as Daniel pretended to busy himself lining up fruit in neat rows. Isaac stole a sugar-apple from his stall and hid the fruit behind his back. Daniel shot Isaac a wink and saluted in return. The people of Nassau had come to know Isaac well. He was loved by many, hated by some, and merely tolerated by others.

Isaac cracked the apple shell open and tore out the fruit. He tossed the creamy white pieces into his mouth and chewed loudly. Wafts of fish stung his nostrils as he hit the dock and wandered down to where Popino would be, unloading crates.

"Isaac Carver, I haven't seen you in weeks!" Popino held out his arms to greet his oldest friend. Isaac hugged Popino back, still gnawing on the apple flesh. Bits flew out onto his friend's back.

"You're all dirty Pino, what's that all about?" He feigned shock as he brushed the apple off.

"Oh, you know... busy day, everything is fine though. Same old really." He shifted awkwardly and Isaac thought he looked a little suspicious. "Wait, why are you covered in blood, Isaac?"

"Why are you wearing another man's shirt, Pino?"

"Enough said... Rose is good, she's excited to see you tonight." Popino changed the subject. "Come see what we found this morning in a crate." Popino led Isaac over to the end of the dock.

"Why's it all the way back here?"

"No one has dared to touch it. Reckon they'll be cursed." Popino elbowed Isaac.

"Pff." Isaac didn't care. He reached down inside and picked up the paper which covered the contents. "What's it say, Pino?"

"If you see Thad, tell him I'm coming for him," Popino read the note aloud.

Isaac peered in the crate and gave the brown leathery object a poke. "Looks like someone's missing their tongue."

"Is that what that is?" Popino recoiled in fear and disgust. "Who do you think sent it?" he asked, his voice wavering. "I've never seen that skull with three snakes before." Popino pointed to the top corner of the note.

"Me either but it's a great find, Pino." Isaac gave him a pat on the back. "Anyhow, in other very exciting news... I think I've nearly found it." Isaac grinned and grabbed Popino by the shoulders in excitement. "Well, I'm close at least," Isaac continued. "I just need to find the man, talk to him, do some mission, and then I'll have it."

Popino shook himself away from Isaac and handed him a crate. "Help me with this, would you. Walk with me."

Isaac rolled his eyes and dragged his feet as he held the box and followed Popino down to the shore. Isaac gazed with envy at the docked ships. The Fancy was in. The grand vessel didn't move far nowadays, but when it had they'd said it was the fastest on the ocean. The ship had long been stripped of its guns, but it was still magnificent. He was lost in thought as he considered what it would take to commandeer such a ship. "One day," he told himself.

"Now, what in the world are you talking about?" Popino snapped Isaac out of his daydream. He hadn't even noticed that they had reached the shoreline.

"I told you, I've nearly found it!" Isaac placed the crate down on the sand and retrieved the weathered map from his pocket. "Look." Isaac's eyes sparkled as he unfolded the parchment. "There's only two places left." He pointed to each of the islands in turn. All but two were crossed with black Xs.

"C'mon then, hand it over." Popino took the map from Isaac's hand. Narrowing his gaze, he soaked in the information. "Remember that day? My god, things were simple then," Popino reminisced.

Isaac nodded. Most of his childhood memories were fuzzy to say the least but that day remained a standout, even after all the rum doused years.

"So, let me get this straight. You're saying that there's only two possible locations for Captain Kidd's treasure?"

Isaac snatched the map back. His paranoid eyes darted around. "Shh, don't say that so loud." He leaned in and got closer to Popino's face.

"Are you two about to kiss?" A beady-eyed shore worker with a heavy beard and an upturned nose teased and pointed to them. He was standing with a group of men who all whistled and heckled the pair. Isaac moved his face away from Popino's and glared in the man's direction.

"Go slam your head on a marlinspike, pig-face!" Isaac turned back to Popino. "Anyway..." Isaac folded the map up.

"What did you say?" the bearded shore worker interjected as he cleaned off his hands on a rag.

"Isaac, why'd you go and do that?" Popino sighed and took off his shirt, revealing his tanned, rippling muscles.

"Because I know you love any excuse to take your shirt off. Besides, he does have the face of a pig," Isaac joked as he tucked the map back in his pocket and opened a small bag attached to the right side of his belt.

"Just like old times, Pino?" Isaac winked.

"You never fail to get me in trouble."

"What did you call me?" The shore worker walked over with two of his friends in tow. His manner was calm but his small, black, beady eyes told a different story. He stroked at his bushy beard with one hand and balled and flexed the other. His friends readied their fists in support and wore their meanest grins but none of this bothered

Isaac in the slightest. Not one of them came even close to his height and they certainly didn't look agile.

Besides, he had a pocket loaded with tricks and traps ready to be unleashed, though he was starting to run low on his infamous blinding powder after the day's events.

"Deaf too! I said you had the face of a pig." Isaac's tone was matter of fact. "Did your father and mother both sleep with a pig when they made you?" Isaac mocked as violence erupted.

The beady-eyed shore worker made straight for Isaac, tackling him to the ground. The pair wrestled and rolled, throwing punches and gathering sand until Isaac came out on top. He straddled the bearded man, trapping his arms with his knees, and snorted like a pig as he brushed sand into his face. The shore worker struggled. He kicked his legs and tried to wiggle his arms free, but Isaac just increased his thigh grip and laughed.

Isaac watched as Popino knocked one of the smaller men unconscious with a knee to the face. "Behind you!" Isaac warned, as the other small sidekick ran at Popino with a stick. Popino snatched the stick off him and attempted a strike in retaliation but the man sped off.

Isaac, still sitting on top of the bearded man, punched him in the face. "Don't start things you can't finish, fella," Isaac said, knocking him around some more.

"It's going well." Popino shouted encouragement and stood with his hands on his hips, catching his breath and watching the scene unfold.

The beady-eyed man reached boiling point. He found the strength to push Isaac off and grabbed him by the throat. "You're gonna regret talking to me like that." He pinned Isaac to the ground by his neck and raised his fist to strike his jaw but was met with a gob of spit to the eye.

"What the—" The man released his grip to wipe his eye clean.

Isaac dug his hand into his open pouch and hurled a handful of his infamous blinding powder into the man's beady eyes. Isaac turned his face to shield himself from the dust fallback as the man copped a smattering of the lava-like substance. He screamed at the top of his lungs as it took hold.

Isaac looked over at Popino who stood with his hands on his hips, resting.

"Pino? Were you just watching me?"

"I knew you had him." Popino held out his hand to help Isaac up. He placed his arm around Isaac once again as the bushy-bearded man sprinted toward the ocean to bathe his burning eyeballs. "Now, where were we? You were about to tell me something."

"Right, as I was saying before we were so rudely interrupted..." Isaac brushed off the sand which had gathered in the patches of blood on his treasured captain's jacket. "There's only two locations left. And I know someone, who knows someone, who knows more. I just have to meet them and do some mission... I think. Details are a bit foggy." Isaac couldn't hide his excitement. "Do you understand what I'm saying, Pino? After all these years we're finally going to get our hands on it."

"You know someone who knows someone, and you have to complete some sort of mission, you think? But you don't know what it is. That's what you came to tell me?" Popino stopped in his tracks and crossed his arms, scrunching his eyes shut. "That's got to be the worst plan I've ever heard."

"Better plan than your plan."

"I don't have a plan."

"Exactly, therefore my plan is better."

"I suppose by that logic you're right." Popino shook his head. "Well, here's a good plan; dinner at my house tonight, old friend. You promised. Plus, you can let me know how it goes with this someone who knows someone."

"I will talk to this someone who knows someone, and then you'll be jealous that I know someone who knows someone, but you don't know someone who knows someone."

"You're not making any sense."

"No, *you're* not making any sense." Isaac smiled and crossed his arms.

Popino laughed. "Just meet me at my place tonight okay, Rose really does miss you Isaac, you don't come by enough."

"Sounds good. Oh, one more thing." Isaac patted his jacket down. "Where am I meeting him?" He produced the small piece of paper Nelson had written on and held it out for Popino to read.

"Excellent choice—*The Squat and Gobble*. Maybe you can get something other than rum in that stomach of yours." Popino raised his brows and nodded knowingly.

"But I'm saving myself for the feast at yours tonight!" Isaac winked and waved to Popino as he walked away.

The Inn sat alone in a side street down from the center of Nassau. It had a reputation for excellence, and whilst Isaac could never afford to stay there himself, he had heard countless tales of its hearty fare, plump feather mattresses, and fine linen sheets from the folks at the tavern.

His thoughts were preoccupied as he made his way there. He had often considered acquiring himself a ship and a crew and exploring both of the possible locations left on the map but the distance between them had always stopped him. Plus, one of them was Devil's Cay and since only three people in all of Nassau had ever made it back from there alive, he wanted to avoid going if he could.

The Inn's sign creaked in the wind as he turned down the street. He tried to keep a lid on his excitement. "Don't get drunk and forget," he told himself and wagged his finger.

Inside, a plump, ruddy-faced man sat alone at a table, his back to the door. He was feasting on potted meat, spreading it thickly on bread. His white shirt was tight, though not due to any bulging muscle. Over the top he wore a burgundy waistcoat, which hid a multitude of sins, and a matching bandana. Isaac couldn't remember his face for the life of him but assumed this was the man he was to meet since no one else was around.

Isaac strode in brimming with confidence and took a seat opposite him. "Good afternoon." He dared not attempt his name.

"Isaac, hello again." Nelson wiped the crumbs from his mouth and swigged his rum. "Drink?" Nelson didn't await a response and signaled to the barkeep who wandered over with two full glasses.

"Why thank you, fella." Isaac lifted his glass and gulped down the dark liquid.

"Not sure if you remember me but I'm Nelson."

"Yes of course, that's why I'm here." Isaac bluffed. "So, you've got some information for me I believe?"

"Umm, I will have, we haven't discussed what exactly

it is you need yet. Remember?" Nelson nodded and sipped his drink, his gaze fixed on Isaac.

"Of course," Isaac replied, he couldn't for the life of him remember the details of their previous conversation. "So…"

"Tell me what is it you need, and we'll go from there." Nelson leaned in.

"I need some information on a location. I have a…" Isaac hesitated, it hadn't even occurred to him that he would have to share the map in order to get what he needed. He hadn't ever shown the map to anyone but Pino. Joy had caught a glimpse here and there but nothing more. She never asked him any questions for fear he might talk about it more than he already did.

"You have?" Nelson fumbled with the collar of his shirt.

"I have a map and I need some location information." Isaac's heartbeat increased as the words left his mouth.

"Oh. Well, the captain and I can certainly help with that. There isn't much we don't know or can't find out." Nelson smiled.

Isaac's heart raced at the prospect of gaining the final piece of information. "Great! And what do you need from me?"

"Show me the map first. Better I double check we can definitely help, otherwise we're just wasting your time."

Isaac nodded. He had to risk it and show him. He scanned the room for signs of anything suspicious, but all seemed well. "Alright." Isaac pulled out the paper from his pouch and unfolded the tattered edges. He placed the map on the table, his fingers pressed into it as he stared at Nelson waiting for his reaction.

Nelson's eyes lit up at the very sight of the map.

"Perfect." Nelson smiled and looked up at Isaac, his

eyes crinkled and his face even redder. "I know someone who can help cross off one of those locations." Nelson nodded, his eyes bright.

"Okay, now what do you need from me?" Isaac withdrew the map, and quickly tucked it away as Nelson dug his hands deep in his pants and stood up rather abruptly.

"Woah, let's be calm about this, fella." Isaac put his hands up.

"I'm looking for something, where on earth is it?" Nelson seemed panicked. "Oh, here it is." He pulled out a small piece of paper and handed it to Isaac. "You know a man named Popino don't you?"

Isaac was taken aback by the question. "Yeah?" He didn't know where this was going, but it didn't sit right.

"He owes us a coffer of coin and we need it returned... he's not to know."

"What? But how do I even find his coins?" Isaac asked, confused. "Why can't yo—"

Nelson cut him off. "Do not ask any more questions about the whys of this request. Simply do so and we shall exchange information at the location on that paper." Nelson fanned himself with his shirt. "You're an intelligent man, Mr. Carver, I trust you'll find a way." Without another word Nelson headed for the door, leaving a bemused Isaac to sit alone with his thoughts and a now empty glass.

MOLLY WEAVER

Molly found a seat tucked away in a corner of the inn. She positioned herself so she had a clear view of Isaac but was hidden enough to not draw the attention of Nelson, or anyone else for that matter. It always posed a challenge for someone of her stature but the stack of papers and pot of ink on the table made for a good excuse should she need one.

The Squat and Gobble was an ideal spot to get some writing done. It wasn't boisterous like the many taverns in town due to the higher drink prices and lack of busty waitresses.

She beckoned to the barkeep and ordered a beer. It was the only thing she ever drank in public places. She figured it was cleaner than the water and not quite as potent as the rum. Molly wasn't much of a drinker. She liked to keep a clear head. It kept her mind sharp and her reactions fast.

She made a start and watched the scene between Nelson and Isaac unfold. They were focused on a piece of paper of some sort. Molly busied herself sealing some letters.

"Ma'am. May I sit?" Roy tottered over to her table.

"Of course."

Roy dragged a stool from the neighboring table and hopped on it. Molly thought he looked like a child sitting across from her. Despite running the best bounty office in town, Roy certainly wasn't threatening. He was, however, a source of great information. Roy knew everybody.

She pushed a bunch of sealed letters across the table to him. "Vella's very happy with how things have been going."

"Excellent. We aim to please. Or kill, rather!" Roy chuckled as he gave the letters a shuffle and tucked them into his satchel. Molly ignored his attempt at humor.

"Thank you, Roy. So, did you catch much?"

"I did."

"What did you learn?" Molly leaned in closer. Out the corner of her eye she saw Isaac sat with his head in his hands, nursing an empty glass.

"Well..." Roy lowered his voice. "Nelson wants Isaac to steal from Popino. You know Popino, right?"

Molly nodded.

"Apparently Popino owes them. And if Isaac succeeds, Nelson will lead him to someone who knows a location that he needs." Roy shrugged.

Molly sat back in her chair and folded her arms as she contemplated what this could mean.

"When's he supposed to meet with them?"

"Not sure. I think it was written down." Roy scratched his head.

"Interesting..." Molly checked the room and shielded one side of her mouth as she whispered. "Did anyone take the bounty on Jane?" She sat back in her chair again in a bid to look inconspicuous.

"Ah yes." Roy's eyes gleamed with delight. "Do you know Joy?"

"Isaac's ex-lover? The one who lives with her younger sister Raven?"

Roy smiled. "Yes, her. She took it."

"Do you think she'll be able to pull it off?" Molly took a sip of her drink.

"Oh, she's good Molly, you should meet her someday."

"Maybe someday. Sounds like she'll have her hands full for a little while."

"Ha! Yes, well." Roy glanced at the floor. "If that's all for today I'll head off now. I'll be seeing you." He gave a nod of respect, hopped off the stool and made for the door.

Molly strode over to where Isaac sat. He propped his head on his hands and stared down at the table, seemingly deep in thought. He jumped from his seat as she smacked her hand on his shoulder. "Ah! Molly. Here to buy me a drink?" Isaac winked and held up his glass.

"Sure." She nodded to the barkeep. "Just for him. I'm leaving, thanks."

"Ah, you're the best, Molly." Isaac grinned.

"Want me to tell you what that note says?"

"Oh this..." Isaac hung his head. "You know I—"

"I know, let me help." Molly grabbed the paper. "It's a location."

"I knew that much." Isaac snatched the paper back and sighed.

"Well, you know those shipwood shacks? Down from the center of town, weather-beaten old things?"

"Yeah, I do actually."

"Well, that's where the paper says to go."

"Right. Well, that's easy. Ah, thanks, Molly. You really are the best!"

The barkeep brought over a fresh glass of rum and winked at Molly. "This one's on me."

"Thank you." Molly looked the barkeep hard in the eye and nodded.

"He must like you, I never get any free drink, well, unless I take it." Isaac gave a wink and raised his glass to her.

"Nothing like that. I'll see you around, Isaac."

"Sure thing!" Isaac grinned. She gave him a slap on the back and walked toward the exit as a grimy looking man charged through the door and ran straight into Molly. He bounced off and fell to the floor.

"I have news!" the grimy man declared as he looked up at her, his eyes dizzy from the fall.

"Otis, what is it? You know not to..." She grabbed his arm and led him outside.

"I know but a lots 'appened. Here you go, ma'am." He reached into his pocket and handed her a piece of paper covered with fingerprints and smudged ink. "For your eyes only. I've written down all the details for you." Otis was missing an eye, several teeth and hard of hearing. People paid him no attention which made him a great informant.

"Thank you, Otis. Appreciated." Molly tucked away the grubby piece of paper and pulled out a fresh piece. She scribbled on it and handed it to Otis. "Can you give this to Johnny? He'll want this information." She gave him five reale with the expectation he would leave. Instead, he stood grasping his hands together, eagerly awaiting her next instruction. "That's everything. Thank you, Otis." He bowed his head and made off in the direction of the center square.

People liked Molly, they respected her and knew she

paid well and without question. She used her income from selling her potions and powders to learn what was happening in Nassau. The more she knew, the more useful she became. Molly stepped outside of the Inn and leaned against the wall. She retrieved the grubby bit of paper and read.

Popino seen entering house of Eva Boucher before her and Lucien Boucher found murdered.
Three of Thad's main men have been murdered by Jane and new recruits - Anna and Jose.
The entire Milky Way has been slaughtered by Thad's men.

Molly put her hand to her mouth and stood in silence. Rage pulsated through her. She crumpled the note and clenched her fists tight. Her nails dug into her palms as she tried to compose herself. She needed to walk off this temper and see Vella before she did something she'd regret.

Molly opened the door to Vella's place. "Georgia, is Vella upstairs?" Georgia looked at Molly and nodded, her giant lip ring and dreads swung as she nodded her head up and down. "Can I go up?"

"Yeah, but tread lightly. She's angry."

"What's happened?" Molly didn't always let on what she knew.

"Well, you know Emma? Started with us a while back now."

"Yes." Molly thought hard about who Emma was. She remembered the girl had started off in the brothel, but her temper was ferocious and she often tried to fight the men. Eventually Vella realized her anger could be better directed and recruited her to join the clan. "She was the feisty one, yes? Liked to fight."

"Yeah, that's her, well, was her... she's dead."

"Oh yes, I did hear that. Heard it was Jane Hatch," Molly lied. She didn't know if it was Jane, but she knew Vella needed a push to attack. The war between Jane, Vella and Thad had been brewing for months and someone needed to take the first step.

"What?" Georgia looked confused. "How do you know?"

"That's what people are saying. Not sure though. It's just what I heard." Molly shrugged. She knew Georgia couldn't spot her lying, she never did.

A crash came from upstairs. "She really is angry, isn't she?"

"She's been breaking things all day I'm afraid," Georgia said with concern.

"Alright, I better head up." Molly made her way up the stairs, her heavy feet making every step creak. I would be useless if ever I had to sneak around, she thought to herself. She approached the door to Vella's office and could hear more thuds.

"Vella?" She pushed the door open to find Vella lying on the ground, breathing heavily, surrounded by her books.

"Who's that?" Vella sprung to her feet and unsheathed a dagger from her side. "Oh, it's you, Molly." She put the dagger away and moved to her chair. "Please tell me you have good news?" With a dramatic sweep of her arm, she brushed the papers off her desk onto the floor and sat down with her arms crossed, her eyes filled with despair.

From the corner of the messy room Molly grabbed a chair that had been knocked over and placed it across from Vella. She sat down and tried to lower her posture to make herself seem smaller. "What's the bad news?"

"You haven't heard?"

"I haven't no, I just arrived," Molly lied. She always waited for Vella to bring matters up.

"Emma's dead." Vella removed her hat and tossed it on the ground. Her dreads hit the desk as she placed her forehead against it. "The Milky Way, Molly. Everyone's dead."

Molly shook her head. "The Milky Way? Sophia.... Grieves... are they dead?"

"All of them... I think." Vella banged her forehead on the desk. "This is a disaster... uh... Do you know how much this is going to cost me!" Vella groaned.

Molly remained silent.

"Sorry, Molly. Are you okay? I know you worked with all of them." Vella snapped out of her own anger and walked over to Molly. She wrapped her arm around her. "I know. It's brutal."

"I'll be okay, Vella." Molly grabbed Vella's hand and gave it a light squeeze. "Thank you."

"So, what are we going to do about this?" Vella paced around the room, stepping all over the torn books thrown from their shelves in rage. "You know Thad's the one who had his men slaughter everyone at The Milky Way?" Vella's face was expressionless, but Molly could see the deep hatred burning in her eyes. "I wish we knew what that prick looked like."

Vella bit at her knuckle in rage. The man was more of a myth than a reality at this point. Whilst many had worked for him few had seen him in the flesh.

"That bastard." Molly shook her head. "I think... I might just have a plan."

"Don't hold back on me now." Vella paused and looked at Molly with intensity.

Molly scratched her neck. "We should ask Crow and his men to help us take down Jane."

"You think?" Vella cocked her head.

"Yes. It's time, we need to act now."

"But why Jane first? If anything, we should go after Thad!"

"We know how to get to her. Plus, she killed Emma."

"What?" Vella shook her head, confused. "I thought you hadn't heard the news and now you're telling me it was Jane?" Vella crossed her arms.

Molly threw up her hands. "Vella, I'd heard about Emma. Not The Milky Way though. Georgia mentioned it and I…" Molly looked away.

"Georgia? She never mentioned anything to me about Jane." Vella sat back in the chair and bounced her leg in agitation.

"Probably too scared. I don't want to get her in trouble. She's a good girl."

"Yes. Look, it's been a rather tense day so far." Vella looked around at her ransacked office. "I can see why she wouldn't say anything."

"Yes. So going back to the plan, I think with Crow's men we can at least take on Jane first." Molly leaned back in her chair.

"Crow will never agree to that." Vella shook her head.

"Well, I've heard that a man named Johnny Ives is gunning for captaincy. We can always back him. I know for a fact he will help me."

"I'll think about it..." Vella paused as if she was waiting

for her thoughts to catch up. "Do you really think Jane would kill Emma for no good reason?" Vella eyed Molly intently waiting for a reaction.

"I heard she killed some of Thad's men too."

"She killed Thad's men too? I don't know what to think anymore." Vella sat with her head in her hands. "Maybe you're right. I can't just sit here waiting to be attacked."

"Well, you know what they say… those who strike first, strike last."

"I need to think about this mess some more before I get us all killed!"

"I think that's wise," Molly agreed, "but I wouldn't wait too long."

POPINO BELTRAME

"Clara, I just have to pop out for a bit. I won't be long."

"Of course, sir. Rose and I will prepare everything for tonight."

"As nice as it is, remember you don't have to call me sir. Popino's fine." He grabbed his jacket in one hand and patted Rose on the head with the other. "You ladies remember all of Uncle Isaac's favorites, yeah?"

Rose nodded and grinned. "Food! And lots of it."

Popino laughed. "Exactly, dear."

"Bye, Papa." Rose grabbed Clara's hand.

"I'll be back soon." Popino slung on his jacket as he made his way out. The sun had disappeared for the day. The sky was thick with clouds and the sprinkles of rain made the ground muddy underfoot.

He broke into a jog. He needed to be back in good time so as not to arouse suspicion and Vella's place sat on the outskirts of town.

He reached the beautiful beige stone house and knocked three times on the thick blue door. His stomach churned with anticipation.

"Hello, we were expecting you." The door girl eyed Popino up and down.

He smiled and stepped inside. Her gaze didn't falter, it never did. He had noticed how she eyed him, but he could never move past the ring in her lip. It jiggled as she spoke and bothered him more than it should.

He supposed some men might like that, but it didn't do it for him.

"Thanks. Should I go right up?"

"Yes, but be warned she is not in the best mood today. We had an... incident earlier. Several actually."

"Oh? Can you tell me what happened?"

"Not really."

Popino leaned on the counter she had tucked herself behind and propped his head up with his hands. He stared in her direction and tried to imagine her without the lip ring.

She shifted in her seat and leaned toward him. "Okay, I really shouldn't be saying anything." She scanned the reception and lowered her head. "One of ours was killed today. She'd been with us four years. Wasn't even on a job, we just found her body hidden in the bushes down the road."

"That's horrible, any idea who was responsible?" Popino asked and leaned in closer.

"Yes, but I shouldn't be talking about this." She bit at her lip and brought her face in close to meet Popino's. He could almost taste her lips against his.

Popino touched her hand and whispered in her ear, "Well you can tell me, I promise I won't say a thing to anyone."

He often used his good looks to his advantage and getting hold of the right information was precisely what he needed today. Popino brushed his lips against the side of her cheek as he pulled back and fixed his eyes on hers.

She smiled. "Come back here," she said and beckoned to him with her finger. She brought her lips to his ear. "It was Jane Hatch." She stroked her hand over his. "She wants to send Miss V a message. But now we're planning an attack." She backed away and held her finger to her lips. "You can't tell anyone I told you though."

Popino smiled and mirrored her actions, putting his finger to his lips. "You have my promise." He backed away and shot her a wink as he made his way up the stairs.

I'll save that snippet of information for later, Popino thought as he climbed the staircase toward Vella's office. At her door he knocked and took a deep breath.

"Come in," she said.

"Vella, my dear, how are you?" Popino strode in with open arms awaiting an embrace but his charm was lost on her. The girl downstairs was right—she was in no mood to be trifled with today.

"Shut up, sit down. You're late on your payments." Vella pointed to a chair in front of her desk.

Popino sat down as instructed and stopped smiling. He knew it would only anger her. She stood over her desk and shook her head. "Do you think I'm a joke, Popino?"

"No, no of course not."

"You owe me three-hundred doubloons. Three-hundred!" She smashed her fist into her desk. "You were supposed to pay the complete amount as of yesterday. What happened to this investment you were going to make, huh? What happened to the wealth of riches it was going to bring us?"

Vella took out a dagger and stabbed the blade into her desk. "I'm done, Popino," she yelled. Popino flinched.

His shoulders felt so tense they could almost touch his ears.

She grabbed her ledger and opened it up. "Let's see, shall we. Oh, look, just one whole page dedicated to you," she said with sarcasm. "You and your cock-and-bull schemes." She hurled the book at the wall.

Popino's hands shook and his heart raced though he tried not to show signs of weakness in front of Vella. At that moment he wished he had not come to see her today, but he knew time was running out and he'd hoped to charm his way to some sort of extension. "I tried," he said with a voice that was not his own.

"I knew it was a stupid idea trusting you." She pulled the dagger out from the desk and scraped the blade across her palm. "I should just kill you now." She walked over to where he sat and stood behind him.

Popino turned his body to look over his shoulder. "Face forward!" she barked. Popino stared ahead, his body motionless. His heartbeat pounded in his ears.

Vella held the knife to Popino's throat. "I had hoped things would work out." She pushed the sharp blade into his neck and grazed the skin. He could feel the blood pool and didn't dare to swallow. She applied enough pressure to draw blood but not so much that it would be fatal.

"Vella," Popino uttered. It was hard to speak with the pressure against his neck.

"What is it? What are you trying to say?" she pushed his chair to the ground and returned to hers. "Hurry now, before I get really mad."

Popino clambered to his feet and clasped his hands behind his back. He wanted to appear strong yet respectful and his shaking hands showed neither.

"I have thirty doubloons. I can pay you right now if you need me to."

That was all Popino had left. The investment he told Vella of didn't exist. In truth, he had met a doctor who promised to save his ailing wife for a hefty sum. Popino had handed over the coin but the doctor took off, leaving them in debt and Elizabeth to die. Since then, he'd kept living beyond his means, borrowing more and more, spiralling further and further until he dug himself in a hole so deep that it was becoming impossible to get out.

Vella seemed to have calmed down. "Thirty? That's barely enough but it'll do for now." She didn't bother to write it down. "Tomorrow morning, you'll come by here with thirty doubloons. If I don't see you, I'll come find you... and Rose. I'll kill her and then... I'll kill you. Don't try me, Popino."

Popino knew he had no other choice. It would leave him with nothing, but better that than dead. "Sounds fair, I'll see you tomorrow." He stood up and walked to the door. His entire body was drenched in nervous sweat. "Sorry about your loss by the way. That wasn't very nice of Jane." Popino opened the door but Vella stood up, just like he'd hoped.

"Excuse me? Who told you about that?" Vella said with furious curiosity. She walked over to the door and closed it on Popino, blocking his exit.

"I just heard in town, something about Jane attacking one of your people on your own ground. Everyone seemed to think you'd never dare retaliate," Popino lied. He knew this would get a rise out of her, maybe even get him a few jobs, so he could pay off some of the debt. He needed something, anything to take the heat off of him.

"Is that what people think?"

"Yep, apparently she's bragging about it too. Bad taste if you ask me."

She looked stunned and opened the door. "Go!" She waved her hand and dismissed him. Popino nodded and walked out the door, leaving Vella to brood.

This would surely shake up Nassau to some degree, he thought. Maybe it would finally force the feud between Thad, Jane and Vella and he would end up debt free. Especially since he not only owed money to Vella, but to Jane too.

ISAAC CARVER

Isaac knocked on Popino's door and waited. The same question played over and over in his mind. How could he justify stealing from his oldest friend?

He told himself Pino would understand. He had lots of coin and a beautiful house. He probably wouldn't even notice it was gone... Well, he'd definitely notice, but it wasn't going to change *his* life. Besides, Isaac could share the wealth once he found it.

The door swung open and Popino held out his arms in welcome.

"Isaac, come on in, we're delighted to have you over." Popino patted his friend on the arm with affection. "Rose, honey, Uncle Isaac's here."

"Nice scarf, Pino, makes you look exotic," Isaac remarked.

"Thanks." Popino looked to the floor and nodded as he adjusted his neckerchief.

Popino's home was quite the contrast to Isaac's shack. It was filled with ornate furniture, exquisite paintings and fine glassware.

Popino had been working down at the docks since he was of age, but the real wealth had come from his parents and, more latterly, Elizabeth. When they all passed, he inherited more than his fair share of doubloons and, judging by his abode, he had spent more than his fair share too.

Rose ran down the stairs and over to Isaac, hugging him tight. Isaac enjoyed her company; she was such a dear little girl. "Oh, Rose, your dress is beautiful. You look just like a princess." He ruffled her hair a little. "How are you?"

"Uncle Isaac, I missed you. Why don't visit anymore?" Rose asked bluntly, her bottom lip stuck out.

"Oh, you know, Rosy, I've been very busy, adventuring and the like," he lied. "I have something for you." Isaac placed his hand behind her ear and snapped his fingers. She shrank into her dress a little with embarrassment at the attention but was delighted when he produced a silver brooch in the shape of a rose.

"It's so pretty!" She clasped the piece with both hands and clutched it to her chest with delight. "Look, Papa, look what Uncle Isaac got me."

"Yes, that's quite beautiful, isn't it?" Popino attached the brooch to Rose's dress and sent her off to the dining room. "Where did you even get that?" Popino raised his eyebrows and shook his head.

"Are you jealous, Pino? I can get you one too if you'd like." Isaac smiled. "You don't really want to know, do you?"

"I don't think I do, do I? Thank you, however. She clearly loves it."

"Something smells good," Isaac changed the subject. He was starving and couldn't wait to tuck into some actual food for a change.

"Come through, dinner is ready."

Isaac stepped into the dining room and scanned for potential hiding spots, though he doubted Popino would be foolish enough to store his coins anywhere other than his bedroom.

"You sit beside me, Uncle Isaac!" Rose tapped on the chair next to her. Isaac shuffled around to be next to Rose, grabbing a plate of chicken as he went.

"So, how did your meeting go?" Popino asked. His hands shook as he passed plates of food around the table.

"It was a bust," Isaac sprayed chicken pieces everywhere as he spoke.

"That's too bad." Popino's eyes looked vacant, as if he were someplace else.

"How was your day, Rosy?" Isaac chewed with his mouth open, heaping his plate with stew and hunks of bread. He needed to divert attention from any discussion of the meeting earlier that day, and he couldn't help but worry that Popino suspected him of concealing information. Something about his behavior just seemed a little off.

"Uncle Isaac..."

"Yes, dear?" Isaac responded with half a chicken leg sticking out from his mouth.

"Can you pass the food please? I haven't gotten any yet."

Isaac stopped chewing and looked at the plates which he had piled next to him without thought. "I'm sorry, deary, here you go." He handed her several dishes and chewed his remaining chicken feeling awkward.

To have dinner with others was a novelty and something he wasn't entirely comfortable with. He joked his way through the rest of the meal, but he felt like a monster. A horrible selfish monster. How could he steal from those that showed him the most kindness? He stared down at his empty plate, his belly full and his heart heavy.

"Pino, I need to use the john. Where is it again?" Time was running out. He had to strike now and begin his search.

"Just down the hall to the left."

"Thanks." Isaac plastered on a fake smile and pushed himself out of his seat. "It's quite the feast, isn't it, you eat like this every night?"

"No," Popino and Rosy chorused.

"It's a special treat for you." Rosy smiled and looked down at her brooch, beaming.

"We'll be tightening our belts around here soon though, should probably get rid of some of this stuff." Popino tugged at his neckerchief, as if it were tightening around his neck.

Isaac nodded, stunned. He didn't know what to say or why Popino would want to get rid of the beautiful things he owned. Maybe they reminded him of Elizabeth?

"Well, you're too kind," he said as he made his way down the hall.

He spied the stairway, which from memory led up to Pino's bedroom. He crept up the stairs, being careful as to only tread on the well-worn spots. His mind cast back to the time he brought a girl here. The chicken coop didn't quite do it for the ladies, and Pino was away so it had been a prime opportunity. That was until Popino came home early and they'd been forced to flee out of the window mid romp.

Inside the room, he started his silent search. He checked under the bed first, but it was too obvious. He wedged his hands under the heavy feather mattress but the weight made it near impossible to move. He fumbled about but decided realistically nothing would even fit underneath it. Next, he tried the dresser, opening each drawer in turn with a soft hand. Then he tried the chest of drawers.

Where could it be? Isaac wracked his brains, conscious of how long he was supposedly taking in the john.

"You okay, Isaac?" He froze at the sound of Popino's voice coming from downstairs.

"Isaac?"

"I still can't find the john," Isaac lied. He was good at playing dumb when he needed to.

"Are you upstairs?" Popino asked. Isaac scanned the room, checking everything was as he found it, then walked out into the hallway to meet Popino.

"It's not where you said it was, you liar! Quit fooling around, I'm busting," Isaac lied again.

"You're so ridiculous, Isaac. I said it's downstairs, down the hall." Popino led the way. "My mother would have said you have cloth ears."

"She'd have been right." Isaac rolled his eyes and mocked a sigh of relief.

"Made room for some more." Isaac patted his stomach and belched as he returned. His eyes darted around the dining room for potential hiding spots when an idea struck. "Pino, this is embarrassing to ask, but do you think I could borrow like three or four reale from you?" Isaac made the saddest face he could muster, hoping to win some pity from his friend.

Popino scratched at his head, a wash of concern spreading across his face. "Um... sure."

"Are you sure? You don't seem it." Isaac hadn't expected any hesitation.

"Yes, yes of course. Sorry, I just couldn't remember if I had any coins lying around. I've paid Clara you see. It's been a busy day," Popino rushed the words out and walked over to the cabinet which housed the abundant collection of glassware, plates and now dust. He stood motionless as if stunned.

"Pino, are you okay?" Isaac couldn't tell if his own nerves were throwing him off or if in fact Popino was acting rather strangely.

Popino nodded. "Just don't spend it all on one girl," Popino hushed his voice and gave Isaac a wink as he removed the golden coffer and fumbled in his back pocket for the key.

Isaac watched his every move like a hawk. "Thanks, Pino. I owe you one." Popino dropped the coins into Isaac's outstretched pouch.

"Rose, dear, would you like to help me clean up?"

"Yes, Papa."

"I can help too if you'd like." Isaac picked up a glass, hoping Popino would refuse.

"No, no, you sit, we'll only be a few moments."

"Well, if you insist." Isaac sat down and waited for them to leave the room. Once the coast was clear, he tiptoed to the cabinet and snuck the small golden box out. He held his breath, hoping the coins inside wouldn't move, and tucked the coffer in his jacket.

"Uncle Isaac..." Rosy ran in.

"Yes, deary?" He coughed in a hope to muffle any rattling coins as he swung around to face her.

"Do you want custard?"

"Is it for pie?" He held the coffer tight in his armpit.

She nodded her head.

"Well then, yes please, can't wait!"

Rose sped back to the kitchen.

He breathed a quiet sigh of relief and shifted about trying to make the coffer as inconspicuous as possible, but it's shape and weight combined made it difficult.

He couldn't sit through dessert like this. How would he lift a spoon to his mouth? He'd already disgraced himself enough with his animalistic eating habits and didn't want to top it off by tipping an entire plate of hot pie into his face. Besides, it was both incredibly uncomfortable and incredibly obvious. He spied the small window next to the cabinet, retrieved the coffer from his armpit and dropped it to the ground outside. "Genius." He would return for it later once Popino was sleeping. That way he could make it look like someone had broken in and stolen it.

He returned to his seat where a plate of steaming custard and fruit pie now awaited him. He smiled as he savored every luxurious morsel and let his mind drift to the mountains of doubloons soon to be in his reach.

After dinner he lay in wait outside. He passed the time sipping on rum and searching for the perfect rock to break the window. Once the candles had dimmed, he knew Popino had ventured up to bed. He snatched the coffer from the tufts of grass underneath the sill and hurled the rock through the glass.

The street was quiet, other than the few rotating guards, but it didn't seem to have caught their attention. Isaac kept his cool and made in the direction of the weathered shacks where he would meet Nelson. At least he assumed it would just be Nelson, he realized he had not actually clarified that part.

Isaac patted at his pocket which held the map and fantasized about the treasure. His heart beat fast with excitement as he lost himself in thought... he'd have to get himself a crew... and a ship.

The breeze picked up and sent a shiver through him as the shacks came in sight. He stopped dead in his tracks and put his hand to his mouth. He had been so preoccupied with acquiring the coffer that it hadn't even occurred to him that this might be a set up. He dismissed the negative thoughts from his mind. He was so close. It was just a mixture of excitement and nerves.

"Nothing some rum won't fix." He downed the remainder of his flask and marched onward into the night.

A dimly lit figure stood in the shadow of a towering palm. "Nelson?" Isaac approached with caution. A blanket of clouds blew in and covered the moon. It was now almost pitch black and Isaac struggled to make out the figure. If Nelson was trying to intimidate him it was most certainly working. "Nelson?"

The figure didn't move but cleared their throat.

"Do you have the coin?" It was Nelson.

"I do." Isaac took out the coffer and gave it a jiggle to demonstrate it was full. "It's very heavy and it's all yours once I get my information," Isaac said. He hoped he sounded more confident than he felt. His eyes darted around, trying to make out any familiar shapes. He had been here before during the day, but not at night. It was a place few frequented, and with good reason.

They stood at the start of the dirt road which led to a series of small huts and crumbling houses. Nelson stepped out from the shadows. His face looked tired and his expression was stern.

"Right this way."

Nelson motioned for Isaac to follow him down the path and into the darkness.

"Sure." Isaac made sure to stay close to Nelson. If someone was to strike, they'd likely get the both of them.

They arrived at something similar to what Isaac called home. The familiarity slowed his racing heart. The door creaked as Nelson pushed it open. There was enough light in the room to see that his stubby hands were well weathered, scarred and red from years of combat and sea water, Isaac assumed.

Inside the wooden shack a tall man with a heavy beard stood in front of the lantern, which hung in the corner. He wore a long, black, leather coat and a frustrated frown. A captain's hat sat on the small table in the middle of the room.

"Finally!" the tall man said. His voice was gruff, as if he had been shouting at people for years and it had now been permanently lost.

It dawned on Isaac who stood before him. Captain Crow was a well-known pirate of Nassau. Feared by many but loved by his men. Few dared to cross him.

"Nice to meet you, Captain. My name is Isaac Carver, I've heard a lot about you." Isaac hoped he didn't take that the wrong way. His charm was a little off given the circumstance. "Good things. I've heard good things." Isaac nodded.

"Hopefully not all good." Crow let out a raucous laugh as he circled Isaac like a shark. "We've met before, boy, that rum puddles your brain."

"Ah."

"Do you know why I don't like this Popino friend of yours?"

Nelson tipped the door shut.

"Not at all, sir."

"Well, it's because he stole something very precious from me many moons ago."

"The coffer?" Isaac guessed. A wave of cold sweat swept through him as the realization set in. Crow wasn't just any old pirate captain. He was *the* captain. That day in the square. The map... it was his.

"Oh, if only it was a coffer. No, it was something far greater. Our life's work—a map."

Isaac nodded as Crow closed in on him.

"I hear you're familiar with it?"

"Um, yes. Yes, sir, I am. It's almost complete." Isaac felt the blood drain from his face.

"Is it just? Well, it looks like you saved me some work. And tell me, how exactly did you get your hands on our map?" Crow spoke with an unnerving calm.

"I uh, well, Popino. He gifted it to me for my birthday a few years ago," Isaac lied.

"Ah, of course. Can I see it?" Crow placed his arm around Isaac. "Go on now, take it out."

"I don't know if that's a good idea," Isaac said and walked away from Crow's grasp, the coffer tucked under his arm.

Crow cringed a little, but then a wicked grin spread over his face. "Well, you don't really have a choice at this point, do you?" Crow reached into his jacket and retrieved a small hand-sized flintlock. A golden crow adorned the barrel and glinted as it caught the light from the lantern. The captain raised his arm and stepped toward Isaac.

"Hand over the coffer and the map." Crow pressed the

gun into Isaac's temple. Isaac's mind raced as the cold barrel touched his skin. He reached for the coffer and held it out for Nelson to take.

"Check it," Crow instructed.

Nelson fumbled with the lock but quickly gave up.

"Smash it open," Crow snapped.

Nelson hammered the small gold box on the ground until the lid swung open. Coins spilled out and rolled across the dusty floor.

"Where's the map, boy?" Crow cocked the gun.

"It's right here." Isaac took out his metal sealed pouch and pulled out the map, displaying it to the captain. "I have but one favor to ask before you kill me, Captain."

"Do you think I have gotten this far in life doing favors for people?"

"Well, no, but you see my father passed away long ago, and he left me a pendant. It's just in my pocket and I would very much like to see it again before I move on. Just one last time."

Crow's brows dipped to a frown. "Take the map from his hands, Nelson, we don't want any mess getting on it."

"Yes, sir," Nelson said wide-eyed, placing the final X on the map and tucking it into his back pocket.

"Mr. Carver, it would be foolish of me to think that a man as cunning as you wouldn't be trying to trick me. So no, I can't do you a favor."

"That's fair, no, it really is." Isaac was hardly surprised. His reputation for cheating and trickery preceded him and the captain was no fool. "How about a smaller favor instead?"

"What?" Crow replied, incensed.

Isaac reached into his pocket and took out his prized silver coin.

"Ship or no ship?" Isaac shouted as he flipped the coin in the air.

The bemused captain, distracted by Isaac's escapades, let his gaze falter for a moment. Isaac acted fast and threw the remainder of his blinding powder into the captain's eyes. Crow squinted and screamed. He wobbled back a few steps, lifted his gun toward Isaac and fired.

CAPTAIN CROW

A strong gust of sea air blew in and howled through the shack. The corner lantern swung back and forth causing the shadows to swing like a pendulum across the walls.

Crow, startled by Isaac's antics, watched the thick silver coin flip in the air. Isaac caught the glinting beauty and smacked it down onto the back of his hand.

"Last chance! Ship or no ship?"

Before Crow had a chance to answer he was met with a handful of dust to the face. He tried to blink the powder away, but it was too late. His eyeballs seared with pain as if they were being branded with a hot iron. He shut them tight and didn't dare open them again. He raised his pistol in the air and shot in Isaac's direction. A yelp came from outside the weathered shack. Crow fumbled around for a familiar object to steady himself on.

"Water! Nelson, I need water!" The stinging in his eyes was unbearable. "Did I get him?" He squinted and rubbed at his eyes with one hand as he discarded his used pistol and searched for another within his jacket.

"You got someone, sir."

"Who? Where's the boy?"

"At my feet... I smashed that coffer over his head."

"Then who the bloody hell did I hit?"

Nelson tossed a jar of water into Crow's eyes. Despite the lack of warning, the water came as a welcome relief. He regained some of his vision and stared down at Isaac's unconscious form.

"He might come in useful, you know, sir."

"Oh, I didn't want to kill him, just give him a bit of a scare but you're right, he might." Crow wiped his face with his shirt. "Nelson, can you smell that?"

Smoky wafts of air breezed through the shack. Crow sniffed again. The air grew thick as an acrid smoke seeped in through any cranny it could find. He readied a fresh pistol and reached for the door. He pulled it open only to be met with an explosive force. His body launched backwards into the far wall, as if hit by the boom of a ship in a high wind. Shards of shattered lantern glass flew through the smoke-filled air, the only source of light now gone. It fell quiet for a moment before another deafening bang ricocheted through the shack.

Boom!

Weak spots in the walls burst open and splinters of wooden planks tumbled down from the roof. Crow sat slumped on the floor, his breath knocked from his body, his old bones battered and bruised. He opened his eyes to see the door frame crumbled and the roof above it collapsed. He patted down his jacket, searching for a weapon. "Nelson!" He peered through the dust and debris and saw Nelson's body. "Nelson?"

The smoke faded with the breeze as several shadowy figures approached. They stepped over the discarded furniture and planks of smoldering wood toward Crow.

He tried to stand but his legs wouldn't cooperate. His head throbbed as the room spun around him. A deep booming laugh cut through the smoke. "Ives!" Not only did he recognize the voice, but it belonged to one of his own. Crow winced.

"Crow, my old friend." Johnny Ives strode in and stood with his hands on his hips, his muscular frame illuminated by the moonlight. Crow struggled to see as far as Johnny's face, but he knew a smug grin would be plastered all over his stupid mug and it killed him inside.

Johnny walked over to Nelson and bent down to his level. "Looks like your friend got hurt in the blast." He flipped Nelson over with surprising ease. "That doesn't look good does it?"

"Nelson!" Crow scrambled to stand and wobbled toward him, but Johnny pushed him back down.

"Now, now. We've things to discuss first." He smirked, muscles bulging as he pinned Crow to the ground.

"Johnny, now's not the time! Nelson's hurt."

"I never did understand you two, bit weird if you ask me."

"Yeah, well no one asked you, did they Johnny?"

Johnny punched Crow either side of his face. Crow's teeth banged together as the fist hit him, again and again. Blood pooled in his mouth and trickled down his face.

Johnny paused. "Boys!" He snapped his fingers and pointed to Nelson. Three men gathered around Crow's faithful quartermaster. Crow's men.

He turned his head and shouted in their direction. "You'll regret betraying me, you spineless rats!" Spit and blood flew from his mouth with every word. "Don't you dare touch him!" Crow couldn't stand seeing Nelson hurt. He would take all the beatings in the world to protect him. He tried to struggle free, but Johnny pinned him down.

Two men grabbed a leg each and the other tucked his hands under Nelson's shoulders. They heaved his limp body up off the ground and stumbled away with him into the night.

"That's the last time you'll see your little friend." Johnny punched him again.

Crow's mouth filled with blood and he spat it into Johnny's face. "You couldn't even wait for a vote!"

"Why would I when I can do this?" Johnny wiped the blood off his face with his shirt.

"There's a code, Johnny, pirate code."

"Fuck the code." Johnny punched Crow in the nose.

Crow's eyelids drooped then shut. He forced them back open, but he could feel himself slipping away with every blow. Getting hit was one thing but the darkness made it near impossible to recover. He needed to find a focus, but the shapes all blended into one. "What do you want, Johnny?" he blurted the words out as they echoed in his head.

"Lots of things really. Mainly you dead."

Johnny snapped his fingers and four men gathered around them. The youngest held a big black lantern which creaked as it rocked. He looked to the other three in turn as they raised their rifles and pointed the brass barrels at him. He recognized every single one of them. There was not a part of him that didn't feel broken. He lay still, trying to conserve his energy and figure a way out, but for once nothing came to mind.

Johnny walked over to where the coffer lay upturned, doubloons spilled everywhere. "Very nice. I'll take this." Johnny snapped his fingers again and two men rushed to his aid. They picked up the loose coins and loaded them back into the coffer.

Crow couldn't believe his men would betray him like this. Ives was no leader. Sure, he was good-looking and brash but no captain. Who did he think he was? Snapping his fingers at men as if they were dogs.

"What else have we got?" Johnny crouched and scanned the floor. "No! Surely not?" He picked the map up off the ground. "Is this what you've been banging on about all these years? Wait... Where's the rest of it?"

Through swollen eyes Crow made out that a substantial part of the map was now missing. "It's worthless now!" Crow laughed a little and was met with a sharp twinge in his chest. "You reap what you sow, Ives," he spluttered through coughs.

"Shut him up!" Johnny ordered, and tucked the tattered map remnants in his pocket. The four men looked at one another, unsure what to do.

Johnny walked over to where Isaac lay motionless and gave him a kick. "Aw, Molly will be sad. Fucking drunk." Isaac didn't move or make a sound.

Crow looked into the eyes of the men standing over him. His men. He'd be sure to remember each and every one of them. His blood boiled. "Was what I provided never good enough? Were you not some of the richest pirates in Nassau? You'll live to regret this day." His blood-soaked face felt swollen and tight with each word. It took everything in him not to rise up and take them on, but he needed to recover.

The four men looked at one another, worry spreading across their faces. They'd seen Crow get angry before, and they knew what he was capable of.

"After everything I did for you!" Crow shouted. He

curled his hands into fists and slammed the ground beneath him. He couldn't contain it anymore. The men looked uncomfortable and took a step back.

"What's wrong with you lot? This old man worry you?" Johnny finished his hunt around the shack and stuffed a couple of loose coins into his pocket.

"Crow, Crow, Crow." He walked over to him wagging his finger. "You need to calm the fuck down!" He drew his leg back and booted Crow in the ribs.

Crow jolted and clutched at his aching sides. He had no more breath left in him. "You bastard." He wheezed and clenched his jaw to tolerate the pain.

"So, it seems I've got my hands on the famous map." Johnny circled Crow as he rolled on the ground. "Doesn't look like much... but I'm sure I can find someone around these parts who'll help me out."

"Ha! Good luck with that! They're all dead!"

"Oh, stop being so bitter, Crow. No one likes a sore loser!" Johnny gave him another kick.

His smug, smarmy smile enraged Crow. He tried to stand but a rifle pushed him back down. The men dug their gun barrels into his chest and pinned him to the floor.

"Thanks for everything, Crow." Johnny snapped his fingers and the men who had so obediently gathered the doubloons followed him faithfully into the night.

"You bastard!" Crow shouted, his teeth clattering together.

"Kill him once I'm out of sight," Johnny said from the shadows.

"What about the boy?" one of the rifle-wielding men piped up.

"Him too. He'll only cause me trouble."

"You won't win, Johnny. People like you never do!" Crow yelled.

"I already have." His booming laugh carried through the still of the night. Crow winced in pain and clutched at his chest as Johnny and all but four men vanished from sight.

"Boys, now's your chance." Crow eyed the men towering over him. "You with me? Or are you going to let that pretty prick boss you around?"

Crow looked to Tim. They'd known one another for years. He thought he was loyal. "Tim?"

"Captain," Tim replied, breaking his silence. He had a long beard nearly down to his groin and thick bushy eyebrows which talked when he did.

"What's it going to be?"

"We're with him. With Johnny." Tim nodded.

"Yeah? And what's that prick going to give you that I haven't?" Crow turned his head and spat out a mouthful of bloodied spittle.

"He pays us, Crow. Gets us the girls too. You're not fit to be captain no more. Just an old fool, gone soft."

"Don't speak to him like that," a man with a crooked and scarred nose spoke up. "Crow's been good to us."

"Shut it!" Tim slapped him on the back of the head. "We haven't seen any coin for months!"

"You with the nose. I know your face. I'm no good with names. What is it again?" Crow asked, his voice hoarse from all the bruising and beatings.

"Walt, sir."

"Don't speak to him." Tim slapped Walt on the side of the head again.

"Walt, how did Johnny convince you to join him?"

"Well, he—"

"Shut the fuck up!" Tim turned his gun on Walt.

The remaining rifle-wielding man stepped between them.

"Move, Remy!" Tim ordered.

"Stop being an idiot and just shoot the old man!" Remy replied.

"I'm not an idiot." Tim pointed his gun barrel down at Remy's feet.

"That's what Johnny calls ya." Remy laughed.

Tim pulled the trigger and blasted Remy in his foot. Remy yelped in pain and grabbed at his injured limb. He lost his balance and hit the floor hard.

"Why'd ya do that?" Walt said and raised his rifle.

"Lower your gun, Walt." Tim fumbled to reload his.

"What the hell, Tim?!" Remy held his foot and tried to pull off his boot.

Crow seized the opportunity and with a swift kick swiped at the men's feet. Tim and Walt were so fixated on one another that they didn't see it coming and tumbled to the ground. The lantern-holding young lad made a run for it and dashed into the darkness. He didn't want to wait around and face Crow's wrath. The pair scrambled to their feet, searching for their lost rifles in the darkness.

"You're on your own, Remy!" Tim yelled and sped off.

"Sorry, Remy!" Walt made a dash for where the door once stood and stumbled over the piles of debris. Crow grabbed at Walt's legs, but he kicked himself free and ran into the night.

Crow stood up, his battered body doubled over in pain. He turned to Remy who had managed to remove his boot and lay propped against the wall.

"Just leaves you and me, boy."

"And me!" Isaac's voice cut through the darkness.

Remy reached into his jacket and pulled out a flintlock. "I'm sorry, Crow, I have to."

Isaac sprung to his feet and kicked the pistol from Remy's hand. The gun flew through the air and smacked down out of Remy's reach. Isaac scrambled and snatched up the flintlock.

"Were you conscious this whole time?" Crow gripped his middle as he spoke.

"Most of it."

A strong gust swept through the shack and took the clouds with it. The moonlight beamed in and Crow caught sight of the pistol barrel Isaac now had pointed at his chest.

"What are you going to do to me, boy?" Crow struggled to stand, sharp stabbing pains cutting through him with every breath. His jaw throbbed from clenching his teeth to bear the pain.

"I... I want a truce."

"What?" Crow couldn't understand why. He had held a gun to his head, taken his map and now put him in the middle of this mess. Maybe the boy wasn't so sharp.

"We've both lost the map... for now. And I don't need any more enemies in Nassau." Isaac relaxed his grip on the gun.

Crow didn't move or draw breath. The sharp stabbing pain in his chest consumed him.

"I bet you're wondering how you can trust me. And believe me, I'm thinking the same of you." Isaac grinned.

Crow grunted, clutching at his ribs. "Well, I don't have too many friends right now. I'll take what I can get. Truce it is."

"Great!" Isaac lowered the flintlock and extended his hand. "Shake on it?"

"Sure." Crow grabbed his hand and used his remaining strength to shake it.

"Excellent. I'll be off then." Isaac slapped Crow on the back nearly knocking him to the ground.

"I... I could do with some help here," Crow said, though it pained him to ask.

"And what would be in that for me?"

"You stole my map! It was my life's work, boy, I could say you owe me," Crow replied.

"I guess you make a good point. I'll stay and help you with this. Then I'm out." Isaac rubbed his hands together and turned to Remy. "Now what?"

"Now you point that pistol at him." Crow motioned to Remy who sat nursing his bloodied foot. "I want answers, Remy." Crow searched for some way of making light. He stumbled over to his bed which looked more like a few battered planks of wood thrown in a heap at this point. He fumbled for the tinderbox and candles underneath it. "Keep that gun on him, boy." Crow patted around until his hand struck the metal container. "Gotcha!" He sparked the flint, showering sparks into the small box.

"Do we really need light? Can't you just shoot him and go?"

"Just hold on. We need information from him first." The sparks took and Crow lit a candle with the splint. He went straight for his flintlock and dusted it off. "Right. Where have they taken Nelson?"

"I dunno, Crow," Remy said.

Crow cleaned off his pistol. "It's hard to believe what comes out of your mouth." Crow shook his head as he tipped powder into his gun muzzle. "You do know, and you'll tell me."

Remy eyeballed the crumbled door frame and rolled to the side.

Crow shot Isaac a warning look. "Don't shoot him, boy! We need answers first."

"I won't." Isaac pulled a bag out from his belt and retrieved a tiny vial. "Drink this, it will help with the pain." Isaac held the vial out to Remy.

"Don't give him anything! Let him suffer until he tells us where Nelson is!"

"You trying to poison me?" Remy asked.

"Why would I bother?" Isaac shrugged. "I could just shoot you if I really wanted."

Remy took the tiny vial and tipped the contents down his throat. His chin dropped to his chest and his body fell to the side.

"Boy! Why'd ya do that? Did that kill him?" Crow asked.

"No, just knocked him out for a bit." Isaac picked up the vial and tucked it away. "He'll be out for about five minutes or so. Not even. Hopefully."

"But it's not like he was going anywhere!"

"Now we have time to form a plan." Isaac smiled.

"Okay, well, good job, boy." Maybe he wasn't such an idiot after all.

"What should we do with him?" Isaac dug into Remy's pockets, found some reale and put it in his pouch. "Nice." They clinked together as they found their new home.

"Help me bring him to the bed." Crow grabbed Remy's still booted foot with one hand and kept hold of his side with the other. He hadn't managed to straighten up fully yet.

"Um, okay." Isaac wedged his hands under Remy's shoulders and helped Crow move him to the bed.

"If you go under the mattress, there should be some rope."

"What? Okay... interesting." Isaac brushed away some of the debris and gave it a slight lift. He stuck his hand in and felt around.

"It's not what you think, boy."

"Aha. Got it." Isaac threw the coil of rope to Crow. "Now what?"

"Help me restrain him. Tie him up." Crow wound the rope around Remy's wrists and secured them to the wonky bed posts.

"First time for everything." Isaac chuckled. "Bit weird."

Crow shook his head.

"What are we going to do with him?" Isaac asked.

Crow smiled and the dried blood crinkled on his face. "Watch and learn, boy. I've got a few potions of my own."

MOLLY WEAVER

Molly sat at her kitchen table trying to devise her latest concoction. She hadn't moved from her workspace in hours. Her back ached from hunching and her fingers throbbed from all the intricate work.

Papers and apothecary bottles covered every inch of the timber countertop and surrounding floor. Above her hung a wrought iron candelabra which lit the open room. She twisted and reached down to dig through a pile of dusty papers. She knew where the article ought to be.

"Why isn't it here?" Molly thumbed through the pages of a notebook, tipped it sideways and gave it a shake. Her frantic movements knocked a large brown bottle off the table. "Damn it!" The glass bottle shattered and sizzled as orange liquid flowed out onto the floor. She would usually grab a rag and carefully clean the spill, but time was of the essence today. Instead, she reached down to pick up the broken pieces without giving it her full attention. Her hand hit a jagged piece of glass which cut into her palm. "Ouch! Stupid thing!"

Molly struggled to keep her temper. She had already

spent so many hours trying to perfect her latest potion and she would stay here all night if she had to.

Blood pooled in her palm. She took out her handkerchief and applied pressure. That would stop the flow long enough for her to continue. She was determined to follow through with her idea. Her new creation would change the way battles were fought. She planned to formulate a potent elixir which would eliminate the unwanted after-effects of drinking alcohol. The idea behind it being that people could stock up on liquid courage the night before, or even during a battle, and they wouldn't feel groggy or need time to recover. It would make them not only courageous but invincible. And with the impending war between Vella, Jane and Thad looming, now seemed like the ideal time to perfect such a thing.

"Molly!" The door swung open. Startled, she dropped the handkerchief on the ground and blood poured out from the wound once more.

"Johnny?" Molly picked up her cloth and re-applied it to her hand.

"Molly, I need your help!" Johnny Ives stood in her doorway, sweating through his thin, pale yellow shirt, which was stained with blood. Beside him stood several men, three of which held an overly round man between them.

"You could have knocked!" Molly shook her head, unimpressed with the interruption. "What did you do now, Johnny?" Molly waved him in. "That lot can stay out there!"

Johnny held out his arms and the three men dropped the unconscious man into them. Despite his strength, he nearly toppled over under the weight and staggered through the doorway. His eyes searched the room, desperate for somewhere to dump the heavy load.

Molly cleared the rectangular, dark wooden table in her living room. A once white cloth, now stained with a sea of murky browns and reds from her lotions and potions, covered the timber top. She typically reserved this spot for eating since every other surface in the house was covered by something or other but there wasn't really anywhere else to put this man. "Put him down here and tell me what happened." Molly scanned the unconscious man's body.

"It's Nelson, Crow's man." Johnny heaved him onto the table.

"Yes, I can see that." Molly felt eyes burning into her back and turned to find her living room filled with Johnny's men.

"Tell your men to give us some space."

"Out of here, boys." Johnny nodded his head in the direction of the door. "Leave the coffer."

"Otis found you then? Gave you my note?" Molly grabbed the cleanest cloth she could find and applied it to Nelson's gaping head wound.

"He sure did. Told me where Crow was then I followed this one and Isaac. Have a look at this." Johnny reached for the coffer filled with doubloons. His eyes marveled at the glinting golden coins. He seemed lost in them.

"Quite the score." Molly observed Johnny as she continued to apply pressure to Nelson's wound. He lifted his shirt up to mop the sweat from his face. She tried to stay focused on the matter at hand, but the sight of Johnny's firm torso made it difficult. Molly checked Nelson's pulse. The beats were faint and slow. "Hold this, would you?"

"What?" Johnny snapped out of his daze.

"If you want him to live, hold the cloth to his head. Why did you bring him here anyway?"

"I don't know. I just thought you would know what to do... Can you even save him?" Johnny did as he was told and applied pressure to Nelson's leaking wound.

"Probably." Molly walked over to a dusty, dark timber dresser and opened the top cupboard. Bottles and dirty rags filled any space possible with plates of half-eaten food piled awkwardly around them. Some would call Molly's house a mess, but she didn't care. It had been years since it functioned as a home. To her it was simply somewhere to create.

"He knows a lot, Molly. In the wrong hands he could be dangerous but by the same token he could be exceedingly useful... to us." Johnny flashed Molly a wicked smile. "Though once he finds out about Crow..." His face dropped.

"What exactly did you do to Crow?" Molly pulled out a large bottle from the dresser.

"Knocked him about a bit, well, a lot actually." Johnny looked to the floor. "Then had the men kill him." He rubbed at the back of his neck.

"Yes, well, you're right. Nelson's not going to be too forthcoming with information, but under the right circumstances I'm sure he will be." She threw Johnny a few clean rags. "I think he'll be very useful, let's see if we can save him."

Molly made her way over to the kitchen table. She recalled the first few weeks in the house, they were absolute chaos. Her thighs had been covered in bruises from bumping into furniture and her head filled with lumps from bashing it on places others would miss. She had since spaced out the room perfectly to accommodate her stature. She collected several tiny vials from her workspace. They were labeled and organized by use: *Explosives*, *Traps*, *Tricks*, *Poisons*, *Healing* and *Smells*.

"Perfect!" Molly held up a small vial to the light.

"What is it?"

"This should stop the flow." Molly motioned for Johnny to move over. She removed the blood-soaked rag from Nelson's head, grabbed the tiny vial and uncorked the top. She tapped lightly and a dark brown, sand-like substance tipped out and spilled onto the wound. The fine grains absorbed the blood in an instant. "It's like a permanent self-holding cloth, I suppose. It seals off the wound completely."

Molly tapped a little on her own palm, secured a cloth around her hand then tied a fresh cloth around Nelsons' head. "With a bit of luck, he'll see sunrise."

"Great." Johnny stood with one hand on his hip and combed the other through his hair.

"What happened to Isaac?" Molly asked.

"Just about vanished, couldn't find him."

"I see." She put her hand on Nelson's cheeks, they were warm to the touch. A good sign.

"Help me move him to the bed?" Molly asked. In the corner of the kitchen sat a small bed where Daniel had slept once upon a time. She missed her boy but wherever he was he wasn't a boy anymore. She still had so many unanswered questions. There wasn't a day which passed where she didn't think of him.

She pushed such thoughts from her mind.

"Righto." Johnny grabbed Nelson by the arms and Molly took his legs. She couldn't help but stare at Johnny's shirt tightening around his bulging arms as they lifted Nelson onto the bed.

"You're a lifesaver, love." Johnny released his grip on Nelson and shot her a smile.

"He'll have a use." Molly cleaned her hands. "Nelson has a sharp mind. I believe Crow relied on him for most of his thinking."

"Yeah, and who knows, maybe he'll be happy with a new captain?"

"I very much doubt that but give it time, maybe he'll come round." Molly gave a light shrug and took a seat.

Johnny pulled out the half-torn map from his pocket. "Have a look at this, would you? Can you make out what it says?"

Molly studied the tattered paper for a moment. "*C. Kidd treasure not found*." Molly's eyes widened. "Kidd?"

"C. Kidd..." Johnny crossed his arms and looked to the ceiling. "Captain Kidd?"

"Of course!" Molly stood up in a flurry of excitement. This map was stuff of legend in Nassau. "Captain Kidd, remember the day they hanged him?"

"Not really, I was only a boy at the time."

"Johnny! What a find!" Molly slapped him on the shoulder and knocked him off balance.

"It's only half." Johnny steadied himself.

"Kidd buried his treasure somewhere. 'Thirty-thousand doubloons' he shouted from the gallows as they hung him. The rope even snapped the first time around. What a day." Molly smiled as her mind cast back. She remembered the touch of Daniel's hand in hers. The excitable crowd edging closer to the platform. The treasure had been all anyone spoke of for weeks after that. "This must be some of the islands they've searched — Crow's searched, I suppose."

Molly handed the map back and paced around the room. Johnny's eyes darted from island to island.

"But it's only half the map."

"So that's what Crow's been up to." Molly walked over to Nelson and watched the rise and fall of his chest. His breathing had returned to normal and a flush of red broke out in his cheeks.

"But we can't do anything with half a map." Johnny slammed his fist on the table causing the bottles to rattle and the candlelight to flicker.

Molly turned to face Johnny. "You have men, you have a ship."

"Well... the ship isn't close to being fit to sail. Needs a lot of work. A lot."

"Won't this cover it?" Molly walked over to the coffer full of doubloons. She flipped open the lid and counted. "There's about thirty here."

"That'll probably cover half. There's a reason Crow's men turned on him, Molly. It's been awhile since they've sailed. Nearly a full year."

"I see." Molly closed the gold box and pushed it aside. "I know how we can get you the rest."

"How?"

Molly had Johnny right where she wanted him. "We're finally going to make our move. Vella has decided to attack Jane and Thad. If you and your men help, Vella will pay handsomely."

"You're crazy!" Johnny waved the idea away with his hand. "Take on those two?"

"Not at the same time. First Jane. Recruit her people to join ours, and once she's taken care of, we'll move in on Thad." Molly needed to convince Johnny, him and his men were crucial in her plan.

"I don't know. Sounds like a sure-fire way to get yourself killed." Johnny fixated on the map.

"Imagine you do this. Vella will pay you. You can fix the ship. And with a little help from our friend over here," Molly looked down at Nelson, "you can find the thirty thousand doubloons. Captain Kidd's treasure! I don't think you realize how famous you'll be, Johnny. Or infamous rather. You'll be the pirate captain they write books about."

Johnny's eyes lit up. "Books, you say?"

"Think about it, Johnny."

"Oh, I am, love." A smirk spread across his face. "So, what's my part in this then?"

Perfect. Molly tried to keep the joy from her face. She had worked her charm, told him what he wanted to hear. She learned long ago that it was key to getting people to do the things you want in life.

"Since you have Crow's men, that'll double our current size, so between your men and Vella's women, it puts us at about two hundred. Double what Jane has."

"What's Jane at?"

"Half. Half of that." Molly's brow crumpled in a frown as Johnny nodded. She had long known he was more muscle than anything else, but she didn't think basic numbers were beyond him. Still, she couldn't help but stare. Those muscles were really something, plus that strong jawline, the hair. Not only was he handsome but charismatic and charming too. She could be the brains; he was most definitely the brawn.

"Maybe you don't need us if you've already got more than Jane?" Johnny said.

Molly snapped out her trance.

"No! We very much do. Jane may have less people than Vella, but every single one is highly skilled. They're trained killers. It will still be close but with you on side, I think we can do it."

Molly recognized the look on Johnny's face, he loved nothing more than flattery.

"I'm in! The men won't take much persuading, especially when they hear about the map. Maybe they can even help convince Nelson to steer the course with us." Johnny pounded his fist into his open palm.

"Quite possibly. Do me a favor and just keep quiet for a bit though. Gather the rest of your men and prepare them for battle but maybe don't let on why exactly."

"I'm not sure they'll like that."

"Don't give them a choice, Johnny. You are captain after all. Oh, and I need you to find Isaac."

"Okay... why?" Johnny crossed his arms.

"Strategy." Molly chose not to elaborate.

"Isaac? That drunk lad? You want him for strategy?"

"You'd be surprised." Molly retrieved a stack of papers from the floor and flicked through them as she spoke.

"Damn right I would. I am!"

"We play chess together; he wins every time. That lad can beat anyone at a game." Molly busied herself looking for the missing article. That blasted paper held the key to her final ingredient, and she couldn't for the life of her remember what to use without it.

"Maybe everyone else is just bad?" Johnny laughed at his own suggestion and looked to the floor, eyes wide. Molly's face didn't falter.

"Just gather your men, Johnny, and try to find Isaac. Then send him my way... please." Molly looked up and smiled.

"Alright, love, sounds like a plan." Johnny looked over toward Nelson and pointed. "What do we do with him? And the coffer?"

"Leave them both here, it's too risky taking them out now, there are guards everywhere."

Johnny opened the door. His men we're still standing outside. "Are they back yet?" The men shook their heads. "Robert, you've a good aim. Go back to Crow's shack and make sure the job's taken care of." Johnny turned to Molly. "What will you do, love?"

"I need to talk to Vella. Time to get everything in order."

JANE HATCH

Jane blinked in astonishment. She couldn't believe what she read.

Take this as a message. Some of us are not pleased with your direction. Needless risk, needless deaths. It's time for a new leader. We need someone stronger, someone smarter.
An uprising is coming.

She scanned the words again and fought her instinct to tear up the note in a fit of rage. She needed to study it closer first. A thousand questions raced through her mind. She needed to calm down, but how could she? Had she really started to lose control of her mercs? After all these years of seemingly unwavering loyalty, was it finally falling apart? A leader without control is no leader at all, she panicked.

Jane looked at where Margaret was lying. Leon had fetched a sheet and covered her body with the thin cloth. What sort of monster would do this to one of their own?

"Ma'am? What's it say?" Leon asked. Jane could tell he

was hesitant, but she knew how him and Margaret had gotten along. He'd only want to help, but she couldn't breathe a word of a traitor in the ranks. Not yet.

"It's just a threat. A cowardly threat."

"Ma'am?" Leon approached her, scratching his arm with his hook. "I know this is terrible timing, but I really have to go. The trial's about to start."

"What trial?" Jane stared through him; her mind lost in thought.

"For the new recruit's, ma'am." He bowed his head. "May I be dismissed?"

"Sure." Jane nodded and waved him away.

Leon shut the door behind him and an eerie silence filled the room. Only moments ago, some pig was in here, brutalizing Margaret. How did nobody come to her aid? Or Maddy's? There must be more than one of them. Jane's eyes darted around the room—looking for signs—but the words written in the note clouded her judgment. They echoed in her every thought: *an uprising is coming.* Jane wasn't one for tears but for the first time in a long time a small part of her wanted to sob. However, a much larger part of her wanted to scream then slaughter the bastards responsible. Some time to sit and gather her thoughts would be ideal but she needed to act now and fast. Everyone would be expecting her to step up and lead... at least, those that still believed in her.

Jane walked out of her armory, pushing the heavy oak double doors wide open. In one breath her heart was heavy, in another it burned with rage. Margaret had been her confidant, her only true friend in this lifetime. And everyone knew it. Death came with the territory, but treachery within her crew?

It evoked a different kind of emotion.

Maddy's body had been removed. Jen, her housekeeper, mopped up the remainder of the blood with a rag and bucket. A crowd was forming along the staircase. "Downstairs everyone!" Jane commanded. "Not you, Jen." Jane beckoned her over.

"Yes, ma'am?"

"I need the armory cleaned up. Get someone to help you. And set up a proper burial. For both of them."

"Of course." Jen scurried away.

Jane made her way to the mezzanine which overlooked the grand marble-floored foyer and stood tall. She needed to address the issue head on. Her mercenaries lined the bottom set of stairs and milled about in the entrance below, all staring at her with questioning eyes. Word had obviously spread. Which of these sick bastards had slain Margaret? Were they the same ones that killed Maddy? Her thoughts jumped from one to another. She drew in a deep breath and focused. "Can I have your attention!" She always tried to remain polite with her mercs—firm but polite—until people showed her that they needed to be spoken to otherwise.

A light smattering of chatter continued on the stairs.

"Everybody! Shut the hell up!"

The noise ceased. All eyes were on her.

Jane paused. "Good," she uttered under her breath. "Maddy, and now Margaret, have been murdered."

She eyed the crowd for their reaction. Anyone who would have done this wouldn't be shocked, or they'd try to feign shock, but Jane would see through it. Her eyes darted around looking for any overtly suspicious behavior but she struggled to home in on just one person.

"I need everybody to keep their eyes and ears open. Anything suspicious, come straight to me." Jane nodded.

"We will find out who did this." Some of the crowd began to chatter but Jane held up her hand. "We won't kill them though!" People turned and looked at one another. "Not right away." Jane faked a smile.

The crowd responded with laughter. They all seemed to be eating up what she was saying. It was hard to believe there were traitors amongst the ranks.

"First we will torture them." She threw in a sinister laugh and the crowd followed suit, nodding toward each other as she spoke. "Then we will question them. I always find people are more willing to talk after they've lost a finger or two." Jane wiggled her fingers and the crowd responded with more laughter. "Once we have found out what we need, then... and only then... we will end their lives!" Jane paused for effect. She had mastered giving speeches. "We will avenge our girls!"

The room erupted in cheer. She lifted her fist in the air and everyone followed suit. They were all riled up, ready to take on anything. A round of applause erupted and deafening whistles of encouragement bounced off the walls.

"For now, it's business as usual. I'll share what news I have later," she shouted over the noise of the crowd then turned on her heel and made for the staircase down to the foyer. The stairs were lined with people. Her people. Their faces filled with emotion. Some with glazed eyes, sad from the loss of their friends. Some with mischievous grins, excited by the prospect of hunting down those responsible. The crowd slowly dispersed, back to training, eating, fornicating, whatever they did when they weren't working.

The first step in her plan sprang to mind. She needed to find her newest recruits. People who hadn't made too many friends or allies as yet and she had just the pair in mind. As she made her way down the stairs and across the foyer, she nodded to those who crossed her path. She recognized most of them but as business boomed, she had to admit there were a few she didn't. Jane reached the door and as she did a black-haired woman rushed by with her head down, clearly avoiding eye contact.

Jane stopped. "You're Patricia, right?"

The woman froze in her tracks.

"Yes. Yes, ma'am." Patricia corrected herself.

Jane put her hands on her hips and eyed her up and down.

Patricia continued to avoid eye contact and kept her gaze to the side.

"I'm sorry about... about the girls." Patricia bowed her head as she spoke, but her face didn't show any signs of remorse.

"Yes. Me too. Tell me, Patricia, how long have you been with us now? Two? Three years?"

"Just a year, ma'am."

"Right. And would you say you're happy?" Jane crossed her arms.

Patricia responded by crossing her own arms. "Yep, no complaints, good place to lay my head, good food, good job I guess, if you can call it good." Patricia smiled, but Jane saw through it. No crinkles appeared at the corners of her eyes and no teeth showed.

Jane uncrossed her arms and clasped her hands behind her back. "Do you have any family, Patricia?"

"Just my father, he lives not far from us."

Jane looked to the floor. The toe of Patricia's boot pointed away from Jane and to the door. It signaled to her that not only was she uncomfortable but would escape quickly if needed. It wasn't a behavior people were typically aware of, but Jane had observed it many times. Everything about Patricia felt off, but she couldn't act now. The words in the note ran through her head: *needless risk, needless deaths*. This might not be the best time to lash out, Jane thought.

"Life can be tough out there. I hope he's doing well." Jane kept her eyes fixed on Patricia. "And do let me know if you hear anything about the trouble we're having."

"I will." Patricia flashed a forced smile.

Jane reached for the door and yanked it open. Maybe she was reading into things too much? She was normally so good at reading people, but her detection skills were off today. She needed some air, and more importantly she needed to find Anna and Jose. Jane had her reservations about the pair. They were a little unpredictable, but they did at least seem fiercely loyal. Right now, that was exactly what she needed.

JOY LAFITTE

"Listen up, you weak pieces of shit!"

Joy let every booming word glide over her. She hated being shouted at, but she refused to fall victim to these scare tactics. She kept her gaze straight ahead, occasionally catching a glimpse of his bald, thick skull.

He was the tallest man she'd ever laid eyes on and mean looking too. He wore a green short-sleeved shirt, tucked into faded blue pants. His clothing strained over his bulging frame. Joy had never seen arms like them, his biceps were the size of two human heads. He wore a dark leather baldric draped across his chest. It housed five pistols at the front and two daggers and an ax at the back. Multiple pistols and blades hung from his belt. Joy marveled at the treasure trove of weaponry. The only thing that made him somewhat less intimidating was his attempt at facial hair—a thin strip of a beard stretching from the middle of his lip down to his chin. Hardly worth the effort, Joy thought.

So, this was the man who filtered out the recruits. If he was anything to go by she had a tough few weeks ahead.

He strode up and down the line of wannabe mercenaries and continued yelling.

"You!" The booming giant grabbed the smallest man in the line-up by the throat.

"Y-y-yes, sir," the small man stammered between breaths.

"Say my name!" the large man shouted.

"Th-Th-Thunder, sir."

"Say it again. Louder and clearer." He dropped the man from his grip.

"Thunder, sir!"

"That's right!" Thunder yelled.

He turned his back on the line-up of potential recruits and stared off into the distance. For a moment it was as if he had a change of thought. Joy felt the recruits breathe a collective internal sigh, but it was short-lived. Thunder turned on his heel and grabbed the small man's shirt, pulling him into his chest and holding his cowering frame under his chin. "Do you think you have what it takes?"

"I've got what it takes, sir."

"Do not dare call me sir!" He released the man, who stumbled backwards.

"Thunder! Thunder is my name."

Joy couldn't stand it. The whole rigmarole irritated her no end. She just wanted to know what she needed to do to get through and to get it done.

Thunder walked up and down the row of potential recruits. "When I challenge you, you will follow my orders. If you so much as hesitate for even a moment you're out!"

Joy's chest tightened as he walked past her, but she didn't flinch.

Thunder walked back to the small man and punched

him in the stomach. "I don't like being disrespected." The weight of Thunder's punch knocked the man to the ground. "Let that be a warning to you, next time it won't be my fist." A grin crept over Thunder's face. "Do you all understand what you are here for?"

Everyone in Nassau knew that only the best joined Jane's crew, and if you made it in you were set for life. Not only were you well-paid but housed in the finest quarters too. Food and any beverages of your choosing came in a near unlimited supply. You slept on a proper bed and had all the weapons you dreamed of. The only downside being that you had to do things that a lot of people were not comfortable doing.

"Yes, Thunder!" Joy yelled toward the beast of a man. She ran through her priorities in her head. Get to Jane, get the coin, get revenge.

"Good." Thunder cracked his knuckles as he continued to circle the recruits. "If you're serious about joining then you must be willing to take a life... any life. Might even be someone you know. Are you capable of such a thing?"

"Yes, Thunder!" the recruits shouted in unison.

"Let's test that then." Thunder pulled out the top flintlock strapped to his chest and walked down the row. He held the pistol to the head of the unlucky soul standing at the end of the line. The boy couldn't have been more than seventeen, Joy thought. "It's not much fun having a gun to your head," Thunder said. The boy's legs shook. "That's why you want to be the one doing the shooting."

Thunder lowered the pistol and handed it to the boy. "Th... thank you, sir. Thunder! I mean Thunder," the boy quickly corrected himself.

"Better. So, are you willing to kill on behalf of Jane Hatch?" Thunder asked.

"Ye... yes!"

"Then now's the time to prove it." Thunder grabbed the arm of a man from the line-up and dragged him in front of the boy. "I want you to shoot this man."

"What?" The boy looked at Thunder, then back at the man.

"There's a doubloon in it for you." Thunder took out a gold coin and held it in the air.

"Don't do it!" The man raised his hands. Thunder gripped the back of his shirt and held him in place.

Joy couldn't believe her eyes. She hadn't thought for one moment that they would just be shooting one another. Dueling maybe but this didn't seem fair.

"Go on!" Thunder ordered. "This is what we do, we're mercenaries, we get paid to do things other people wouldn't. It's simple. You kill someone. You get the doubloon. You don't and..." Thunder eyed the boy and waved the golden coin at him.

"I can't..." The boy let the pistol hang loose. "It doesn't seem fair."

"I see." Thunder handed a fresh flintlock to the other man. "You shoot him then."

The man grabbed the pistol and looked at Thunder.

"If you don't, I'll shoot you both." Thunder smiled and stood back to watch who would shoot first.

The young boy's legs quivered and a stream of liquid pooled around his crotch, darkening his pants.

"I'm sorry, I've a family to take care of." The man raised his gun and shot the boy in the stomach. He dropped the pistol on the ground. "I'm so sorry."

"Pathetic." Thunder looked to one of his assistants. "Take 'em both out, clearly not strong enough to handle it."

He looked at the boy wounded on the ground,

clutching at his side. "He'll live, take him to the doctor and you can keep the doubloon for your trouble, and for your silence." Thunder walked over to the boy. "You'll keep your mouth shut won't you, boy?"

The boy nodded.

"That goes for the lot of you, we don't want word getting back to that smarmy captain about what goes on here."

Joy had tried to prepare herself for the worst, but she hadn't expected this. She focused on her reason for being there: Raven. Her sweet sister had been through hell, kidnapped, enslaved. This was nothing in comparison. Joy had what it took to get through this. She stood tall as Thunder sauntered down the line eyeing the recruits up and down. His assistant fetched five fresh pistols.

"One of these is loaded, but lucky for you the other four aren't." Thunder laughed. "I'm a generous man."

Joy's heart pounded a little harder than usual as he stopped in front of her. Sweat formed at the back of her neck. It was showtime. Joy stood still. Unflinching. Unwavering. She was ready.

"Our first and only woman of the day. Let's see how this goes." Thunder placed a pistol to Joy's forehead. He pressed the barrel into her skin. "Are you scared yet?" Thunder whispered into her ear, his rancid breath striking her nose. Onions and garlic — well-fed. He reached around to grab her rear, cupping it with his hand while the pistol remained resting against her head.

"No, but you should be," Joy whispered in reply and grabbed him by the balls.

Thunder dropped the gun. His eyes watered as Joy continued to squeeze. He bit his lip and looked at her with begging eyes. She gave them a twist, and he fell to the ground. He cupped his crotch with his hands and rolled on the ground in pain.

The recruits were silent and still. Joy didn't know if her move had been incredibly courageous or incredibly stupid. A barrel pressed into her back. Stupid it was.

"Thunder?" his assistant called out. "Shall I do the honor or save it for you?"

Thunder didn't reply. He rolled on the ground, red-faced and glassy eyed. The gun pressed harder into her back.

"Maybe I'll make that call," the assistant said. He sounded smug and it sickened her. She didn't flinch, didn't move. They wouldn't get the best of her.

"No, no." Thunder roared with laughter as he clambered to his feet. "You." He stood, hunched, cupping his balls with one hand. "You'll fit right in here," he said, his voice a little softer than before. "Free pass to the next round for you."

Joy's racing heart returned to normal at his declaration.

"Never had that happen before." He smiled and wiped away his tears.

He finished working his way through the line-up of recruits. Joy watched on in horror as people struggled to shoot one another. She looked around and counted four others left standing.

"Looks like we're done for the day! Down to five and one is a woman. That's rare, very rare." He shot Joy a wink. "Good on you, darling."

Patronizing bastard, Joy remarked internally.

Thunder addressed the surviving recruits. "You'll be spending the next few days... trying to impress me." He smirked. "And I'll be spending the next few... trying not to kill you." He beckoned his assistant. "Show them to the bunker."

Joy sat on a plank of wood with a thin sheet tossed over it. This was where she would be resting her head for the next few nights and no doubt trying to fend off any unwanted night-time predators.

On a group of beds as far away from her as possible, three of the men who had survived the first round sat eyeing her. One was a tanned, wiry, older man. He looked somewhat sharp but the other two left a lot to be desired. Another was what Joy could only describe as deranged. His neck sat low, almost hunched between his thick shoulders. He breathed through his mouth which was permanently open, revealing a few top teeth. The man next to him looked like your everyday brute around Nassau, he was unremarkable other than a scar through his top lip which made it appear almost split in two. They avoided any eye contact with Joy and kept to themselves. She hoped for their sake that they were apprehensive, even a little scared of her after what went down with Thunder today.

Joy watched the small fire crackle away in the center of the room and played out the forthcoming scenarios in her head. If she were to make it through the next few days, she needed to form a plan. The wind picked up and the bunker's cloth walls flapped back and forth with each gust. Her thoughts were interrupted as the youngest survivor from the day's events approached.

"Good job today, you're a brave one, aren't ya?" He was an average looking man of average build. The only thing not average about him was his distinct lack of hand. In its place was a hook with a handkerchief wrapped around the pointy end. The man extended his hook to Joy. "Nice to meet ya, the name's Leon."

Joy wasn't sure what to do so she extended her hand out of politeness and gripped onto the hook.

"Ah just kidding." Leon laughed and pulled his hook back. He outstretched his hand and shook Joy's. "Confuses people every time."

His grip crushed into Joy's hand. "How'd you lose your hand?"

"Ha! Just an accident." He looked at the hook with fond eyes. Not the reaction Joy had expected. She'd remember that. Leon let go of Joy's hand. The release of his tight grip left a sting. "Mind if I join ya?" He grinned, revealing a full set of teeth. Interesting.

"No, not at all." Joy moved over and made room on her bed, if you could call it that.

"The name's Joy." She tried not to stare at the hook and distracted herself with her surroundings. She counted twenty beds in the bunker. Not many looked used. Her mind wandered. Were they ever full or did Thunder shoot most people dead in the first round? The three other men in the room sat huddled together, speaking in low whispers.

"Joy, what a nice name." Leon leaned in and whispered in her ear. "Good job with Thunder today, I didn't expect that one." He gave a soft chuckle.

"I don't think he expected it either." Joy smiled. She kept one eye focused on the three men the whole time. Intermittently they glanced over at Joy and Leon, then nudged one another and laughed. A classic sign that trouble would be coming their way soon, she thought.

"So, what do ya think our odds are of getting through?" Leon asked.

"How should I know?" Joy shrugged.

"Well, there's five of us, and they're only looking for three."

"Really? How'd you come to know that?"

"Did my research."

"Right." Joy's mind spiraled. This could prove problematic. Her odds were good, but she still needed to beat two of these brutes at whatever Thunder would throw at them next.

"Ever since I got this hook my prospects for most jobs have been pretty grim. So, I did some research on this place before signing up," Leon continued. He waved his arms as he spoke. Joy sat back to avoid losing an eye.

"Pay is good, you're fed, roof over your head too. And most of all, they'll allow a cripple like me in if I can pass the trial." Leon nodded and smiled.

"Yeah. I'd heard the pay would be good." Roy hadn't told her anything of the trial specifics. "Did you know they would shoot people during the trial?"

"I did."

"Yet you still came?"

"No choice. Need to make a living."

"Doesn't seem right to me," Joy said.

Leon shrugged.

"I'm surprised the governor isn't onto them."

"Ha, probably paying him off. Plus, people keep quiet, they're paid for their troubles. A doubloon's a lot to most folk," Leon replied.

"True," Joy said.

The three whispering men stood up and strode over to where Joy and Leon sat. They weren't the most terrifying men Joy had laid eyes on, but they still weren't exactly the kind you wanted to be alone with in a bunker. They were all here to prove themselves as skilled killers, after all.

"Here we go." Joy rolled her eyes at Leon who smiled.

"Only a matter of time." Leon stuck his hook into his pocket.

"Well, well, well, look at you two lovebirds," the hunched man taunted.

"Fuck off, Joe!" Leon spoke up, his voice deeper and more assertive than when he spoke to Joy.

"Little baby wants me to leave them alone." Joe stuck out his bottom lip. He picked Leon up by the neck and lifted him off the bed. "Poor little baby only has one hand." He threw Leon on the ground with ease. Leon wasn't a big man, but the fact Joe was able to lift him with one hand was still impressive. "I could just kill you both, and then we three automatically make it through." Joe pointed toward his two friends who stood on either side of him and kept his other hand behind his back the entire time.

"Auto-what?" the man with the scarred lip asked. He must be the stupid one, Joy thought.

"Shut up, Roe!" Joe shouted.

Roe? What kind of name is Roe? Joy cocked her head and stared at the trio.

"Well, Joe." Leon got to his feet and dusted himself off. "That wouldn't be very clever, seeing as how if one of us dies in the bunker... we all do."

"What?" The older, more reserved of the three spoke up. "You didn't say anything about that, Joe."

"You disrespecting me, Moe?"

Joe, Roe and Moe. Is this a joke? Joy couldn't believe her ears.

Moe shook his head. "You didn't say anything, that's all."

Joe whipped out the dagger which he had been hiding behind his back. Joy had assumed as much. "Everybody's gonna be real quiet soon," Joe said.

Joy considered whether she should help Leon. He probably wouldn't make it through the rest of the trial so keeping him around for now would at least increase her chances. Plus, he seemed like a nice enough guy. Joy reached into her jacket and gripped the handle of her favorite blade.

Leon didn't so much as flinch and pointed to the dagger Joe held. "I've done my research on all this. If any of us die tonight we all die. So, I'd put that dagger away and get the fuck back to your bed."

Joy tried to hide her shock. Leon had quite the mouth on him. He seemed fearless.

Joe glared at Leon and spat at his feet. "Back we go." He eyed Roe and Moe and motioned with his head for them to return too.

"We'll take care of you tomorrow then. And you, darling." He turned to Joy.

It took everything in her to keep quiet and not slice her blade into his back.

The trio walked away and Joy and Leon sat down, side by side. "Thanks." Leon rubbed the back of his neck.

"I didn't do anything. Looked like you had it under control."

Leon shrugged.

"So, if one of us dies? We all die?" Joy asked.

Leon nodded in agreeance and looked at the three men. They returned to sitting with their backs to Joy and Leon. He leaned and whispered, "Nah, made that up."

"Smart." Joy was beginning to like this man. "I think we're going to get along just fine, Leon."

"I think so too." Leon walked to the bed next to Joy's. "Mind if I sleep here?"

"Not at all." Joy took off her jacket but kept her vest on. It had a dagger within easy reach and a few poisoned blades, should they be needed. As the fire died down and the light dimmed, her mind wandered. She couldn't stop thinking about tomorrow. What would they have her do? Today worked out well in the end, and she was one step closer to Jane. She still hadn't decided whether to take her in dead or alive. For now, alive seemed like the better deal but Joy realized that might not be possible. She tried to fight sleep for as long as possible but as snoring filled the bunker, she drifted off, dreaming of vengeance.

"Arghhhh!" A voice shouted, waking her. She pulled out her blade, wielding it into the darkness.

The cloth door was thrown aside as masked figures ran into the room. The glowing embers from the fire lit the bunker ever so slightly but not enough to tell who these people were. One person lunged at Leon and lifted a sword above his head, ready to slice him in two.

Joy hurried to untangle herself from the sheet to help him. "Leon! Wake up!"

JANE HATCH

The warm breeze swept through Jane's hair as she stepped out the door and onto the rough gravel path. Wafts of soups and stews from the mansion's kitchen filled the air. Sea salt carried in the breeze stung Jane's lips. She had been chewing on them all day, she always did when frictions were high. For once, she felt clueless as to who was on her side and who wasn't. Now would be the perfect time to confide in Margaret, she thought as she took the shortcut through the tall grass to where Anna and Jose were cleaning up the bloody mess they had made.

"Thad," Jane said and curled her lip in disdain. She brushed her hand through the grass as she considered the mounting tensions between them. It wouldn't be long now before things blew up with him. This, these slayings. They would be the final straw. With each step Jane's thoughts grew a little clearer. A blast of air always helped. Maybe it was all those years locked up that made her appreciate it so much.

Snap.

The sound of a flintlock firing cut through the air and

interrupted her thoughts. Jane's heart raced. It was happening. Word had already spread. She drew her pistol from her hip holster and ducked, hidden amongst the grass. As her eyes searched for signs of the incoming attack, she recalled that today was in fact recruitment day and the fading sun meant that Thunder would be running through the final stages right about now. She rose to her feet and tucked her pistol away, embarrassed by her overreaction.

Her mind cast back to the day Thunder approached her with his new and rather novel idea. He wanted to make sure that the new recruits were ruthless. The best of the best. They needed to be able to kill absolutely anyone on command, so he devised a plan to have them shoot one another during the trial. Jane thought he was mad but when he explained it would all be an act, her interest piqued.

Thunder had heard around town that it was possible to fake a pistol shot, and when coupled with bags of animal blood he figured he could make it seem like people were being murdered. When in truth, half of the recruits were already part of Jane's crew and acting. Jane had still been reluctant. It had seemed far too risky, not to mention time-consuming, but Thunder had kept on, and in the end she had decided to try it for just one round. To her surprise it had worked. She needed more people like Thunder; they set her and her mercenaries apart from the likes of Thad and Vella's people.

Jane realized she hadn't yet moved and picked up her pace.

"Anna! Jose!" she called out as she approached the pair.

"Nearly done, ma'am," Anna replied and looked up. Her brow was soaked with sweat and she had strands of dirty, blonde hair stuck to her face. She tossed a final shovel of dirt over the shallow grave and patted it down. "Now we're done." Anna discarded her shovel and grinned at Jane.

"Like it never happened." Jose followed suit and threw down his shovel and took off his black bandana. His face was covered in a mix of dirt and sweat, which he wiped away with the black cloth.

"Good." Jane had half expected to find them at it and was surprised by their efforts. "Now that's taken care of, tell me, any good recruits today?" Jane blocked out the sinking sun with her hand and looked to the training camp.

"Yeah, it's been very entertaining." Anna laughed.

"How so?"

"Well." Jose pointed toward a woman wearing a striking tricorn hat with a plume of feathers. "You see her over there?"

"Yep." Jane narrowed her eyes.

"Thunder grabbed her behind." Jose raised his brows.

"Pig!" Anna remarked.

"But get this." Jose stifled a laugh. "She grabbed him by the balls and squeezed them until he fell to the ground!" Jose slapped at his thigh.

"What?" Jane's eyes went wide. "The mighty Thunder fell to the ground?"

"You should have seen him drop, ma'am." Anna wiped her hands clean with a rag from her pocket.

"So, she's good then?" Jane asked.

"Best I've seen so far." Anna kicked at a patch of dirt to cover some remaining blood splatter.

Jane nodded. "How are you two finding everything here at the camp?"

"Good," Jose replied and Anna nodded.

"We were sad about Maddy, we liked her but guess it's part of what we do." Anna shrugged.

"Yes." Jane paused. "Unfortunately, when I returned to the house early today, Margaret had also been killed. Murdered." Jane folded her arms and poked her tongue in her cheek.

"What?" Anna said.

"But it can't have been this lot, can it?" Jose pointed his thumb at the freshly turned earth where Thad's men were now buried.

"Exactly," Jane replied.

"Who then?" Jose said.

"I'm led to believe it's one of our own. There seems to be a traitor in our camp."

"Who'd do that, ma'am? Dirty fuckers!" Anna raised her voice.

"Believe me, I'm as angry as you. Anyway, the reason I'm telling you this is because I need your help. Since you were both out here when the incident happened... I figure I can trust you?" Jane cocked her head to the side.

"Yeah." Jose grinned. "Nobody else does though, we don't know many of the others yet."

"Even better." The more Jane interacted with the pair, the more she knew she had made the right decision in choosing them to help her. "No one will suspect you if you already keep to yourselves, and no one would think I'd trust you with such information given how new you are."

"Makes sense. We'll find 'em, ma'am. You mark my words." Anna looked over to Jose whose eyes sparkled with mischief.

"What's next then?" Jose asked.

"Give me until dinner. I need to come up with a plan...

On second thoughts, let's head down to the camp." Jane motioned toward the training camp where the new recruits had now turned in for the night.

Jose dusted himself off and rubbed his hands together.

"You making yourself look nice for him?" Anna teased, her voice hoarse. She spat and wiped at her mouth with her sleeve.

Jane shook her head. She couldn't keep up with everybody's sleeping arrangements, nor did she care, but seeing Jose potentially prettying himself up brought a wry smile to her face.

As they made for the camp a booming voice cut through the air. "Miss Jane!" a large man called out and walked toward them.

"Thunder! I've just been hearing all about your day." Jane had a soft spot for him, many at the camp did, at least once they'd made it through the trial.

"How are your balls?" She smirked.

"Bit sore actually. She didn't half squeeze 'em."

"And rightly so, I heard," Jane said.

"She's a feisty one that Joy. I like her. I think you will too," Thunder said.

"So, the one who took the mighty Thunder down is named Joy? Pretty name," Jane said.

"Joy Lafitte. I told Leon to keep an eye on her in the bunker, befriend her as part of the character test," Thunder replied.

"Think we might need to improve on the character testing actually." Jane put her hands on her hips and looked to the floor.

"How come?" Thunder tilted his head to the side.

"Long story short," Anna interjected. "Maddy and

Margaret are dead. Someone is betraying us, and we've got to find out who." Anna gave a coy smile.

Thunder's face dropped.

"Might want to work on your delivery. Margaret was a good friend to many here." Jane turned to Anna and stared her down.

"Anna's not known for her tact." Jose winked.

"Someone in the camp did it? Our crew?" Thunder asked.

"Unfortunately so. And there's possibly more than one traitor amongst the ranks," Jane replied.

"I see." Thunder covered his mouth with his hand. "It's hard to believe." He crossed his arms and widened his stance. "What's the plan then? I'll help where I can but no one will breathe a word to me. They know where my loyalties lie." He stroked at his chin in thought. "What if we got Joy to help out?"

"Joy?" Jane considered the new recruit. "We really need to get something happening soon though. We can't risk losing anymore."

"We could speed up the trial? Set the next part in motion tonight?" Thunder said.

"Is she really that good?" Jane asked.

"I reckon," Thunder replied.

"Okay." Jane didn't like resting on matters for too long. She trusted Thunder. He was a good judge of character and had proven himself to be endlessly loyal over the years.

"And what are you two going to be doing?" Thunder looked to Anna and Jose.

Jose shot him a wink. "You, hopefully."

Thunder shook his head.

Jane ignored Jose and pressed on. "Apparently no one

trusts Anna and Jose." She looked to Thunder who smirked.

"Makes sense, you two certainly have a reputation." Thunder eyed the pair.

"Yes, they do." Jane considered for a moment how the pair could be of most use. "I want you two to keep watch for anything suspicious, and I mean anything. If you have so much as a hunch about anyone, you come straight to me." Jane nodded. "You two should be able to do that, yes? I don't want to hear of you taking matters into your own hands." Jane looked to Anna and Jose.

"Of course!" Anna grinned and took out a dagger from inside her jacket and polished the blade.

"Thunder, what about Leon? He won't be expecting phase two until tomorrow night," Jane asked.

"Good point... He'll just have to improvise, I suppose. He's quick, he'll figure it out." He let out a boisterous laugh. "He won't be happy at all!" He continued to laugh and it echoed through the camp. "There's a few odd ones in there with them too. Should be interesting." He wiped a tear from his eye.

"Can you send Patricia in there tonight, for the ambush?"

"Patricia?" Thunder thought for a moment. "Black hair? About your height?"

"Yes, that's the one. Unless we have more by that name?" Jane smirked. "In that case, send them all in."

"I don't think we do." Thunder cocked his head. "Any reason?"

"I don't trust her. She needs to go and if Leon's not expecting an ambush tonight, I'm sure he'll take care of her. We can kill two birds with one stone, as they say."

Thunder scratched his head "Two birds and a stone?

That's a new one. I like that! I'll go find her myself," Thunder said.

Jane turned to Anna and Jose who looked bored by all the talk and lack of killing. "You two, go get something to eat, drink... whatever you need to prepare for the coming days."

"Yes, ma'am," they said in unison and jogged off toward the mansion.

"See you soon, Thunder," Jose shouted back.

"Got yourself a fan?" Jane said to Thunder who shook his head in response.

"Guess we all need one." He turned and made his way to find Patricia.

Jane stood alone for a moment. "We do."

ISAAC CARVER

The candles flickered in the night breeze and illuminated the carnage within Crow's shack. Isaac rummaged through the rubble and grabbed himself a battered wooden chair. He looked to Crow who muttered to himself and shifted the belt which held up his pants.

"What are you looking for?" Isaac asked as he tried to catch Crow's gaze. "You said watch and learn but you're just fumbling with your pants!" Isaac contemplated making a run for it. There wasn't a great deal stopping him, and he had what he wanted.

He still couldn't believe it, after all these years he finally knew the island where Captain Kidd had buried his treasure. All thirty-thousand doubloons worth. It didn't even matter that half the map was missing, he had the important part.

"I'm going to take a seat." Isaac perched on the crooked wooden chair he had retrieved. He looked over to Remy who had awoken to find himself shackled to the bed. "Do we really have to do this? Not that I know what exactly it is that we're doing but it all seems a bit odd."

"Hang on! I've nearly got it." Crow shifted his belt and pants some more.

Isaac put his head in his hands. "We're going to be here all night," he muttered under his breath.

"Got it!" Crow announced and shook a small bottle which he had retrieved from somewhere deep in his pants.

"Now, Remy." Crow knelt and put his face close to his. "I'm going to ask you a few questions."

"Well, this is less weird than I thought." Isaac shrugged and sat back. The chair wobbled.

"Johnny will kill me," Remy slurred, writhing in pain from the shot to his foot.

"You're still worried about him when I could kill you in an instant!" Crow yelled. "You never were very smart."

Crow uncorked the small bottle and grabbed Remy's cheeks. He pushed them in with his fingers, causing Remy's mouth to fall open, and tipped the liquid in.

"What is it?" Isaac asked.

"Truth serum, boy. He'll tell us anything we want once we give this to him." Remy gave in and swallowed the serum with a shudder.

"Now what?" Isaac stood up and looked at Remy as he ingested the concoction.

"We wait, boy."

"How do we know it worked?"

"I don't know actually," Crow said.

"What do you mean you don't know?" Isaac threw up his hands.

"I've never actually used one of these." Crow showed Isaac the inside of his pants where ten tiny vials hung, hidden away.

"That's not a great place for them."

"Yeah, that's what Nelson said, but it keeps them hidden."

Isaac leaned over the bed and looked into Remy's eyes. He held out two fingers. "How many fingers am I holding up? Wait, this isn't going to work."

"T... t..." Foam spewed from Remy's mouth and his body convulsed.

Isaac withdrew from the bed and looked to Crow. "Is this normal? He looks... um..."

"He's fine!" Crow yelled as he grabbed Remy by the shoulders and shook him. "Snap out of it, man!"

The foam from his mouth turned to blood. His eyes bulged as the convulsions grew violent.

"I don't think he is fine," Isaac mumbled.

"Dammit! Must've been the wrong vial! I never have this trouble when Nelson's here!" Crow panicked. "Remy! Where's Nelson?" Crow shook Remy but his eyes were gone. The color faded from his face and the convulsions slowed as his body grew limp.

"I think that ship has sailed." Isaac shook his head. "How did you get the wrong vial?"

"They're not labeled. My memory, well, it's not what it used to be."

"You don't say," Isaac mumbled under his breath, trying not to crack a smile.

"I need to find Nelson! And the map. I didn't get a good look at it," Crow said as he gathered his belongings. "Let's get out of here."

"Stop! I will shoot you both dead," a voice came from what was once the doorway and a rifle hammer clicked into place.

Isaac and Crow looked at one another and both put their hands in the air.

"Turn around, face the wall," the man said in a high-pitched voice which almost squeaked.

Both Isaac and Crow did as they we're told.

"I'd know that voice anywhere!" Crow said.

"Shut it! Face the wall."

"How'd he get you, Robert?"

"I said shut it! Johnny sent me to check... check you were dead."

"He knows it would take more than a few men to get rid of me." Crow smiled.

"Now turn around, the both of you," Robert yelled, his voice shaking.

"Okay," Isaac said and rolled his eyes at Crow.

Isaac and Crow turned to face Robert.

"I don't want no trouble, Crow." Robert lifted the rifle and aimed the barrel at Crow's head.

"Says the man pointing a gun to my head."

"I'm just... following orders, we don't have a choice! I've a family to feed." The rifle shook in Robert's hands. "What happened to Remy?"

"Took a turn for the worst." Isaac chuckled and stole a glance at his jacket pocket. He caught sight of the map, along with the three cards Pont Neuf had given him. 'Death, it surrounds you.' Her words echoed in his ears. Hopefully not my death, he thought as he looked to Crow who leapt forward and attempted to snatch the rifle and disarm Robert. He missed. Robert jumped back and clutched the rifle tight.

"I will shoot you, Crow, I mean it!" Robert yelled. His finger twitched on the trigger. "I'm sorry."

Crow closed his eyes, held his head high, and braced for the impact.

"Hold on!" Isaac retrieved the map from his pocket and

waved the tattered paper in the air. "Don't do something you'll regret, Robert. We're all friends here you know? Crow's my friend, he's your friend too, so now we're friends."

"We ain't friends, stranger." Robert relaxed the trigger and pointed the gun at Isaac, then back toward Crow. "What's that? What you waving at me?"

"This?" Isaac smiled. "This is the other half of the prized map. I think your boss might quite like this."

"You had it the whole time?" Crow glared at Isaac.

"If you don't shoot us, how about I give it to you? You can pass it on to Johnny, you'll be the hero!"

"What's the catch?" Robert narrowed his eyes.

"We get to live?" Isaac shrugged.

"And you tell us where Nelson is?" Crow interjected. Isaac glanced at Crow whose eyes were clouded with sadness.

"It's not worth it. Johnny would kill me. Map or no map." Robert kept the rifle held high, switching his aim from Crow to Isaac. "I could just shoot you both and take the map."

"Not sure about that, Robert. I mean, you can shoot Crow—he hasn't done me any favors lately—but by the time he goes down, I'll be long gone with this map. I'm very quick."

"What? You just said he was your friend," Robert said as heavy lines formed between his eyebrows.

"I think you're missing the point."

"Listen to the boy, Robert. He may be a drunk but he's talking sense, for now." Crow nodded.

"Well." Robert pointed the gun toward Isaac. "I'll shoot you first then."

"Ah, you could." Isaac smiled and held the map up in

front of him. "But you're going to need to reload that thing to take care of Crow, by which point he'll probably have killed you."

"Ugh." Robert shook his head. "If Johnny finds out I told you where Nelson is, he'll kill me."

"And if you don't tell us, we'll kill you." Crow tapped his foot.

"Fine, fine." Robert relaxed his gun but didn't lower it. "Walk toward me with the map and place it on the ground. Then I'll tell you where Nelson is."

Isaac did as instructed. He stepped forward.

"Slowly!" Robert yelled. His eyes darted from Isaac to Crow and his hands shook. His nerves seemed frayed.

Isaac placed the map down on the ground with one hand and kept the other hand in his pocket. He remained close to the map and looked to Crow and winked.

"What's wrong with your eyes, boy?" Crow tilted his head like a confused dog. Isaac winked a little harder, his heart racing. Was Crow trying to get him killed? On purpose?

"Why you winking, boy? Is it sand? I hate it when I get sand in my eyes."

"What?" Robert looked at them both.

"It's nothing!" Isaac quickly dismissed the whole thing and swallowed the nervous lump in his throat. "So, where's Nelson?" Isaac stared at the map, memorizing the last location. He still couldn't believe he had it, after all these years.

"He's with Molly Weaver, at her house."

"Molly? Okay." Isaac was a little confused but wasn't going to think too hard about it just yet.

"Johnny's gonna thank me for this and thanks... for not pulling nothing, y'know."

"Of course! I'm a man of my word." Isaac pulled out his hand from his pocket and produced a pouch. He ripped it open and it expelled thick blinding smoke. He closed his eyes tight and hoped Crow had got the hint to close his eyes too, otherwise he wouldn't be able to see for at least a couple of days.

As the smoke took effect Crow and Robert yelped in pain.

"Sorry, Crow!" Isaac shouted blindly into the shack whilst steadying himself on a plank of wood. He sniffed at the air. The smell needed to completely disappear before he could re-open his eyes. After a few moments, the air cleared and the pungent, burnt smell faded into the night.

Isaac opened one eye. No stinging. He opened the other and saw the map intact on the ground beneath him. He snatched the paper up and tucked it back in his pocket then ran over to Robert and grabbed the rifle from him. "Thank you!" Robert lay on the shack floor rubbing at his eyes.

"What've you done to me?" Robert screamed. "Am I blind now?" He sobbed.

"Your vision will come back in a few days." Isaac looked over at Crow who had seemingly gotten the clue.

"Is it safe to open my eyes now, boy?" Crow stood doubled over with his head tucked in his jacket. "I can hear Robert crying. Ha! Not the first time." Crow let out a coarse laugh.

"Yes, the smoke has cleared. How are your eyes?"

"Oh, it stings a bit, kind of like that powder from before."

"Yes. And I'm out of both now!"

"Maybe that's good for me, not sure these peepers can take much more!" Crow laughed again and this time swung his arm into Isaac's back. "Good work, boy." Crow walked over to Robert who lay on the ground, sweating in pain, his eyes shut tight.

"Should we kill him?" Isaac kicked the rifle toward Crow. "I'd rather not."

"No, he's a good enough man. You hear me, Robert? I'm going to spare your life. You owe me!" Robert rolled over and lay on his side. He curled up like a sleeping cat and rocked with his head in his hands. "Robert!" Crow knelt down and placed his hands on Robert's shoulders. "If you tell Johnny about any of this, I'll have you killed, you hear me? You and your family. Keep quiet and I'll shower you with riches." Crow nodded.

"He can't see you," Isaac reminded Crow.

"I know! Robert, what do you say? Keep quiet and you'll be the richest man on my crew, I'll make sure of it."

Robert nodded his head, still clutching at his face.

"Is that a yes?"

"Yes," Robert managed a faint reply.

"Excellent." Crow picked up the rifle and clambered to his feet. His eyes were heavily swollen and his face was covered in dried blood.

"Boy..." Crow said. His face filled with concern. "Come with me to free Nelson?"

Isaac couldn't help but feel sorry for Crow. He looked a thousand years old after the day's events. There was no way he'd survive Molly's wrath alone. "It's just I'd rather stay out of trouble right now. Plus, what's in it for me? You of all people should know you don't get any thanks for doing people favors around these parts."

"That's not true. My crew. My men, we're different. There's a code."

"That hasn't really worked out of late though, has it?"

Isaac looked around at the blown apart shack with Robert huddled on the floor.

"I've been doing this for a long time. I'll make it worth your while."

"How? I have everything I need. Everything I've ever wanted is in my pocket right now."

"I know you want that treasure more than anything and believe me, I do too but you can't do it alone!"

"I wasn't planning on being entirely alone."

"Then help me get Nelson back, and we can go together. When I kill Johnny, I'll have a crew. Do you have a crew, boy?"

"Not yet..."

"Do you have a ship?"

"Again, not yet but I'm working on it."

"I've got a ship and once Johnny is out the way, I'll have a crew too." Crow grinned.

Isaac could make out a sparkle in his swollen black eyes. He considered Crow's proposition. He was right. He did need a ship and a crew too. Maybe teaming up with Crow wouldn't be such a bad move?

"Yes!" Crow said.

"Hang on, I'm thinking," Isaac replied.

"No, I mean yes, I finally realized where I remember you from."

"You're a very confusing man," Isaac said.

"A crow never forgets a face, boy, and I remember yours now. You were with Popino, the day they hung Kidd."

Isaac looked away. "It was a remarkable day," he said as he recalled his father leaving him. "What does that have to do with anything?"

"Well, I know you've been dreaming of that treasure

nearly as long as I have which means you're willing to do what it takes to find it."

Isaac scratched the back of his head. "And how do I know you won't just toss me overboard once we get close?"

Crow put the rifle down and put his hands up. "You don't. I'll have to earn your trust, just like you'll have to earn mine. That's how it works, boy."

"What do we do when we find the treasure?"

"We split it equally amongst the crew," Crow answered immediately and with such certainty that Isaac wondered if he had planned his answer or, if in truth, that was what he always did. Isaac had heard numerous stories of the captain. Some labeled him a ruthless, unpredictable man but others spoke of his generosity and reputation for bringing in the finest loot to Nassau.

"You always do that?" Isaac said.

"Ask anyone, boy. I stand by my word."

"Fine, but on one condition."

"What's that?"

"Popino has to be on the crew."

"He's rich! He doesn't need anymore! Have you seen his house?" Crow shot Isaac a disgruntled look.

"Yes of course. Wait, why? Have you?" Isaac asked.

"Never mind!"

"Anyway, I owe him... a lot." Isaac raised his brows and stared at Crow who met him with a frown and muttered a grumble.

"I can't do it. He's a thief!" Crow clenched his fists and stood firm.

"So am I. And you're a pirate!" Isaac shrugged.

"Yeah, but there's a code, plus I've been hating him for years now." Crow gritted his teeth and waved Isaac's proposition away with his hand. "It's hard to forget all them years of hate, just like that."

"It's my one and only condition."

Crow kicked at the upturned table. "Fine!"

"Then we have a deal!"

"If he so much as steps out of line... well, I won't be held responsible for what I might do," Crow said.

"I'll warn him." Isaac shrugged and extended his hand to Crow. "Oh, and I'll be captain of course."

Crow walked over to shake Isaac's hand. "No."

"Yes." Isaac gave Crow a hard look.

"In your dreams, boy."

"How about we flip for it then?" Isaac took out his treasured silver coin and polished it on his jacket. "If it lands on the ship you get to be captain."

"Let's deal with this later. First, we need to get Nelson. We'll be useless without him."

"Fine." Isaac grabbed Crow's hand and gave it a firm shake. "Luckily, I know exactly where to find Molly's place." The pair left the shack and made for the main road into town. "You know, I thought he was called Nellie." Isaac slapped Crow on the back as they staggered up the road in the darkness.

JOY LAFITTE

A hand gripped Joy's ankle. "Leon, wake up!" she screamed at the top of her lungs. She kicked into the dark and must have struck whoever it was as the grip released. A thud of someone hitting the deck followed.

Joy scrambled out of the makeshift bed and crouched by its side. She peered into the night, trying to make out what was happening. The clang of a blade striking and scraping against another metal object came from Leon's bed. He must have blocked it, she thought, but why wasn't he saying anything?

Joy's eyes searched for whoever had grabbed her ankle, but they had disappeared. Scared off by a kick? Odd. Joy tried to piece together what exactly was happening.

The sword wielding figure who towered over Leon cried out in pain and fell to the floor. "That wasn't supposed to happen yet..." Leon said. He appeared to be sitting up in bed.

"Leon?" Joy whispered as she reached for her jacket and hat and dragged them toward her. "What's going on?"

"Joy, we have to get out of here." Leon grabbed his

belongings and made for the back of the bunker. Joy kept low and scurried over to where Leon was crouched, waiting for her. She clutched a blade in either hand. What did Leon mean by 'not supposed to happen yet'?

"Get off me!" Joe called out from the far side of the bunker.

"They got me again!" It sounded like Roe's stupid voice.

"Joy, we have to go!" Leon held a cloth flap open at the back of the bunker. The glimmer of moonlight revealed his blood-soaked shirt. "Don't bother with them, they're bastards! C'mon." Leon motioned for her to follow him.

Joy looked him in the eye. "There's something not right, Leon." What if this was a test? She couldn't shake the nagging feeling that it might well be. Who would ambush them on Jane's property? No one would dare, and then to be scared away by a kick? None of this made sense.

"I think it's a test, Leon. Stay!" Joy urged, her eyes wide, trying to convince Leon.

"You're mad! Who'd do this?"

"That thick-skulled fucker Thunder, that's who!" Joy crept back in and turned to Leon who didn't follow. "Hold the door flap open then, give us some light."

Yelps of annoyance and injury came from the far side of the bunker. Joy stormed over to where a masked assailant was seemingly running circles around Joe, Roe and Moe. A figure roughly the size of a child clutched a dagger in each hand and kept running at the men, slashing at their ankles, then rolling out of sight underneath the bed frames. It was almost comical. Every time one recovered, the tiny assailant struck another.

"Oi!" Joy shouted. Roe had just been struck again and the figure had rolled away under the bed out of their reach. Moe fumbled around trying to find some candles to light. At least he was smart, Joy thought.

The masked assailant took a run at Joy and was met with a kick to the face. Joy moved fast and grabbed their arms whilst they flailed on the floor. She slammed their wrists into the ground causing them to drop the daggers. "Mask off!" she ordered as they tried to struggle free.

Joy released her grip on one arm. It was a risk, but something told Joy that the tiny assailant may have been testing them. No one would dare to attack on Jane's land, let alone be able to get close to do so.

The assailant pulled down their mask.

"Who are you?" Joy looked at the young girl's face, she wasn't quite a child but couldn't have been much older than sixteen.

"I'm a merc," the young girl said.

Joy observed her closely.

"It's a test. We get paid extra," the girl continued, trying to convince Joy. "Nipper's the name."

"Well, that's fitting. Sorry about the kick." Joy smiled; she believed her.

"Hold the bitch." Joe came stomping over.

"Don't you dare touch her." Joy rose up and turned to face him. "Step back, Joe."

Nipper bolted out of the bunker. "I'll tell them you passed," she shouted back.

Joe moved close to Joy and pressed his body against hers. "You're no fun. Maybe we can change that." He stared down at her chest licking his lips. His breath was foul.

"You were defeated by a child. I'm not scared of you!" Joy smirked and held her ground. There was nothing more satisfying than bullying the bullies.

"Joe, leave it," Moe said. "We won't get through if we kill her now."

Joe backed off.

"We knew it was a test," Roe said.

"Sure you did." Joy busied herself searching for candles. She lit a few more and made her way back to her bed.

Leon stood over the assailant he had taken down. They'd bled out. "Fuuuuck," Leon whispered under his breath.

"What's wrong, Leon? Not part of the test?"

Leon jolted out of his thoughts. "Good work, Joy. I would've let these three bastards die." He looked at his arm with the hook and shook his head. "I'm useless in these things. Or at least I normally am." He looked down at the dead body.

"Yes, well," a woman's voice came from outside the bunker and pushed the cloth entrance open. A striking woman with sleek, cropped hair walked in with Thunder at her side. Joy couldn't help but stare. "So, we have three buffoons and a capable woman, no surprise there."

Joy knew exactly who she was looking at. Should she just strike now? A quick slit to the wrist with one of her poisoned blades and the mighty Jane Hatch would be dead in a couple of hours. Thunder was a problem though. A big, beefy one. Plus, that would only give her fifteen doubloons and after the day she'd had she deserved the twenty.

"Leon!" Thunder pointed to where Leon's attacker lay cold. "You stab her with your hook?"

"I wasn't expecting it! Not tonight!" Leon yelled. "Fuck! Who'd I get?" Leon pulled the mask off revealing a pale-skinned, dead-eyed face. "Patricia." Leon shook his head.

Joy looked at him wide-eyed. He avoided her gaze.

Thunder gave Leon a friendly smack on the back. Leon surprisingly stood firm, only rocking forward a little. "Don't worry, we had to rush. There was no time to warn ya. Besides, you did us a favor." Thunder led Leon out of the bunker through the back door flap.

"He got her. You'll see," Thunder said from outside.

A tanned man with a black bandana appeared, followed closely by a wiry woman with dirty, blonde hair heaped on top of her head. She grinned at Joy and winked. They grabbed Patricia's body and dragged it out through the back entrance.

Jane stood, eyeing each one of them up and down. She gave Joy the slightest hint of a smile. "There's been a change of plan. We'll be concluding the trial tonight. Thunder will be back in a short while. He'll let you know what's happening." Her voice was firm, commanding yet soft. Jane nodded to Joy as she turned and left the bunker.

Joy made her way back to her bed and took a seat. She needed to catch her breath and be alone with her thoughts, just for a moment. She liked being alone. It wasn't always the case but lately she needed it. She took in a deep breath and felt the energy rising back to her chest. So, Leon had tricked her. This whole set up was good. Really good. Jane was much smarter than she anticipated. They all were.

Her moment of calm was interrupted by the presence of Joe's crotch at her eye level. "Charming." Joy sat back on her bed and crossed her legs. She rested her back on the wall and ignored Joe.

"What do you think the odds are for us all getting in?" Joe breathed through his mouth and cracked his knuckles.

Joy closed her eyes and ignored him. She didn't want anything to do with these bastards. Even if she were to befriend them, they'd turn on her in a second. She didn't need their help. They needed hers and she wasn't feeling generous.

"The boss is talking to you." Moe tittered. Joy opened one eye. She hadn't noticed before but his eye twitched. He appeared antsy. She had thought him smarter than to come looking for a fight that he wouldn't win.

"I heard him." Joy leaned back and placed her hat over her face.

Crunch. Crunch. Crunch.

Joy could hear the footsteps coming toward her. It was hard to move quietly on the dirt floor. She guessed they belonged to Roe, coming to join his friends.

"You can't ignore me, bitch." Joe knocked the hat from Joy's face.

"Every time you open your mouth, another little gem falls out, doesn't it?" Joy sat up.

"Get her!" He nodded. Moe and Roe lunged at her and tried to grab her arms. In a single heartbeat Joy flicked both wrists and threw two of her delightfully small poisoned blades. One for Roe and one for Moe. The pair dropped to their knees and keeled over.

Joy stood up as Joe backed away. He fell onto Leon's bloodied bed. "You bitch!"

"Again with the mouth. I don't think you're in any position to be mad with me." Joy grabbed her hat from the ground and tucked her hair into it. She reached inside her jacket. She would need a much bigger blade to take this one down. "Joe, there's no need to attack me. We've both made it through."

Her words only angered him. He erupted and grabbed her bed, tossing the wooden plank aside. "You're for it!" he yelled and stormed at her. His eyes bulged and the veins in his muscles surged. He charged like a bull and swung at her face. She ducked and swiped at his sides but missed. He was surprisingly fast. Joe lifted his fists and hopped from one leg to another.

"Joe, I will hurt you."

He swung low, then high, then low again. Joy jumped back, copping the tail end of a blow to the stomach. It knocked her to the ground. She wasn't winded and rolled back to standing. Joe swung again, this time at her face. Joy anticipated his predictable pattern and held up her dagger to meet his fist. Joe punched into the sharp edge and the blade sliced deep into his clenched fingers.

He clutched his bloodied hand with the other. "Fuck!"

"What's going on here?" Jane ran in, followed by Thunder and Leon, who grinned at Joy's handiwork.

"You weren't wrong, Thunder. She is good." Jane crossed her arms and stood before Joy with an approving smile. "And you..." She walked over to Joe and grabbed his injured hand. He clenched it tight in an attempt to stop the bleeding. "You won't be any use to me... with or without that hand." Jane drew her pistol, raised it and shot him in the face. His meaty body crumpled and hit the dirt.

Joy didn't move. "Sorry, ma'am."

"Don't be sorry. I'm impressed with how you dealt with them."

Leon smiled, admiring Joy. "Those three bastards tried to attack us earlier."

"Too stupid to have any place here." Jane looked at their bodies as she spoke.

"Great work. You passed!" Jane put her hand on Joy's back. "Now walk with me, would you?"

"Of course, ma'am." The grin crept over Joy's face. Every time the corners of her mouth twitched, she reminded herself of her purpose. The excited part of her screamed inside: you've done it! You passed! You're one of Jane's mercenaries! But the sensible part told her she needed to focus, regain composure. Now might even be the perfect time to strike?

"Let's go, Leon." Thunder motioned for them to leave but Leon stayed rooted to the spot staring at Joy.

"I've got questions for you, Leon," Joy said quietly and smiled. She cleaned off her blade and tucked it away.

"Come, let's enjoy some air." Jane led the way out of the bunker's main entrance.

There were far more people out here than Joy anticipated. Jane led her to a patch of land just out of earshot of anyone who might want to listen.

"You see, Joy, I have a problem and I think you can help."

"Okay."

"I think I may have one or two traitors in my crew."

"Oh." Joy's mind raced. Was Jane onto her?

"That black-haired girl Leon killed... I thought she might be one, but I think there are more. Patricia didn't seem smart enough to pull off such a thing on her own."

"Right." Joy nodded and wondered if others had caught wind of the bounty on Jane's head.

"You're new here so no one will suspect you. You can befriend people. Find out who's got a problem with me and then let me know. Sound like something you can do?"

"Yes, definitely. I like a challenge." Joy took a big breath of air in. It soothed her aches and pains from the night's activities. She blinked as her eyes adjusted to the moonlight. Maybe this was the best chance she would get to take out Jane? But something told her not to. Stick to the plan, befriend her, take her in alive, she reassured herself.

"So... I can trust you with this then?" Jane grabbed her by the shoulders.

"I haven't killed you yet." Joy laughed.

"I admire your spirit."

"Yes, you can trust me and I will find out what's going on for you, ma'am." Joy extended her hand to shake Jane's.

Jane looked at Joy's hand. "Not yet."

"Of course." Joy snatched her hand back.

"There's one more thing I need before that. Before I can fully trust you."

Joy looked sideways, unsure and uneasy. "Go on."

"I need you to kill a man. Should be simple enough for someone like you. He owes me a lot of money." Jane's eyes grew cold. "Do this for me, and then you're in, fully in. You'll be looked after for good. Your family too."

"Sure. Who's the guy?" Joy had done this kind of thing countless times. She couldn't imagine anyone in Nassau would be too much of a challenge.

Jane handed over a folded piece of paper. "All the details are on there."

Joy recognized the paper. It was just like Roy's. "Thank you, ma'am. I'll deal with this right away."

"No need. First thing tomorrow's fine. Go sleep. I'll have the kitchen fetch you something too. You've earned it."

Joy didn't know what to say. Jane seemed to be fair and kind. Not at all what she had expected. "Thank you. I'll report back to you once it's taken care of." Joy turned and walked back into the bunker.

She wasn't sure she could get much sleep after all that had happened. Inside the bunker, logs had been added to the fire and a fresh sheet was thrown on her bed. The bodies were gone and all the furniture had been returned to its upright position. She smiled and took a seat. Everything ached. She tossed her hat on the nearest bed and kicked up her legs.

"So, who's in trouble now?" Joy unfolded the paper and scanned the details. "Oh no." Joy shut her eyes. She hadn't for one second imagined this. She re-read the details then quickly folded the paper and tucked it away. She shook her head and rubbed at her face. "Shit." Joy sighed. "Popino Beltrame... you absolute idiot."

POPINO BELTRAME

Sunlight blared through Popino's bedroom window as he opened his eyes to the day. For a moment his mind was free. He gazed out at the peaceful blue sky. A faint bird chatter cut through the silence and brought his thoughts to Elizabeth. He smiled as if he were smiling back at her. She had been the greatest wife anyone could ask for. Nothing but kind and patient with him and their darling girl Rose.

Thoughts of Eva crept in. Her charming French accent purred in his ear. He shook his head as if trying to shake the images of their sordid affair away. He pulled the sheet over his face. Her blood drenched body flickered before his eyes and blinded his vision.

Popino's mouth grew dry. He stroked at his neck which was still sore from where Vella had pressed her blade in. He wanted to scream at his own stupidity. How! How do I keep getting myself into trouble?

He poked his head out from the sheet and stared at the ceiling. At least you got out of work today. You can head to Vella's then spend the day figuring the rest of this out, he told himself. He put his hand to the side where Elizabeth used to lay. He still left room for her. He pulled his hand back and pushed away any thoughts of her.

The guilt was too much.

Popino swung his legs out of bed and sat on the edge. His mind jumped to last night. Isaac had been acting oddly at dinner. He didn't spend much time with him nowadays, but he knew his friend well enough to recognize when something wasn't right. He threw on his linen shirt and his pants and tied a ruby red neckerchief to cover Vella's handiwork. He didn't want to risk any questions about what had happened yesterday, and the scarf did quite suit him.

"Morning, Rose," he shouted as he passed by her door. No answer.

He jogged downstairs to find Clara on her hands and knees in the dining room, scrubbing at a mud-stained floor.

"Oh sir, I didn't know you were home today." Clara looked up at Popino.

"Sorry for the mess, Isaac was over last night. Must've had dirty boots." He stared at her chest. Her bosoms jiggled as she scrubbed back and forth.

"It's coming out, sir. Don't worry." Clara noticed him staring and covered her chest. "Sorry."

"No, I'm sorry, sorry to have startled you. No work for me today." He made his way to the kitchen and poured a small glass of rum.

"Fancy a bit?" Popino poked his head around the corner and shook the rum bottle at Clara. "Rum, that is."

"Not whilst I'm working, sir, but thank you."

He downed the contents of his glass and considered if he should give Vella every last bit of coin he had. Why did he promise her thirty doubloons? That would leave him with nothing. He topped up his glass.

"Have you seen Rose?"

"She's playing in the backyard, sir, with my son Lucas," Clara replied.

"Ah, good." Popino swirled his drink and stared into the whirlpool of brown liquid. Another matter which he had ignored for some time came to mind and that was Jane. He still owed her one-hundred doubloons and there was no way in hell he could get that back to her anytime soon. Should he save ten for her? A gesture maybe? She'd throw them in his face. Especially given their history.

Pangs of shame gnawed at his heart. If Elizabeth could see him now she'd be disgusted. His parents would have disowned him too. Popino took another gulp from his rapidly emptying glass.

"Sir?" Clara stepped into the kitchen. "Did you break something last night?"

"Not that I remember. We just had dinner, nothing too wild." Popino raised his eyebrows and smiled. Clara's face didn't falter, her eyes filled with concern.

"Why, what's broken?" Popino asked.

"Come see for yourself." She walked through to the dining room and over to the cabinet. Shards of broken glass were scattered across the floor.

"I didn't notice before because I was too busy cleaning up the dirty footprints."

Popino followed the trail of glass with his eyes. The small window next to the cabinet was broken.

"It's broken. The window's broken, Clara."

"I'm sorry, sir, I didn't see it before."

Popino eyed her with suspicion. "Look, if you or Lucas broke it, it's fine. Accidents happen."

"No, sir, truly. This is the first time I'm seeing it."

"Who would break it then?" Popino panicked and took a closer look at the glass on the floor. "No, no, no." He yanked the cabinet doors open. Nothing. He pulled open the drawers. "Clara... the coffer. Where's the coffer?" Popino could hear the blood pumping through his body. His heart punched in his chest.

"I don't know, I haven't seen it." Clara shook her head, her eyes wide.

"You're the only other person who knows where it is!" He grabbed her shoulders and gripped them tight. "Please," he pleaded and increased his grip. "If you know where it is, I will forgive you, I won't be mad. Please, I just really need to know." He stared into Clara's big brown eyes. They were filled with fear and sadness. Tears welled in his own.

"Sir, you must believe me. I wouldn't do this." Clara put her shoulders back and took a deep breath in. "You know me. I'm no thief." She held her head high.

"I know. I know." Popino released his grip and put his head in his hands. He breathed into them as he moved from one leg to another. He looked to the ceiling as if looking for answers. He needed to calm down. He couldn't think. His skin prickled, it felt icy cold.

"Sir..."

Popino wrung his hands together and paced faster.

"The window suggests it's stolen. Are you sure no one else knows where you keep it?"

"Certain!" Popino was sick with worry. "I have to go. I think you're right, Clara." He trusted her, for now. She could have stolen from him at any time, and she never had. "Would you watch Rose for me please? Maybe get the children inside?"

"Why, sir? What's going on?" Panic spread over Clara's face.

"It's fine. They'll be fine. I'm just being ridiculous." He searched for his boots.

"I'll be back soon." He pulled his boots on and slammed the door behind him. He needed to hold off Vella until he had a chance to figure out this mess.

Popino gave three sharp raps in quick succession on the thick oak front door. He hadn't come up with a plan yet. What would he tell Vella? The truth? It just didn't sound plausible. Maybe he should have taken Rose and ran. His thoughts were interrupted as the door creaked open.

Georgia, the lip-ringed door girl, stuck her head out. "Back so soon?" She opened the door fully. "You just couldn't keep away, could you?" She crossed her arms and leaned on the door.

"Yeah, great seeing you again... I wanted to have a word with Vella, if I may?" Popino forced a smile.

"You're out of breath. Did you run all this way?"

"Aha." His flirting was off today. For once, he didn't have it in him. He tried to work his usual charm and smiled, but he was a bundle of nerves. "Can I come in then? Happy to wait." Popino looked past the girl and into the foyer.

"Just because it's you, I'll let you come in for a bit and see if Miss V will see you."

"She's expecting me." He nodded and followed her in. Thick drapes adorned the windows and sheltered the room from the blazing sunlight. The foyer was cool and quiet which was exactly what he needed right now. He took a seat in the worn upholstered armchair, grateful for the rest.

"Don't go anywhere, I'll be right back." Georgia wandered off out of sight.

"I won't," he sounded desperate. He needed to be charming. He was Mister Charming. Vella would smell his weakness. His mind jumped back to the coffer. What about last night with Isaac? He was acting rather strange. There's no way, he told himself. Someone must have broken in. Maybe it was one of Vella's girls? That would make sense.

Georgia re-appeared. "You can head on up."

"Thank you so much. I owe you." He almost leapt at the stairs in his haste.

"Anytime. You know where I am."

He felt her eyes burn into the back of him as he climbed the stairs. His chest tightened as he approached Vella's door and gave a knock.

"Come in," a muffled voice came from behind the thick wooden doors. Popino was lost in the carvings upon them. Intricate naval ships. Must have cost a fortune, he thought.

He opened the door to find Vella sitting behind her desk with a loaded pistol which happened to be pointing right at him. "I can explain!" He raised his hands.

"Oh, it's just you." She disarmed the flintlock and placed it back under her desk.

"I thought the girl let you know?"

"Yes, well, you can never be too careful. Not nowadays."

Popino thought he saw a hint of relief on her face. Maybe he should be honest after all.

"I trust you've brought your offering. I'd call it a payment but it doesn't even come close." Vella scoffed. "Wait, what can you explain?"

"Exactly that." He walked toward the chair opposite her and took a seat.

"You have the coin don't you, Popino?" She reached under the desk.

"Vella, please. Please just hear me out."

She grabbed the flintlock and lay it down, pointing at Popino. "Go on then. Don't let the pistol put you off. I won't shoot. Have to get Rose first, don't I?"

"You... you see..." Popino stammered. The thought of anything happening to his dear girl unnerved him. He clasped his hands together and steadied them in his lap.

Vella tapped on the desk. "Yes..."

"There's a slight problem. I lie—it's a big problem but I'm going to sort it." He leaned in toward the flintlock. Maybe he could snatch it away from her?

"Yes, you do lie, Popino. That's all you fucking do!" Vella stood and grabbed the desk with both hands.

"Well, it's not that ea—" He leapt across the desk and went for the flintlock, but Vella snatched it away before he could lay his hand on it. The cold barrel pressed into his forehead.

"Did you really think that would work? You're so predictable."

"Vella. I had the doubloons. They were in my coffer at home, but last night someone stole them."

"How convenient. You have to pay up and suddenly they vanish." Vella withdrew her pistol and sat down.

Popino stood, bolted to the spot, shocked and confused at what to say or do next.

"It's true, Vella. You have to believe me."

"I don't have to do anything."

"No, of course. I would like you to please believe me when I say they were stolen."

"By whom? I'm finding this all rather difficult to believe." Vella kicked up her legs and crossed them on her desk.

Popino wracked his brains. Who could he blame? What would Isaac do? He always got into scrapes and managed to find a way out.

"Well, I've been told it was Jane."

"Hatch?"

"Yep." Popino nodded.

Vella took her feet off the desk and tapped one on the floor. This was exactly the reaction Popino had hoped for. She was annoyed.

"When she found out I was going to give them to you she came looking for them. When I went to my coffer this morning it was gone and there was a note in its place left by her or one of her mercs." Popino was used to lying but this was a risky one. "They broke my window. If you send someone to my house now, you'll see."

Vella stopped tapping her foot and leaned forward, resting her arms on her knees.

"And how would they know where to look for the coffer?"

"Maybe... my housemaid?" Popino winced, he didn't mean to say that. Clara didn't deserve to be dragged into his mess. He scratched the back of his head.

Vella nodded. She seemed to be buying it. "Makes sense." Vella stood up and put her hands on her hips. "I'll have her killed then. Tortured first to find out if this is all true. Then killed."

"No!" Popino sprang to his feet.

Vella glared at him.

"Just let me deal with her. I need to find out some other

things. Some jewelry went missing too." Popino's stomach churned.

"I'll give you a week to get me my coin."

"Thank you. I'll get it sorted." Popino turned to leave.

"And a day for the maid."

"Wha—"

"Well, you should be able to get the information from her today. Might take a little longer to get the coin back from Jane. You can't say I'm not generous."

"But it doesn't make sense? You said I could deal with my maid?"

"And you can. I expect her to be dead by tomorrow if what you're saying is true."

Popino was glad he had his back to Vella. He couldn't hide the horror on his face.

"And if it's not true, I'm having you killed along with Rose."

Popino couldn't respond. The lump in his throat choked him.

"I'll send somebody by yours tomorrow to check."

"Yes, Vella," he managed to blurt out and rushed for the door. He darted down the hallway. He needed air. He sped past Georgia without uttering a word and closed the door behind him. The hot sun seared at his skin. The heat didn't usually bother him but today it felt insufferable. "What have I done!" He pressed his fingers into his temples and tried to force the stress away. "It's okay, I'll figure something out, I always do," he reassured himself and set off on his walk toward home.

He mulled over his potential options. Maybe he could hide Clara? No, too risky. Maybe he'd say she fled before he even got home? That way he didn't have to account for a body. It did mean Clara would be out of a job, but better that than dead. She would understand, she'd have to. That didn't solve the problem of the coin though. What if he couldn't hunt down the coffer? Maybe he could borrow from Thad? He'd drained all other sources dry. "Terrible plan," he said and was met with an odd look from a passer-by who just so happened to be a rather attractive woman; chesty with a plump behind. Nothing he loved more. His groin throbbed. Not now, he told himself. He closed his eyes and tried to get back to the matter at hand. He needed to concentrate. He needed to save Clara and himself, not to mention Rose, but he wasn't thinking straight. Why was he always so easily distracted? "Fine," he muttered to himself in annoyance. He knew the quickest way to clear his head and that was with a visit to the brothel. Maybe a little morning delight would help before heading home to face the music? The Milky Way was out of action, however, The Silky Swallow had just opened and there was talk of it hosting the finest women in all of Nassau. Right, decision made. I'll go there, get the job done and come out with a clear head. Then no more distractions and I can figure this all out.

MOLLY WEAVER

Molly approached the sandy-beige stone house and gave her usual knock. The sun had sunk long ago but candlelight still flickered away inside.

Vella kept her reception manned at all times. Both Molly and Vella survived on little sleep. They preferred to pour themselves into their work until late.

The door opened and out popped Georgia's head.

"I have news," Molly said.

Georgia nodded. "Go on up, Miss V will know it's you. No one else comes at this hour."

Molly made her way up the stairs, knocked on the door and poked her head around it. "Vella?"

"Molly, I know when you're here so late it's never good."

"Crow's dead, Vella." Molly walked over to Vella and took a seat across from her.

"How?" Vella put her hand to her chest and rose to her feet. "I just spoke to him a few days ago."

Vella blinked back tears and turned away from Molly, her hands shaking. She walked to her overflowing

226

bookshelf and propped herself up on a thick leather-bound book which stuck out from the shelf. She stifled a sob and hung her head low.

Molly readjusted herself in the well-worn and slightly uncomfortable seat. She hadn't quite expected this intense of a reaction. She knew Crow and Vella had been romantically involved over the years, but she assumed they loathed each other now.

"It was Jane," Molly said and held her breath, waiting for Vella's reaction. She knew this would be the push Vella needed to attack. There wasn't enough business in Nassau for Thad, Jane and Vella and someone needed to strike first.

"Why would Jane take out Crow… of all people?" Vella asked.

Molly shrugged. "Maybe she thought you two were still together?

Vella grabbed a book from the shelf and threw it on the ground. "She's trying to push me and it's working!"

She caught her breath and looked at her shelf. She selected a tattered book with a dark green cover half hanging off and took it back to her desk.

"What's that?" Molly asked.

"A map of Nassau." Vella tossed the book down and took a seat. She opened the book and retrieved a folded piece of paper from the middle, then cleared most of the contents of her desk onto the floor and spread the map out for them to observe. "Do you know anyone that's good at strategy?"

"I do actually."

Molly took a peek at the information on the map. It was surprisingly detailed. She noticed Thad's name written in a few peculiar places.

"What's that?" Molly leaned into Vella's desk and tapped on the map edge.

"Oh, there's another map for Thad's base. It's in one of the other books."

"This is extensive. Where did you even get something like this?" Molly asked.

"That doesn't matter right now. Can you find me a strategist or not?"

"I can." Molly dropped the matter despite her intrigue. No need to upset her further, she thought. "Vella, I should tell you something else."

"What?" Vella propped her chin up on her hand and tapped on the map. Her eyes darted from one spot another. "What is it?"

"Johnny Ives is now in charge of Crow's men."

Vella looked less than impressed at the announcement. "I remember that cocky charmer. He annoys me."

"I happen to be good friends with him actually."

"Right," Vella's reply was curt.

"He could help us attack Jane?" Molly pushed.

"I see."

"He'd behave, don't worry about that." Molly tried to catch Vella's eye.

Vella sat back in her chair and looked to Molly. "I trust you."

"Do you?" Molly cocked her head to the side.

"Of course." Vella stared down at the map and sighed.

"Shall we get the map of Thad's base out too? You know once we get rid of Jane, he'll be our next target." Molly couldn't quash her curiosity.

"Please, not now, Molly. Let's just take this one murderous army at a time."

Molly smiled. "Yes, of course. I always get a little ahead of myself. Just like to be prepared."

Vella swung her head back and stared at the ceiling. Her crown of dreadlocked hair bounced and flowed down her back.

"It's hard to hunt down someone when you don't even know what they look like. Thad slipped right under our noses. I've never understood how but he has. What I do know though is that fortress of his is impenetrable." Vella let out an exasperated groan. "Problem for another day."

Vella slid her desk drawer open and tossed three carved wooden pieces on the table. "We can use these."

Molly picked up a roughly carved wooden fox. It was about the size of a chess piece. "Is this to represent Jane?"

Vella nodded. Molly placed the fox where the merc mansion sat.

Vella placed a wooden dog-like creature on the table and moved the piece over Thad's name. "Not sure why Thad chose this creature as his symbol but it's all over the fortress. I've never seen this thing before." Vella shrugged. "I looked it up in one of my books, turns out it's a coyote."

"Interesting." Molly picked up the final carved creature, a rough, rugged wolf. "And this is us?" She eyed the piece with mischievous glee and placed it on the map.

"Do you know the numbers?" Vella asked. "If we're to attack Jane, I want to know what we're up against."

"We have just over one-hundred strong women at our side, with Johnny and his men we'll double that figure."

"Pirates! The craziest of men." Vella looked annoyed.

Molly chuckled and widened her eyes. "Yes, they are, but we could use that to our advantage."

"I just don't see how we need him when we have over a hundred strong women of our own."

Molly nodded. "I agree, it seems unnecessary if we look at the numbers alone. Jane has around a hundred on her crew too." Molly looked over her shoulder to the door, checking they were truly out of earshot.

"Please don't take offense, Vella. I'm not trying to be rude, but Jane's people are highly skilled killers. They're very well-paid, they're well-fed and their training... well, I've heard it's brutal."

Vella crossed her arms and glared at Molly.

"I think they could win if we don't have Johnny's crew of savages. They're not all bad, he does have some skilled swordsmen actually. He's one of them."

"Trained by Crow." Vella's eyes glistened with tears which she blinked away. She tapped her foot in annoyance. "I know there's been talk around town that I'm the weakest leader of the three, but I don't believe it. It's men spreading that rumor. Frightened by a woman being in control."

Molly cocked her head to the side. "You're probably right, but that doesn't mean we should dismiss Johnny. We want a guaranteed victory, and this does that. Plus, it minimizes injury to your own women." Molly could see the shift in Vella's mood. She knew what Molly said made sense.

"Fine," Vella agreed and stared blankly into the distance. "But you need to keep him under control."

"Of course."

"He'd better not come in here and try to take over. My people won't stand for it." Vella sprang to her feet and grabbed the coyote. She clutched it in her hand and walked around the room. "What about this one?" She waved the piece at Molly. "Won't he attack whilst we're distracted with Jane? That's what I'd do."

Molly felt a rush of excitement. She had been waiting years for this. Finally, Vella would take out Jane. It might even bring her closer to finding Daniel. She often wondered if he was part of Jane's crew but could never get close enough to find out. Molly had found out the hard way that Jane's land was well protected at all times.

"I don't think so." Molly's eyes followed Vella around the room. "I heard he wants to take out Jane too. He'd be more concerned with her. She took out some of his men... apparently."

"Molly, how do you know this?" Vella turned to face her. Molly's body tensed.

"People talk when I sell them potions."

"Ah." Vella seemed satisfied with the answer. "So, when do we get Johnny? When do we attack?"

"I think we'll need two weeks to plan and prepare. I need to find our strategist first." Molly scrunched up her face and contemplated where Isaac might have run off to.

"I thought you had someone in mind?"

"I do, he's... Johnny will find him for us." Molly dismissed Vella's concern. "He's one of the smartest men I know when it comes to strategy. Other things not so much, but this is his forte."

"If you say so. And what about Thad? We can't just hope he doesn't attack."

"I think we'll have to. Plus, once Jane is out of the picture we can recruit some of hers to join us. Maybe if you loosen your rule on women only, then we can recruit at almost triple the rate we do now?"

"Never!" Vella smashed her fist into the table. "Men cause too much trouble, they get drunk, they spit everywhere and honestly they can be very... primitive."

Vella thumbed some pages of a nearby book. A tell-tale

sign she was annoyed. "You must stop pestering me to bend that rule. It's not going to happen. Johnny helping us out is one thing but recruiting men? It's out of the question."

"Fine." Molly held up her hands as a sign of defeat. "Once we've recovered from the battle with Jane we can proceed with a plan of attack against Thad, but from what I hear we'll need a lot more help."

"Miss V?" A muffled voice spoke followed by a hard knock on the other side of the door. The knocking persisted. "Miss V, it's urgent."

"Sorry, Molly." Vella shook her head. "Not now, Georgia!"

The door slowly opened and Georgia poked her head in. Molly looked to Georgia and gave her a head shake of warning.

"Sorry Miss V, but it can't wait."

"If it's about Crow, I already know." Vella waved Georgia away.

"No, it's not. You might want to be alone for this?"

Molly stood up. "Of course. We're about done here anyway."

"Sit down, Molly. Whatever it is just let me have it, this day can't get any worse." Vella sat in her chair and put her hand over her face.

Georgia walked over to Vella's desk with her hands behind her back. She lowered her head in respect.

"It's your son, miss."

Molly's eyes nearly jumped out of her head. She knew everything about everyone in Nassau, or at least she thought she did, but she never knew Vella had a son.

Georgia's eyes grew wide as she looked to Vella then to Molly then back to Vella.

"What happened? What did Thom do now?" Vella shut her eyes and massaged at her temples. "Is he diseased? Does he want more money?"

Molly's mind raced. She had so many questions bubbling away inside and there would never be a good time to ask.

"That stupid boy is always getting into trouble!"

"He's... he's..." Georgia clasped her hands and wrung them together.

"He's what? Getting married... again? Spit it out, please!"

"He's dead, miss."

Molly didn't know where to look. Vella covered her face with her hands. They were shaking. Molly couldn't believe her ears. How had Vella kept her son from her all these years? And now he was dead.

Vella took her hands away. Tears ran down her face and her mouth quivered. "How? Georgia, do you know how?" Vella moved from her seat and crouched on the floor. She forced her head into her knees and sobbed.

Molly cleared her throat. "Georgia... do we know anything? Any details?"

"Apparently his body was found in Eva and Lucien Boucher's house."

"Popino..." His name slipped out before Molly could catch herself. Eva and Lucien had been found dead in their home and Popino had been seen there that day. It was on her note from Otis, her informant.

Vella stood up. Her face was stained with tears and her eyes glowed red. "What? Why did you say his name, Molly?"

"He..." Molly didn't know what to say. She couldn't let on that she essentially spied on everyone in Nassau.

"You clearly know something, Molly. Did he do it? He was here not long ago." Vella curled her hands in rage, her breathing quickened.

"He... he was apparently seen entering the Boucher's home. Right before they died." Molly threw her hands up. "What would your son have been there for? Did he have business with Lucien?"

"More likely he had business with Eva, if you catch my drift. Thom fucked anything that breathed, it would seem." Vella's tears dried up.

"Georgia, would you leave us please?" Molly motioned to the door.

Vella pulled out her knife and scratched at her desk with it. "I'm going to kill him, Molly," she spoke with an icy calm. "He's fucking dead."

"Yes. Do you need my help in this?" Molly still couldn't believe Vella had a son that she knew nothing about.

Vella shook her head. "He dies by my hand." She took out another blade. "Him and everyone he loves."

CAPTAIN CROW

Drunken men stumbled about the streets of Nassau. The center was not as quiet as Crow hoped considering the taverns had long closed. Sounds of slurred sea shanties and fighting blurred into one as they walked up yet another street.

"I thought you knew where Molly lived?" Crow followed Isaac. "Boy, are we lost?"

"Of course not! I've been here a thousand times, it's just..."

"You're sober?"

"Yeah, could be that. Everything's a bit foggy!"

Crow caught up to Isaac, grabbed his flask from his inner pocket and smacked it into Isaac's chest. "Have that."

"This is fancy, Crow." Isaac hesitated before taking a sip. "You first, I don't want what happened to that fella back there happening to me."

"It's not poison, boy."

Crow snatched the flask back and took a sip. They stood in the middle of the street and waited. "Still breathing." Crow held out the rum filled container to Isaac.

"Yes and no foam spewing from your mouth, it's your lucky day." Isaac took the flask and swigged the contents in one loud gulp. "Thank you."

Crow caught sight of the polished pewter vessel as Isaac handed it back. He recalled the day Nelson gifted it to him almost ten years ago. He tucked it away and his heart sank at the prospect of what state Nelson might be in once they found him.

Isaac put his hand to his brow and peered up the street into the darkness. "Crow... why do you like crows so much?"

"They're smart. They never forget a face and they hold grudges."

"Crows do? Right." Isaac nodded and turned to the captain.

"Why do you call me boy?" He wagged his finger in Crow's direction and put his hands on his hips.

Crow ignored the question. Isaac stepped toward him and jabbed his finger into Crow's chest. "Don't touch me, boy."

"Pff. You don't scare me."

"I should." Crow kept his temper. "Look at you!"

Crow pointed toward Isaac's feet. "You have no soles left on your boots and there are holes in your pants. Even your vest looks half chewed off! You're a boy."

Isaac shrugged.

"Jacket's nice though. I'm sure whoever you stole it off misses it." Crow stroked at his beard, a wicked glint in his eye.

"Probably not actually, he's dead!" Isaac laughed. "Anyway, I'm no... nooo boy," Isaac slurred. The rum was doing the trick or so Crow hoped. "I could call you an old man, but I don't."

"I wouldn't if I were you." Crow clenched his jaw and gnashed his teeth together. He didn't have time for this now.

"Well let's look at you, shall we?" Isaac's bravery seemed to increase as the rum took hold.

"Your boots are... well, they're pretty good actually."

Crow narrowed his gaze to a scowl.

"Your pants are just as wrecked as mine, a little stretched even! And your shirt looks like it's permanently stained with who knows what." Isaac grinned. "Jacket's nice though." He took a few steps backward and stumbled. Isaac held his finger up in the air, his eyes half closed. "I remember now, we passed it. Follow me!" He pivoted and jogged up the street. "You coming?"

Crow grumbled and did his best to run up the street after him. The beating from Ives had knocked a lot of life from him but he wasn't going to let it stand in his way of finding Nelson.

Isaac broke into a sprint and ran at full pelt down the street, almost tripping over a man who lay belly up in the middle of it.

"Boy, watch out!" Crow shouted to him. Isaac stopped in his tracks and made his way back to the man.

"Who... who's this?" Isaac swayed a bit and grabbed the man by the face.

"Leave him!" Crow nudged Isaac away. "He's just had a bit too much."

"Hey, don't push me." Isaac nudged back a little too hard. Crow tripped over the man and fell smack down onto him.

The man came round and tried to push Crow off. "Get off me!" He was only of slight build and Crow didn't budge. "I can't breathe!" the man said, his voice muffled under Crow's six foot four frame. Crow wiggled his arms free from underneath him and tried to get up but the slight man pummeled Crow's back with his fists, throwing wild and surprisingly forceful thumps.

"Hang on!" Isaac grabbed at Crow's back and reached for his arm to help him up.

"Stop hitting me!" Crow reached boiling point and head butted the slight man with all his might. The thumping ceased and Isaac dragged Crow off by the arm. They stood over the man's slight frame. He didn't move and looked pale, almost gray in color.

"Can you hear me?" Isaac yelled. Silence followed. "You must have knocked him out cold."

Crow scratched at his head and gave the man a push with his boot. "I think he's dead, boy."

Isaac put his hand to his mouth. "No!"

"I knocked his head pretty hard." Crow took off his hat and ran his fingers through his hair. "You were annoying me! I was angry, I blame you for this!"

Isaac bent down and tapped at the man's face. "Wake up, fella! C'mon?"

"Look at his face!" Crow barked at Isaac, angry with himself and furious with the whole situation.

Isaac stepped away.

"Leave him be, let's just hope he has no family." Crow sighed and walked up the road.

"I feel terrible," Isaac slurred.

"C'mon, boy. Nelson will be dead before we even find him."

Crow felt guilty and annoyed. Annoyed that he had to put his trust in this drunken idiot. Annoyed that his men had turned on him, and guilty that he had just killed some poor sod by sheer accident.

"We'll pretend it didn't happen. That's what I usually do." Isaac caught up to Crow and put his arm on his shoulder. Crow shrugged it off.

"Down here, we're nearly there." Isaac skipped ahead and beckoned to Crow. He pointed to a plain house with bare walls. No decorations or patterns adorned the wooden exterior. There were no plants, no gate. It was really quite remarkable how unremarkable it was.

"This one?"

"Absolutely. Bet my life on it!"

"You think Molly's home?" Crow lowered his voice and checked for passers-by. "There's no light inside."

"Let's see." Isaac strode over to the door and gave a knock. "Molly?" he yelled through the closed door.

"Shut up! Shut! Up!" Crow marched over and grabbed Isaac's arm, his eyes fierce. "Are you trying to get us killed? She's not just going to hand him over," Crow said in an angry whisper, increasing his grip on Isaac's arm.

"We're friends." Isaac tried to shake free of Crow's grip. He flailed his arm up and down, then to and fro. Crow let go at such a point that it knocked Isaac off balance, and he tumbled into the dirt.

"Ouch!" Isaac looked at his hands, now brown from the fall.

Crow tiptoed forward and put his ear to the door. "She's not home, you could hear a pin drop. Any good at picking locks, boy?"

"Move it, old man! Breaking into places happens to be my area of expertise." Isaac tried to nudge Crow aside but bounced off him instead.

Crow smiled. "I might be older than you but I'm not weak. Don't you forget it!"

Isaac rolled his eyes. "Carefully step aside, good sir."

Crow stepped away from the door and folded his arms, ready to watch Isaac's handiwork. Isaac dusted off his hands and ran at the door. He slammed his shoulder into it, but instead of flying through, he bounced back and tumbled to the ground. Crow put his head in his hands. Now was not the time to lose his cool. They were so close to finding Nelson, but the boy was an idiot!

"Let's try another approach." Isaac scrambled to his feet, picked up a rock and hurled it through the front window. Shards of glass flew in all directions. Crow didn't have time to shield his face and copped a gash to the cheek from the shattered remnants. Isaac poked his head in and turned to Crow, grinning.

"You!" Crow wiped his cheek and dusted the glass from his beard. "You'll be the death of me." He couldn't keep it in anymore. He turned and punched Isaac straight in the stomach.

Isaac doubled over and clutched at his middle. "Nel... he's in there," Isaac said and pointed through the window. Jagged glass lined the edges of the frame. Crow found a stick and beat the remaining glass away.

"It's definitely him... maybe." Isaac returned to standing upright.

"Well go in and check." Crow knelt next to the window. "I'll boost you in."

"No." Isaac held his stomach. "Not until you apologize."

"You..." Crow's eye twitched. He closed it and pressed his lips together. He did feel a bit bad for hitting him, but he was such an idiot... sometimes. Crow let out a sigh. "I'm sorry I hit you."

Isaac smiled and walked over to the window. "Boost me in." Crow gave him a push and Isaac clambered through the opening.

"Need new boots!" Isaac whispered as he crunched across the floor of shattered glass.

Crow peered through the window. "Is he in there, boy?" he asked, his stomach knotted in anticipation.

The front door swung open. "Please come in." Isaac politely waved Crow in. "Welcome, if you could take off your shoes, I just cleaned."

"Now's not the time to be funny, boy." Crow nudged Isaac and shot him a look of disapproval as he crept inside. "Nelson?" he whispered into the dark.

"I can't see anything in here," Isaac said and stumbled into the darkness. "Ouch!"

"What is it?"

"Table, I think." A clattering of glass followed.

"Careful!"

"There's stuff everywhere!"

"Find us some light, boy. We need some light."

Crow's chest tightened. If Nelson was here, he wasn't responding. It reminded him of when Vella ended it. He'd felt sick for days, weeks even.

A candle flame flickered and illuminated the room. "Fire poker was still hot." Isaac walked over with candles in hand.

"Good work. You're not totally useless after all." Crow took the candle from Isaac who lit himself another.

"There!" Crow pointed to a small bed in the corner on which Nelson was lying. He rushed over and put his hand to Nelson's burning hot forehead. "It's me, Nelson."

"Crow?" Nelson's eyes flickered open. "You're alive!" he mustered.

"It will take more than Johnny Ives and those rats to get rid of me. You were right." Crow nodded. "The boy did come in handy." Nelson managed a smile. A surge of relief rushed through Crow and he gave his arm a squeeze. "We need to get you out of here."

Nelson nodded and tried to move. "Yes," he replied, his voice hoarse.

"Um. Crow..." Isaac scampered over to the jagged window frame. "I think someone's coming."

"Hide the light." Crow flapped his hands. "Keep quiet." He sat Nelson up and put his arm around his shoulder. "Can you walk?"

"I... I think so." Nelson seemed groggy. "Where am I?"

"Molly Weaver's. We have to go. We don't know where she is." Crow hoisted Nelson up and the two of them limped toward the doorway and hid out of sight.

"They're getting close." Isaac peeked through the window. "There's three of them."

"Shh," Crow hushed.

Isaac sank low and scuttled like a crab over to where Crow and Nelson stood. Crow propped Nelson up with his hip and listened. The footsteps drew closer, then stopped. Isaac looked at Crow with fear in his eyes. He gave him a knowing nod. They had to be ready for a fight.

"I might have to put you down," he said to his quartermaster. Nelson nodded and grasped at the wall to steady himself.

The sound of glass crunching underfoot followed. "Anything good?" a voice came from outside. "Dunno, there're some bottles of liquid. It's a right mess."

Crow cocked his pistol.

"Let's keep going," another voice from outside spoke up. The sound of footsteps picked up and disappeared into the distance.

Nelson let out a big breath of air. His head bobbed about, tired and confused.

"Right." Isaac snuck back into the room.

"Sir?" Nelson leaned on Crow. "I don't think I can make it very far."

"Boy!" Crow propped up Nelson's drooping frame. "We have to go!"

"Of course." Isaac pulled out two empty pouches from his pocket.

"But first..." He dug his hand into the coffer tucked away in the corner of the room. He scooped up a handful of doubloons and stuffed them into one pouch.

"We don't have time for this!" Crow said as Nelson's eyes fell shut. "I don't care about the coin; we have to save Nelson."

"Hold on." Isaac stuffed the second pouch. He legged it back to the door and held out a pouch for Crow. "These are Popino's!"

"Fine, just help me with Nelson." Crow snatched the pouch and tied it to his belt.

Crow grabbed Nelson's arm and threw it across his shoulder. Isaac ducked under his other arm. They struggled to move. Nelson's feet didn't touch the floor.

"Let's grab him by the waist," Crow said and lowered his grip.

"Let's go!" Isaac heaved Nelson's frame with one side of his body and reached out for the door handle with the other, nearly toppling over.

They staggered away from Molly's house without closing the door behind them.

"Thank you... Isaac." Crow really did appreciate him, for once.

"Stick to boy, it doesn't sound right." Isaac pointed to the street on the right. "I know a place where we can rest."

"I know a place where you can rest too," an unfamiliar voice came from around the corner of Molly's house.

Crow and Isaac stopped dead in their tracks.

Click... click... click...

The sound of several rifle hammers locking into place ready to fire carried through the night. A line of five rifle-wielding men stood before them, all pointing their barrels straight at them.

"Isaac Carver!" A tall, well-postured man stepped out from the shadows. He wore a red jacket with large turned-back cuffs. Intricate gold braiding trimmed the jacket edge and its buttonholes.

Crow recognized such attire well.

"My name is Relocke Smith. I am the captain of the guard here on Nassau, and I'm here to arrest you."

"For what?" Isaac passed his bag of doubloons to Crow behind Nelson's back and put his hands in the air. He let go of Nelson whose full weight fell onto Crow. Nelson's bobbing head jolted, and he briefly opened his eyes.

"What's this all about, gentlemen?" Crow turned on his very best charm as he stuffed the bag into his pocket. "We don't want any trouble. Our friend's had a bit to drink, you see." Crow placed Nelson down on the ground and took a step back.

"Don't move!" Relocke spoke with great authority. "Isaac Carver, you are being arrested for the murder of John Finch."

The rifle-wielding men took a step toward Crow and Isaac, pointing their loaded rifles at their chests. Nelson lay on the ground, his breathing labored.

"John who?" Isaac walked toward Relocke and his men.

"Stop!" One of the men shot into the ground, barely missing Nelson. "Next one won't be a warning."

Isaac placed his hands in the air. "Who's John Finch? I genuinely have no idea!"

"The man from the tavern you stabbed with that poison blade of yours. Ring any bells?" Relocke stepped toward Isaac, his head held high and his hands behind his back. "We've had our eye on you. You've been very busy." Relocke grabbed Isaac by the shoulders and drove his knee into Isaac's stomach. He fell to the ground, winded.

Relocke stomped his foot into Isaac's back and dug his knee in as he bound a rope around his wrists.

Crow panicked. He couldn't get away with Nelson in tow, but they'd all be on the gallows if he did nothing. He snuck his hand into his pants and fumbled for the vials. They were both right, he thought, this was the worst place possible to keep them.

His hand settled on several of the tiny bottles. He gripped as many as he could hold without making it obvious and smashed them onto the ground in front of the gun-wielding men. They shattered on the dusty path. Orange liquid spilled out and fizzed a little before it disappeared, absorbed by grains of sand. "I'll come back for you!" Crow yelled.

"What was that?" Relocke pushed Isaac's head into the ground.

"Failure." Isaac laughed.

"Shoot him!" Relocke pointed toward Crow who had already made it up the street. The guns let rip, blasting Crow with a barrage of shots, but everyone missed. It might have been a failure but it had confused them and that was enough. Crow ran and ran, his feet pounded the ground, his legs grew heavy with each step, but he had to keep on going. A lump welled in his throat as he thought of Nelson. He tried to save him, and he'd keep trying. The boy would look after him, he reassured himself as he turned a corner and darted up an alleyway into the night, leaving Isaac and Nelson at the mercy of Relocke and a date with the gallows.

POPINO BELTRAME

A fleeting moment of peace and relaxation swept through Popino as he walked out of The Silky Swallow with a swagger in his stride. This might just be my new favorite place, he thought as he took in a deep breath and let the air flood his body.

"Hey, out the way!"

Popino looked up only to see a man with a hook for a hand standing before him.

"I'm heading in." The man nodded toward the door as he wiped at his hook with a bloodied rag.

"Sure..." Popino stared at the cloth covered in blood. "Busy morning?"

"Yeah, ya could say that." The man gave a mischievous smile before heading through the brothel door.

Popino shook his head. You always come across someone strange in this town, he thought as he made his way out of the alley and onto the main streets of Nassau. People rushed by, their crates loaded with wares to sell by the shore. A band of rather savage looking men were already rolling drunk, pushing at each other and yelling.

247

Popino didn't recognize any of them. A ship must have docked early, he thought.

Popino was dreading returning home and having to dismiss Clara. She had been with him since Elizabeth passed. Her life had been nothing but hard, and he was about to make it a whole lot harder. He wasn't sure how he would take care of Rose without her, but he'd have to make it work. That was if he found his coffer. His heart sank. Maybe he should take Rose and flee now. But where would they go? He looked up and realized he'd taken a wrong turn. He turned around and headed for the wealthy part of town. He needed to pay attention and get home, tell Clara the news then pay an afternoon visit to Thad. Maybe. That was a last resort.

"Popino!" His neighbor, Antoine, rushed toward him, waving his arms.

"Antoine!" Popino extended his hand to greet him.

Antoine was a wealthy and currently a rather sweaty individual who had grown rich from distilling the finest rum in Nassau.

"Popino, I came to find you." Antoine was too out of breath for a handshake and instead leaned his hands against a nearby wall and caught his breath. "Have you found Isaac?"

"No. I haven't been looking for him. Should I be?"

"The broken window at yours. I saw Isaac throw a rock through it late last night and there were guards milling about at your place."

"What? Are they still there?"

Antoine shook his head. "I don't think so. There was some commotion earlier but nothing for a while now."

Popino was still processing the information that Isaac had been the one to break his window. Why would he do that unless he had stolen the coffer? Surely, he wouldn't have.

"It's odd that the guards came over today. I didn't mention the window to anyone. Did you tell them what you saw?" Popino's mind searched for answers.

Antoine shook his head in response as his breath restored. "No, no, I know Isaac's your friend. That's why I came looking for you. Maybe your housemaid told them?"

"Clara wouldn't dare approach them." Popino's mind jumped to Vella's words: 'I expect her to be dead by tomorrow.' It had only been a few hours.

"I have to go, Antoine. Something doesn't sound right." Popino sped off up the street as fast as his legs could carry him.

His home came in sight and he stopped running. Maybe he was overreacting? His hands shook as he looked for guards but he couldn't see any. No noise came from the children playing outside. In fact, everything seemed unusually quiet. His heart raced and his vision started to blur as he reached for the door handle. "Rose, darling? Clara?" he called out as he tried to open the door, but something was in the way. He pushed a little harder and wedged himself through the small gap he had made. He looked to his feet only to see what was blocking it.

Clara lay on the kitchen floor, her throat slit and her body covered in stab wounds. Popino stared in disbelief. "Oh god, no. Rose!" He whipped out his blade as he stepped through into the dining room. His heartbeat echoed in his ears. He needed to find Rose, but he couldn't bring himself to look. "Rose?" He sobbed as he made his way down the hallway. He held his breath and covered his mouth as he checked the bathroom. Nothing. He crept upstairs, to her bedroom. "Please, if there is any god, please let my girl be alive." Tears streamed down his face. He pushed and the door creaked open. Nothing. No trace of anyone or a struggle. Maybe she ran off? With Lucas, Clara's son? Popino poked his head into his bedroom. Nothing. He ran downstairs and out the back. Two guards lay in a heap, their throats slashed, but there was no one else in sight. No sign of Rose and no sign of Lucas. Popino turned and went back into the house. His head spun and his legs trembled.

"Rose? Lucas?" he shouted. He didn't care who heard him now. He just wanted to see his beautiful girl and her sweet smile.

How could Vella do this? She said he had the day. Why had she broken her word? The lump in his throat throbbed. He stared through to the kitchen where Clara lay covered in blood. "I'm so sorry." He put his head in his hands and sobbed. What had he done? He peered through his fingers at the upturned room. His memories of home were replaced with horror. He needed to find Rose. He steadied his breathing and wiped at his eyes.

Where would she go? Maybe she'd try to find Isaac? He looked the other way as he stepped back into the kitchen, he couldn't bear to see Clara like that. His foot slipped as he navigated over her body. He steadied himself on the table and noticed a note covered in bloody fingerprints. He snatched it up. His fingers shook as he opened it and read.

"Popino," a voice came from outside. The door pushed open. "I need to talk to you."

ISAAC CARVER

The grazing of the rope against Isaac's skin became difficult to ignore. He shifted his shoulder blades back and tried to work out if he could somehow struggle free, or at the very least stop the burning. A guard's sharp finger prodded him forward as they marched down the hallway of the Nassau jail. His eyes fixed on the empty cell ahead. "I don't even know a John Finch," Isaac repeated for the umpteenth time.

A hand pushed into his back and he stumbled into the cell. The guards let out a sigh of relief as they offloaded Nelson, the well-rounded quartermaster, who continued to slip in and out of consciousness. Nelson smacked into the cell wall and his eyes shot open for a moment before he slumped to the ground.

"Can I at least get rid of this rope?" Isaac said as he took in his surroundings. Despite his years of mischief, he had managed to avoid the Nassau jail. He sniffed at the stale, musty air, wet with decay. "Delightful."

"Be quiet!" Relocke said. He tugged at the cuffs on his bright red jacket and stared Isaac down.

Isaac stared back. Everything about Relocke irritated him, from his arrogant tone through to his pathetic thin mustache, which somehow suited his fancy black captain's hat.

"Search them. I'll be back shortly," Relocke said.

Isaac mimicked Relocke under his breath as the captain strode back up the hallway, leaving two guards behind to take care of the prisoners.

"Now, don't try anything funny!" one guard said as he patted down Isaac's dirtied blue jacket. He dug his hands into the deep pockets. "Ow! What the hell is that?" the guard withdrew a handful of small balls covered in spikes.

"Keep them! And maybe in exchange you can untie my wrists?" Isaac said.

"You going to check the other one?" the guard shouted to his friend and pointed to Nelson.

"Nah, he looks half dead. Not too worried," the other guard replied and took a seat.

The guard pocketed the spiky balls and continued his search. "You don't have much! Few reale though, I'll take those. Hang on! What's this?" He retrieved a couple of worn out pouches.

Isaac closed his eyes as his heart sank to the pit of his stomach.

"Where did you get this?" The guard pulled out Isaac's prized silver coin and waved it in front of his face.

He shrugged.

"What's in this next one?" The guard peered inside. "Nothing! Wait. What's that powder?"

"Sand, I think. Keep everything you like! You can put your new-found reale in those pouches too," Isaac said.

The guard scrunched up his face. "You a bit funny in the head?"

"No, no. Well, maybe. I'd just like my wrists untied please?"

"Fine."

The guard stuffed the reale into the pouches and tucked them in his pocket. He locked the cell door behind him and took out a small blade.

"Turn around," the guard said.

Isaac shimmied his back up to the bars and held his wrists out. The guard sawed at the rope. It dropped to the ground and his wrists fell free. A wave of relief washed over Isaac. He still had the map, plus the remnants of that powder might coat the reale and inadvertently end up in the guard's eyes, maybe even make its way to his crotch.

Isaac's eyes searched the walls of the dank cell. They moved to the floor. A layer of dark brown, almost black sludge covered every inch. There looked to have once been a bench to sit on but only the wrought iron fixtures remained. Isaac stood on his tiptoes and peered out through the small window in the top corner of the room. A speck of moonlight shone in, which was broken up by the footsteps of passers-by and a rat poking its nose in.

He turned to face the neighboring cell which contained a malnourished man asleep in a heap on the ground. The guards sat either side of a small wooden table and chatted amongst themselves.

"Nelson?" Isaac crouched and placed his hand on Nelson's shoulder. "Nelson, can you hear me?"

Nelson opened his eyes and groaned. "Where am I?"

"The rather delightful Nassau jail," Isaac replied as a rat scurried in through the bars.

"Why, why am I with you?"

"I don't really know. They seem to think I murdered some fella and just dragged you along with me, I guess?"

253

He helped Nelson to sit up and propped him against the wall. His head lolled forward and his chin tucked into his chest, almost resting on his belly. "Have we been here long?" Nelson asked and moved his hand to push himself up. It landed in a wet pile of sludge.

"Just a short while," Isaac replied and feigned a smile. "Could use a drink!" A big brown rat gnawed on something in the corner of the cell. Isaac crept over and the rat scurried off, leaving behind a bone of some sort. He picked it up and tossed it through the bars of the neighboring cell.

"Hey! You!" Isaac peered through the bars. "Hey, fella!" Isaac whispered. The man didn't stir. "Dammit!" Isaac stomped his foot.

"Oi! No talking to 'im," the guard who had searched Isaac said.

Isaac rolled his eyes at Nelson and plonked himself down on the floor next to him.

"Any plan?" Nelson let out a sigh. "My head isn't right."

"Well, I've been trying to think... Not looking like there's too many options right now. I really could use that drink." Isaac put his head in his hands and rubbed at his face.

"I've seen it ruin many a man," Nelson said and shut his eyes. He shook his head a little before he drifted off.

"You and me both." Isaac gave a wry smile.

A few hours passed with no movement other than the visiting rats. Light snores came from Nelson and the one remaining guard. The other had left to get food but never came back. The malnourished man in the next cell hadn't flinched and Isaac started to wonder if he was still alive.

He'd been creeping about the cell, trying to come up

with a plan, looking for any way out, but there was nothing.

He sat himself back down next to Nelson who stirred from the interruption.

"Still here?" Nelson opened his eyes.

"Unfortunately so," Isaac replied.

"So..." Nelson said. Some color had returned to his face after the brief rest. "Why'd you kill that man?"

"I didn't."

"Then why are we here?"

"I don't know. They seem to think I did it."

"So, you didn't kill him?"

"No!" Isaac replied. "I don't know who did. I don't even know who he is. Sure, I was at the tavern but I always am." Isaac's stomach churned and his chest fluttered. He couldn't believe that after all these years he finally had the missing piece of the puzzle and now he'd be hanged for the murder of someone he didn't even kill.

"Ah." Nelson seemed to believe him. "Well, thanks for coming to rescue me. Or trying to, at least." Nelson patted at his head wound.

"You and Crow... seem... how should I put it?" Isaac smiled. "Very friendly."

"Yes." Nelson cleared his throat and looked around. "We are." His face flushed.

"How long have you been together?" Isaac asked.

"Well." Nelson counted under his breath. "About twenty-two years or so."

"Wow! That's loyalty." Isaac nodded, impressed.

"Crow's a good man." The corners of Nelson's mouth drooped. "He took me in when nobody would. Saw the value in me. He knew I wasn't a fighter but he didn't care. Said he'd always look after me... He has."

255

Isaac's brows fell to a frown. He paused for thought and checked around. "Do you think he'll come for us?" Isaac kept his voice as low as possible.

"He'll do what he can, I know he will." Nelson smiled. "How about you? Any friends? We might as well focus on the good."

Isaac sighed. "Can't say I have too many. And since I stole from my only real friend, probably, actually, no one." He pressed his lips together.

"Ah, Popino, of course. Well, you were quick to betray him," Nelson said, in his matter of fact tone.

"I know, but that treasure is all I've ever dreamed of. He has a home, people respect him." Isaac hung his head between his knees.

"Don't you?" Nelson asked.

"Nelson, I live in a chicken coop or wherever I happen to wake up. I'm a nobody with nothing to my name... The map was a chance. A real chance... My chance. Something for people to respect me for. They'd talk about me. The boy who had nothing and made something of himself. I wanted someone to be proud of me for once in my life." Isaac's eyes were glassy. He didn't dare move his head for fear of tears spilling out.

"I'm a nobody." Nelson shrugged. "It's not so bad."

"You're part of a notorious pirate crew! People at least fear..." Isaac stopped himself and looked to Nelson.

"No one fears me! I know that! People fear Crow. I'm just his sidekick." Nelson gave a light shrug. "We're a team."

"I'm too sober for this. All of this." Isaac shook his head.

"Here." Nelson reached into his bloodied burgundy waistcoat and retrieved a tiny thin flask. "One sip left each."

"Oh, thank you." Isaac tipped the brown liquid into his mouth and savored the sweet burn.

Nelson took a sip and gasped. "That's good."

"Isn't it!" Isaac gave him a light elbow.

The sound of footsteps marching down the hallway echoed in the cell.

"Right!" Relocke stood at the cell door with two men behind him.

The guard on duty sat up and wiped the drool from his mouth. "Captain." He wobbled to standing, still half asleep and gave a salute.

"At ease." Relocke nodded. He looked pleased with himself. "Nelson! You haven't been up to much of late."

Nelson's eyes went wide with hope.

"Wouldn't mind having a chat with your captain friend though."

Nelson's face dropped.

"Haven't quite decided what to do with you yet. But you, Mr. Carver... well, there's only one place you'll be going."

"Back to the tavern?" Isaac joked.

"What, so you can kill another innocent man?"

"I didn't kill him!" Isaac yelled. "I know you don't believe me but for once in my life I am telling the truth."

Nelson placed his hand on Isaac's shoulder. "There's no point arguing."

"That's right, Mr. Carver, you'd do well to listen to your friend here." Relocke crossed his arms. "Speaking of friends, you've been keeping some rather interesting company."

"Have I?" Isaac shrugged.

"Molly Weaver, Popino Beltrame, Joy Lafitte and now the dear old captain you both know so well."

"And?"

"Well, they all have very interesting lives. Seems nobody can stay out of trouble around here. Lucky for me!" Relocke laughed.

"Tell me, why exactly does Popino owe quite so much?"

"What?" Isaac stood up, his mouth falling open.

"Yes, up to his eyeballs in debt that one. And how about your old flame, hoping to claim the bounty on Jane Hatch's head."

"Joy," Isaac said to himself, his eyes growing wide. How did Relocke know all of this? "Popino's rich, extremely wealthy. I think you've got the wrong man!" Isaac shook his head in disbelief. "Just like I'm the wrong man! I don't know where you're getting your information but it's wrong."

"Oh, I don't think so." Relocke shot Isaac a smug smile and stroked his annoying thin mustache. "And how about Molly, guess you don't know anything about that one either?"

Isaac stared at the floor. He couldn't muster a clear thought. "The potions?"

"Ha! We went through her house after you lot had been."

"We'd just stopped by to collect something." Isaac held his head high but his mind raced.

"You don't know, do you?" Relocke said.

"Know what?" Isaac replied and looked to Nelson whose face was as puzzled as his own.

Relocke turned his back on the pair and addressed the guard. "Keep a close eye on him." He swung around and glared at Isaac. "You'll be hanged bright and early tomorrow morning, Mr. Carver."

Isaac's breath stopped. He tried to swallow but his

throat grew tight. It felt like it was closing in. It all did. "I..." Isaac managed but words failed him.

"I'll have a think about the other one." Relocke turned on his heel and marched out the door and up the corridor.

"I..." Isaac slid down the wall and sat back down next to Nelson. Relocke's footsteps rattled through his head.

"It'll be okay. It has to be, we've treasure to find." Nelson put his hand on Isaac's shoulder.

"Not this time. I... I think this is it." Isaac put his hand to his mouth, stunned. He closed his eyes. His mind cast back to the day his father left him. He'd locked him in that chicken coop with not a crust to his name. Maybe he should have just given up then.

"Crow will come for us. He'll find a way," Nelson said, his voice shaky.

"He won't get into this place without your help." Isaac buried his head into his knees. "I'm sorry."

JANE HATCH

Jane caught a glance of her reflection in the armory window. Her cropped, blonde hair stuck out in all the wrong places and her eyes glowed red. She hoped no one would notice the dark bags underneath them.

The fact was she hadn't slept in days. Rest was out of the question until she discovered who was responsible, which sick bastard had slain her only friend.

She longed for a drink and fantasized about the sweet liquor hitting her lips, but she knew the hold it had on her. Margaret had kept her accountable and, without her around, the call of the bottle came creeping back.

She paced around the room with her hands clasped behind her.

"I want to be clear, I'm not blaming you, I'm merely trying to establish how we can improve our... security. I don't want what happened to the girls happening to any of you."

"Of course, ma'am."

She circled the young man who sat patiently in front of her desk. "Where were you when everything happened?"

Jane stopped in front of him and leaned back onto her desk.

"Out training, down near the camp for new recruits. It's where I spend most of my free time." He nodded.

"I see. And how do you think Thad's men got away with what they did?" She tried to catch his gaze.

"I don't know. Unless maybe they knew Maddy? That was all I could think of. I dunno. It don't make sense."

"It certainly doesn't. Did you know Maddy?" Jane readjusted her stance and folded her arms.

The man shrugged. "Not well. I'd never been on a job with her or nothing."

Jane nodded. Her line of questioning had led her to understand that Maddy was known by many but no one had been close to her.

"What about Margaret?" The question wrenched at Jane's insides every time.

He looked down. "Everyone knew her, ma'am. She was like your shadow." He looked to Jane and forced a half smile. "I'm sorry."

Jane stared through him. Nothing had ever affected her quite like this. Losing Margaret was something she had never even considered. They'd been through so much together and now images of her bloodied body slit from throat to stomach haunted her mind.

"What do you think we could do to make things tighter around here?"

"Me?" the man responded, shocked. "Err well, I guess, I dunno. Didn't expect you to care about my opinion."

"Well, I do, so now's your chance to speak up." Jane feigned a quick smile.

"I..." he hesitated. "I think everything you do is smart. Maybe just get an extra couple of guards."

Jane sighed. "Yes, I think I will be doing that. Thank you, James. You're free to go."

James stood up and bowed his head in respect. He made his way out and pulled open the thick oak door to a mean-faced Thunder who stood with his legs wide and his arms folded.

Jane had questioned everyone about their whereabouts that day. Her mercenaries were told Thad's men were responsible for the murders and that she was gathering information to make their operation tighter. This way she hoped people might be more forthcoming with the truth, but so far she hadn't discovered anything of interest and had started to wonder if they saw through her lies.

"Thunder, can I have a moment with you, please?" Jane took a seat at her desk.

Thunder strode in and closed the door behind him.

"Nobody's saying anything. I haven't had so much as a hint of anything!" Jane said.

The more she analyzed everyone's behavior the more she started to doubt her own. How had she not seen any signs of a traitor in the ranks? Were they still fooling her now? She had always been so confident in her abilities. At times people even thought she could read minds. Was she losing her touch?

"Do you think it's our approach? Maybe we need to put a bit of fear in them?" Thunder narrowed his gaze and pounded his fist into his palm.

"We can't do that to our own. We'll have no one left! Plus, we need everyone we can get with what's about to go down. Vella, won't hold back," Jane said.

Thunder walked over to the window and stared out. He cracked each of his knuckles in turn.

"Don't get me wrong. I'd like to instill some fear into

people right now, but we need a lead before we go down that path." The words came from Jane's mouth but she was detached from them. It was as if she was watching herself from outside of her body. She shook her head and buried it in her hands.

"I think you need to eat something, Miss."

Jane looked over at Thunder. "Probably."

Thunder continued to stare out of the window. "I'm starting to think that it wasn't one of ours ya know?"

Jane shook her head. "It has to be. Thad's men didn't do it. They can't have killed Margaret. Think about it!"

"Maybe they killed Maddy, then someone else killed Margaret thinking they could get away with it and blame them?" Thunder said.

Why hadn't this thought occurred to her before? She was shocked she would miss such a thing. "That is a very good point. I'd just assumed it would be the same group of people responsible for both. Unless—" A knock interrupted her. "Yes?"

"Can we come in, ma'am?" Anna's muffled, raspy voice came through the door. Jane nodded to Thunder who marched over and pulled open the thick oak door with ease to a grinning Anna and Jose.

"Hello." Jose raised his eyebrows and addressed Thunder.

"Come on in. Tell me you have news?" Jane rose to her feet and paced around the room. Her eyes fixed on the floor.

"We do!" Anna said. Jose stood next to her, silent. He clasped his hands behind his back and didn't take his eyes off Thunder. "We made a friend." Anna took a seat and made herself comfortable.

"Well, that's certainly something. And?" Jane said.

SOPHIE & CHRIS BROUSSEAU

"You know Tim?" Anna replied.

Jane stopped. "Remind me."

"Short... no hair really. Walks funny. Think one of his legs is shorter than the other," Anna replied.

Jane tapped her index finger on her lips and thought for a moment. "Spends a lot of time down at the tavern? A little too much."

"That's the one. Turns out he used to go drinking with one of those men we killed. Thad's men. They'd meet down at The Rusty Trombone but never talked business or nothing. There's a group of ours that meet a group of theirs, so I'm told."

Jane's brows dipped. Her lips pursed. "And he offered up this information to you, wanted to make friends with you knowing that you'd killed his friend? I use the term loosely."

"Well, he was worried you'd think it was something to do with him and was trying to figure out why we'd done it," Anna said.

"Hmm. Go on," Jane said. She didn't like that some of her mercs drank with the enemy, but she figured she couldn't control them entirely and at times it may even prove useful.

"Apparently there was a guy that hung around when both groups would meet up. He wasn't with Thad, and he's not one of ours. Name of Jiffy." Anna scratched her head. "It sounds like he's part of a different crew, one we don't know about. Tim said that Jiffy is working with someone close to you. This person works for him... and us too."

Jane pressed her lips together.

"I guess there's a secret crew in Nassau we don't know about." Anna shrugged.

"Secret crew? This Jiffy is part of a crew we don't even know about?" Jane looked down at her boots.

"Apparently." Anna nodded.

"And Tim didn't think to mention this?" The rage welled up in Jane. She pushed her clenched fist against her lips. "Even though they're a traitor!"

"I think Tim knew what would happen to him." Anna's eyes lit up. "Seems it is an inside job. Someone close to you too."

Jose looked at Thunder and nodded.

"Don't look at me like that!" Thunder scowled at Jose.

Jose cocked his head to the side and raised his eyebrows.

"What exactly are you accusing me of?" Thunder stormed over and grabbed Jose by the scruff of his neck. He smashed him into the wall. "Huh?"

"Nothing! Relax!" Jose said. Thunder released his grip.

"Leave him, Daniel. Tensions are high. No one thinks that of you. We're all a bit on edge." Jane took a seat at her desk.

"Don't call me that." Thunder stepped away from Jose, his face filled with fury.

"Sorry, Thunder," Jane said with a hint of sarcasm.

"But Daniel's such a nice name," Jose said.

"I'd shut your mouth if I were you." Thunder shook with rage.

"Or what? You gonna pin me down again?" Jose winked.

"I'll fucking knock you out if you don't shut your mouth!"

"Okay, okay." Jose put his hands up.

"We've no time to be joking around. We need to prepare ourselves for what's to come," Thunder said.

"And what exactly is that? To come that is?" Jose said.

"War! That's what." Thunder turned his back on Jose and walked toward Jane. "I'm sorry, Miss Jane."

"Like I said. We're all a bit tense right now. So back to Tim. Did you threaten him to obtain this information?" Jane asked.

"A bit. Like I said, we're friends now." Anna gave a wicked smile which Jose returned.

"So he's still alive?" Jane asked.

"Of course! Maybe not for long." Anna winked. "You said no killing."

"Yet." Jane's face dropped. "What sort of man would keep that information to himself."

"He's a traitor, regardless of whether he did it or not!" Thunder spoke up.

"Agreed. We'll take care of your new friend. Thank you both," Jane said. Anna and Jose looked disappointed.

"Are you sure we can't take care of him?" Anna asked.

Jane couldn't help but smile. "There will be plenty of people to take care of in the coming weeks. Just leave this one to us."

"Of course," Anna replied. The pair turned on their heels and showed themselves out. The door shut behind them.

"This isn't good," Thunder said.

Jane didn't know how to respond. She eyed him up and down. It couldn't be him, could it? She trusted him... didn't she? But he was smart. Smarter than her? Probably not. "Any word from Joy?"

Thunder shook his head. "She's not back yet but I hear he's been taken care of. Guards all over the place."

"We can confirm that later." Jane chewed at her lip. "Do you think Thad has someone posing as one of ours too, or do you think this secret crew—whoever the hell they are—is solely responsible?" She leaned forward on her desk, interlaced her fingers and propped her chin up.

"I don't know, both are possible." Thunder clenched his fists. "I hate that bastard!"

"Thad?" Jane nodded. Her mind jumped from one subject to another. "And how is the increased intake of new recruits coming along?"

"Good. We're getting double what we used to, at the cost of quality. Still, Vella won't know what's hit her."

"That's the plan. It's been a long time coming... but first, sounds like we need to pay a visit to Tim. Meet me in the dungeon?" Jane said.

"Don't have to ask me twice!" Thunder replied.

POPINO BELTRAME

"Popino?" The door handle rattled. "I can hear you in there." A voice came from outside and whoever it belonged to tried to push the door open but Clara's lifeless body blocked the way.

Popino bolted to the door and smashed his weight against it. He recognized Joy's voice but he didn't know what to do. She couldn't see this. What if she thought he was responsible? What if Joy was responsible?

"Joy, why are you here?" Popino said through the closed door. He wasn't sure if he could trust her.

"I need to talk to you. Can you please just let me in?" Joy said.

Popino opened the door a crack and poked his head out. Joy stood with her hands on her hips. "You by yourself?"

His eyes shot from one place to another. The street seemed empty but Joy alone was dangerous enough.

"Aren't I always?" Joy replied.

"You need to know this wasn't me, okay?" Popino said.

"What wasn't you?"

Popino opened the door further. "Squeeze through. Watch your step."

"What the hell happened?" Joy looked down at the blood covered floor where Clara lay.

"I don't know, but Rose is gone. They've taken her." Popino tried to steady his hands to show Joy the note. His eyes filled with tears. "My girl's gone, Joy." The thought of Rose scared and alone ate away at his insides.

The corners of her mouth turned down. "She never mentioned..." The words spilled from Joy's mouth as she stared at the floor.

"Who never mentioned? Why are you here? I haven't seen you in forever and then you just appear at my door. Do you know something? Do you know where she is, Joy?"

Joy put her hands up. "I don't know anything about Rose. I'm sorry, Popino. I'm... well... Jane Hatch sent me."

Popino drew his blade and held the pointed end out at Joy. "Get back!" he said and took a step back toward the dining room. "I mean it, Joy, put your weapons on the table. All of them!" Popino recalled Joy's penchant for tiny, poisoned blades. "Those blades of yours too."

Joy folded her arms. "I'd have killed you by now if I was going to."

Popino's whole body shook. "Great! So, Jane wants me dead too."

Joy removed her hat and popped the feathered tricorn down on the table. Her thick, brown hair tumbled down onto her shoulders. She ruffled her hand across her scalp and let out a sigh.

"She does, but lucky for you she sent me. I can't kill you, Popino, I know you too well. Plus, I couldn't do that to Rose, wherever she is." Joy took a step toward him.

"Losing Raven was... awful. She's all I have. I can try to help you but you need to trust me."

Popino nodded. "Weapons, put them all on the table." Even unarmed Joy was still dangerous.

"Fine, if it makes you feel better." Joy removed the blades from her jacket along with three pistols and placed them on the table. She stepped toward him with her hands up. "Now, show me the note." She held out her hand.

Popino took a step forward and handed the bloodied paper to her. He then immediately stepped back, still brandishing his blade.

I have your daughter. If you want her back, you'll have to pay me.

Joy placed the note on the table. "This can't be Jane. She would have said."

"It's Vella." Popino fell to his knees and discarded his blade. "I thought I had more time. I don't know what to do."

"Oh, Popino." Joy stepped forward and bent down to join him. She gave his shoulder a squeeze. "Vella is much more dangerous than she lets on. You must owe her a lot? Surely not more than Jane?"

"I don't have it. Any of it." Popino sobbed. "The small part I had left was stolen last night. My neighbor said he saw Isaac throw a rock through my window and when I woke up this morning it was gone!"

"What was gone exactly?" Joy asked.

"My coffer of doubloons. It's a small gold box. I keep it hidden from everyone! Everyone but Clara."

"I can't believe Isaac would steal from you. You two..." Joy said.

"I know. The oldest of friends. I don't want to believe it but Antoine has no reason to lie."

Joy rose to her feet and walked back over to the table. She swirled her hair into a bun on top of her head and put her hat back on. Popino had always found Joy intoxicating. Her soft face with those sparkling green eyes. It had always been beyond him how Isaac had snagged such a beauty.

"I know Isaac, and he wouldn't do it unless he was desperate. But this, this wasn't him, was it?" Joy pointed to the body on the kitchen floor.

Popino shook his head. "Never! Vella said I had the day to take care of Clara. Her son is gone too." Popino scrunched his eyes shut. "What's wrong with her!"

"A lot apparently. I'll help you but first you need to help me out with Jane."

"Sure." Popino pushed himself up and searched for the rum on the kitchen counter. He gulped the sticky brown liquid straight from the bottle and savored the burn as the liquor slipped down his throat. He thrust the bottle in Joy's direction.

"It's all yours. I think you need it more than me right now." Joy tucked her blades back into her various jacket pockets. "I need to tell Jane that you've been killed, and we need to make it look like you have."

"Did she ask for proof?" Popino said then tipped the remainder of the potent liquid into his mouth.

"Just the usual." Joy smiled awkwardly.

"Which is?" Popino asked.

"Your cock or your hand with your wedding ring on it."

Popino's jaw dropped in horror. He looked down at his ring and covered his crotch with his other hand. He couldn't survive losing either, surely? He'd bleed to death and if he did survive, he'd be near useless with a hook hand down at the docks. The other was out of the question, though maybe he wouldn't be in this mess without it. "Is there a third option?" He looked at Joy with concern.

"Just kidding!" Joy said and forced a laugh. "Sorry, I couldn't resist. You never were very nice to me."

"Joy!" Popino put his hands on his head. "This really isn't the time for a joke. Poor Clara is dead at our feet, my daughter is missing and you're joking about cutting off my cock!"

"I'm sorry. Look, Jane doesn't need proof but you need to disappear for a bit."

"I can't though. I've nowhere to go! I need that coin for Vella. Oh god, I don't know what to do, Joy." Popino panicked and motioned to the dining room. Joy followed him. "I can't think looking at that. At Clara. It's all my fault." Popino perched himself on a dining room chair. "Where could I hide? Your house?"

Joy shook her head. "Too risky. I know a place." Joy checked her jacket. "I'll write you his details." She riffled through the writing desk in the corner of the room and found a sheet of paper. "I need ink!"

"In the top part, flip it open." Popino sat with his head in his hands. Vella had Rose. Alive. That was something, he tried to reassure himself. Hopefully Lucas too.

Joy snatched up a cuttlefish bone and scratched down some details. "Here." She handed the scrap of paper to Popino. "Roy's used to this kind of thing. Tell him Joy sent you."

"And what about Vella? What if she gets word that I'm dead? Surely she'll..." Popino fell silent. He couldn't bring himself to say what he thought.

"As soon as I've told Jane that you're dead I'll go find Isaac. When he hears that Rose is gone, he'll give the coffer back. He'll be horrified. Probably thinks you're rich and that you wouldn't miss a few doubloons. I know I did. Then I'll make him come help us get her back. Sound good?"

"It's a plan." Popino nodded. "When will you come for me?"

"I don't know exactly. Just lie low at Roy's until you hear from me," Joy said and headed for the door.

"I'll gather my things and head straight there."

"Be careful, Popino. Jane has people everywhere."

"Same goes. And thank you. I owe you," Popino said.

"I'll hold you to that." Joy turned and flashed him a smile before closing the door behind her.

ISAAC CARVER

A well-rounded, rosy-cheeked guard sauntered down the hallway. He held a jug in one hand and balanced a plate of bread and meat in the other. His shrill whistle as he waddled toward the holding cells caused Isaac to withdraw his head from his knees. Isaac watched as the guard unloaded the items onto the table.

"Food's up!" The chirpy guard took a seat.

"Most 'ave dozed off, Phin," the sleepy guard said.

"You don't say," Phin replied.

Isaac couldn't take his eyes off the jug. Maybe it contained Bumbo? Or even better, straight rum! If he was to be hanged tomorrow, he was going to at least try his luck for one last drink. "What's in the jug, Phin?"

"Never you mind!" Phin poured the brown liquid into cups and the pair swigged it down.

"This bread's still hot," the sleepy guard said as he topped a large piece with a hunk of meat and shoveled it into his mouth.

Nelson came to and sniffed the air. "I'm starving," he said and rolled his eyes at Isaac.

"You ever been on the gallows, boy?" the sleepy guard asked. He looked at his friend and laughed as they munched away, slurping their drinks and spilling crumbs all over themselves.

"No, can't say I have. Don't think I'd be here, would I?" Isaac found it hard to believe how stupid some people were. How did they have power over him? It didn't seem right.

"Don't be smart with me! You'll be dead soon enough," the guard replied.

"Ha!" Phin added and laughed.

"It's true, I will." Isaac pushed himself up and stood at the cell door. "So maybe, since I will, there's no harm in asking for one final drink. Please?" Isaac flashed the most genuine smile he could muster.

"Not a chance!" Phin said.

Isaac's shoulders sank.

"Try begging at the window," the sleepy guard said. "Never know your luck." The guards both laughed.

"I hope you choke," Isaac muttered to himself. He turned to the small corner window and, as he did, he caught sight of a bag flying down the hallway.

"Close your eyes," a mysterious voice instructed. Isaac snapped his eyes shut and fumbled his way to Nelson.

"Cover your eyes, quickly," Isaac whispered and shoved Nelson's shirt over his head. "Keep them shut until I say otherwise." The pair crouched low as pungent smoke seeped down the hall and into the cell.

"What the bloody hell is that?" Phin said.

Isaac heard a rush of footsteps.

"What in the..." Phin screamed out in pain. "My eyes!"

The sleepy guard must have run to his aid as Isaac heard a clatter of the jug and plate smashing on the cold stone floor, followed by a yelp of pain. "I'm blind! Everything's gone!" The guards' cries of panic and pain filled the cell.

Isaac pressed his shirt into his eyes and squeezed them as tight as possible. If he was correct, the bag contained the same blinding concoction he had used on Robert. And there was only one person in Nassau who made such a thing. Molly.

"Isaac!" a booming voice came from what sounded like the hallway.

"Nelson, who's that?" Isaac said.

Gunshots rang through the cell. "Keep your head down!" the booming voice ordered.

The guards' screams stopped.

Isaac sniffed at the air. The burnt smell had faded. He peeled his shirt away from his face slowly. "I think we're okay, Nelson."

"It's Johnny!" Nelson said as he removed the shirt from his face.

"Ives? Why's he here for us?" Isaac said and opened his eyes fully to see the two guards dead on the floor.

"Because..." Johnny took the keys from the guards' table and unlocked the cell door. "Apparently, you're good at chess."

"What?" Isaac replied, stunned.

Johnny walked over to Nelson. He clenched his fist and punched him in the face. "Not you though."

Nelson fell to the floor.

"Wait!" Isaac ran to shield Nelson. "Don't do that to him."

"Boys!" Johnny snapped his fingers and five men wielding flintlock pistols stormed into the cell and pointed their barrels at Isaac and Nelson.

276

"Molly wants you and only you," Johnny said. "I suggest you step away from him right now. We need to get you out of here quick."

Johnny lunged forward and grabbed Isaac's arm. "C'mon," Johnny said and pulled Isaac toward him. Isaac struggled.

"No! Can't we just bring him? He's useful." Isaac looked Johnny in the eye.

"If I don't get out of here soon, there's going to be a bounty on my head bigger than the one on Jane Hatch! Come! On!" Johnny dragged Isaac who stumbled past the men.

"What do we do with him, boss?" a black-toothed, crusty looking man asked, pointing to Nelson.

"You know what to do!" Johnny replied and stuck his pistol into Isaac's back. "Follow me with this one, make sure he doesn't try anything."

Johnny eyed two of his men who turned their pistols to Isaac's head as Johnny attempted to march him out of the cell.

"Please, Ricktor, I didn't do anything wrong," Nelson said.

"Johnny, don't do this!" Isaac pleaded and tried to turn his head to Nelson.

"Ricktor, remember the Thiggins heist?" Nelson said. Johnny stopped in his tracks and turned to face Nelson.

Isaac looked at Nelson and nodded for him to continue.

"Remember the riches we scored on that one? That was me. My brains behind that. I led that," Nelson said.

"He's got a point, boss," Ricktor said.

Nelson knelt before Ricktor and continued. "Remember the day we set sail for Whale Cay? That was some storm, but we made it through, our crew, together." Nelson forced a smile.

Ricktor lowered his gun. "Boss, I can't. We can't!"

"Molly insisted! Says he knows too much. Something about the map. He's competition. Just kill the bastard!"

"Molly? I can talk to her. She'll listen to me," Isaac said. He looked at the two men pointing flintlocks at him. "Don't suppose you have a drink, do you?" Isaac tried his best to distract them. "Reckon that fella in the next cell does? I bet he does." Their eyes lit up.

"We'll check," the smaller of the two replied.

"There's no time! We have to go!" Johnny shouted. "Shoot him already!"

Ricktor raised his pistol.

"I won't come with you! Unless Nelson comes with us." Isaac tried to wriggle free of Johnny's grasp.

"I'll fucking knock you out if I have to," Johnny said. "Hold this fucker, boys. I'll do it myself."

The five men rushed to Isaac and pinned him down.

Nelson looked around and scrambled backwards into the corner. "Johnny, you don't have to do this," Nelson pleaded.

"I don't have a choice!" Johnny yelled and pointed his pistol at Nelson. "Now that Crow's dead, I can't have you hanging around trying to turn my men against me."

"Crow's dead?" Tears spilled from Nelson's eyes.

"The boys took care of him," Johnny said and puffed out his chest, yet his hand shook. "I wanted to keep you alive, you damned fool. I tried to save you. I brought you to Molly's house to save you."

"If he really is gone then I guess I'll join him." Nelson closed his eyes. Tears trickled down his face.

"I'm sorry. Molly's orders." Johnny aimed and looked

away as he pulled the trigger. The bullet hit Nelson's head and his body flew backwards. Johnny unloaded another shot into Nelson's chest.

"Shit!" Isaac turned his head away.

Johnny grabbed Isaac by the arm and dragged him past the men. "Shut your mouth!" he said and dug his pistol into Isaac's back.

"Fuck." Isaac blinked back tears. He hadn't let a drop spill from his eyes ever since the day his father left him, but this was a lot. He felt torn. Nelson hadn't deserved that, but he couldn't help feeling relieved for his second chance. Maybe he could make things right with Pino? He could find Crow and take out this bastard Ives together. "Fine." Isaac shook off Johnny's grip. "I'm coming, you don't have to manhandle me." Isaac put his hands in the air.

"I need to get that pouch from the guard though." Isaac pointed to where the guard who had frisked him lay belly up, dead.

The smallest of the men ran over to the body and patted down his pockets. "This the one?" He held a rusty earth-colored pouch in the air.

"That's it. Thank you." Isaac held out his hand.

"Check it first! Don't just hand it over to him," Johnny said.

"Big silver coin."

"He can have it," Johnny said.

Isaac held out his hand and smiled. "Appreciated." He took his worn pouch with his prized silver coin and re-attached it to his belt.

"What's going on here?" The malnourished man from the next cell came to. He wobbled to his feet. "Let me out too would ya?"

"Boss?" Ricktor said.

"No witnesses," Johnny replied.

Ricktor raised his gun and shot into the neighboring cell. The emaciated man dropped to the floor.

"Not completely useless then, are you?" Johnny huffed. "Let's go!"

Isaac took one final look at Nelson. "So, does anybody please have a drink?"

JOY LAFITTE

The flutter in Joy's stomach increased as she approached the mansion. She hoped Popino had been discreet and made it to Roy's unnoticed and unharmed. As she set foot on the rough gravel path, her mind raced with possibilities, none of them good.

Crunch. Crunch. Crunch.

Each step felt alarmingly loud.

"Joy!" Leon waved to her with his hook. She smiled at the sight of his face. He seemed to be welcoming her at least.

"I heard there're guards everywhere?" Leon said.

"What?" Joy pretended to look around and seem distant.

"At Popino's. That's where you've been, right?" Leon said.

"Yes, it's a bit of bloodbath over there," Joy replied. She sounded overly confident. It was intentional but maybe a bit much? It wasn't an exaggeration though; it was a bloodbath. The spilled blood just happened to have nothing to do with her nor did it belong to Popino.

"What's been going on here? Why's everyone outside?"

"Practicing, we're finally going to attack Vella."

"Vella? Of course," she played along. "When?"

Leon shrugged. "Soon. You ready for it?"

"As I'll ever be. Guess it was only a matter of time." Joy folded her arms and gave them a comforting squeeze in a bid to quash the rising dread in her chest. This news meant she would have to get to Jane sooner rather than later.

Leon brushed the hair from his eyes and straightened up his baggy waistcoat. "I'll walk you in."

"Thanks," Joy said.

Leon ran ahead and held the door open for her. "After you, m'lady."

"Ha! How kind of you, Leon." Joy stepped through the rich dark wood double doors and into the marble-floored foyer.

Her eyes widened as she took in the room. She looked to her feet and admired the black and white checkered floor. Her eyes followed it to the bottom of a black wooden banister wrapped around a curved staircase. Her eyes shot to the other side of the room where another staircase mirrored its opposite. The dark red stair carpet struck a brilliant contrast against the wood. Her eyes stopped at the mezzanine which overlooked them.

"Beautiful, isn't it?" Leon remarked. "Just like you," he said under his breath.

"What was that?" Joy said.

"Nothing! Follow me, I'll show ya where she is," Leon said.

"You're too kind." Joy followed Leon. He turned to her as he sidestepped up the stairs, and she watched as he tried to avert his eyes from looking down her corset. He nearly tripped a few times which lightened her otherwise somber mood.

"So, you've never been in here. What do you think?" Leon said.

"It's impressive." Joy slid her hand across the banister. A glittering glass chandelier hung above the mezzanine. Ornate candelabras and fine paintings lined the walls. Joy started to consider if she was out of her depth. Jane wasn't like her other marks. The sort of wealth she had amassed and the power she wielded over others led Joy to think that kidnapping her unnoticed might be harder than she first anticipated.

"She's been questioning people in here all day." Leon pointed to the armory door and gave a solid knock.

"Yes?" a muffled voice said.

"It's Leon, ma'am. I have Joy with me."

"Come!"

The door was pulled open and Thunder stood there. He turned to Jane and saluted, then squeezed himself through the door past Joy and Leon. Thunder gave Joy a wink as he brushed past. Joy tried not to roll her eyes.

"Come in and have a seat, Joy. Leon, please give us some privacy," Jane said.

"Of course." Leon gave Joy a smile and closed the door behind him.

"I hear congratulations are in order. I know you and Popino had a history."

Joy kept quiet and nodded her head as her brain tried to think of how to play this one. How much did Jane have on her? She didn't think she would look into her past. Did she know about Raven?

"I always do my research." Jane stood up. "Come sit." She motioned to the chair in front of her desk. "I learned quite a lot about you actually, about Isaac." Jane looked up as if thinking and moved toward Joy. She sat on her desk in front of her.

Joy's face flushed as she took a seat. Did she know about Roy too? About the bounty? She cleared her throat. "Isaac was a long time ago. We all make mistakes." Joy tried to play it cool, but she could feel the sweat start to accumulate.

"We do, but I wasn't sure you'd be able to go through with what I'd asked given Isaac and Popino's friendship," Jane said.

At that moment, Joy could have sworn the temperature in the room had increased. She hoped she wasn't showing her nerves. She calmed her mind and focused on her mission. "Well, a job's a job and I really want to work for you, ma'am." Joy removed her hat. She needed to appear respectful, obedient even. She also needed easy access to the blade she had hidden away inside there.

"Why? Why do you want to work for me?" Jane asked and sprang to her feet. She walked over to the window.

Joy wondered if this was another test or if Jane simply wanted praise. "Because... I know I can be of service to you and I hear the pay is good," Joy said and stroked at the inside of her hat. Her finger traced over the blade.

"It is. Seems you'd be a fine addition to the mansion." Jane leaned on the windowsill.

Joy scoped Jane up and down. Now would be a perfect time to sneak up but the distance was too great, plus several muskets were within easy reach on the wall. She didn't look to have any other weapons on her which was odd considering they were alone. Maybe it was because she was surrounded by weapons and didn't think for one second anyone would try anything. She did look exhausted though. Maybe her reflexes wouldn't be as sharp?

"Thank you, ma'am," Joy replied.

"I just have something I'd like to clear up first though." Jane turned from the window and looked straight at Joy.

"Oh?" Joy replied. Her heart raced.

"It's been brought to my attention there's a bounty on my head." Jane put her hands on her hips and walked slowly toward Joy. She could feel her eyes burning into her.

"Oh really? Does this shock you?" Joy asked.

"It does actually. Let's just say it's known by those who open bounties that I usually find out who opened it, and who took it too." Jane leaned back on her desk in front of Joy, her arms folded.

"That makes sense." Joy nodded. She tried to remain calm but her damp palms told a different story.

"I know for a fact that Roy is the one who has taken the bounty." Jane didn't take her eyes off Joy. "Do you know Roy?"

Joy wasn't sure how to play this. "I know a few Roys."

"I see." Jane returned to her seat and opened up her desk drawer. She withdrew a pistol. "Let me jog your memory. He's short, size of a child."

"Yes, I do know that one actually. I've seen him around the old part of town here and there." That wasn't a lie, Joy thought, she had seen him around. Should she push it? "I don't know him personally though." It was a gamble, but from memory she had kept her meetings with Roy secretive.

"You're lying."

"What?" Joy said and let her mouth fall open as if shocked by the suggestion.

"You're lying to me." Jane picked up the pistol and pointed the barrel at Joy. "I can read people like a book, so it's time to tell the truth or face the consequences." Jane cocked the pistol.

Joy flicked her wrist and the small dagger from her hat flew out. The blade hit Jane in the neck and embedded deeply as planned. Jane clasped her neck with one hand and fired the pistol with the other.

The shot narrowly missed Joy who ran to Jane's side and caught her body as she slumped to the ground. Jane's eyes fell shut and her body went limp. Joy laid her down and rolled her onto her stomach. She ripped off Jane's heavy jacket and patted her pockets for weapons. She needed to be as light as possible, plus she might wake up sooner rather than later and she didn't want her to be armed when she did.

A wave of panic rushed over Joy. How could she get her out of here alive? Was that footsteps, running? The gunshot. Could she hide?

The door to Jane's office burst open and at the door stood an out of breath Leon, holding a pistol in his hand. "Joy?"

"Leon, please close the door." Joy flicked her other wrist and three small blades came out into her hand. She held each one in between her fingers and showed them to Leon. "I don't want to kill you."

Leon looked behind him and closed the door. "What are you doing? Is she dead?" He pointed the flintlock upwards but didn't put it down.

"Just paralyzed. I don't have time to explain everything right now but I can reward you handsomely if you help me out."

"I don't need a reward, but I doubt you'll make it out of

here alive." Leon put his pistol back in its holster and rushed over to the pair. "I do know a way out where we won't be seen, but you owe me an explanation after this."

"Anything, anything you want."

"Drag her over to the bookshelf," Leon said and ran over to it. He scanned the shelf up and down as if looking for something in particular.

Joy hurried along and dragged Jane's body across the ruby red carpeted floor. "Let me guess, a secret door?"

"Sure." Leon grabbed what looked like a book and smacked Joy across the head. That wasn't a book, she thought as her eyes grew heavy and she slumped to the ground.

CAPTAIN CROW

Desperate times call for desperate measures, Crow told himself as he hid in a row of short bushy trees opposite the guards' tower. Breaking into the Nassau jail would be no mean feat, but he was Nelson and the boy's only hope.

After passing out from sheer exhaustion in a field of palms, Crow had returned to his decimated shack, bound his wounds and grabbed all the weapons he could carry. His jacket had never been so heavy. Now he waited outside of the fort-like jail, eyeing for an opportunity to strike. He scanned the high, flat walls for a way in. There was nothing other than the front door, a thick wooden slab with wrought iron panels. He narrowed his eyes. The door looked to be slightly ajar. Maybe they were taking in a new prisoner? Now might be the perfect time to strike.

He ran as if propelled by a great force and stuck his back to the wall. He pressed his body into the stone blocks and side-stepped toward the door with a pistol readied in each hand. He sprang into action and kicked the door. The thick slab didn't budge. He threw his whole weight into it and the door begrudgingly moved a few inches. He forced his way through the gap only to see a guard with his throat slit slumped and blocking the way. Had someone got here before him? Had the boy fought his way out? He sure as hell hoped so.

"Stop right there!" An out of breath guard ran down the hallway toward him. Crow aimed and shot. He never missed. The guard copped a bullet to the head and went down. Crow's eyes darted around. The hallway stretched far and looked to split off into different directions. The cold, dank air sent shivers down his spine. As he crept forward, he hoped Nelson had survived. He was so close now. He stepped over the dead guard and continued down the hallway.

In the far distance a door swung open and four men came hurtling through. Crow unloaded his pistols into two of the men and dropped to the ground, belly down. The two injured men tumbled to the floor as the others showered him with incoming shots. He rolled to avoid the fire and withdrew two fresh pistols. He raised both barrels and fired. Cries of fallen men echoed through the hallway, bouncing off the thick stone walls. He pushed himself up, rushed toward them and checked their bodies for spare weapons. Nothing. He only had two shots left and needed time to reload but the sound of footsteps meant that wouldn't be happening.

Another two men came running through the door. This time Crow had a different strategy in mind. He reached down into his pocket and grabbed an earthy brown pouch, freshly labeled to avoid any mix ups. He threw the weighty sack ahead of him, hoping for thick smoke to come pouring out and render the guards useless. Instead, the contents hit the floor, made a loud bang followed by a flash and fizzled out. "Dammit!"

The guards laughed. "Not so tough now are you, Crow?"

"I don't know about that," Crow said as he walked toward them, firing twice. The pair dropped to the ground. "I'd say I'm pretty tough, boys." The adrenaline pumped through his veins. With each surge came that feeling of power he had missed. These dogs wouldn't destroy him and Nelson, or the boy. He ran toward the men, hoping to score a loaded pistol. Nothing.

He reached the end of the hallway. The dank corridor split off in two directions. Crow peered down each in turn as he paused for a moment to reload. Which way would take him to Nelson and the boy?

"Help me?" a voice cried from the shadows. He took the left and ran toward the pained cry. His eyes fixed on an emaciated man slumped in a cell bleeding out.

"Help me! End it..." The starved man reached out to Crow who replied with a shot to the chest.

"Poor bugger," Crow said to an otherwise silent corridor. He tiptoed down the hallway constantly checking behind, ahead, behind, ahead. Those cells that were visible seemed to be empty but there were a lot of closed doors with no noise coming from them. Crow shuddered at the thought of being shut in.

At the very end of the corridor, he spied what looked like a foot poking out of a set of bars. Crow ran to what he assumed must be the holding cells. Two guards lay belly up on the ground. A malnourished man was dead in the middle cell and a familiar body was slumped against the wall of the one closest to him. He didn't want to believe it. "Nelson..." Crow's hands shook as he walked toward his faithful quartermaster. "I'm sorry. I'm so sorry. I took too long." Crow couldn't breathe. His body felt like he was drowning. He dropped to his knees and placed his shaking hand on Nelson's chest. He closed his eyes as tears spilled down his face. "We had the best of times, didn't we?" He hung his head, doubled over. Pain consumed him. He fumbled to remove the burgundy bandana which hung around Nelson's neck then placed the well-worn cloth in his inside jacket pocket. "You'll always be with me. Always." He put his hand to his chest and closed his eyes. The pain seared in his heart. He steadied his breath and, as he did, his sadness turned to fury. "I'll find those bastards, Nelson. I'll hunt them down." He couldn't bring himself to look at Nelson's body again.

Hot anger was burning within him. He stormed over to the guards' table and smashed his fists into it. "You bastards!" he shouted. The wood cracked in two. He picked up the splinters and hurled them into the wall. He wanted to rip the guards apart. Tear them limb from limb. Instead, he cocked his pistol and shot their lifeless bodies. The pain engulfed him. He'd had hope. Hope that he could save Nelson. Hope that they could go on many more adventures together before their time was up. It wasn't meant to end like this. Crow sobbed. His old bones ached. His heart torn into pieces. "What would Nelson do? What would he advise me?" he said to himself through shaky breath.

"He'd tell you to pull yourself together!" a voice came from behind Crow.

Crow unsheathed a dagger and his final pistol and pointed in the direction of the voice. "Well, if it isn't the captain of the guard himself," Crow said. His tears dried in an instant at the sight of Relocke.

"Don't shoot, Crow! I'm alone and I need to talk to you," Relocke said and put his hands up. He walked closer to Crow. "I'm not here to kill you. I'm unarmed so please lower your weapon."

Crow didn't flinch. He wanted to hear from this bastard. "Where's the boy?"

"Gone!" Relocke said.

"I can see that. This doesn't make any sense. Why are you here unarmed?"

"Because I think we can help each other out," Relocke replied.

"Go on." Crow lowered his pistol and dagger but kept them ready.

"We both want the person who did this to hang," Relocke said.

"I have other ideas for them," Crow replied.

"Either way, we want them to pay. My men are dead, your man too."

"Yes." Crow avoided looking in the cell again.

"And it just so happens I know for a fact that Johnny Ives was responsible. And he has taken Mr. Carver with him."

A blinding fog of rage came over Crow again. He wanted to scream at the top of his lungs. To smash everything in sight. "That smug prick!" he said through clenched teeth.

"Yes, he is rather."

Crow looked at Relocke's face. He couldn't trust him. He was another Johnny Ives type. A pretty prick who would turn on you in a heartbeat.

"I was thinking that since I'm a few men down, as you clearly are, we could hunt down Ives together?"

"I can do that myself." Crow tapped the barrel of his pistol on his leg. He grew more and more agitated by the second.

"I want vengeance just as much as you do, Crow. I may be the captain of the guard but I'm still human."

"Debatable," Crow muttered to himself. "Why'd you need me?"

Relocke moved away from the door and leaned his back against the wall. He folded his arms and smirked. "Well, you probably have a little more insight as to where Johnny might be. Plus, if I help you out with this, you'll owe me. And once you have your crew back, that could be pretty handy to me."

Crow considered Relocke's words for a moment. His eyes wandered to the cell where Nelson's body lay. He could hear Nelson's voice as if he were speaking to him one last time. "Fine," Crow replied and stuck out his hand.

"Really? Excellent. You won't regret it at all, my good man." Relocke stepped forward and took Crow's hand. Crow gripped Relocke's hand tight and pulled him in and onto his blade. He dug the sharp steel dagger deep into his stomach. "I'm a pirate not a fool," he whispered into Relocke's ear as he withdrew the blade and stuck it in again and again. He watched as the life drained from his eyes. Crow expected to feel something but he was numb. He dropped Relocke's body and walked away. Don't look back, he told himself as he touched the burgundy bandana stuffed in his pocket and walked down the hallway with vengeance in his heart.

MOLLY WEAVER

The overpowering scent of pipe smoke hit Molly's nostrils and the lanterns flickered as she followed Roy into the room. His office was the ideal place to do business: windowless, discreet and away from prying eyes.

"Has anyone claimed the bounty on Jane yet?" Molly asked and sank into the hole-filled chair opposite Roy's desk. Her eyes hovered over the papers strewn across the wooden top.

"Not yet. Although I heard that she has gone missing, so might only be a matter of time now." He rubbed his hands together. "Joy's a fine one, I have every faith in her."

"Good. And who have they appointed in her absence?" Molly said.

"Not sure actually. Otis, what's the new merc crew leader called?"

Otis sat in the corner of the room and fumbled with a brown leather satchel.

"Otis?" Roy said.

"Otis!" Molly yelled and waved her arm to catch his

attention. Her temper teetered on the edge of explosion with all the recent events.

"Wha?" He looked up. "You want me? I'm sat on my bad side." He pointed to his left ear and grinned.

"Tell me again why we use a half deaf informant?" Molly muttered to Roy.

"I heard that, Molly!" Otis shifted in his seat.

"Of course you did." Molly rolled her eyes.

"Who's in charge at Jane's camp now that she's missing?" Molly said.

"Last I heard it was Thunder," Otis replied.

"That can't be his real name, what's his real name?"

Roy hopped off of his chair and went over to a small cupboard. He pulled out a well-used black book and waved it in the air.

"What's that?" Molly watched as Roy tossed the book on the desk and sat himself back down.

"This is one of my favorite things." He thumbed through the pages. "It's a who's who of everyone in Nassau."

"Oh." Molly leaned back in her chair and folded her arms. Sweat formed around her hairline. "Everyone in there?" Molly said.

"Almost." Roy carefully turned through the pages muttering as he went. "A... Bob... C... no... no." He took his time and eventually reached the last page. "And... nope! That one isn't in there."

He snapped the book shut and stroked at his chin. "No Thunder."

He looked over to Otis who continued to fumble with the satchel. "What's his real name, Otis?"

"I don't remember. Wait... actually..." Otis looked up in thought and scratched at his chin. "Nup, it's gone." He shrugged and tipped the contents of his bag onto the couch.

Roy swiped the air in annoyance. "Anyway, not to worry. Jane is gone and this Thunder character is in charge."

"Should be good for us." Molly put her hands behind her head and leaned back. "It's taken years to convince Vella to attack and now Jane's out of the picture I can't even see it being difficult."

Roy scrunched his face up and squirmed in his seat. "Now, don't take offense to this, but they're still highly skilled killers. Don't underestimate them, Molly. Even without Jane, I think they'll put up a fight," Roy said.

"Of course. I've got a new weapon that should help though." Molly grabbed her satchel. "Want to see it?"

"Yes!" Roy clapped his hands and rubbed them together. "You're really very talented."

"Thank you, Roy." Molly produced a clam shell out of her brown leather satchel.

"A clam?" Roy laughed.

"On first inspection." Molly opened the shell and placed the rough brown and white-flecked halves on Roy's desk. "You see how there're two powders in here?" She pointed to the halves in turn.

"Yes." Roy nodded and squinted. "One black, one white."

"That's right. Well, once you press the two halves together..." Molly clapped her hands and Roy jumped in his seat. "Boom! They react and create an explosion, three times the size of a cannon."

"Three times?" Roy jerked away from the clam.

"Don't worry, this one isn't active. It's just to show you. The white powder is just salt."

"Ah, thank goodness." Roy closed his mouth and let his shoulders sink.

"Plus, you have to smack the two halves together. A little tap won't do it. I thought we could lay them as traps on the battlefield. And when people run over them, they'll explode!" Molly snatched the clam up and tucked the shell back in her bag.

"Impressive." Roy stuck out his bottom lip and nodded.

"I've named it the clam bam! What do you think?"

"Oh... well, it's very clever, Molly." Roy leaned into the desk. "Though I'm not sure about that name." Roy tipped his head back and gave a laugh.

"I like it. It's catchy." Molly wished she'd never asked.

"It's your invention, Molly. I couldn't do it!" Roy laughed.

Exactly, Molly thought to herself. No one in Nassau could. She pulled out a handful of letters from her satchel and threw them on the desk. "Usual rate?"

"Never changes... for you." Roy scooped them up and smiled.

Molly leaned over and dropped the reale into his hand. "Thank you, Roy."

"I meant to ask, did you find Isaac?" Roy opened his drawer and dropped the coins in.

"I did, or rather someone else did the hard work for me. He's being brought to Vella's as we speak."

"Very good. I am puzzled as to why you want him though?"

"You're not the only one." Molly stood up. "It's important not to take everyone on face value, you know."

"Yes, I suppose."

"He has a mind for strategy. We play chess."

"Oh?"

"I'm good but he wins every time, without fail. I figure he can help us plan our attack on Jane's camp... and win."

"Weaver!" Otis blurted and held his finger in the air.

Molly shook her head. "That's my last name, Otis, you know that."

"No! Not you, Molly." Otis sat with his repacked satchel on his knee. "I'm talking about Thunder. His last name is Weaver."

"Thunder Weaver?" She paused for thought. It was a common enough name in Nassau.

"No, Daniel Weaver. That's his real name. People just call him Thunder."

Molly's eyes grew wide and searched the blank space which flashed before her. "That's my Daniel! It has to be!"

"I don't know who your Daniel is but that's Thunder's real name."

Molly's heartbeat thumped rapidly, the noise pounding in her ears. She threw her satchel onto Roy's desk. "I need something to write with."

Roy hurried. He grabbed a stick of graphite and a piece of paper from his drawer.

"I have to stop what I've started!" Molly shouted. Her hands shook as she wrote.

"What do you mean?" Roy asked. "Who's your Daniel?"

"It's my son, Roy," Molly yelled as she frantically wrote. "I can't go to war with him. I can't have him killed. I thought I'd lost him. I can't do this again!" Molly folded the paper. "Add this to the pile. I have to go!"

"Okay." Roy didn't move. Molly could see the shock on his face as she rushed out the room. She slammed the door behind her and ran down the street in the direction of Vella's house. She slowed her run to a fast walk as she grew out of breath. "What the hell was I thinking? Idiot!"

"Molly?" a passer-by said.

"Not you!" Molly yelled.

The small man shrank back into himself. "I just wanted to buy..."

"Not now!" Molly yelled and stomped up the street.

She'd often wondered if Daniel worked for Jane. She had a sense he was still in Nassau. Her heart told her so, but he clearly didn't want to be found. Why hadn't Otis made the connection? Why had he never mentioned this until now? Until it was too late!

"Dammit, Otis!" Molly huffed as she quickened her pace. She turned a corner and onto the rough dirt road which led to Vella's. Her legs couldn't keep up with her mind. She passed field after field of palms. Finally, her house came in sight.

"That's her!" a voice said from behind.

Molly's knees almost buckled. She wasn't expecting this. "Get off me!" she screamed, enraged as two men tackled her legs. They had grabbed onto them like a small child would. Molly tried to kick herself free and as she did, fell to the ground. Her head hit a rock on the rough path and blood spilled out. Molly put her arms out in front of her and tried to push her body up. A rock flew into the back of her head. More rocks followed. Her veins rippled with rage. She knew she was about to lose it and unleash her wrath on whoever had dared to mess with her. It would be the last time they did.

Despite the dizzying pain in her head, she used all of her strength to rise up. She pummelled her fists into the two idiots still clinging to her legs, over and over, until they fell silent. She stumbled a few steps forward before a heavy blunt object cracked across the back of her head. Her face smacked down into the dirt once again. She looked around. Pairs of boots surrounded her, including one within a wooden post for a leg.

"Gotcha! You old cow," the voice said.

Molly recognized that spiteful twang.

"Don't stop now, boys! She needs to pay."

"I knew it was a mistake leaving you alive, Jacky Boy," Molly uttered through a mouthful of sand.

"It was. Got me a new leg though. Weren't gonna stop me," Jacky Boy said.

Molly couldn't believe her bad luck. She needed to get to Vella's place like it was yesterday and now this disgusting pig of a man (and his no doubt equally disgusting friends) were about to take her down. Did she have anything in her bag that could help? She shuffled her hands underneath her body.

"What we gonna do with her, boss?" a man's voice said.

"Hold her down. Somebody get the rope!"

Molly's hand struck her bag. She dug her hand in and landed on a pouch. Perfect. She gave the small bag a shake and threw it up in the air.

Boom!

An explosion carried through the air. Pairs of boots scurried away.

"Quickly!" Jacky Boy screamed. He wobbled away. "Get the net!"

Molly panicked. It was now or never. She needed to make a break for it. The explosive noise had startled them but it wouldn't cause any damage. She pushed her body up and charged through them like a bowling ball striking skittles.

The crew were too frightened to grab her. They didn't want to end up like Jacky Boy. Molly ran toward Vella's hoping no one would pull a pistol on her. She could hear her blood pumping in her ears. She'd never run so fast in her life. Footsteps followed. The men were coming. If she got close enough to Vella's, the girls might see her. They might come help.

"Now!" Jacky Boy screamed from the distance.

A heavy net pelted her back and stopped her in her tracks. She scrambled to break free of the rough rope but its four weights in each corner made it difficult.

Five men rushed Molly, thick ropes in hand. They tried to push her over but it didn't work. She widened her stance and stood slightly hunched with the net draped over her. "I'll snap your fucking necks, each and every one of you!" Molly flew into a rage. She stuck her hands through the net and grabbed the two men in front of her. She lifted them off the ground and threw them aside. "Come on! Is that all you've got!" Another man rushed at her and Molly met him with a fist to the face. The remaining men backed off and yelled back to Jacky Boy.

"Boss?"

"Fine!" Jacky Boy yelled. "Do it!"

Click.

Molly braced for the impact of the bullet.

"Fuck you all!" Molly closed her eyes as hot pain flooded her calf. She'd never been shot before. She toppled over and clutched at her leg. A wounded leg wouldn't stop her. She wasn't far from Vella's. She'd drag herself there if she had to. She heaved her body up the path and heard Jacky Boy laughing.

"How does it feel, you old bitch?"

The words rang in Molly's ears as her arms suddenly stopped working. Her vision faded to black and the world went dark.

ISAAC CARVER

TWO WEEKS LATER

Isaac leaned into the wall and admired the fine cut beige stone. Vella's house had not been at all what he expected. It seemed better suited to a wealthy family rather than a crew of man-hating killers. He often wondered how she'd acquired such a place but never dared to ask. "So fancy," he said to himself as he swayed and dripped a little amber liquid on his boots. "Whoops!" He fastened his pants back up and could have sworn someone whispered his name. It happened again. He turned around but couldn't see anyone. "Yes?" he said to no one.

"It's me! Come here!" a voice came from behind a thick hedge.

"Pino?" Isaac said and stepped cautiously toward the bushes. He had been drinking an awful lot of late and it was possible no one was really there. Isaac stumbled toward the glossy green foliage only to find a bedraggled Popino crouched among the leaves.

"What are you doing here?" Isaac asked.

"I could ask you the very same question." Pino glared.

"Pino, what's wrong? You look wrecked!"

"You know exactly what's wrong. How could you steal from me after all these fucking years?" Popino's hands shook as he reached for his blade.

"It's not what you think. I'm sorry, Pino, I had to." Isaac's heart twisted into knots.

"And now Rose is gone, Isaac! She's fucking gone! Vella took her!"

"What? News to me."

Popino's bottom lip quivered. He leapt forward and grabbed Isaac by the scruff of the neck. He pulled him in close and looked him straight in the eye. "Have you seen her? Do you know anything? You have to tell me!"

"I don't know anything! No one's mentioned Rose. Pino you must believe me!" Isaac shook his head. It had been two weeks since Isaac had been brought to Vella's place. They'd plied him with more rum than he could dream of, and he had even been given a fancy title too. He was the 'Master Strategist', and for once in his life people actually listened to what he had to say. But this was news to him. He hadn't thought Vella would do something quite so despicable. Rose was just a child.

Popino loosened his grip. "I believe you." He put his head in his hands and sobbed. "Where is she Isaac? Where's my sweet girl?"

Isaac put his arm around his oldest friend. "I didn't know she was missing. I've just been here, oblivious. Now, tell me exactly what happened?"

"I owe Vella coin, a lot of it. I was meant to give her the coffer full but you took it!" Popino's eyes blazed. "How could you?"

"I'm so sorry. I was doing it for... for us. I'll explain later, keep going."

"Vella gave me time to find the coin but said she'd kill

Rose if I didn't have it by the week's end. But when I got home later that day, I found Clara dead and Rose gone. Clara's boy too! He's gone!"

"Maybe they saw what happened to Clara then ran off and hid somewhere? That's what I'd do," Isaac said.

Popino shook his head, his eyes wet with tears. "No, there was a note which said I have your daughter and you'll have to pay to get her back!"

Isaac put his hand to his chest.

"And then Joy said she'd help me but she was meant to kill me and I've been waiting at Roy's."

"What? Joy? Why was she going to kill you?" Isaac asked.

"She's working for Jane. I owe Jane coin too," Popino blurted out.

Isaac was speechless. He thought about the past two weeks at Vella's. He hadn't seen or heard any signs of a child.

"Joy never came back," Popino added. "I got sick of waiting, so I came to find Rose myself."

"Pino, I don't think Rose is here. I've been here for a while; I would've seen her. Vella never mentioned anything. I mean not that she'd tell me, but something would have slipped." Isaac pulled out his flask and held out the weathered vessel to Popino.

Popino gulped down a few mouthfuls.

"We're going to attack Jane's camp tomorrow."

"What?" Popino said.

"Maybe Jane's got her?" Isaac said.

"I guess it's possible," Popino said and wiped some spilled rum from his chin. "Why are you even here?"

"I was about to be hung. Molly said I was good at

chess, so Vella wanted me here and yeah, here I am. Turns out I'm a master strategist!"

Popino looked at Isaac. His eyes vacant. "You were about to be hung?"

"Yes. Honestly, Pino, I don't know what I'm doing, but they seem happy with my plans," Isaac said.

"You have to help me, Isaac. You have to make things right. If that coffer wasn't gone, I wouldn't be in this mess!"

"Well, that's not strictly true." Isaac cocked his head to the side in disagreement.

"Fine! It's both of our faults. My own stupidity."

"I didn't even know you were in debt. I would never have done what I did if I'd known." Isaac questioned himself. Was that a lie? Would he have? Maybe. He thought of Rose's sweet face. Guilt stabbed at his heart. "Anyway, I got your coin back!"

"Really?" Popino's eyes widened.

"Yes! Except Crow has it right now. You know, the pirate captain we stole the map from all them years ago?"

"What? Why on earth does he have it?" Popino said, his eyes wide in disbelief.

"We're friends now, he's going to keep it until we meet up again and then return it to you," Isaac said as if it were the most normal thing in the world.

Popino rubbed his palms over his face and pressed his fingers into his forehead. "So, the pirate captain we stole from now has my coin which I desperately need to get my five-year-old daughter back?" He threw his hands in the air. "Great. That's just great."

Isaac nodded.

"Are you out of your mind? Why would he give it back!" Popino shouted.

Isaac covered his mouth. "Ssh!"

Popino grimaced at the touch of Isaac's grubby hand on his lips.

"He will, alright. He keeps his word," Isaac said. He looked Popino in the eye. He'd never seen his friend so distraught. "We're going to come up with a plan, okay? Like old times. Together."

Popino nodded. "I'm all ears."

"Great. Well..." Isaac looked around. "Who knows your face here?"

"Vella. Oh! And the door girl. She loves me."

"Georgia?"

"Maybe? Has a lip ring. Can't get past that to be honest."

"Okay, well, we can't go in through the front door then. The back door leads to the kitchen and the cook isn't my biggest fan for reasons I'll refrain from going into right now. So that's out."

"What about a window?" Popino said.

"Yes! Maybe. Follow me! We'll have a look around and see if they're any clues that suggest Rosy was here," Isaac said and checked around for prying eyes. He motioned for Popino to follow. "Stay close behind me." The pair scampered along the edge of the house. The grass was slippery underfoot but quiet at least. They arrived at a half-open window. "Stay back here, I'll check it out." Isaac ran ahead and poked his head through the small gap. He turned to Popino and waved for him to join. "This is much easier than I thought. I really don't think Rose is inside the house, Pino, but maybe you'll notice something I don't."

"We have to try." Popino placed his hands on the windowsill and jumped. He twisted and landed sitting on the sill edge, his legs dangling down. He reached his hand for Isaac to join.

"Shift over, I'll do the same." Isaac clambered in the window a little less gracefully. He joined Popino. The room looked identical to every other in the house. Beige walls and wood-trimmed naval paintings. Grand but odd, Isaac thought. It certainly didn't suit Vella, it was as if she was trying to be someone else. He'd often wanted to ask about her choice of decor, but she wasn't the most approachable of people, and he certainly got the feeling she wasn't too happy with the arrangement of him being there. "What should I look for?"

"Anything—notes, paper, clothing," Popino said.

"Yeah, alright."

They rummaged around the room checking anything and everything. Isaac opened the door of a beautifully carved wardrobe. Inside hung heavy corseted dresses of all colors and fabrics. "Well, this is nice." He took one out and stepped into it. He pulled on the arms and patted down the train. "Pino, look." Isaac grinned and took a swig from his flask. "Am I beautiful?" He waggled his eyebrows in a suggestive manner.

"This is not the time to be joking around. My daughter is fucking missing and you're trying on dresses!" Popino paced the room, his eyes frantically searching for clues. "You know, you and Joy are actually perfect for one another. She's just as... as thoughtless!"

"Ouch." Isaac brushed his hands over the ruffles on the dress. Popino's words stung. "Well, I guess that's what happens when you come from nothing and have no one." Isaac spun around in the dress and the skirt billowed out.

"That's a very fair point," Popino said and stifled a smile.

"See? I gotcha, little smile." Isaac stopped twirling. "Pino, let's just focus on finding Rose. That's what matters." Isaac shuffled over to the wardrobe and peered in. He riffled through the contents. "Nup, nothing much." He got down on his knees and searched the dusty base. His hand struck a few rat droppings and some rags heaped in the corner. He pulled at the pile. "What do we have here?" Isaac retrieved a small brown chest, similar to that of a coffer but a little more sturdy. He unhinged the latches and flipped the lid back to reveal a sea of golden coins.

Popino ran over and joined Isaac. "Perfect! This is perfect. How much is in there?" They took out their pouches and were about to scoop in the glinting, golden beauties when the door kicked open.

"What the fuck is going on in here," a booming voice startled the pair.

Isaac stuffed the chest under the skirt of his dress. "Johnny! I haven't seen you all day."

"What the fuck are you doing in that dress, Isaac? Who's this?"

"Um." Isaac threw his arm around Popino whose hand was moving toward his blade. "I brought a boy home."

Johnny scrunched up his face. His lips curled up and the corners of his mouth pulled down. "What's with the dress?"

Isaac shrugged. "Felt like a change."

"Don't play stupid with me. If it weren't for Molly you wouldn't even be alive right now."

"Aw, don't be like that," Isaac said and turned to Popino. "I'm the favorite you see."

Johnny marched over and grabbed Isaac by the arm. "Get up!"

"No need to be like that." Isaac pulled away from Johnny's grip and stood up. He carefully pushed the chest back toward Popino with his foot and came eye to eye with Johnny. "They need me. Remember that."

"They don't need your friend though." Johnny unholstered his pistol.

The clink of coins tumbling followed as Popino lumped doubloons into two pouches as quickly as possible.

Johnny pushed Isaac aside. "Are you stealing?"

Isaac acted fast, throwing the dress off and over Johnny's head. "Run, Pino!"

Johnny squirmed and shot blindly but Popino fled out of the window. A barrage of footsteps running down the hall followed. The door flung open. Isaac leaned on the wall and tried to look as casual as possible.

Johnny finally untangled himself free of the dress. "You!" He clenched his jaw and stormed over to Isaac.

"Not so fast, Johnny! Turn around. Hands where we can see them," Georgia said. The lip-ringed door-greeter stood with four other women by her side, all with muskets in hand, raised and pointed at the pair.

"I caught him." Isaac pointed to Johnny. "He was trying to steal from the chest, and I stopped him with the dress."

"That's a lie!" Johnny said.

"You know what these pirates are like. Can't help themselves," Isaac said.

"Hands on your head, Johnny," a dark-haired woman said.

"It was him, you fools!" Johnny pointed to Isaac who was doing his best to side-step over to the window unnoticed.

Isaac put one hand on the window ledge and tried to peer out over his shoulder.

"Why would I steal from you ladies? I'm one of you," Johnny said.

"You may fight with us but you'll never be one of us," a woman with thick, dreadlocked hair piled on top of her head said.

Isaac leapt onto the window ledge ready to hurl himself out.

"Not so fast, boy." Vella stood before him on the outside of the window with a flintlock pistol pointed at his head.

He wondered if he could run past her, unharmed? Probably not. "I was just getting some fresh air, bit heated in there."

"Back inside!" Vella said.

Isaac nodded and swung his legs back into the room. This time all musket barrels were on him. Johnny smiled that smug, sickening grin of his.

Isaac jumped down from the window ledge as Vella followed him in. She grabbed the scruff of his neck and held the pistol to his temple.

"I just saw this one's friend running away. And not just any friend... Popino Beltrame." Vella pulled Isaac into her. "He was meant to be dead!" Vella yelled.

"Surprise," Isaac said and choked a little as Vella increased her grip. She let go and he stumbled forward.

"Sorry about that, Johnny." She wandered over to the chest and picked it up. "You've had your use, Isaac." Vella walked to the door. "Girls, come with me." She looked back. "Johnny, he's yours. Do whatever you want with him."

Johnny looked at Isaac with a wicked smile. "Excellent."

THUNDER

The breeze picked up and swept through the training camp grounds. Storm clouds blew in and the sky grew dark.

"Alright, you filthy lot!" Thunder yelled. He stood tall with his chest puffed out and biceps bulging. In one hand he held a well-polished saber, and in the other a spear large enough to skewer two people at a time.

"We're gonna take down that bitch! And her pathetic crew!" Thunder raised his spear for emphasis. He hadn't mastered speeches like Jane. He usually just yelled at people. "They're vermin!"

Jane Hatch's crew of elite mercenaries stood in rows before him. It was hard to believe she had disappeared without a trace. Some had questioned if she had abandoned them and hidden herself away, but most believed she'd been captured at the hands of Vella, or worse still, Thad.

Thunder looked to Anna and Jose who grinned as they sharpened their blades. Jose shot him a wink and for once the gesture didn't annoy him. Today they were all one.

United in their goal for victory and their desire to rescue their fallen leader.

"Vermin! Vermin!" Jose chanted. Everyone joined in as they clutched their weapons of choice tight, ready for action at any moment.

"Vella has already reached our gate so we're only moments away. Does everybody remember the plan?" Thunder shouted.

The crowd erupted in cheer. "Kill the bitch!" one man piped up. Laughter followed.

Thunder raised his hand. "Now remember, they're no match for us, but they still won't go down without a fight. We're on our land. We know our land."

"Yeah!" The crowd cheered in unison.

"Now, you must only retreat to the mansion if injured. Otherwise, you stay and fight. If you're tired, I don't care. If you run out of ammunition, kill 'em with your hands! We are not cowards! We are the finest fighters in Nassau!" Thunder nodded. "Brothers and sisters of the white fox, are you ready?"

"Yes, sir!" The crowd yelled back, their eyes full of fire, ready to decimate Vella and her people.

Despite his rousing speech, fear infiltrated Thunder's heart. He hadn't slept in days. He couldn't. Everything now fell on his shoulders. Jane would never abandon them. She'd worked long and hard to build her crew of the finest mercenaries in Nassau and was proud of it, but her disappearance really was a mystery. He couldn't figure out how someone had kidnapped her right under their noses. Then there was Joy. She'd vanished that day too. He'd wondered if it was her? Had she kidnapped Jane? Was she working for Vella? Sure, it was possible, but something told him it wasn't so simple. He pushed such thoughts from his mind and turned to the main gate. He held his hand up to block the glare from the cloud and narrowed his eyes to a squint. A sea of women swarmed at the gate's edge and he assumed more marched behind them. He looked back to the mansion and raised his hand in signal to the two men positioned by the front door. They waved back.

"Now remember," Thunder said, "that hill over there." He pointed behind the bunker where the new recruits would normally sleep. Behind it a thick row of trees blocked the mansion and grounds from the outside world. And further beyond that sat a high mound where Thunder had positioned an injured merc to keep watch. "If there's a green cloud, we're in the clear. If it's red, there's an ambush. Remember, you need your eyes everywhere." Thunder dug his spear in the ground and raised the blade in his other hand high above his head. "Weapons at the ready!"

The merc crew put their heads low and held their weapons high. "Charge!" Thunder yelled. Everyone ran toward the gate to the outside world. Arrows came whistling in. "Don't look back! Push on!" he yelled as screams of fallen mercenaries filled his ears. Thunder searched for the source of the arrows. Their accuracy suggested they couldn't have come from the gate. "There!" he yelled and pointed to the bushes behind the bunker where two women hid amongst the foliage. Anna and Jose hurled a blade a piece in their direction. Screams followed.

"Yes!" he shouted over the battle carnage. His heart soared with fear and pride. Pistol shots and clangs of blades rang in his ears. Hordes of Vella's women hurtled toward them wielding axes and pistols. Their battle screams deafened him.

Thunder ripped his spear from the ground, flipped it to horizontal and charged into the crowd. He impaled two at a time. Only someone with his strength and stature could manage such a feat. He pulled out the bloodied implement and struck another woman down with a slash of his saber to her neck. A surge of adrenaline shot through him "Yes!" he roared. Chaos surrounded him and it satisfied his soul. He repeated the battle plan to himself as he charged forward. Draw the fighting group in tight. Make sure all Vella's people were as close to the black line as possible. Then fire the cannons. They had drawn the black line in the middle of the training camp long ago in the event something like today should happen. Thunder couldn't take any credit for the plan. Jane had drawn it up long ago. She was a master of strategy.

Up ahead Thunder eyed a large wooden monstrosity being pushed toward them. A heavy triangular structure something of the likes Thunder had never seen before. At the very top stood Vella. Her body looked to be shielded by a sheet of blackened iron, like something from a ship. She held a long rifle and fired into the crowd. She shot and reloaded over and over. Jane had told him she was quick, but he had never seen anyone with the ability to reload at such a pace. Plus, the vantage point she had was genius. At differing points in the structure stood more rifle wielding women. They too fired into the crowd of mercenaries, but their shots were haphazard.

Out of nowhere a short woman with a mass of dreadlocks ran at him. He stabbed her in the gut with his spear with minimal effort. He looked over to the mansion. The two men positioned at the door had vanished. "Dammit!" Thunder said as Vella continued to unleash her fire on the crowd. He would have to take care of her himself.

"Fall back!" Thunder shouted and ran back toward the black line drawn in the camp's ground. They needed to draw her in. If they retreated, Vella would only push harder. Those that remained ran back to join him. They looked around the field. Carnage surrounded them. The sky rumbled and raindrops fell from the stormy sky. Heavy drops landed on his back and ran down his shirt. The mercenaries hovered low to the ground. "We're winning! Might not feel like it, but we are. We'll draw them back here. Obliterate them!"

He turned and addressed the group of civilians he had recruited at the last minute. They were a ragtag bunch he found in the center square, but they could hold a weapon and right now, that's what mattered. They stood underneath the cannons, hands over their ears. "You ready?" Thunder yelled. They nodded. It didn't look like they could hear much, but they'd get the idea once Vella and her crew came hurtling at them.

The ropes which heaved the bizarre wooden structure Vella had been on top of stopped moving and her crew climbed down and hurtled toward them. "Retreat! Retreat!" Thunder ran to the rear of the training camp's ground. His mercs followed.

Vella and her hordes of women ran at them screaming. They hacked and slashed with their axes. With no time to reload, pistols were out of the question. Thunder threw a small bag into the air and shot. A cloud of blue mist erupted. "Fire!" he yelled and pointed his saber toward Vella.

Cannon balls whizzed through the air, aimed perfectly to decimate anyone on that line. He watched as her crew smashed into the mud, their limbs crushed and bodies broken. Cannon balls continued to whirl through the air. He looked for Vella but she had vanished.

The smoke cleared. Thunder saw Vella glaring in his direction, clearly furious. She threw a bag into the air with such force that it disappeared from sight. In one seamless move she withdrew a pistol and shot at it. The bag exploded and a cloud of heavy purple smoke filled the air. It must be a signal, Thunder panicked. Were they about to get ambushed? He looked to the mound but saw nothing. The purple smoke hung thick in the air. Vella's crew stood with confidence and reloaded their weapons. Thunder looked at his mercs. They knew what to do. "Let's fucking kill her!" Thunder shouted. His heart soared with pride as his people erupted in cheer and stood by his side.

ISAAC CARVER

Isaac's head bobbed onto his chest as the cloth hood disappeared. The white light flooded his eyes and temporarily blinded him. He blinked and looked up at the angry clouds rushing by.

"What the fuck is this?" Johnny slapped him in the face and waved a bag so close to his eyes that he couldn't see anything but the color of the cloth.

"If you stopped slapping me, I could maybe tell you," Isaac said and spat out the blood which had started to pool in his mouth.

"Don't play smart with me you, you good for nothing drunk!" Johnny said.

"Rum... don't remind me," Isaac muttered to himself. Raindrops pelted his swollen face. The stormy sky brought him comfort. It suited his mood. "Why haven't you just killed me then? If I'm good for nothing?" Isaac asked.

"Shut it!" Johnny replied and wiped a bloody knife on his pants.

Isaac didn't recognize this part of Nassau. There was a tall grassy mound either side of him. He assumed they were near Jane's place since that had been the plan. He recalled seeing something similar on the map they had made him pore over again and again. According to memory, there would be a row of trees beyond the mound which protected Jane's property. A high hill sat behind those trees which dipped to a small valley and then rose to another smaller hill and that seemed to be where they were right now.

He recognized a lot of the surrounding faces from the tavern and a couple from the explosion at the shack. A rough motley crew of men with plenty of scars, cutlasses in one hand and flasks of rum in the other.

A couple of men's bodies lay next to Isaac, their throats slashed.

"I said, what is it?" Johnny waved the bag at Isaac.

"Who were they?" Isaac asked and motioned with his head to the bodies.

"Jane Hatch's people, lookouts. They were carrying this bag." Johnny mushed the bag into Isaac's face. He really was the most unpleasant of men, and Isaac had come across more than his fair share.

Isaac withdrew his face. His bound wrists chafed. In fact, everything in his body hurt in some way or another. "Untie my wrists and I'll tell you."

Johnny held a knife to his throat. "How about I don't, and since I'm the one with the knife to your throat, you'd better fucking tell me."

Isaac wanted to spit in his face. He wanted to tell Johnny how stupid he was. How he should figure these things out for himself, but instead he decided he would play along and hope that he might somehow manage to break free.

"It's a—" Isaac said as pistol shots rang through the air.

A cloud of thick purple smoke erupted and spread across the gloomy sky.

"Whoa!" Johnny and his men all looked up. "That's our signal boys!"

Johnny tucked his blade back in his leather baldric and withdrew his sword. "Get ready!"

"That bag, it's a signal too!" Isaac said.

"What? Not now!" Johnny said.

"But maybe it will confuse them?" Isaac hoped it would do something, anything to escape this. Dragged into a battle with your hands tied behind your back. If Joy really was working for Jane maybe she'd save him? Something had to happen. This couldn't be it. Dead in a ditch. No treasure. No rum. Nothing.

Johnny tossed the bag into the air, whipped out his flintlock and shot it. A cloud of green smoke puffed out. "Best shot in Nassau." He smirked.

"Are you though?" a gruff voice came from on top of the high hill, followed by a wicked laugh.

All eyes shot to where the figure stood. They wore a long black captain's jacket which flapped in the wind and a three- cornered tricorn hat.

"Crow!" Johnny said.

"That's right, boys," Crow replied.

"Finally!" Isaac shouted.

"Shut the fuck up!" Johnny turned and kicked Isaac in the face. He rolled onto his side and lay still. He could make out Crow through Johnny's legs. He tasted that iron-metallic liquid once again as blood streamed from his nose. Don't mess it up Crow, please, please, please, he thought. Not this time.

"You were meant to be dead!" Johnny shouted as Crow slowly descended the hill.

"Maybe I am?" Isaac heard a voice similar to Crow's come from behind him.

"What the fuck?" Johnny backed away from Isaac. His men looked over their shoulders and did the same.

"You're looking the wrong way, Johnny," another voice came from the other side of the hill. Isaac blinked. More than one of Crow? He shook his head. Was he finally losing it? He counted. There were three men all slowly walking toward them who all appeared to be Crow! He couldn't believe his eyes.

"Wha... what's going on?" Walt stammered and panicked. Isaac recognized him from the shack explosion. He'd been frightened then but he looked petrified now.

"He's come back to haunt us!" Tim yelled. His bushy brows waggled frantically with each word. Isaac recalled he hadn't had the balls to pull the trigger on Crow that day. He was sure to regret that now.

The three versions of Crow laughed as they tossed the bags they carried at Johnny and his men.

"Shoot them!" Johnny shouted and fired ahead. Thick smoke erupted from the bags and formed a dense low-lying fog.

Isaac smiled as the thick gray smoke engulfed him.

"I have twenty doubloons to split for whoever wants to join me!" Crow said. His rough voice cut through the smoke. "And I've got an extra doubloon for whoever gives me Johnny." Crow's familiar maniacal laugh erupted from three different directions.

Johnny fumbled with his pistol. The thick smoke made it near impossible to reload. Isaac rolled himself over, dug one knee into the ground and maneuvered the other underneath him. He pushed himself up on his knees and wobbled to standing. He ran at Johnny, smashing his body into him. Johnny fell to the ground, startled. Isaac threw himself on top of the smarmy so-called captain and drove his elbows into his head with such force that Johnny's eyes fell shut.

"So, who's got Johnny?" Crow shouted. "Time's up!"

Storm clouds rolled in and the rain picked up again. The fresh breeze blew away the smoke and the three versions of Crow appeared in full sight. Isaac still couldn't believe his eyes.

"Crow! Here!" Isaac shouted. Johnny came to and Isaac pressed his elbows together and smashed them down into his face again. Johnny's eyes fell shut once more.

A hand grabbed his shoulder. "You did good, boy."

Isaac had never been more relieved. For the first time in a long time his hope returned. Hope that he would make it through another day. Hope that he wouldn't die in this ditch today and hope that he would taste another drop of sweet rum once again. A blade sawed at the rope around his wrists and released them. His arms ached and his shoulder blades crunched as he let his arms swing free. "How are there three of you?"

Crow handed Isaac his flask.

"Sweet rum!" Isaac took a gulp and peered through swollen eyes as Crow put his foot to Johnny's throat. The smoke had cleared, and he stared in disbelief as the two Crow lookalikes grabbed a couple of men trying to flee.

Crow towered above Johnny and increased the pressure on his neck. Johnny gasped as his eyes burst open.

"You should be dead," Johnny said and tried to pry Crow's boot from his neck.

"You wish!" Crow increased the pressure further. "I've

never met a man more despicable than you. Who'd turn on his own! Who'd kill his own!"

Johnny swished his head from side to side as if trying to catch the eye of someone to help.

"No one's going to save you now." Crow withdrew his dagger from his belt then changed his mind and tucked it back in. "For Nelson, you spineless rat!" Crow screamed as he pounded his fist into Johnny's face over and over.

Isaac sipped his rum and stared blankly at the brutal scene before him. Blood poured out from Johnny's busted nose. His mouth. His ears.

Crow kept going. "You killed him! You!" Crow raised his fist, his eyes filled with tears.

Rain bucketed down around them. Isaac couldn't move. He just stared in a trance as life disappeared from Johnny's body.

The splash of pelting cold raindrops on his face snapped him out of it. "Crow," Isaac said.

Crow raised both fists in the air and let out a scream. He brought them down and Johnny stopped moving.

Isaac placed his hand on Crow's shoulder. "Stop, he's gone."

Crow hung his head and gave a soft nod. He looked up at Isaac glassy-eyed.

"Help me up, would you?" Crow held out his swollen blood-drenched hand.

"Of course." Isaac pulled him to standing. "Do I get the extra doubloon?" Isaac raised his eyebrows and gave a small laugh. "So, who were those other Crows?"

"That's for me to know. Stick with me long enough and you'll learn a trick or two, boy," Crow said.

"And the smoke, it worked! You finally got it to work!" Isaac looked at the old captain's weathered face. He looked exhausted and beaten but his eyes crinkled as he gave Isaac a brief smile.

"We've still business to take care of, boy. Ready your weapons," Crow said.

Isaac looked around. The motley crew of men surrounded them.

"We're with you, Captain," a man with ragged, ginger hair and a bushy beard spoke up.

The men placed their weapons on the floor in a show of respect.

Crow's doppelgangers dragged two men before them. "These two tried to escape," one said.

"Tim, Walt, it's been a while. Should have killed me back at the shack when you had the chance." Crow raised his pistol and shot Tim in the forehead. Blood gushed from his wound into his bushy eyebrows and beard. His body slumped to the ground. Walt dropped to his knees. "I'm sorry, Crow. I had no choice. I didn't do it, did I?"

"There's always a choice." Crow raised his pistol and fired. "You know, boys..." He looked around at the faces of the men he'd known for so many years. Isaac could see the fear in their eyes. "I didn't use to be a violent man." He smirked. "Well, not unless I had to be, but it was hard, hard to keep that down, that rage." He stretched out his hands and looked at them. "My father always told me violence was the way and I've decided I tend to agree."

Isaac could see the fear written on everyone's face. No one wanted to be next. He leaned over to Crow and gave him a nudge. "He needs to go!" Isaac pointed to a man he recognized from the prison cell.

"Which one, boy?"

Isaac pointed to a haggard, black-toothed man. "He didn't stop Johnny from killing Nelson," Isaac said.

"Really? Well, that's the same thing in my book, Ricktor," Crow said. The men parted and Crow walked toward him. Ricktor turned and ran. "Coward," Crow said and fired his pistol into his back. Ricktor screamed and dropped to the ground.

"Anyone else?" Crow held his arms out and laughed. The men shook their heads and looked to the floor.

Isaac walked away and dusted himself off. He reached into his pocket to check the map was safe when his hand brushed the cards from Pont Neuf. His gaze fixed on the crow pecking at the dead. "Hmm." Isaac looked at the surrounding carnage. "Let's hope that was all she was right about."

POPINO BELTRAME

Popino tried his best to blend in. He'd dirtied his clothes and not washed in days. Volunteering for battle had been the last thing he wanted to do but it seemed like the only possible way to get onto Jane's property and up to the mansion unnoticed. He stayed in position along with the rest of the civilian crew. Thunder had ordered them to stay back until told otherwise.

He couldn't help but wonder if anyone would recognize him. He'd kept his business with Jane discreet over the years, and he hadn't shown his face for a while since he owed so much coin. Even so, it still pricked at his mind.

He winced as the cannons fired again and again. The scent of burnt gunpowder filled the air. He was sure he'd go deaf, stood back here, but he didn't have a choice. This was for Rose. He still couldn't believe he hadn't found her. He'd been so sure Vella had taken her but it didn't seem so. His heart told him she was still alive. He just didn't know where.

A sea of shots rang through the air. Popino started to

stuff some cloth in his ears when the man next to him gave him a nod.

"You..." The man looked around.

"What?" Popino rechecked his pistol and patted at the blade tucked in his belt. He carried several more of each. Thunder had given them their pick of weapons. He'd never seen so many.

"You with..." The man raised his eyebrows as if trying to signal something.

"Of course." Popino nodded and looked around to see if anyone else was looking at them. He had no idea what the man was talking about but figured he'd play along.

"Ah good, I think most of us are with... you know." The man got closer to Popino and held out a piece of what looked like a brown leather strap. "Have this, Thad says it'll give you that boost you need." The man tore off a strip from the leathery material with his teeth and chewed. "It's dried meat." Bits of the half gnawed blackened meat flew from his mouth as he spoke. "Thad says we're to protect him." He signaled with his head toward Thunder.

"Him?" Popino pointed to Thunder.

"Yeah, Thad's son. At least that's what I was told." The man stuck out his hand. "The name's Gil, who are you?"

"Popino," he said and flinched. He shouldn't have given his real name. "So that's Thad's son? Does he know?"

Gil shrugged.

Popino had never seen Thad but if this man was anything to go by, he'd be terrifying.

"You lot ready?" Thunder shouted.

Popino half ignored him and tried to figure out how he could get up to the house without being seen. He was starting to think that volunteering was a very bad idea.

"I heard Jane Hatch is missing. We think Thad's got her, but she hasn't said. Wants Vella next."

"She?"

"Ah, you know."

"Not really." Popino shook his head. "So, we're to protect Thunder but kill everyone else?"

"Pretty much." Gil grinned. His teeth filled with the gnawed meat. "He doesn't know it yet, but we're going to charge into action then try to capture him and bring him back to Molly." Gil cringed and cowered. "Bad habit. Thad. I mean Thad. Don't let her catch you saying that. You'll pay the price," he said, his eyes wild.

Popino couldn't believe his ears. Surely not, he told himself. This Gil was probably high off that weird meat.

Thunder stood off to the side out of earshot. He turned to them. "Now!" he screamed. His neck veins throbbed as if they were about to burst.

The surrounding men readied their flintlocks and blades.

"Let's fucking go!" Gil yelled. "Wooooo!" He laughed as he ran ahead and fired.

Popino followed along, though he wasn't laughing. He kept on high alert. Firing and reloading over and over as Vella's women came running at him. Cannonballs whistled over his head. The heavens opened and rain pelted down. The thick mud made it difficult to maneuver. A bag exploded mid air and covered the sky with purple smoke.

"Let's fucking kill her!" Thunder shouted and pointed his spear.

Popino looked to the wooden structure Vella had stood atop but it was now empty. She appeared from nowhere and continued to fire, over and over. Popino ran off to the side up a slight incline and kept low to the ground.

"Execute order sixty-six now!" the men from the supposed civilian crew shouted. Thad's men. Gil and his men turned their weapons on Jane's crew and shot. They shot whoever came before them. Jane's people. Vella's people. Popino looked to the mansion. It was too far away to make a run for it, though now would be the perfect time to look for Rose in there.

"Fuck!" Popino needed to hide, or he was sure to get killed. He watched as Thunder's crew of mercenaries crumbled and five men pounced on Thunder. Blood splattered on Popino's face as a man beside him copped a bullet to the face.

"March on!" Vella shouted. She was close, far too close. If she laid eyes on Popino, even for a second, he'd be gone.

Popino ran to a nearby tent. He crouched inside, out of sight. Footsteps and gunshots filled the air outside. "This was a fucking terrible plan," he said.

"Where's Johnny's men?" Popino overheard Vella. His heart jumped into his mouth.

Johnny's men? That guy who'd caught them at Vella's place. Oh great, another one who wants me dead. What should I do? I can't just hide in here forever.

"Fuck it," Popino said. He realized he didn't have any other option than to fight. He was fit, strong and a damn good shot. He'd take out Vella alone if he had to. And Johnny. That was it. He didn't care about the rest. He'd make them his aim and not stop until their bodies hit the ground.

He poked his head out of the tent and saw Thunder, trapped underneath a giant net with a mass of men holding him down. Dead bodies surrounded him. Vella had disappeared from sight. He had to free Thunder. They both wanted Vella out of the picture, and this was the way to do it.

He aimed his pistol at the men holding him and shot.

He reloaded, shot, reloaded, shot. One by one they fell limp on the muddy ground. Thunder stuck his hands out of the net and grabbed two by their throats. He squeezed until their bodies no longer moved.

Popino continued to fire from the tent's edge and then tucked himself back inside. It was the perfect spot, protected from the rain which hadn't let up and would have otherwise clouded his vision. Popino kept firing until the remaining few men fled, not wanting to face Thunder's wrath alone.

Thunder untangled himself from the net and looked around. He spied Popino and gave a nod.

Not many were left standing. Popino didn't want to come away from the tent. Vella was nowhere to be seen and he worried she might strike from any direction.

Thunder turned to the people firing the cannons. "One! More! Round!" he yelled. Cannonballs whizzed through the air and exploded, smashing apart any remaining fighters. Limbs flew in all directions as bodies smashed into the mud. The fire stopped and the ground fell eerily quiet. No more gun fire. Only cries of the fallen. Popino's ears rang with a high-pitched shrill sound. He still couldn't see Vella. Maybe they'd got her? Maybe she was dead?

Thunder walked out into the carnage. He stabbed his spear into bodies of those still breathing.

Popino had survived. He'd fucking survived this. He walked out, looking down at the surrounding bodies. Looking for Vella. He walked in Thunder's direction, stunned and deafened.

"We did it!" Popino said. His throat scratched from all the smoke.

"We won!" Thunder looked around. "Looks like we lost almost all of ours though." Thunder turned to Popino. "Thanks for helping me back there. Some of them must have been working for the other side. Name's Thunder." He stuck out his hand and gripped Popino's so tight that his fingers cracked.

"So, I hear. Did we get Vella?" Popino asked, still on edge.

"That's who I'm looking for." Thunder scanned the bodies and walked away from Popino. "Ha! Here she is."

"You!" Vella lay covered in blood, her arm twisted in the opposite direction to what it should be. Blood flowed from a wound to her upper chest. "Congratulations, you piece of shit." She spat toward Thunder.

"Good fight." Thunder lifted his spear about to strike it down.

"You, you killed my son," Vella said, her voice faint. She lifted a flintlock and shot at Popino. He flew backward with the impact. For a moment everything went numb. He felt nothing. Thoughts of Rose and Elizabeth flashed before his eyes. Then the pain came. It flooded his body.

"You bitch!" Thunder screamed.

Popino tried to speak but words didn't follow. Hot pain seared through his gut. His eyes wanted to shut. He wanted to sleep, for a very long time. He gave in and his vision of the world around him faded as thoughts of Rose skipping in their garden played over and over.

JANE HATCH

Jane's eyeballs throbbed as her lids fluttered open. Not again. She closed her eyes and took a deep breath. Another fucking cell. She thought someone would have come to rescue her by now, but then again, given the number of times they had moved her, nobody probably knew where to look.

As she pushed herself up to sitting, her hand slipped a little on the wet, sludge covered floor.

Jane had been alone up until this point but now in the far corner lay Joy, curled up, out cold. In the neighboring cell lay a huge beast of an individual. They faced the wall and looked to be asleep. Jane couldn't see much other than some blood splatter throughout their mop of curly, gray hair. She put her head in her hands. Her insides longed for a drink, just something to take the edge off. Even if Margaret were here she'd understand, she told herself. This was extreme circumstances. A familiar voice interrupted her thoughts.

"Shut the fuck up!" Jane recognized Leon's voice screaming in the hallway.

"Shut up, Reg, ya bastard!" Leon yelled.

"Prick," she muttered. She pushed herself to standing and pressed her head to the cell bars but couldn't make out much. She turned and looked to the small window at the top of the grimy wall. Maybe if she stuck her hand out someone might help. Maybe they'd then see who she was? She had no idea where she even was, but it was worth a try. She looked at Joy who lay disheveled and bruised, breathing softly. Jane tried to work out what she should do with her. If it wasn't for her, she wouldn't be in this mess in the first place, she thought.

"Wake up!" She gave Joy a shove with her boot.

Joy stirred. "Where am I?" She shielded her face with her arms. "Oh fuck." Joy scrambled to stand.

"Oh fuck indeed," Jane said. She wanted to be angrier than she was with Joy. "So, I finally get to speak to you."

Joy slid down the wall and crouched. Whatever they had given them had clearly knocked her around. "I nee... ded the coin, okay?" She slurred a little as she spoke.

"So I assumed. The bounty, you took it?" Jane said. She bit at her bottom lip and stood firm.

Joy nodded in reply.

Jane crouched and pressed her face close to Joy's. "I ought to tear you limb from limb but, quite frankly, I don't have the energy; I'm going to save it to get out of this hellhole," Jane said, her voice faint.

"And what makes you think... I won't try anything?" Joy smirked, her eyes still half shut.

Jane thrust her arm forward and grabbed Joy by the throat. "Because I could strangle you to death right now, but I'm choosing not to," Jane said through gritted teeth and smashed Joy into the wall. Joy's eyes burst open. "You had your chance. You blew it." Jane released her grip.

Joy gasped for air and frantically patted her pockets.

"They've taken all our weapons so don't waste your time." Jane sprang to her feet and stood over Joy with her arms folded.

Joy stared up at Jane. "My sister. I was doing it for my sister. Someone took her. Made her a slave." Joy let out a big breath. "There's a guy who knows who did it, and he'll tell me for thirty doubloons. There was twenty alone for bringing you in alive." Joy shook her head.

Jane remained silent. She couldn't deny she wouldn't have done the same. After all, her entire business revolved around killing people for money. Her hands were hardly clean. "Well, you were brave to even try. I didn't think anyone would dare take that bounty on me."

Jane tapped her hand on her folded arm. "You're a bit too impulsive though." She brushed at the wound on her neck. "Had to learn that lesson myself." Jane met Joy with a frown. "Tell me, did you even kill Popino?"

"No." Joy put her head down. "His daughter's gone, you know?"

"It doesn't surprise me. That slimy bastard owes coin all over the place."

"He's a charmer that one," Joy said.

"Don't fall for it." Jane folded her arms. Her lips pursed. "Look... I think we're stronger if we're together." Jane uncrossed her arms and extended her hand to Joy.

Joy stared at Jane as she returned the handshake.

"What?" Jane asked.

"I'm just shocked that you would forgive me so easily," Joy said.

"Who said anything about forgiveness? But I'll certainly forget... for now." Jane couldn't help but smile at Joy. She reminded her so much of her younger self. "This business isn't for everyone. You can hold a grudge but not to your own detriment."

Joy looked at Jane. "I can't believe how composed you are. How do you do it? How do you keep it together?"

Jane shrugged. "Who says I am?" She gave a wry smile. "Anyway…" She clasped her hands together as if hoping to find strength. "I think I know the man you speak of. Not the one who kidnapped your sister but the one who knows his identity."

"What? How?" Joy cocked her head to the side.

"He works for me. Name's Grimm, right?" Jane said.

Joy nodded.

"He told me about people coming to Nassau and stealing children. I wasn't sure whether to believe him. He's a bit of a… trickster. Talks a lot. It's hard to be sure what to believe with him, but he does know a lot of people so it's possible he has your information."

Jane reached into her inside pocket and handed Joy a small button-sized coin with a fox head and three notches scratched into it. "Show this to anyone who works for me and they'll do whatever you ask. They have to. Save you having to kill me to get your answers." Jane raised her eyebrows.

"I don't know what to say," Joy said and steadied herself on her feet.

"Just take it and help me get the hell out of here. I detest these places."

"I've never been in one," Joy said.

"Trust me, it's not somewhere you want to see again." Jane rubbed at her face with her palms. "Right, we've got to get out of here fast. I heard Leon screaming at someone before so he's still close by." Jane marched over to the window.

"I can't believe I ever trusted that fucker," Joy said.

"He had us both fooled." Jane shook her head and chewed at her lip. "Give me a foot up, I'll try to stick my hand out. Grab someone's leg or something. Maybe we can bribe them?"

"Sure." Joy rushed over and knelt down to give Jane a boost.

They both froze at the sound of voices.

"Put the girl in the cage. We'll sell her in Devil's Cay later," the voice said.

Jane and Joy looked at one another, their eyes wide in horror.

"Now, now, ladies. Don't be trying nothing here," Leon said as he walked into the room, a cup in his good hand and a piece of steaming hot bread sitting on his hook. He took a bite and chewed with his mouth open. "I'm glad you're finally awake. I missed ya."

"Fuck you!" Jane curled her fists into balls.

Leon smiled then took another bite of the bread. "You know, I still can't believe I managed to fool ya for so long." He took a seat and placed his cup on the table. "I mean, ya really trusted me. And you're normally so good at reading people. Ya pride yourself on your judgment. Jane Hatch, the famous mind reader."

Jane's face grew hot. She wanted to scream. She wanted to smash his head into that table. Tear that hook clean off.

"How many years have we been together?" Leon smirked.

"Fuck. You." Jane turned her back on him. She needed to think. To block out his drivel.

"And my beautiful Joy. Thank ya for setting this all up for me. I've been waiting years, but there was never a right time. Too risky. But then you came along and did half the work for me." He took another bite of the bread. "Never thought you'd be charmed by an old hook hand, but ya don't seem to be too picky." He shot Joy a wink.

Joy dusted herself off and stood at the bars. "You're very good, Leon. Had me going."

Jane watched as Joy pulled down her top a little and bent over. "Maybe we could be a team?" Joy shot him a wink back.

Leon stared as if mesmerized. "Nup, nah. Not falling for it!" Leon said.

"Don't waste your time on that no cocked waste of air, Joy," Jane said.

"Worth a try." Joy shrugged.

Jane paced the cell. "What is it you want?"

"Me?" Leon placed his hand on his chest. "I don't want for much, but The Boss on the other hand..."

Jane put her face as close to the bars as possible and eyed Leon's reactions. "And who's that? Who's your boss? Vella?"

"Pf, please. She's half cracked! I think she's slaying your people as we speak though, so not all bad."

"Is it Thad then?" Jane narrowed her gaze and homed in on Leon's face. "It's Thad, isn't it?"

"Wrong again! You're really not very good at this. Thad's right there." Leon pointed to the neighboring cell.

Jane stared at the huge, lifeless body. "No!" She covered her mouth. "I can't believe after all these years I'm finally looking at him."

"That's Thad?" Joy walked over to the other side of the cell and peered through the bars. "He's huge!"

"She," Leon corrected her. "Thad's a woman. Goes by the name of Molly. Not quite so intimidating, is it?" Leon laughed.

Jane glared in Leon's direction. "Makes sense. Of course Nassau is run by women." Jane chewed at her lip. "Still doesn't answer who you work for though?"

"The Boss."

"Their name is 'Boss'?" Jane asked.

"Yup." Leon took a sip of his drink. "Boss wants you all out of the picture. You, Vella, Thad." Leon rolled his eyes at the mention of the last name. "Can't believe we've pulled it off!"

"I wouldn't be so quick to celebrate," Jane said.

"Still feisty, even when you're locked up with no way out. Still got that spark, I always did admire that in ya." Leon looked into his cup. "And ya thought I was just a sad cripple."

"I wouldn't have hired you if I thought that," Jane said. She tried her best to stay calm as her eyes searched for a way out. Something. Anything. She looked back at Leon, sipping away with a smug grin plastered across his face. Every breath he drew infuriated her. Her temper flared. "Did you kill Margaret?" She knew the answer, but she needed to hear the words from him.

Leon gave a telling smile.

"How fucking could you!" Jane screamed. "You piece of fucking shit. She trusted you. She was nothing but kind. You should have kept her out of it." Jane grabbed at the cell bars and started to shake them. "Let me fucking out of here you, you..."

Jane struggled to stand as waves of sorrow flooded her body. She felt a hand on her shoulder.

"Save it." Joy caught her eye. "No cocked waste of air, remember?"

Leon stood up and tapped his cup against the bars. "Looks like I need a top up!"

Jane stuck her arms through and reached out to grab him. Leon dodged her grasp.

"Y'know. I've been working for The Boss for years. Slowly sabotaging ya." Leon reached into his baggy waistcoat and pulled out a flask. "Remember the raid on Nassau?" He took a sip and tried to speak but choked a little. "Few of ya best went missing then." Leon gave a nod.

Jane pulled at the bars, as if trying to pry them apart. He'd been under her nose all this time. She could have stopped him. She could have saved Margaret.

Leon took another sip from the flask and started to cough. "Phew, that... tastes awful." Leon winced.

"You're more fucked up than I ever imagined," Joy said and stood by Jane's side.

"I'll take that as a compliment. I mean, ya both kill people for a living too." Leon returned to his chair. "Business is business. The Boss wanted me to cause trouble for ya, so I did. He paid me. You also paid me. Nothing personal."

"It is fucking personal when you lie to me and kill my people!" Jane screamed. She dropped to the ground and unlaced her weighty black boot then hurled it through the bars. The boot hit Leon square in the face. He sat stunned.

Joy let out a laugh. "Ha! Good one."

"Well, well, well, quite the mouth on you. I didn't expect that." A tall man strode into the room. He wore a beautiful black captain's jacket and a striking red and black tricorn hat. In his hand he held an embossed black wood flintlock.

"And who the fuck are you?" Jane said.

"So feisty." He smiled revealing a missing front tooth. She eyed him as he paraded in front of her cell with a swagger in his stride.

He sported the confidence of a far better looking man. Jane got the impression he thought himself charming, but in truth he came off as nothing but creepy and smug.

"I'm the one you've been hearing about. The Boss." He turned to face her.

"The Boss of what? Bunch of bitches?" Jane waved her finger in the direction of Leon.

"That's funny." His laugh quickly turned into a sneer as he leered through the cell bars. "You're both very easy on the eye, aren't you?"

"She's not with me. Leave her out of this," Jane said and pointed in Joy's direction.

"I've been trying to get you for years, you know," The Boss said.

Jane wracked her brains. Did she know this man from somewhere? There didn't look to be anything familiar about him. She noticed a gold snake pinned to his jacket lapel. What family did it belong to? Someone in Nassau? She pondered as he peered in at her.

"And how lucky of us to have captured the infamous Thad too." The Boss walked over to Molly's cell. "What a giant of a human. Surprised she's still sleeping though."

"Yeah, I'm not." Jacky Boy limped into the room and waggled a small brown bottle. "We gave her a triple dose. Strong as ten men. Old bitch." He gave a slow nod and fixed his gaze on Jane. "I see our entertainment's awake."

Jane recoiled at his words. He was a grimy man with a peg leg who oozed sleaze.

"Keep a lid on it, Jacky Boy. These two will have your dick off!" The Boss smirked and stroked at his chin. "What shall we do with them, boys?"

The Boss, Jacky Boy and Leon grinned and leered at Jane and Joy. Jane had been in a lot of bad situations with a lot of bad people, but something told her she wasn't getting out of this one unharmed.

"Who even are you?" Jane eyeballed the men. "Why hide behind a name?"

"I don't. Just a nickname," The Boss said.

Jane thought about what she could do to get herself out of this situation. She heard Joy shuffling about behind her and hoped she had figured something out. She'd keep them talking. Keep them distracted.

"What's with the snake?" Jane asked.

The Boss walked over and pushed his face against hers through the bars. "So many questions."

His eyes blazed with a venomous hate. He seemed aggravated and clearly didn't like being probed. She'd bargain with him instead, though it was hard to tell what a man like this wanted other than power and right now he had a lot of that.

"I have a lot of resources at my disposal, you know. Coin too. What's say we strike a deal?" Jane nodded and tried to break through his hateful stare.

He raised his flintlock and pushed it through the bar and into her chest. Typical man relying on weapons to solve problems, she thought. She'd use her brain to get out of this just like she always did. He pressed the barrel deeper and glared. She needed to bargain and fast. "We could team up even? Wouldn't you like an army of mercenaries at your command? And they would be, I'd make sure of it."

His glare didn't falter.

"What is it you want? Land?" Jane swallowed the rising lump in her throat. "How about the mansion?" She forced a quick smile though it felt more like a grimace. His eyes changed and a wicked grin spread across his face.

"Too many questions." He pulled the trigger and the deafening snap bounced off the walls as blood splatter erupted and Jane's body slumped to the ground.

MOLLY WEAVER

The snap of gunfire awoke Molly from her heavy slumber. She peeled her face away from the grimy floor which smelt worse than the dock. "What's going on?" she mumbled and cleared her throat. Her wounded leg throbbed and her entire body ached. She pushed herself up to sitting and saw a man standing outside of the neighboring cell dusting off a black wood pistol. A woman's body lay on the ground in the next cell surrounded by a puddle of blood, and a brown-haired woman stood pressed into the corner, staring at the lifeless body.

"You… you bastard!" the brown-haired woman yelled.

"Boss! Look who's awake."

Molly rolled her eyes. "Jacky Boy." She sighed. "Seems I'll be forever haunted by you and that peg leg. Pff." Molly smirked. "What a joke."

The pistol-toting man strode over to Molly's cell. He wore a black and red captain's jacket with a matching tricorn hat.

"How the mighty Thad has fallen," he said. His gruff voice was surprisingly eloquent.

"I'd let me out of here quick smart if I were you," Molly said.

"Why would we do that? You don't scare us!" Jacky Boy peered through the grubby bars.

Molly stomped over and made a grab for him. He wobbled backwards.

"Ha! Missed!" Jacky Boy taunted.

His spiteful, whiny voice wound Molly up. She gripped the cell bars tight. "Let me out of here or you'll be sorry!" She tried with all her might to pry the bars apart, to move or twist them just an inch, but nothing. She released her grip and counted in her head. Don't let them see they've got to you, she told herself.

"You'll pay," she said under her breath as she turned away. The exertion made her leg throb harder. She looked down at the wound which they had cleaned up for her, though she wasn't sure why they'd bother.

"Now, now, Thad, or is it Molly? It's very confusing. What shall we call you?" The black and red-hatted man asked as he holstered his pistol.

"Whatever," Molly said and walked to the back of the cell. She needed a way out. If she played nice for now, maybe they would let their guard down. Maybe that brown-haired girl would help her. "Molly, call me Molly." She strained to sound remotely pleasant.

She peered into the other cell. "Was that Jane Hatch?"

"Certainly was. I've been waiting years to get my hands on you lot," the man said. He interlaced his fingers and gave them a crack. "You've made my job difficult, I'll give you that much. You're sneaky." He nodded as if impressed and flashed Molly a devious smile which revealed a missing front tooth.

She stared at his crinkled face. There was a familiarity

about it that she couldn't shake. Her eyes jumped to his jacket and stopped at the lapel which had a small golden object pinned to it.

"What's on your jacket?" Molly asked.

"Ha, never you mind." He brushed his hand against the pin.

"Do you have a name?" Molly pushed.

She needed information. Something to help piece this puzzle together.

"I'm The Boss." He put his hand to his chest and gave a little bow. His tanned skin crinkled as he spoke.

"Right. Well, that's as clear as mud. Care to elaborate?" Molly said.

"Ha! Haven't heard that one before. I'm surprised you don't know me."

"That makes two of us," Molly muttered to herself.

"Do you like your new lodgings? Rather nice, isn't it?" he said and flung his arms in the air.

"It's disgusting, as it's no doubt intended to be," Molly replied. She looked over at Jane. "Whoever killed her should go see Roy. There'll be some doubloons waiting from me."

"Roy?" The brown-haired woman in the corner shot Molly a glare. "How do you know Roy?"

"Who are you?" Molly nodded and turned away from The Boss and his men.

"Joy. Lafitte."

"Ah yes, Roy told me about you." She nodded. "Shame you've ended up here but take the credit for this one when you get out." Molly pointed toward Jane.

"Ha! You're not going anywhere! Neither of you!" Jacky Boy stood at Joy's cell door and licked his lips.

"We'll see," Joy said.

"Aw don't you want to stay with us, Joy? I thought you liked me."

A man with a hook hand sauntered through the door and shot Joy a wink.

"Who'd like you?" Molly said and took a seat on the sludge covered floor. Her leg blazed with pain.

"Now, now, Molly, Leon has many redeeming qualities!" The Boss said.

Jacky Boy hobbled over to Molly's cell door. He gripped the bars and peered through the gap. "Did you get my messages?"

"Maybe?" Molly shrugged.

"Those severed tongues in boxes, that was me," Jacky Boy said.

"Bravo." Molly looked over to Joy. She rolled her eyes. "Truly terrifying... clearly."

"Why can't we just kill her? You miserable old cow. I should have shot you myself, finished the job off!" Jacky Boy yelled.

"Enough!" The Boss raised a hand. "Make yourself comfortable, Molly. You're going to be here for a while. Can't kill you just yet." He flashed a wicked grin in her direction and made for the door.

Molly ignored his attempt to scare her and instead cast her mind back to where she might know him from. That smile of his was all too familiar.

"We'll leave you with Jacky Boy, he'll take good care of you until I return. I've got some... questions I need answered." He cracked his knuckles. "Don't let her out of your sight. And figure a way to clean up that mess." The Boss waved his finger in Jane's direction.

Leon followed him out and closed the clunky, thick door behind them.

"Yes, sir," Jacky Boy said and slapped his thigh with glee. "Look who's in charge now! Me!"

Molly shook her head and peeked through the bars at Joy. She looked shaken. "You okay?" she asked.

Joy walked over and pressed her head into the bars which separated the two cells. "I can't believe he killed her. It was so quick."

"I thought you wanted her dead? I know I did." Molly shrugged. "When you kill people for a living, you can't expect that others won't do the same."

Joy blew out her cheeks and let out a loud puff of air.

"You liked her, didn't you?" Molly said.

Joy cleared her throat and avoided Molly's gaze. "I think they've got children here. In cages."

"Shut it!" Jacky Boy yelled.

His voice infuriated Molly. She eyed her surroundings. The small window in the corner of Joy's cell suggested they were at least close to the outside world. She paused and listened. The hum of the bugs which came out at night had started up. Molly's eyes shot to her satchel, dumped in the corner of the room.

"Found anything good in my bag, Jacky Boy?" She wasn't going to waste her energy giving him the reaction he expected.

"What bag?"

"That brown leather one in the corner." Molly nodded her head. She wondered if he was really so stupid that he hadn't even checked the contents.

He looked at the bag but didn't move.

"Ha! Are you scared of touching it, floppy boy?" Molly said.

"I'm not scared of nothing." He snatched up the bag and tipped the contents on the ground.

"Think your boss might be interested in that bit of paper."

He grabbed the worn piece of parchment and fumbled to unfold the tattered edges.

"Careful now, it's very old," Molly said.

"Half a map!" He rushed to the door and wobbled away down the corridor.

"Hey! Boss!" he yelled.

Molly's ears pricked up at the sound of faint cries. They sounded like those of a child.

"Hear that?" Joy ran to the cell door. "I can't stand it," she said and covered her mouth.

"Shh!" Molly put her hand to her lips and pushed herself to standing. "Listen." She pointed toward the corridor.

"Boss, come here!" Jacky Boy yelled.

Molly bent down on one knee. Hot pain seared through her injured leg. She braced as she stuck her hand through the grubby bars and tried to grab her bag. The strap lay inches away from her grasp. She prized her arm through. Further and further but to no avail.

"Oi!" Jacky Boy yelled. He wobbled back in the room and lunged at Molly's arm.

She pulled it back fast. The snug fit of the bars tore at her skin. "Fuck!" Molly said through gritted teeth.

The Boss strode into the room. "What is it?"

"A map." Jacky Boy thrust the paper into The Boss's hand.

The Boss held the parchment toward the candlelight. "*C. Kidd treasure not found.*" He stroked at his chin. "Oh, this is good." His eyes narrowed. "But where's the rest of it? There's only half a map here!" The Boss scowled at Molly.

"That's all I've got for now but I have it on good

authority that the other half is complete, and I just so happen to know where to find it."

"Is that right?" The Boss grinned.

"If you let me out of here, I can take you to it?" Molly said in her nicest voice.

Leon came through the door. "What is it?"

"Half a map. Apparently, Thad knows where the other half is too!" Jacky Boy said.

"Oh sure. And what, we just need to let her out and she can show us where it is? Pff. I don't think so!" Leon said.

"You hook-handed little fuck!" Molly said under her breath.

"Don't be so hasty, Leon. I think we're talking about Captain Kidd's thirty thousand doubloons." The Boss tapped his tanned, leathery finger on his chin. "I'll think about it. But for now, make the preparations for Devil's Cay, we need to set sail soon."

"Tide's about to turn ya know," Leon said.

"Then quickly, load the irritating cargo on and make sure you get that pretty young thing. She'll fetch a lot. He'll be pleased." The Boss smirked.

"The Beltrame kid?" Leon asked.

"Beltrame?" Joy grabbed the bars. "Do they all go to Devil's Cay? Is that where you take them? Is that where you took Raven, you sick pieces of shit!" She shook the bars and screamed. "Let me out, you fucks!"

"Shut her up, Jacky Boy! She's annoying me," The Boss said.

"Can't I start torturing this one first?" Jacky Boy looked to Molly, his eyes filled with a lust for vengeance.

"Soon enough. Needs to weaken a little first and I'm sure a few more days without food will help with that."

The Boss walked out with Leon who slammed the door behind them.

Jacky Boy turned to Molly and gave a chuckle. "Who'd of thought I'd be the one in charge of you. Should have let me have my fun that day, shouldn't you?"

"What say we strike a deal?" Molly said and clenched her jaw. She loathed being nice to this prick. "Just you and me this time."

Joy shot Molly a look of confusion.

"How about I give you another bit of treasure and in exchange you give me some food?" Molly tried to make her voice sound somewhat pleasant though it pained her.

"Not gonna give me my leg back, is it? Cow!"

Molly tried to hide her smirk. "Just grab yourself that clam shell."

Jacky Boy gave the shell a poke with his boot. "What is it?"

"I use them to smuggle jewelry. Inside is a very expensive ring that would fetch a pretty price." Molly pointed and nodded in encouragement.

"You want to give me this ring in exchange for a bit of food? Don't make sense."

"Well, I don't have a choice, do I? I'm hungry!" Molly yelled. She stood up and pulled out her handkerchief.

"You gonna cry?" Jacky Boy laughed.

"Just stomp on the fucking clam to open it. The ring's yours." Molly turned away and feigned a sigh filled with sorrow.

A stomp, a crack and a crunch followed.

Boom!

The room erupted in smoke. Molly pressed the handkerchief over her face and burrowed her head into the wall. Coughs came from Joy's cell.

Molly waited a moment then tucked her handkerchief away, squeezed her eyes tight shut and fumbled for the bars. Her hands landed on the rough iron. She patted them down hoping for a gap, but they were all still in place. She pulled one, then another. They were at least looser than before.

She made her way down the row, shaking each in turn until her hand stopped on one that moved a lot. She gave the bar a yank and it came clean out. She tossed it aside and sniffed the air. The smoke seemed to have dissipated, so she slowly opened one eye. She peeked through the gap in the bars. Jacky Boy lay at her cell door, bloodied and at the least unconscious. Dead, she hoped.

She looked to Joy who was following her lead and shaking at the bars, but with no luck. Molly thrust her arm through the gap and dragged Jacky Boy's body toward her. She reached into his pockets and found a set of keys then fumbled to unlock her door. "Calm. Just keep it together," she said through gritted teeth as her strained hands tried another key in the lock. And another. She held her breath as she waited for that click and turn. "Yes!"

Molly flung the door open, grabbed her satchel and tossed the set of keys into Joy's cell. "My part's done."

Joy snatched the keys up. "Fuck! Fine."

Molly scrambled out of the clunky main door. Ahead lay a dimly lit corridor with a ceiling so low she could touch the roof with her hand. She limped down it, gritting her teeth to bear the pain of her wounded leg. Her body tensed, not only with the pain but the suffocating, small space.

As she hobbled down the corridor her ears pricked up. She could hear those muffled cries again. Those of a child. It sickened her. The people she dealt with had chosen this life. They wanted the riches. They wanted the power, but these children didn't ask to be dragged into this mess. They were innocent. She'd been innocent.

Her mind cast back to sobbing on the street, being kicked, beaten and starved like an unwanted dog. She'd never fought back. She hadn't had the strength, but now was a different story.

She listened intently and located the cries. She crept over and pressed her ear to the door. The muffled sobs were on the other side. A surge of adrenaline rushed through her. She smashed her weight into the door and burst into the room.

"What in the..." Two guards stared at her in shock. They sat atop a six-foot-long cage. The room was filled with them, all stacked upon one another. Inside, children cowered, a couple in each.

"You bastards!" Molly grabbed them both by the neck and smashed their heads together, knocking them out.

She closed the door behind her and held her breath as footsteps rushed by. They rushed past in the direction of the cells. She didn't have much time. She put her finger to her lips and motioned for the children to be quiet. Their frightened eyes made her heart heavy. "It's okay," she whispered. "We'll all get out of here."

She searched the guards' pockets for the keys. "Yes!" Her hand struck a heap on a rope. She frantically unlocked the cages. "Be quiet, follow me and stay close." They reached out for her hands and clung to any body part they could. "Okay, you can't all grab onto me. Hold each other's hands down the corridor, then we run," she whispered and listened at the door. Clangs of swords and screams followed but they at least seemed distant. She peeled open the door and poked her head out. The men all looked to be busy with Joy. In the other direction the corridor stretched far but no one was in sight.

She opened the door and waved the children through. "Follow me." She led the way and broke into a hobbled run. The children stayed close behind. They reached a large room filled with tables on which abandoned plates of food and jugs of drink sat. To the right-hand side there was a large door which Molly assumed led to the outside world. A small boy with a dirty tear-stained face tugged at her sleeve. He couldn't have been more than six or seven-years-old.

"I came through here." He pointed to the door.

"Does it go outside?" Molly asked.

He nodded in response.

"Excellent." Molly put her arms out and herded the children together. "Now, I'm going to open that door and if the men are on the other side I want you to run as far as you can from here and don't look back." Molly nodded. Their eyes were filled with terror. "I'll take care of anyone who gets in our way, okay?"

They nodded and gripped any part of her they could.

"You need to let go of me, be brave, one last time," Molly said and crept forward.

She reached the heavy door and heaved it open, ready to face an army of men. Nothing. She ushered the children outside. In the far distance she made out what she assumed to be the city of Nassau. She'd never ventured this far. There was no reason to, there was nothing here. Or at least so she thought.

Molly signaled with her hand for the children to follow her. They ran toward a dark, leaf-filled field and hid amongst the foliage. Through the otherwise still night she could hear a ship being loaded. They hadn't been missed yet. She turned to the children. The fear in their eyes had receded slightly. "Now, we've a long walk ahead of us, but we're free!" Molly said. It would be a slow half day walk back to town through the rough fields of palms, but she was free. They were all free.

CAPTAIN CROW

Crow stood in the grassy valley and cast his eyes over the carnage. Lifeless bodies littered the ground around him. Johnny's included. The sky rumbled and the breeze picked up. His eyes moved upwards to the pockets of smoke which now swirled in with the clouds creating a thick, heavy sky.

"What's happening beyond the mound, boy?" he asked Isaac whose back was to him with his head focused down. "What you looking at?"

"Nothing." Isaac turned to face him and tucked something away in his pocket. "Jane Hatch's people are at war with Vella."

"Then let's go help her." Crow turned to his men and nodded. "Boy?"

Isaac scrunched up his face. "Vella? Why?" he asked. "I say we finally go find that treasure!" Isaac rubbed his hands together. "You with me, fellas?" He patted down a couple of the bodies at his feet. "Besides, I'm not sure she'll want my help." A few of the men grinned and nudged one another at the mention of treasure.

"We owe her!" Crow was so used to including Nelson in everything he said. "Well, I owe her. Nelson and I struck a deal," Crow raised his voice.

"I see. Guess me being kidnapped and held by her doesn't matter." Isaac's hand landed on a flask. "Finally!" He tipped the contents into his mouth.

Crow stormed over and stuck his face inches away from Isaac's. "We made a deal, okay? I don't go back on my word."

Isaac rolled his eyes. "What's to stop her killing me down there?" he said and tossed the empty flask.

"Me!" Crow's gaze didn't falter. He made sure his eyes burned into Isaac's.

"Okay." Isaac sighed. "Guess you did just save me from that prick."

"Exactly." Crow turned to face his men who had drawn their weapons, ready to charge.

"Men! Stay clear of any women with dreadlocked hair or a 'V' stamped on their jackets. They're Vella's girls. Take out anyone else. Then we'll get V onside and get that treasure." He raised a blade and pistol above his head. "You with me?"

"Yes, Captain!" the men cheered.

They ran up the grassy mound and stood on top. Below, swarms of people were hacking and slashing at anything in sight.

"We run down on my command." Crow scanned the grounds of the infamous merc mansion, his eyes searching for Vella. He saw the bizarre wooden structure she'd been building for so long but never used. It was empty. The smoke-filled air made it difficult to make out anyone clearly. A flurry of cannonballs shot through the air and erupted. Bodies tumbled and smashed down into the mud.

"Are we sure we want to go down there?" Isaac said.

"We're no cowards!" Crow said. "Right, men?"

"Yes, Captain," the men agreed.

Crow raised his pistol in the air. "Go!" Crow yelled and charged down the hill. The men hurtled down with him, Isaac included.

It hadn't looked far but it seemed to take forever to reach the bottom, and when they finally did, the fire stopped. Bodies lay bleeding out in the muddy earth. "We're too late." Crow panicked, his eyes searching for Vella. Not again, he thought to himself. I'm always too late. Thoughts of Nelson pricked at his mind.

"Over there!" Isaac said and pointed, interrupting Crow's thoughts.

A huge man stood over Vella with a spear raised above her. Next to him stood a smaller man. "No!" Crow yelled and ran toward them as fast as his legs would carry him. He needed to be closer to have a clear shot.

"Pino!" Isaac yelled and sprinted toward the men. "It's Popino!"

Crow couldn't get there fast enough. He watched as Vella raised her arm and shot. The smaller man flew backward with the impact.

"No!" Isaac screamed.

"You bitch!" The huge man slammed his spear down into Vella.

Crow stopped dead and shot. The huge man dropped to his knees. The snap of gun fire carried through the air. Isaac sprinted past and dragged the body of the smaller man away. Crow ran over to the huge man who rolled on the ground in pain. He looked at Vella. Her thick hair was matted with clumps of dirt and blood. The handle of the huge spear which had ended it all stuck out from her chest. A few paces away Isaac cradled the smaller man's head in his arms and rocked. A hand reached out for Crow's ankle. "I don't think so." Crow kicked the huge man's meaty hand away. "I should keep you alive, make you suffer!"

"What shall we do with him, Captain?" Several of Crow's men caught up and stood by his side. Others had run off and were checking bodies for weapons and loot.

"Think we can get any coin for him? Is there even anyone left to bribe?" Crow said.

The men shrugged.

Crow lifted a flintlock pistol to end him. He aimed and cocked the gun.

"Oi! Old man! Leave him the fuck alone!" A man wearing a black bandana sprinted toward him, closely followed by a thin-faced, weathered woman with a limp. She clutched a blade in one hand and used the other to help push her leg forward.

"Move any closer and I shoot," Crow said. He caught sight of Vella's butchered body. "On second thoughts." Crow pulled the trigger. The huge man stopped moving.

"Thunder!" The man with the black bandana yelled and ran at Crow. He flew into him with full force and knocked him to the ground. He raised his fists to pummel Crow but several pairs of hands dragged him off.

Crow scrambled to his feet. His men had the black-bandana-wearing man in a headlock. Three others had managed to tackle the weathered woman to the ground. "Take care of them. Both of them."

"No!" The bandana-wearing man cried out and tried to break free. He was met with a blade to the throat.

"I'll see you in hell!" The woman let out a cackle before one of Crow's men struck a blade through her back.

Crow reloaded his pistol and unloaded another shot into the huge man they called Thunder, just to be sure. He watched the breath fade from the man's body. Satisfied he was gone, he walked over to Isaac. "Leave him, boy," Crow said.

Isaac looked up. Tears pooled in his eyes. "This is my fault. I'm sorry, Pino." He held his friend's head and didn't move.

Crow knelt down. He noticed a soft movement of the man's chest. "That wound, just the one in his side?" Crow asked. He checked Popino's body. He wasn't injured anywhere else.

"I don't know, maybe?" Isaac replied.

Crow put his hand to Popino's neck. "I can still feel movement. His blood's still going."

"What?" Isaac said.

"He's still alive! We need to block that gash though. Won't be for long otherwise. Give me your shirt."

Isaac ripped at his shirt. It was fairly tattered so the cloth tore easily. "This do?"

Crow took the tattered strips and bunched them up. He pushed them into the wound. "Men! We need to get this one out of here. Bring Vella too."

"But she's gone?" Isaac said.

"I know, boy, but she deserves a proper burial. Let's take her home. Her girls will see we've helped and let us shelter there," Crow said as the men rallied around them. His men. His tough old heart filled with pride. "You keep the pressure on that wound, boy. I'll lead the way."

JOY LAFITTE

Joy's stomach rumbled and her feet throbbed. She still couldn't believe she'd made it out of that place alive. Her stomach knotted at the thought of those poor children being stolen and shipped away. She still didn't know who in Devil's Cay wanted them, but at least she now knew where to look.

As she trudged through yet another field, she was grateful for the tall palms which sheltered her from the sweltering heat. In the distance, heads of people working in the fields bobbed up and down. The center of Nassau wasn't far away now. Her body longed to head straight for home but the vengeance in her heart wouldn't let her rest.

She dug inside her pocket and her fingers brushed the small silver coin Jane had given her. She hoped what Jane had told her was true. Her hand struck what she had been looking for: a thick brass object which she had taken from Jane's jacket before making her escape. The coin-shaped piece caught the sun and the glint lit up the word 'Hatch'. Joy assumed it to be a sort of family medallion and tucked it back away for safekeeping.

She reached the outskirts of town and made for the center square. First stop would be a visit to Grimm, and Joy knew exactly where to find him. Up ahead she noticed a crowd of people gathered. He would no doubt be in the middle. She pushed her way through and spied his typical set up: cards on the table and heavy-bosomed women with low cut tops to distract the men. The sight of his smug face enraged her. She barged her way to the front and slammed her hands down on the table. "I want a word with you!"

"My! My!" Grimm said, taken aback not only by the interruption but probably by Joy's appearance too. She rarely looked so disheveled.

"Sod off! I was just about to win!" A small grimy man gave her a push.

"Now, now! There's plenty of winnings for everyone!" Grimm gave his best beaming showman's smile. "Joy, dear, if you wouldn't mind stepping aside I'll give you my full attention in a moment." He shot her a wink and didn't move his gaze from hers until she gave a roll of her eyes.

She wanted to push his stupid table over, snap off one of the legs and hit him over the head. Why wouldn't he just give her the information? Why did he even need payment? Did he not care about those children? Joy stepped aside and tapped her foot. Either way he was gutless or greedy, or both, and she hated that she needed something from him.

Grimm scraped the coins across the table toward him. "Same time tomorrow, good people." He scooped the coins into a pouch as the crowd dissipated then gathered the cards and slotted them away into a leather container.

"Finally!" Joy stepped toward him and stood with her hands on her hips.

"Joy, so nice to see you." Grimm looked her up and

down. "Looking a bit worse for wear though, everything okay?" Grimm placed his items into a leather bag. He paused and waited for a response. "I assume you have the doubloons?" He folded his table down and snapped the latches shut.

"Better," Joy said.

Grimm's brow raised. "Really? Follow me then." He walked down a nearby alleyway and checked back over his shoulder every few steps. "This should be interesting," he said under his breath.

Joy followed him down the familiar path until they reached an unassuming doorway. Grimm unlocked the small wooden door and placed his items inside. He held the door open for Joy and bowed his head. "After you my dear."

"Thanks." Joy scanned the dark stone walls and stepped inside. The cool temperature came as a welcome relief. She had been here only once before but recalled the place well. The room ahead was adorned with plump, comfortable seats, crimson drapes and numerous candle-filled lanterns. A large woolen floor covering sat in the middle of the room with two long seats at either side. These were rare pieces of furniture for most people in Nassau. Joy's eyes stopped on a small figure perched on the long seat, eating. "Roy?" She couldn't believe her eyes. "Why are you here?" Joy turned quickly and checked over her shoulder.

"It's okay, Joy. Roy and I are old acquaintances," Grimm replied.

"You look exhausted, Joy," Roy said.

Joy shook her head and hoped her eyes deceived her. She blinked a few times but nothing changed.

"Joy?" Roy said.

Joy walked toward Roy. "I think you failed to mention you knew one another." She balled her hands tight. She felt foolish to have ever trusted Roy. He was well aware of her situation and he had sat there and pretended to not even know Grimm's name.

"Well, you never asked," Roy said in between mouthfuls. Crumbs spilled down his front as he nibbled on what looked like some sort of biscuit.

Joy nodded. "I see."

"It's business, Joy. You know that," Roy said.

She took a seat opposite Roy. He looked away and shifted awkwardly.

Grimm clapped his hands together. "Well, now those awkward introductions are out the way let's get down to business." Grimm walked over to a cupboard and retrieved a tin and a bottle. He returned to where Joy and Roy were sitting and tipped some of the contents onto the table.

"More biscuits! Thank you, Grimm," Roy said and reached for another. "Try one, Joy, they're delightful."

"I think you need a drink?" Grimm said.

Joy nodded. She couldn't find the words right now.

Grimm ripped the cork out from the bottle and poured her a glass. Her hand shook a little as she raised the receptacle to her mouth. She hadn't realized until now just how thirsty she was. She leaned forward, grabbed a biscuit and took a bite. She savored the unusual sweetness and washed it down with the sweet, brown liquid. "I've got news for both of you."

"Exactly what I wanted to hear!" Roy smiled.

"Jane's dead," Joy said and displayed the Hatch brass coin in her hand.

"Well done! I knew you could do it," Roy said.

"Why didn't you tell me it was Thad who put out the hit on her?"

"Oh." Roy sat back and scratched the back of his head. "Joy... you know I do business with whoever gives me money."

"Yeah, but Thad? Well, Molly," Joy said.

"You found that out too? You have been busy," Roy replied.

Joy remained quiet and instead stared at Roy with fire in her eyes. He busied himself and fumbled with his satchel fastening. "It's just business, Joy, please don't take offense." He retrieved twenty doubloons and extended his hands out to Joy with the coins. "Your pay, plus a little extra." His hands shook a little as he waited for Joy to take them.

"Thanks." She scooped them off his palms and didn't take her eyes off him.

"No, thank you." He smiled and brushed the crumbs from his front. "So..." Roy tipped his head toward Grimm. "Ask! You have enough now."

"Oh." Grimm sat back. "You know about that, Roy?"

"I know a lot of things." Roy put his satchel strap over his head and hopped down off the seat.

"What happened to Popino, Roy?" Joy said.

"Oh yes, let's see. I sent him off to hide, and then he vanished," Roy replied and gave a shrug.

Joy wasn't sure what to make of that comment. She hoped Popino simply got tired of waiting and left of his own accord, but Roy made it sound more sinister. Everything he said sounded sinister now.

"It was a pleasure doing business with you both but I must head off. Grimm, the package is on your bed." Roy made his way to the door, paused for a moment and turned to Joy. "I heard that Isaac character you're friendly with is over at Vella's. The battle is done. Seems both Jane and Vella lost." Roy gave a chuckle. "Then again, Jane's entire place has been looted and lit on fire so maybe Vella won actually."

"Didn't she die?" Grimm said and sat up. "I think Thad won that battle, Roy." Grimm sat back and raised an eyebrow to Joy.

"Well for once, I actually think you're right!" Roy laughed and stepped out the door.

Grimm leaned back and put his arms across the top of the long seat. He crossed his legs and winked. "I'm always right."

"Is that so?" Joy leaned forward and took another biscuit. Her hunger had caught up with her and had Grimm's eyes not been burning into her she would have tipped the entire contents of the tin into her mouth.

"You really are quite the beauty," Grimm said.

"I just killed your boss." Joy cocked her head to a side. "And all you can do is comment on that."

"I worked for Jane. She wasn't my boss. I'm my own boss. Top up?" Grimm popped the cork and held the bottle out in Joy's direction.

"Sure." She lifted her glass and watched the liquid tumble in.

"You mentioned that you have something better than those doubloons for me?" Grimm topped up his own glass and sank back into the seat.

Joy pulled out the button sized coin and displayed the piece of silver in her palm. "Recognize this?"

Grimm moved his face close to her hand. "Brothers and sisters of the white fox," he said.

Joy clasped her hand shut.

Grimm smiled. "I see where this is going but I don't know that it will get you much once word spreads of Jane's death. Let me have a closer look."

Joy pulled out a blade. "If you try anything..." She held the blade up.

"I don't think I'd be so stupid." Grimm raised his brows and stuck out his hand.

Joy dropped the coin into his palm.

"This is good for three favors. You see the little notches on the coin? Whoever carries out the favor scratches one out."

"That's what I was led to believe. I just don't understand what the person performing the favor gets out of it?" Joy asked and shrugged.

"Well, if you perform a favor you get to ask Jane for one in return. It has to be considered reasonable though. Could be to forgive a debt, whores for a week." Grimm smiled. "You've got to negotiate well but with Jane that's hard. Was hard."

Grimm rubbed his thumb over the coin. "Ha! One time, I asked—"

"I don't want to hear it." Joy went to snatch the coin from his hand, but he clasped it shut. She lurched forward and grabbed him by his shirt collar and pulled him into her chest. She held her blade to his face. "The coin, Grimm."

He opened his hand. "Of course. I just wanted an excuse for you to get close to me."

Joy snatched the coin and shook it in her closed fist. She looked to the ceiling. "Can this still get me a favor or not?"

"Well, she's dead now, isn't she?" Grimm re-arranged his shirt collar. "How many people know?"

"For now, me, you, Roy. It's only been a few hours," Joy said. It was a stretch of the truth but she wasn't bothered.

Grimm ran his hand through his slick, black hair and folded his arms.

"You want the coin with two favors or the doubloons?" Joy asked.

"But there are three?"

"I need it back," Joy said.

Grimm narrowed his eyes. The corners of his mouth turned down in thought. "Give me the coin and I'll use it to get some favors from people before word gets around she's dead."

"Deal." Joy held out the coin for him to take. "If you give me this coin back and all the notches are ticked, I'll kill you."

Grimm took the coin and grinned. "Means I get to see you again though, doesn't it?"

Joy ignored his lecherous gaze. "The name, Grimm? That's why I'm here. Who was it?"

"Do you know of someone they call 'The Boss'?"

Joy clenched her fists by her side. "I do." She dug her fingernails into her palms. She should have stuck around and finished that fucker off.

"Well, he ships children off to Devil's Cay to a man named Seef. I don't know what exactly happens, or why, but that's where they end up."

"Seef," Joy repeated. "Does he ever come to Nassau?"

Grimm threw up his hands. "I hope not. From what I've heard he's... he's bad, Joy. I don't ever want any of this to come back to me." Grimm shook his head and readjusted his waistcoat.

"It won't." Joy looked back at Grimm. "Thanks for the

biscuits." An icy calm came over her. She was one step closer.

"You're welcome." Grimm sprang to his feet.

Joy could tell her change in mood and sudden politeness unnerved him.

"I'll bring this back to you in a few days." He patted his front pocket where he had placed the coin.

"You'd better. I'll let myself out."

Joy sped through the center. She couldn't wait to get home and see Raven. The streets looked exactly as they did before, but the warm feeling which came with their familiarity had vanished. After everything she'd been through, she wondered if it would ever return. As she reached the old rundown part of town, she picked up her pace.

"Joy?" Raven stood outside of their house cleaning. "Joy!" She dropped her broom and ran toward her big sister.

Joy stretched out her arms and pulled Raven in tight. "Have you missed me?" Joy squeezed her sister and smiled. She caught sight of the front of their house. "Looks like you've been busy. Probably didn't have a chance to notice I was gone!"

"I did! I missed you." Raven pulled away. "You look exhausted, what happened to your face?"

"Nothing much, don't worry."

"Have you eaten? You look starved!" Raven said.

"Of course I have! But I have been saving myself for some of your home cooking." Joy smiled but Raven met it with a frown. Joy recognized the doubt in her eyes.

"Well, you best stick around for some then," Raven said.

"Joy! You're back!" A huge man stood by their front door and waved.

"Remember Tom? And his son Jim? They've been helping fix the place up," Raven said.

Joy swallowed the mounting lump in her throat. "Why?" Her voice broke. Tears longed to escape her tired eyes but she pushed them away.

Jim ran over, a grin spread across his sweet, rosy-cheeked face. "You helped us, we wanted to say thank you."

Joy closed her eyes and nodded. She wasn't used to people being kind and, after what she'd been through, she found it hard to accept. She opened her eyes to Raven and Jim gazing up at her. "That's... really nice of you," she said and smiled.

Raven grabbed Joy's arm and led her toward the house. "Look! We have a door!"

Joy shook her head in astonishment. "Thank you."

"Fresh paint too," Tom said and opened the door. "Take a look inside."

Raven squeezed Joy's arm and buried her head into it. She sniffed loudly. "I think that jacket needs a wash!"

Joy laughed. "It certainly does."

Raven held out her hand.

"Hang on." Joy rushed to empty the pockets into her vest. "All yours!"

Joy took off her hat and tossed it in her room. After so many torturous weeks, it was a relief to be without all the heavy clothing. "This is... I just can't believe it." She walked back out to the front door with her hands clasped behind her back.

"What do you think?" Tom said and took off his hat, revealing a thick mop of hair.

"I think you deserve this." Joy dug into her vest pocket and produced five doubloons. She thrust them into Tom's hand and grinned.

Tom gasped. "That's far too much. I can't accept this."

"What if I was to tell you I need a favor?" Joy gave a sheepish smile.

"Go on, Miss." Tom nodded.

Joy checked Raven wasn't within earshot. "I've been offered another job and it's too good for me to turn down. But it means I'll be gone a month or so and I really need someone to check in on Raven. Could I trust you to do that? I'll make it worth your while."

"Of course! Are you sure you have to go though? She ain't half missed you," Tom said.

Jim came over and caught sight of the doubloons. His eyes grew wide.

"Those are for you and your dad." Joy smiled.

Jim looked over to Raven who stood by the door.

"Did I hear you say you have to go again?" Raven asked. Her voice quivered.

Joy hung her head and sighed. "This will be the last time. I promise." She walked over to Raven with her arms out. "I just want us to have a good life and this will mean we do." Joy brought Raven in close and held her tight. She could feel her body shake as she tried to stifle sobs. Raven pulled away.

"I'm sick of being on my own." She rubbed at her eyes.

Jim ran over and put his arm around Raven. "You're not though, you have us. Right, Dad?"

"We'll check in on Raven for you. Make sure she's safe." Tom nodded. "Come, Jim, let's leave them to it." The pair put away their tools and headed down the path back into town.

Joy reached for Raven's arm, but she pushed it away and stormed inside. Joy caught up to her.

"Why?" Raven stomped her foot. "Why, Joy?"

"I'm sorry but I think this is right for us." Joy's stomach knotted with the lie. She turned and walked toward her bedroom. "Just wait, okay? I've something for you. Wait there."

"Fine. I'll be in the kitchen," Raven said. Her soft voice filled with sorrow. She dragged her feet and disappeared into the kitchen.

Joy ducked in her room. She hated upsetting her sister like this. She'd already been through so much, but she couldn't live with herself knowing other children like Raven were being held at the mercy of that monster. She took out all the doubloons from her vest and counted. She would keep five for herself and give the rest to Raven.

Joy poked her head around the kitchen door. Raven sat with her eyes fixed on the floor, her hands clasped. The occasional tear dripped off her chin onto her skirt. It broke Joy's heart but she had to go.

"Raven?"

"What." Raven didn't look up.

Joy sat across from her. "Here's ten doubloons." She unloaded the golden coins onto the tiny kitchen table.

"What?" Raven covered her mouth with her hands. "How?"

"It was the job."

"We're rich, Joy!"

"Now can I have some of that home cooking? I've been dreaming of your chicken soup."

Raven sprang to her feet and ladled hot soup into a

bowl. She beamed as she set it down on the table for Joy to enjoy.

Joy slurped the hot soup down. "This... I've missed this."

"Bread?" Raven tore off a wedge and handed it to Joy.

"Thank you." For the first time in a long time a glimmer of happiness tickled Joy's heart.

"I still want you to stay." Raven sat back down. "Haven't we got enough now?"

"Like I said, this is the last job. It's on a different island, so I'll be gone a month or so, but Tom and Jim will keep you company. They seem like good people." Joy tried to catch her sister's eye as she spooned in another mouthful of soup.

"They are. They've really fixed the place up." Raven held out her hand to Joy. "When will it ever be enough?"

Joy gave it a squeeze and ignored her sister's question. "I have to leave tonight. I know I've only just come home but next time I'll be back for good."

Raven sighed. "Then I best finish cleaning your jacket."

Joy sat in her freshly painted kitchen savoring her soup. She looked at the stack of doubloons on the table. She was proud of how far she'd come, of what she'd survived, but her mission wasn't done yet. She had to find a way to Devil's Cay and knew exactly who might be crazy enough to help her.

CAPTAIN CROW

Smudges of blood covered the typically immaculate royal blue door of Vella's house. Crow led the way and kicked the door open. His men carried Vella and Popino behind him. Inside, those unharmed rushed about the reception area tending to those injured. Crow's eyes fixed on Georgia, the lip-ringed door-greeter, disheveled and bloodied but seemingly unharmed.

"Captain! We don't want no trouble." Georgia held up her hands.

"Neither do I; we've brought Vella."

Georgia stared. "Miss V? But we lost her."

"She deserves a proper burial," Crow said. His men trailed in behind him. They placed Vella's body on the floor. His eyes shot down. He stared at her muddied, dreadlocked hair and pale face. His heart filled with sorrow. Vella's people ran to her side. Georgia didn't move. She stood shaking her head.

"I can't believe she's gone," Georgia said.

Isaac tumbled in through the door with two of Crow's men who were carrying Popino.

"Popino?" Georgia rushed over.

"You know him?" Crow said.

"Every woman does," Isaac said under his breath. "Where can we put him?"

"Through here, follow me." Georgia led them to a large book-filled room with wood paneled walls.

Crow recognized it well, but he didn't let on.

"Lay him down by the window, draw the drapes," Georgia said. She put her hand to her mouth and shook her head. "Miss V wouldn't be happy having him here. He owed a lot."

"He's not all bad. I stole from him otherwise he'd have paid her back," Isaac said and frantically nodded his head. "You have to help us, Georgia. Please?"

Georgia leant on a nearby desk and let out a huge breath. "He needs help. We have someone. I'll get one of the girls to find them." Georgia ran out of the door.

Crow turned around. His men had followed them in. "There's too many of us in here. Go help where you can. Don't go looting or try anything," Crow said to his men and gave a wry smile. He watched as Isaac knelt by his friend's side.

"You'll be fine, Pino, might even have yourself a new lady friend," Isaac said.

Popino stirred.

"Pino? Can you hear me? Pino?"

Georgia rushed back in the room with an older silver-haired woman by her side.

"This is Grace, she's our healer. She'll fix him," Georgia said.

Grace hurried past them with a basket of cloths and potions in hand.

"Thank you! Please, if the cook is here, tell them I'm

sorry. We just want to make things right. Pino and I both do," Isaac said.

Crow grabbed Isaac by the arm and pulled him to a side. "What did you do to the cook?" Crow said.

Georgia frowned and crossed her arms.

"Nothing!" Isaac smiled.

"It seems I'm in charge now, Captain. Miss V said if she were to die in battle, then all command goes to me." Georgia dug her hand into her jacket and retrieved a piece of tough parchment. "She signed it before we attacked." Georgia held the parchment out toward Crow. "I know about you two, you don't have to pretend."

Crow scratched at his beard and remained silent. He took the parchment and skimmed over the scrawled text, then handed it back to Georgia. He was at a loss for words. He had lost everyone he ever loved in such a short space of time.

A knock on the door interrupted them. A moment of relief washed over him. He didn't want people to think him weak. He sure as hell wasn't, but he was still human.

Georgia made for the door. "Come. Let's leave Grace to work her magic."

Crow and Isaac left Popino with Grace. A grimy looking man stood in the reception area.

"I recognize you! I've seen you about the tavern. Otis, isn't it?" Isaac said.

The man stared through him. "I have a message for you." Otis held out a piece of paper to Crow. "From Thad."

"What if I don't want it?" Crow said and crossed his arms.

"I'll leave it anyway," Otis said.

"Fine!" Crow snatched the paper.

Otis looked side to side then hurried away, hopping over the bodies as he went out the door.

Crow unfolded the paper and scanned the words. He smiled. "Whoops!"

"What's it say?" Isaac asked, his eyes eager.

Crow read aloud. *"You killed my son and now I'm going to kill you. You can try to run but there's no escaping what's coming to you—Thad, or as you may now know me, Molly Weaver."*

"Molly?" Crow looked up, confused. "I've killed a lot of late. I don't even know who her son is at this point."

"Molly's Thad?" Isaac said and covered his mouth. "But I've played chess with her."

"Makes a bit more sense why she had Nelson. Do you think that prick Ives knew?" Crow said.

"He could have been an inside man," Georgia replied. "Either way, we'll stand with you, Captain."

"Thank you, Georgia." Crow fumbled with the paper and considered who Molly's son might be.

Isaac hadn't moved. His mouth fell open so wide that his jaw could have hit the floor.

"You'll catch flies, boy," Crow said.

"I just can't believe it," Isaac replied. He reached into his pocket. "These cards will haunt me. Does Thad have a symbol?"

"Dog, maybe?" Crow replied. The boy seemed more shocked than he expected. Then again, not much surprised Crow. He'd been around long enough to know better, and he certainly wasn't going to be intimidated by threats, even if they did come from Thad.

Isaac pointed to one of the cards and muttered to himself.

A loud thump came from the front door. "I'm not

375

armed," a muffled voice said. Another thump followed as the door pushed open an inch. "Hello? I'm looking for Isaac Carver?"

"Joy! It's okay, I know her." Isaac stumbled over the bodies toward the front door. He pulled it open and hugged the beautiful woman tight. "Are you okay? Why are you here?"

"I can't believe I'm saying this, but it's good to see you." She looked over at Crow.

He paused and stared at her soft face, dumbstruck by her beauty. He didn't think the boy had any friends, let alone one that would dare come and find him here. "Boy! You going to introduce your friend?"

"Joy Lafitte, everybody," Isaac said and held out his arm toward her.

Crow cleared his throat.

"And this is Captain Crow," Isaac said.

"A pleasure to meet you, miss," Crow grabbed her by the hand and bent down to kiss it. She slipped out of his grasp and re-extended her hand for a shake.

"I've seen you around. You and your man Nelson," Joy said.

Isaac shook his head.

"What?" Joy said and looked at Isaac.

"He's dead," Isaac mouthed.

"Oh, I'm sorry, Captain. I didn't know. Seems a lot are," Joy said and looked around.

"Call me Crow. It's a pleasure to meet you, Joy."

Joy gave Isaac a nudge. "You never mentioned you were friends with a famous captain."

Crow smiled and puffed out his chest a little. "Well, I wouldn't say we're friends." He scratched at his beard and laughed. He looked to Isaac who seemed hurt by the comment. "Oh, I'm kidding. We're the best of friends now, aren't we, boy?" He put his arm around Isaac and pulled him in.

"You stink." Isaac pushed Crow away and blocked his nose. "Yeah, we're friends." Isaac rolled his eyes and shook his head. "Popino's here. I know you and him never got along but—"

"Ha! You and me both." Crow winked.

Isaac glared. "He's been shot. His little girl's gone too," Isaac said.

"I know. Well, about Rose, I think it's the same person that took Raven," Joy said.

"What? How do you...? Never mind. Who are they?" Isaac said.

"There's two of them. One calls himself Seef. Lives in Devil's Cay. This man called The Boss ships them to him. That's where Rose will be."

"Devil's Cay!" Isaac said and slapped Crow on the shoulder. "Hear that? Same place the treasure is buried."

Crow stroked at his beard. "Aha."

"We know where the treasure is, Joy." Isaac's eyes were wide with excitement. "Finally!" Isaac scratched the back of his neck.

Crow hadn't seen him like this before. He looked almost bashful.

"I mean, I actually found out a while ago but then Crow's shack exploded, Relocke arrested me, Johnny broke me out then held me captive. Then there was the whole war of course..." Isaac trailed off.

"A lot's happened, miss," Crow added.

"Looks like we're all going to Devil's Cay then." Joy turned to Crow and smiled.

"Now hold up there, miss. I don't know if we'll have

room, there's a full crew."

Joy took out her blade. "I can make room if I need to."

Crow belted out a hearty laugh. "You can have his place!" He pointed to Isaac and wiped a tear from his crinkled eyes. "Have you sailed before?"

"I'm sure you can teach me," Joy replied.

Georgia strode back into the reception area. "Can you lot get out of here? Go be with Popino," Georgia held out her arms and ushered them out. "He's resting."

Isaac grinned from ear to ear and grabbed Georgia's waist. "Resting? So he's okay?"

Georgia nodded.

"Thank you!" Isaac pulled Georgia toward him and threw his arms around her.

Crow led the way into the book-filled room. Isaac's hands pushed at his shoulders as he tried to squeeze past and rush in first. Popino lay underneath the window, resting.

"Pino!" Isaac crept over.

"Leave him be. He's not to be disturbed," Grace said and left the room with bandages and pots of ointment in hand.

"Sorry!" Isaac whispered.

Crow took a seat at the writing desk. Joy and Isaac joined him.

"Is your ship ready?" Joy asked.

"Well..." Crow patted down his jacket. He stuck his hand in his pockets. "It... um... needs a bit of work but I admire your enthusiasm."

"How much?" Joy pressed.

"Sixty doubloons worth," Crow rushed the words out.

"Sixty!" Isaac said and shook his head.

Crow scratched at his beard. He looked down. It had

grown considerably and there was more gray than he last remembered. "I've got that one's doubloons somewhere." He nodded in Popino's direction.

"What do you mean somewhere?" Isaac said.

"Hang on!" Crow untied his pants.

"Okay." Joy looked away.

"I've a hole in my pocket, so I tied it inside," Crow said and retrieved a pouch full of coins.

Isaac shook his head.

Crow tied his pants back up and looked at Joy. "I like your hat."

"I like your jacket," Joy said.

"Well, we've two problems. There's no ship without those doubloons, plus the waters at Devil's Cay are treacherous. Only three people have ever made it there and back alive." Crow held out his hand and counted. "Thad, some man named Leon and..." Crow tapped the table.

"Slim!" Crow and Joy said in unison.

"How do you know him?" Crow asked.

"We're from the same part of town." Joy straightened up her jacket. "I can go talk to him if you like. He's always happy to see me."

"Already proving to be more useful than the boy, might have you take his place after all." Crow laughed. "Now we just need the doubloons."

"Oh, and don't forget that Thad is going to hunt you down and kill you," Isaac said and folded his arms.

"Do you know that Thad is actually Molly?" Joy said.

"Yes!" Crow and Isaac replied in unison.

"Sounds like you need a Master Strategist." Georgia walked in with Grace. The healer scurried over to Popino and changed the cloth on his head.

"I'll get you the map, Isaac," Georgia said and shot him a wink as she left.

Crow noticed Joy's eyes narrow at the gesture.

"We have company!" Georgia yelled and came running back in. "Jane's people are outside! Prepare your weapons!"

"I didn't think any had survived?" Crow said and pulled out his pistol.

Crow followed Georgia as she crept into the reception area. He ran to the front window and peeled back the drape. "They're waving a piece of white cloth. I think they're here to surrender."

"It's probably a trick," Georgia said.

"They don't look armed," Crow replied. He counted a group of twenty or so people. They stood at the front door with their hands up. "Brave coming here... or stupid."

Georgia flung the door open and pointed her rifle. Several women rushed to her side wielding weapons.

"We don't want trouble. We want to join you," a slight dark-haired man said.

"Not interested. We don't take men," Georgia said.

"I'll take 'em," Crow said and stepped away from the window. "Any of you sailed before?"

"No, but we can learn," the dark-haired man nodded.

"Then I'll take the women if you go with him," Georgia said.

The crew of mercenaries nodded.

"Try anything and I'll skin you alive," Crow said and followed it with a hearty laugh. He waved them in and walked back through the reception. "Now, how do we get sixty doubloons?" He scratched at his head and thought of Nelson. What would he do?

MOLLY WEAVER

"What did he say?" Molly looked up from her workspace for a moment. She had been experimenting for days. It kept her mind busy until she could have her day with him. With Crow.

"He wasn't going to take it, the note," Otis said.

"What?" Molly picked up a bottle and hurled the brown glass at the wall. The pieces shattered and scattered across the floor. "That coward! He's not going to know what's hit him by the time I've finished." She picked up a dagger she used to crush up powder and stabbed the point into the desk. "I've had enough of waiting."

She grabbed her chair and smashed the wooden frame into the wall over and over. The spindles splintered and the back fell off. She kept going until there was nothing left intact. Her leg throbbed. She'd tried her best to let the wound heal but it surged with pain each time her anger flared.

She couldn't believe she had survived imprisonment in that filthy rat's nest only to break free and find Daniel gone. Dead. She could never make things right now.

Crow's face haunted her. She threw down the remnants of the chair and stormed out of her room. "Otis!"

"Yes, ma'am, coming." Otis hurried out of the room after her.

Molly walked toward the steep stone steps. The bottom layer of her infamous castle was where she spent most of her time. She was typically alone but those unlucky enough to join her down here didn't usually come out alive. Not only was it the perfect place to torture but also to experiment with explosives or anything else that came to mind.

As Molly climbed the steps she admired the thick stone. This place was solid and sturdy, just like her. The castle stood at the tallest point of Nassau, surrounded by a moat of water. For so long nobody had known she was the one behind this whole operation. People respected her as Molly, but they never knew she was capable of this. Thad was the most feared man in Nassau, and he didn't even exist.

A glimmer of satisfaction brought a wry smile to her face. Her plan to gain Vella's trust then drive her to attack Jane had taken years but she'd finally done it. Though any feelings of victory were short-lived when she thought of Daniel. All she ever wanted was him back in her life, but Crow had taken that from her. Vengeance wouldn't bring him back but it sure would help make her feel better. And once Crow was taken care of she would step out from the shadows and claim Nassau as she so rightfully deserved.

She headed down the long corridor. Otis trod softly behind.

"Ma'am?"

"Yes, Otis."

"I don't fully understand some things. A few of us don't

actually," his voice wavered as he spoke. He quickened his pace to keep up with Molly's huge strides. Even with an injured leg they were still substantial.

"And why do you need to?" She stopped dead in her tracks and turned to face him. He almost smacked into her but stopped just short. "I don't think you're in a position to query my motives. Especially when you withheld information."

"I didn't, I swear, I just never made the connection that he was your... your son." Otis stared up at her.

Molly shook her head and tried to keep her temper in check. Otis had been nothing but loyal for so many years. He'd slipped up on this one, but she couldn't ignore everything else he'd done for her. He was one of the very few she trusted. "What is it you want to know?"

"Why..." He shifted awkwardly and held onto his arm. "Why did you have us slaughter everyone at The Milky Way?" Otis scrunched up his face.

"It had to be done. Drove Vella to finally attack Jane, didn't it?" Molly said and swallowed a surge of bubbling rage.

"But Vella thought it was Thad? I don't..."

Her eyes intensified and burned into Otis. "It drained her of money. Weakened her. She'd never take on Thad first, but her old enemy Jane." Molly's glare didn't falter. "You know this has been the plan. It's been years in the making."

Otis shrank back into himself, fearful of what was to come.

"You delivered thousands of letters for me, helped weave this web of lies to ensure everyone feared Thad yet nobody knew who *he* was."

Otis looked to the floor and nodded.

"Think about it. We opened bounties, we planted seeds of doubt. Look at Jane Hatch. We killed her guard and she ended up dead." Molly smirked.

"Weren't us though," Otis muttered.

"You're missing the point." Molly's hands shook as she quelled the urge not to crush him like an ant.

"We set all of this in motion. Without Johnny on side, without him taking over Crow's crew we would never have had enough men for Vella to risk an attack. And that all came down to knowing where Isaac and Crow would meet that day. We made ourselves the eyes and ears of this island, and yet all you care about is what we did at some brothel?"

Otis cowered and scratched at his head. "We just liked that place."

"Go to The Silky Swallow instead," Molly said through gritted teeth. "I don't expect you to understand everything we've done, but I expect you not to question me." Molly turned away. Her temper simmered. She continued walking. "Besides, we didn't kill them all now, did we?"

"Guess not," Otis mumbled and shuffled behind.

"Ma'am!" A strong looking, dark-haired man walked toward Molly and Otis.

"Patrick." She gave a nod of acknowledgment.

"The perimeter's been lined with that... that clam thing you made," Patrick said.

"You mean the clam bam, Patrick?"

"The name, it's—"

"It's a clam and it makes a loud bam!" Molly smacked her hands together.

Otis and Patrick flinched.

"I'd like to see you come up with something better." Molly crossed her arms and widened her stance.

"Of course I couldn't." Patrick looked to the floor.

"How's the concoction going? The liquid courage. Are the men ready for anything?" Molly asked.

"Seem to be. Few hurled their guts up but that's probably the amount they drank." Patrick laughed.

"To be expected. Have them ready soon, would you? We don't want to give Crow time to plan anything." Molly nodded and proceeded down the corridor. She passed through a tall archway and walked into the dining hall. Rows of dark wooden tables and benches filled the long room. Wrought iron candelabras hung from the ceiling and illuminated the huge space.

"Otis, eat something. I'll call you over when you're needed."

He bowed his head and ran over to where the cook served up the hot meats of the day.

Molly's eyes scanned the room for Arnaud. He wouldn't be hard to spot since he usually wore such unique attire. Molly walked over to the far corner where a slight man was sitting with his feet kicked up on a bench.

"You stand out a mile off," Molly said and took a seat opposite him. He swung his legs down and faced Molly. He wore a bright blue hat with a neckerchief to match and a pale blue, almost gray, linen shirt with the arms rolled up.

"I assume that is because I'm impeccably dressed," he spoke with a thick French accent.

"This is new?" Molly pointed to a glinting gold locket around his neck.

He rubbed at the circular gold piece with his thumb and forefinger. "Bonne chance," he replied and looked down at the sketch he was working on.

Arnaud was quick-witted, astute and an exceptional

artist. These skills not only made him the most valuable informant in Nassau but also the most expensive.

Molly clasped her hands together and leaned on the table. "Tell me Arnaud, do you know of a man they call The Boss?"

"Describe him to me," Arnaud said and pushed his sketchbook aside.

Molly cast her mind back to the cell. "Missing front tooth, weathered—"

"That is everybody in Nassau," Arnaud said.

Molly gave a glimmer of a smile. "True. Dresses head-to-toe in black and red. Hat and captain's jacket as well. Has a gold pin on that jacket. It's distinct."

"A gold serpent?" Arnaud said.

"Could be?" Molly replied.

He grabbed his sketchbook and thumbed through the pages. "Ah."

He stopped and turned the book to face Molly. She cast her eyes over a detailed sketch of three mean-faced men. "That's him." Molly pointed then clenched her fists.

"They're known as The Serpents of Death," Arnaud said.

Molly had never even heard a mere mention of the name. "Go on."

"They've been around for years but don't stay in Nassau for long."

"Where do they go?" Her mind raced in a flurry of intrigue and annoyance.

"I don't know. Though I'd be happy to investigate... find out some more for you."

"I thought you'd have a little more on them considering your detailed sketch?" Molly suspected he was holding something back.

"I draw anything of interest. It doesn't mean I have all the information," Arnaud replied.

Molly nodded and looked over her shoulder. "Otis!" Molly yelled and waved in his direction. He didn't flinch and kept spooning in his stew. Molly rubbed her hand against her forehead. "Why must I..." She stood up and cast a long shadow that engulfed him. He nodded and put down his spoon.

"You want me?" Otis said.

Molly nodded and beckoned him over with her finger. He grabbed his satchel and hurried over. "Arnaud will explain more but I need you to work together on this, find out everything you can."

"Together? Okay, ma'am," Otis replied.

"Yes. It's of the utmost importance. I need to know their every move." She looked at Arnaud. "You will of course be paid handsomely for your troubles."

"Bien sûr." Arnaud gave a tip of his hat and tucked his sketchbook under his arm. He motioned to the door with his head and Otis followed, leaving Molly alone with her thoughts as vengeance boiled in her heart.

POPINO BELTRAME

"Now, how do we get sixty doubloons?" Popino heard a gruff voice say followed by loud footsteps. He told himself to open his eyes, but they wouldn't cooperate. He tried to move but nothing responded. He lay for what felt like an eternity, unable to speak, listening to the chatter of voices. He could have sworn he heard Isaac as he drifted back off to sleep.

He awoke. It seemed like only moments later, but this time his body felt different, more responsive. He focused on moving his hand and gave a small wave, hoping someone would notice.

"I need rum to strategize!"

Popino recognized the chirpy tone. "Isaac?" he said softly and waved again.

"He's coming round, boy," the gruff voice said.

"Pino?" Isaac came hurtling over. He knelt by his side and gave his arm a squeeze. "You're alive!"

Popino winced at his touch. Any movement right now sent throbbing waves of pain through his entire body.

"Get him some water or something."

The voice sounded like Joy's. Popino started to wonder if he was dreaming.

"Where am I?" He stared up at Isaac. His face looked more rugged than ever.

"We're at Vella's place," Isaac said.

Popino's eyes grew wide. Was he in danger?

"It's okay, she's dead," Isaac whispered.

Popino let his eyes fall shut again. "Rose?" he asked.

"She's definitely not here. Joy thinks she might be in Devil's Cay," Isaac said.

Popino scrunched his eyes tight. He just wanted this nightmare to end. "Did..." He took a breath in and was met with a deep stabbing pain in his side. "Did we win?"

"Win what? The battle? Nobody really won. Most are dead," Isaac said.

Popino touched his bandaged side.

"You got shot, but lucky for you the ball seems to have passed right through." Isaac nodded.

"It hurts. A lot," Popino said and tried to sit up. Searing pain blazed at his side. "Think I'll just lay here," he said, his voice faint.

The man with the gruff voice cast a shadow over him. "Remember me?"

Popino stared up at the crinkled face. He had a long, thick salt and pepper beard and a well-worn black captain's jacket. Popino shook his head.

"This is Captain Crow, Pino. Remember? I told you about him." Isaac nodded and shot Popino a wink.

"The map. Sorry," Popino muttered.

"Hmm." Crow gave a disgruntled grunt as he walked away.

A strong looking woman with a spiral of gray beaded dreads strode into the room. Isaac moved aside and she took his place at Popino's side. She tipped a tumbler of liquid into his mouth. The bitter aftertaste wasn't pleasant, but he was grateful to have some fluid back in his body.

"You shouldn't have left Roy's!" Joy walked into view and smiled. "I was planning on coming back, you know."

He nodded. The gray-haired woman gave a tip of her head and disappeared. He cleared his throat. "I'm confused. How do you know she's in Devil's Cay? Did Vella send Rose there?" Popino asked.

Joy shook her head. "It wasn't Vella."

"The note though?" Popino said, his voice strained as a wave of pain surged through him.

"Must have been fake. She's been kidnapped by the same people that took Raven." Joy's eyes fixed on the floor. "I tried to find her but I think she was already gone."

Popino shut his eyes. "Do we know who they are?"

"We do, and I'm going to hunt them down myself." Joy held a clenched fist to her mouth. "They call one The Boss. He's in charge here in Nassau but works for a man named Seef."

Popino nodded and opened his eyes. He took in Joy's beautiful, soft face. Her delicate skin reminded him of Rose's. His poor girl would be scared out of her mind... He wanted to slit their throats. Carve out their hearts. Popino swallowed hard. "So, nothing to do with Vella?"

"I really don't think so. Rest, anyway. You need to get better. Won't survive the journey to Devil's Cay otherwise." Joy gave him a smile and walked away.

Crow scowled. "Who said he could come? Come on, boy, we've planning to do." Crow sat at a writing desk and jiggled a map at Isaac. "Can't let Thad get to us first." Crow frowned and looked to the floor. "She's the reason Nelson's dead." Crow flexed his hand and made a tight fist.

Popino could tell it took everything in him not to smash it into the table. His mind cast back to the battle and what that strange man who gnawed on that weird meat told him. "You know... someone told me that Molly is Thad?" Popino said in a faint whisper.

Isaac nodded. "Yes! I still can't believe it! Now, where is that rum?"

The lip-ringed door-greeter walked in with a bottle in hand. "Here you go!" She handed the bottle to Isaac who took a seat next to Crow. "Oh hello," she said and walked over to Popino. She knelt at his bedside. "Glad to see you're awake." She took the cloth from his head. "I'll have Grace get you another." She placed her hand on his.

"Thank you. Thank you for this." Popino flashed a smile.

"You're welcome," she said and put her mouth to his ear. "I know about Thomas."

Popino's eyes grew wide. He shook his head. "Who?"

"At the Boucher house. Thomas was Vella's son," Georgia whispered and squeezed his hand. "But don't worry, your secret's safe with me. I'll figure out repayment." Her hand wandered down to his crotch.

Popino coughed. "Yes, thank you, okay. Thank you."

"I'll have Grace come with that cloth." She shot him a wink and rose to her feet.

Popino lay still and stared at the beige ceiling in horror. He certainly hadn't forgotten what had happened with Eva and Lucien, but it had been pushed to the back of his mind when Rose was taken. He wondered how many people knew about the Boucher incident. He'd surely be hanged for their murders.

"What's this?" Crow waved something and interrupted Popino's racing thoughts.

"Put it back on the map. It's for planning. Vella, Jane, Thad, they all have one," Isaac said and snatched the small carved wooden wolf from Crow's hand. "The wolf represents Vella's people."

"You can take Jane's away," Joy said and took a seat at the table. "She's dead." Joy grabbed the wooden fox figure.

"Dead?" Popino raised his head.

"Can I keep this actually?" Joy waved the fox at Crow and Isaac. They nodded in response.

Popino put his head back down on the makeshift pillow and closed his eyes. For the first time in a long time a wave of relief washed over him. Jane was dead and with Vella out of the picture too there was no one left to pay. Georgia seemed to want something else from him and he was happy to oblige. Could he finally be debt free after all these years? It didn't bring Rose back, but it would help them once he found her... eventually. He'd need to deal with the Boucher incident though. He hoped it really was a secret.

Isaac swigged from the rum bottle. "I don't know how to even get close to that giant castle. It's surrounded by water."

Crow scratched at his beard. "Hmm. What about the doubloons? I need sixty to fix Black Beauty." His eyes twinkled as he spoke.

"Is that your ship's name? I can't wait to see her. Is she like The Fancy?" Isaac asked.

"Better, boy. You just wait," Crow replied.

"I have some." Popino waved his hand.

"Ships?" Crow said and let out a raucous laugh.

"Doubloons," Popino said.

Crow stroked at his beard. "So do I. Well, they're yours actually." He walked toward Popino and stood over him.

He pulled out the pouch and tossed it on the floor. "Thirty, I believe. The boy said I was to give them back to you."

"How about you keep them as payment. I need to come to Devil's Cay, but I won't be much use until this fully heals." Popino looked down at his side. "I have more too." He patted his belt. "I took them from Vella."

"Ever the thief!" Crow looked around to check if Vella's people were around. "It's our secret, okay?" Crow said. His eyes burned into him.

"Yes, of course. And I can sail with you?" Popino tried to sit up. He closed his eyes tight as pain shot through him.

"Not sure how much sailing you can do but sure. It's a deal. Now don't move, kid, I'll untie that pouch." Crow reached over and fiddled with Popino's belt. Popino turned his head to the side and looked away, hoping that the Captain would just untie the pouch and not slit his throat. "Thank you for keeping your word. Isaac told me you would."

"I always do." Crow shook the pouch and grinned. "Black Beauty will be back on the water before we know it. Now, who's going to see Woodman Jack?" Crow asked and looked at Joy.

Joy scrunched up her face. "Fine!"

"You have certain assets he appreciates. Might help us get a better price. Besides, it seems you can handle yourself," Crow said.

"Yeah, yeah." Joy rolled her eyes. "I'll go see Slim, then Woodman Jack. But first I need a word with you, in private." Joy pointed at Isaac.

Isaac pointed at himself and raised his eyebrows.

"Lucky!" Popino winked and smiled.

Joy and Isaac walked out leaving Crow and Popino alone.

Popino lay there and thought of Rose. He tried not to panic himself, but he couldn't help it. She'd be so frightened. If he hadn't borrowed so much, if he hadn't gone to the brothel that day, he wouldn't be in this mess. The thoughts played over and over in his head. The guilt gnawed at his gut. Occasional grunts came from Crow's direction.

"Can I help?" Popino asked.

"Any good with strategy?"

Popino shook his head. "Good with a pistol though."

"Well, that will come in handy later. Where's the boy? They've been gone a while."

Popino smiled. "You know they're probably just..."

Isaac and Joy strode in through the door smiling.

Joy snatched up the pouches of doubloons and attached them to her belt. "I'll be off then. You three better have a plan for Thad by the time I return," she said as she walked out the door.

"Doubt it." Crow grumbled once more.

Nobody had moved from the room in hours. Isaac occasionally strode around stroking at his chin and demanding more rum. Crow sat scratching his beard, grunting. And Popino lay in his makeshift bed, trying his best to rest.

"Why does Thad want you dead anyway?" Popino asked. He sat up a little and this time the pain was manageable. He propped himself against the wall underneath the window.

"Killed her son apparently." Crow shrugged.

"Thunder?" Popino cocked his head to the side. "Big guy, arms as big as my head?"

Crow looked up and narrowed his eyes in thought. "Is that who it was? He killed Vella so..."

Popino kept quiet. Thunder had done him a favor, but he didn't think Crow would appreciate hearing that.

"That's it!" Isaac yelled. He stopped pacing and stood frozen to the spot.

"Yes, yes, yes!" He ran over to the map. "Joy told me a story while we were—"

"I hope she waited for you to finish." Popino slapped at his thigh and laughed.

Isaac shot him a look of disapproval followed by a smile. "I've got it. I know how to get to Thad."

JOY LAFITTE

"Slim! There you are!"

"Miss Joy! It's been far too long since I laid my eyes on your loveliness."

Slim limped toward her. He was a short, scrawny man who looked underfed, and despite the glorious Nassau weather like he had never seen the sun.

"To what do I owe the pleasure?" He gave a small bow.

Joy peered down the alleyway where Slim crouched beneath a window. "I need your help. But first, what are you doing here?"

"I need to break in, you see. There's something that these men have that I want." He placed his hand on his chest.

Joy crept toward him and kept low. He pointed up to the window and grinned. She stole a glance inside the wooden hut. Three brutish men stood gathered around a table, heads down, assembling weapons.

She quickly ducked as one man turned his gaze to the window.

"What is this place?"

"Thad's weapon store." Slim nodded, his eyes filled with mischief.

"Well, what you want better be worth it." Joy crouched and kept out of sight.

"Oh, it is, Miss Joy." Slim rubbed his hands together and grinned. "Look again and you'll see something on the table to the right."

Joy raised her head and peered in. "There's a big greenish ball, or is that thing a fruit?"

"Melon!" Slim said and licked his lips.

Joy shrugged. "I don't know it."

"It's rare in these parts but I've had a taste before. It's too good to miss." Slim smiled. "If you help me, I'll split it with you."

Joy thought about Slim's proposition. She couldn't care less about tasting that thing, but she did need his help. And if she had to battle these three brutes for that, then she would. "If I do it, will you help me with my request?"

Slim's eyes widened with enthusiasm. "What is it?"

"I need you to navigate a crew of us to Devil's Cay," Joy said.

Slim threw his arms in the air. "Of course! You know my brother's still there, Miss Joy?"

"I didn't, but I know you're one of few to make it there and back alive."

"One of three people!" Slim held his finger in the air. "But first we must have the melon. That's my one and only condition."

Joy rolled her eyes. "You're going to risk it all for that melon?"

"You haven't tasted it! Plus, with your help there's no risk, Miss Joy. I just need you to provide the distraction."

He looked her up and down. "Any man is distracted by you."

Joy let her jacket fall open and pulled down her top. "They're distracted by these. Ha! Let's make our way to the door. Then I'll go ahead and pretend to be lost." Joy led the way. She walked around the corner and assessed the door. The well-worn wood didn't look like it would be hard to kick down, and it had no lock.

She strode over and pushed the door open. To her surprise it swung back and she walked in with her hands on her hips. She stuck out her chest and gave her most charming smile. The men looked up startled. "Sorry, boys, I think I'm lost. Can you help?"

"Oi! You're not meant to be in here," the tallest of the three said and placed a box on the ground. "This is private property."

The other two men wiped their dirty hands on rags in unison and leered at Joy.

"I know but I'm lost and I thought you could help." Joy feigned a pout and looked at them wide eyed. She wasn't scared but she hoped Slim would step in soon. She needed to get to Woodman Jack's before sundown.

"How'd you find us in here? Who sent you?" the tall man asked and walked toward her. The other two stood behind him and folded their arms. She was about to reply and tell them they weren't as discreet as they thought they were when blood burst from their temples and they each dropped to the floor. Joy recoiled as some splattered onto her face.

Slim laughed. "That was much easier with you here!"

Joy turned to Slim. Her mouth fell open. "How did you... How did you get all three at once? I've never seen that before."

"It's my new rifle." He held up a long gun and unscrewed the barrel. "It's very powerful. It comes apart so you can carry it, see?" He took the barrel and shoved the metal tube down his pant leg. He smiled at his handiwork and attached the other part of the gun to his hip. "Plus, they were lined up in a row nicely. Now, where is that sweet fruit?"

"I didn't think you would kill them... for some melon?" Joy wiped the blood from her face with a nearby rag. Slim busied himself cutting the melon open with a thick carving knife.

"How far does that thing shoot?"

"Well, if you're good and take the wind into account, very far. Made it myself I did," he said with pride and handed a piece of the juicy fruit to Joy.

She sniffed at the hunk of thick-skinned fruit and took a bite. "Do I eat these seeds?" she asked with her mouthful. The sweet soft flesh burst in her mouth.

"Spit 'em out. We should save some though, try and plant our own." Slim's eyes went wide with glee as he sunk his teeth into the ripe flesh.

"This is good. Though not sure we should have killed three men for it," Joy said in between a mouthful.

"I'd say it's worth the price." Slim discarded the skin and sliced another piece. "So, who's heading the crew to Devil's Cay?"

"Captain Crow," Joy replied.

Slim grinned and rubbed his hands.

"I'm about to go see Woodman Jack to get the ship fixed. We should be ready to go soon," Joy said.

"I'll meet you later then. I'll go find Crow... and Nelson." Slim grabbed the remainder of the melon and limped out of the building.

"Just Crow, Nelson's dead. Oh, and they're at Vella's," Joy said.

"Nelson's dead? They're at Vella's?" He looked to the floor and shook his head. "If you say so, Miss Joy. I'll be seeing you."

"Bye, Slim."

Joy headed for the old wood yard.

"Well, if it isn't the delightful Miss Lafitte," Grimm said. He stood next to Woodman Jack with his arms folded, staring at a broken ship hull. Woodman Jack was most definitely the bushiest man she had ever seen; a thick layer of white hair covered every inch of him. He wore a scruffy black shirt with rolled up sleeves and leant on an axe.

"What are you doing here?" Joy asked.

"I could ask you the same question," Grimm said.

"Maybe she's come to see me." Woodman Jack gave Grimm a nudge and leered at Joy for an uncomfortably long time.

"I certainly have." She stood with her hands on her hips and stuck her chest out.

Woodman Jack didn't take his eyes off her. He stroked at his beard as he gazed at her chest.

Grimm noticed Woodman Jack's longing stare and shook his head. "Glad I bumped into you. I believe this is yours." Grimm twirled the button-sized coin in the air and caught it with ease. Joy held out her hand, unimpressed. He dropped the silver piece into her outstretched palm and attempted a smile.

"Thanks. Dare I asked what favor you called in?" Joy smirked.

"You don't want to know." Grimm winked. "Anyway, I best be heading off. Thank you, Jack, I'll let you know." Grimm walked away leaving Joy alone to negotiate.

Woodman Jack strode over to the broken ship hull and stroked at the wood. "She's a fine one." He turned to Joy and stared. "Just like you."

"We've business to discuss."

"Maybe a bit of fun first?"

It took everything in Joy not to storm over there and press a blade to his neck. "I need you to fix Black Beauty," Joy said and ignored his vulgarity.

"You can't afford it. Though I'm sure we could come to some arrangement."

Joy took out the sacks of doubloons and tossed them in front of him. "Check the bags, should be sixty." He threw down his axe and greedily snatched the sacks from the ground.

Joy eyed the yard as Jack engrossed himself in counting. Dozens of battered and broken ship parts lay scattered as far as the eye could see. Some looked to be more barnacle than wood at this point and others merely looked damaged from battle.

"You've got enough coin," Jack said and offloaded the sacks into his own.

"I know." Joy smiled though it pained her.

"Tell Crow it'll take a week or two."

"Can it be done any quicker?"

"Well, that depends…" Jack leered at her chest once more.

"I'll come back and visit each day?" Joy said.

"I might take my time then." He shot her a wink which made her skin crawl. She marched over and whipped out one of her small blades.

"Jack! If you do, I'll poke you with one of these!" She held the blade under his chin.

Jack leaned his head back. "It's worth it to feel you press up against me." He let out a longing sigh.

She grabbed his collar. "Don't. Push. It!"

"Fine, I'll have it done as soon as I can."

She released her grip and watched in disbelief as he sniffed at the part of his shirt she had touched. Joy rolled her eyes as she walked away. She loathed his lecherous behavior but he knew ships and that was all that mattered right now.

Joy fanned herself with her jacket as she made her way through the streets of town back to Vella's. The sun was still blazing hot despite the time of day. Out the corner of her eye she saw a man that looked exactly like Isaac rush by. She'd recognize that handsome face anywhere, though she didn't like to admit it. "Isaac!" Joy yelled and ran after him.

He turned and glanced over his shoulder. "Oh, Joy! It's just you. Thank goodness. I mean not just you. You know what I mean." He shrugged and looked a little bashful.

"What's in the bag? Shouldn't you be strategizing at Vella's?"

He shook his head. "I've got it! You gave me the idea."

Joy threw her hands up, confused.

"The story you told me about Jane's camp during the trial with Thunder, y'know? I'll explain, follow me. We need to attack Thad... before she gets to us!"

MOLLY WEAVER

"I bring news." Arnaud tipped his striking bright blue hat as he took a seat opposite Molly in the main hall.

"Already?" Molly raised her brows. "It's only been a few days."

Arnaud relaxed back. "I can take longer if you like? But I don't like to keep a lady waiting."

Molly wasn't used to being referred to as a lady and whilst it had a nice ring to it, she wasn't entirely comfortable with the term. "Very well. What have you got for me?" Molly leaned in to listen. The raucous chatter which filled the hall was near deafening. Her men were polishing their weapons and swigging down drink with gusto in preparation for battle.

Arnaud flipped open his sketchbook. "See this?" He pointed to two ships side by side. "This smaller ship is The Fancy. You know it, right?"

"Of course, but it's not small, it's one of the biggest to dock here. Hasn't moved in a long time," Molly said.

Arnaud nodded. "Yes, but this ship makes it look small." He pointed to the much larger vessel.

"It's an old slave ship which now belongs to The Serpents of Death."

Molly stared at the chunks of brass on the table before her; two custom-made pieces built to slot onto her knuckles. She'd never used them before, but they were sure to make for one hell of a fight. Her brows dipped and she pressed her lips together. "If it's so big then why haven't I seen it?"

"Exactly! Doesn't make sense, but that's because it never docks here. They keep this ship at a nearby island and take a much smaller one here which they keep in the backwaters."

Molly let out a huge sigh and tapped her finger on the tabletop.

Arnaud tipped his head. "It seems The Boss had purposely stayed away from Nassau. Left the island to you, Vella and Jane but now..." Arnaud snapped his book shut.

"What does he want? The island?" Molly clenched her shaking fist.

Arnaud nodded.

She banged her fist on the table. "I've waited too long and sacrificed too much to let anyone take it from me!" She tried to keep her voice low but it was difficult. She had spent years slowly weakening Vella and her people. Years of hiding in the shadows. This was her time, and no man was about to take that away from her.

"Apparently they live in Devil's Cay but come here for trade." Arnaud averted his gaze. "They take children from here."

Molly kept quiet and cracked her knuckles. A storm brewed inside of her. She hated everything about these 'Serpents'.

"Not many make it there and back alive, but they seem to have found a way around that." Arnaud shrugged. "I'm sure none of this will stop you getting what you want though." He smiled though it seemed forced.

"Thank you, Arnaud. Insightful as ever." She took out a handful of coins and dropped them into his hand. "A little extra to—"

"Ma'am!" A slender man with plaited, long, brown hair ran toward them. He clutched a rifle in one hand and used the other to mop the sweat from his brow.

"Yes, Arthur?" Molly didn't like being interrupted, but she knew her men would only do it if necessary.

"There's..." He caught his breath. "There's some sort of battle."

"Yes? That's what we're all preparing for." Molly crossed her arms.

"No! Outside, right now!"

"What?" She jumped to her feet.

"It's Crow and... I don't know. Some others, they're fighting, just outside the gates."

She strapped the pieces of brass to her knuckles. "Men! Prepare your weapons and follow me." She strode out of the main hall and down the corridor as fast as she could. Her leg hadn't fully healed, but she had enough men to make sure that wouldn't be an issue.

"Seems Crow thought he could breach the walls. Ha! For as long as I'm still alive, nobody ever shall! We will show them what we're made of! Why Thad owns Nassau." She let out a howl and the men joined in. She raised her fist as she marched down the hall toward the door. "The call of the Coyote will haunt them, even in death!" She paused as two men pulled thick chains and raised the door to the grounds. Molly stepped outside and into the

405

palm-filled land which separated the house and the main gate.

"Arthur, have they stepped on any of the clams yet?" Molly asked.

"No, they're too busy fighting. Haven't even tried the main gate yet," he replied.

"Keep the gate shut until I say otherwise." Molly stormed over to the twelve-foot-high thick stone wall and climbed the ladder which ran to the top. Her eyes fixed on the guard. "What is it?"

He shook his head in response, his face filled with worry. "They're dead, ma'am, all of them," the guard said and looked away.

"What?" Molly peered over the edge.

"I watched... saw it all happen. Crow and his men were marching toward us, up the hill, and then they got ambushed by another group." He pointed down at the scattered bodies which lay across the grounds outside the wall. "A few went flying into the moat—"

"Ambushed? By whom?" Molly narrowed her gaze. She made out a couple of bodies with Vella's signature dreadlocked hair, some of Crow's motley crew too. "The fox—Jane Hatch's people." Molly pointed to a flag which lay on the ground next to a body. "They can't all be dead! I don't believe it. It's a trick."

"But there's blood, ma'am, I saw them get shot." His hands shook as he stared at the floor. "I'm sorry, ma'am, I should have—"

"Open the gate!" Molly glared at him as she clomped down the ladder. She winced with each rung as her wounded leg flared. Her foot touched the bottom, and she turned to her men. Around thirty stood waiting, ready for action with various blades and pistols in hand. "Shoot the idiot, Arthur. What sort of a guard doesn't alert me sooner?"

Arthur nodded and raised his rifle. "Never liked him anyway."

Molly paused and waited for the snap of gunfire to settle. "Now, do you remember where you planted the clam bams?" she asked.

The men nodded in agreement. Several swayed with their eyes shut. They had been drinking solidly for days now but had downed Molly's liquid courage at the last minute. The concoction supposedly absorbed any ill effects from drinking but still gave them the drunken confidence to give it their all, though it didn't seem to be working.

The main gate rattled open and Molly pushed any thoughts of her men's shortcomings to the back of her mind. She stormed through the gate arch, over the bridge and out into the field littered with bodies. Her eyes searched for any signs of movement. Nothing. Her men followed close behind. "Check they're dead. Take their weapons." The men staggered about the field poking and kicking at the bodies.

Her eyes scoured the area. She made a left and hurried past body after body with no sign of Crow. "Find anyone with a captain's jacket and bring them to me!" she yelled. She narrowed her eyes. They stopped on a black-jacketed man with a blood-soaked, long gray beard. "It's him!" Molly stormed toward his body, blinded with rage. She towered over him. There was no sign of movement. For a moment everything around her disappeared into the darkness as thoughts of Daniel pricked at her mind. She'd been dreaming of tearing Crow limb from limb, making him pay for snatching away her chance to change things with her son. But it was too late.

Her body tensed with rage as she stared down at his face. It wasn't meant to be like this. She needed vengeance. She grabbed his jacket collar and went to lift him off the ground but a hot, burning pain stopped her. The snap of gunfire rang through the air.

"You!" she yelled as she dropped to her knees. Her leg seared with pain. It was unbearable. She toppled to the ground and tried to drag herself away but to no avail.

"Surprise!" Crow rose up to sitting with a smoking flintlock pistol in hand.

Molly tried to reach out and grab him but for once she felt weak. Screams of agony filled the air. She looked around to see her men stumbling about and dropping to the ground. Her breath quickened as pain surged through her body. How could she have been so stupid, so consumed by rage?

She lay on her front and turned her head to the side. He'd shot her good leg. She couldn't even crawl away. "You bastard!" she said through labored breaths.

"You should have left things alone," Crow said and raised his pistol toward her head. "Bye, Thad, or whatever your name is."

ISAAC CARVER

"No!" Isaac leapt in front of Crow, shielding Molly. "We don't have to do this."

"Get out the way, boy." Crow kept his pistol in place. "Don't you want the treasure? If we don't do this, there's no treasure!"

"Can't you just..." Isaac looked back at Molly who lay face down, blood pouring from her leg. "Just, let her live? We'll be sailing away soon enough."

Crow waved his pistol and motioned for Isaac to move, but he stood firm. "You came up with this plan, the fake blood, the playing dead. If you didn't want her killed, you shouldn't have done all this." Crow threw up his arms and swiped at the air.

Isaac rubbed his palms over his face. "I know, I know, but—"

"But nothing, move!" Crow yelled and pushed Isaac aside. "She won't stop hunting us down until we're dead."

Molly turned her head to the side and tried to push herself up. "He's right," she said through gritted teeth. "You killed my only son. I'll never stop until you're dead."

Crow shook his head. "First of all, I didn't know he was your son. I didn't even know you were...you!" Crow looked at Isaac. "She killed Nelson. Remember that, boy. You were there, it was her order." Crow shook his fist at Molly. "He didn't deserve that end."

Isaac shrugged. Crow was right. "Well, I tried." His shoulders sank as he looked back at Molly and frowned. "I'll miss our chess matches." He pressed his lips together and turned away. He'd picked his side, but he couldn't watch this. They'd been friends, of sorts anyway. They had something, a bond. At least he did with Molly but not Thad. Still, Molly had been lying to him for years. How could he ever trust her? He was angry but his heart filled with sadness at the thought of her being gunned down.

Crow took a step forward. "This is for Nelson," he said and raised his pistol.

Isaac tensed and held his breath.

Boom!

A series of explosions erupted. Crow stumbled backwards and lowered his gun. "Don't move," Isaac said and checked the surrounding field for whatever had exploded. Joy ran toward them. "Isaac! Behind you! Run!"

"Don't listen, don't move! I think whatever is exploding is buried around us." Isaac's eyes searched frantically for the source.

"You would be right." Molly gave a wry smile.

"What are they, Molly? Help us get out of here, and we can team up? It doesn't have to be like this," Isaac said as more explosions erupted.

Crow shot him a glare. "In your dreams, boy."

"We've got company." Molly motioned with her head behind them.

"Captain Crow! Don't move another muscle," an

unfamiliar voice spoke. Isaac swung around to see nearly fifty men running out from the dense foliage surrounding the castle. They were led by a tall, weathered man wearing a black and red captain's jacket. Isaac looked to Crow, whose face said it all. Pistols were pointed at them from all angles and explosives surrounded them. There was nowhere left to turn.

Isaac patted at his inside pockets hoping for something to help them out of this mess. He felt the crinkled map and sharp edge of the cards but nothing more. "Do you know him?" Isaac asked.

Crow shook his head.

"Well, he seems to know you!" Isaac said. His heart sunk. Why did they get themselves into this?

"Put the pistol down, Crow. On the ground in front of you," the man in the captain's jacket ordered. This man stared at Isaac but every time Isaac tried to catch his gaze he looked away. Something about him seemed odd yet familiar.

"You put yours down first," Crow said.

"The boy gets shot if you don't," the man said and pointed his pistol at Isaac.

Crow looked to Isaac and lowered his gun without hesitation. He crouched and placed his pistol on the ground in front of him. "We're out of luck, boy."

Isaac searched the faces of the men before him. He didn't recognize any of them. They each wore a black bandana and vest with some sort of snake and skull painted on them.

"Who are you?" Crow asked and put his hands in the air. Isaac followed his lead.

"It's you!" Molly said with a tone of disgust. She tried to push herself up but couldn't.

411

"Indeed it is. I'm sure you thought you'd got away from us." The weathered man smiled and revealed a missing front tooth. "But I never got what was promised to me. I'm still missing half a map." The man took out a piece of torn tattered parchment and held it up.

Isaac's eyes grew wide. He tried to show no reaction but it proved difficult. There was the other half to their map.

"So where is it? You might as well tell us 'cause we're about to ransack your place and find it anyway," the weathered man said.

"It's not in there." Molly scoffed. She grasped at her leg and scowled in Crow's direction.

"Who are you?" Crow asked again and shook his head.

"I'm The Boss, Captain Crow," the man said with confidence and turned his gaze to Isaac. Their eyes met and The Boss quickly looked away. "Round them up, bind their wrists. We'll decide what to do with them in a moment. Get the girl too." He pointed in Joy's direction. Three men dragged her toward them. She kicked and screamed every inch of the way, managing to nick one with one of her concealed blades.

"Pf, didn't even hurt," one of the men said. He wiped a spot of blood from his leg. "Barely even a cut, love."

"Ha! You'll see," Joy yelled as they dragged her over and shoved her down next to Isaac.

Isaac knew Joy's tricks, that blade would most definitely be poisoned.

A man with a hook hand used a wooden club to hit Crow in the back of the legs. Crow dropped to his knees. Isaac saw Crow squint with pain, but he made no sound.

The man with the hook hand moved over to Isaac who knelt before he had a chance to hit him.

412

"Coward," the man with the hook hand said.

"Or clever," Isaac muttered under his breath.

A sweaty man shoved Joy to the ground. She knelt alongside Isaac and Crow.

"Get the beast too!" The Boss laughed.

Several of the black bandana-wearing men ran over to Molly and dragged her to be in line with the others. Molly did what she could to make it difficult, but she couldn't hide the pain in her face as they pummeled her and dragged her through the dirt.

The hook-handed man stood before Joy and waggled his crotch in her face. Joy spat at him. "Fuck you, Leon!"

Isaac's chest tightened as Leon continued to harass Joy.

"That fire in you, I love it." Leon scraped the point of his hook down her face.

"Go any further and I'll bite your cock off!" Joy yelled.

The men all laughed.

"I'd like to see you try," Leon said and turned to the men.

"Ha! Is it too small? Is that what you're saying?" Joy smirked.

The men erupted in more laughter, elbowing one another and leering at Joy.

Isaac squirmed. Joy was full of fire; it was part of her appeal, but it always got them into trouble.

"Shut up!" Leon smacked her across the face. His hook tore at her cheek.

Isaac winced. He hated to see her hurt.

"What do you want with us, Boss? Or should I call you Mr. Boss?" Crow said.

"You're in no position to mock me." The Boss smacked Crow across the face with his closed fist.

413

Crow shook it off. He puffed out his chest and fixed his eyes on the weathered man. "If it's coin, we ain't got it."

The Boss swaggered up and down, grinning. "A poor pirate? Not sure if I believe that one. We're not poor. Are we, boys?" He swung around and looked at his men who cheered in agreeance. "But then again, we're the ones holding the pistols. I think you've lost your touch, Crow. I remember when you used to rule these seas, spend doubloons without a second thought."

Crow shifted from one knee to another and grumbled.

"I don't know what we want with you... yet. What do you think, boys? Any ideas?" He turned to his men and flashed a wicked smile.

Isaac stared at the scene unfolding before him. The name clicked into place. This was the man Joy spoke of— The Boss. He was the one selling children to someone in Devil's Cay. He had Rose. Isaac swallowed the pressing lump in his throat.

"I've got some ideas for her," a toothless man stroked at Joy's face. Isaac could see the rage blazing in her eyes.

"Oh, just kill 'em already, I want to go in that place!" A tall, hairy man pointed to Thad's castle.

"Sounds good!" The Boss agreed and laughed. "Though..." He tapped his forefinger on his chin.

"John!" Molly yelled out of nowhere.

"What?" The Boss said and scrunched up his face.

"You're John fucking Carver!" Molly shuffled a little and tried to steady herself to her feet, but several men pushed her back down.

"John..." Isaac said under his breath. He couldn't believe his ears. He stared at the man's weathered face in disbelief. "My father?"

"I knew I recognized you. I've been around these parts

414

longer than most," Molly said and held her chin up in the air. "You can only hide for so long." She smirked.

"I wasn't hiding! You're the one hiding! Hiding behind this!" The Boss waved his arms in the air. His face grew red and he balled his pistol-free hand into a fist. "Nassau isn't yours anymore... you, you..." He stormed over to Molly and cracked his black wood pistol across her face. "We don't need your help. We'll find the rest of that map ourselves."

She shook it off and tried to headbutt his crotch but with no luck. "At least I wouldn't murder my own son!" Molly spat out a mouthful of blood onto his boots.

"Kill her! Now!" The Boss ordered and looked square at Isaac.

"Gladly," Leon said and picked up his wooden club.

"Beat her to death," The Boss said with such venom that Isaac even saw Crow wince.

"Don't ever trust him, Isaac!" Molly yelled as Leon and five others stormed toward her. Leon swung his club in a circle and smashed it down into Molly's leg. Isaac winced. Anybody else would have screamed in pain but not Molly.

"Not so tough now, are ya!" Leon shouted and smashed his club across her back. The others joined in, kicking at her sides and stomping on any part they could. Isaac watched in horror. He told himself to look away, but he couldn't. Leon screamed as he hit her across the face. They pummeled her over and over until her body lay still.

Isaac wanted to drown out the noise. His stomach knotted and churned. He looked over at Joy who stared down and didn't move. Crow kept his gaze straight ahead. These men were brutal and led by his own fucking father. This monster was the man who had left him with nothing.

The abusive drunk he assumed dead. And now he was to die by his hand.

"Yes!" Leon tossed the blood coated club aside and raised his hook.

"Stop! She's dead!" Isaac yelled.

"Shut it!" Crow snapped.

Leon turned to Crow, his face splattered with blood. "And you're next, old man."

Isaac's vision grew cloudy. His heart thumped in his chest. He shut his eyes. The lump in his throat throbbed. Isaac sensed a presence close. He opened his eyes to see his father standing before him.

"It's just business, son. She would have done the same."

Isaac looked over at Molly. Blood poured from her head and seeped into the ground. Business or not, no one deserved that kind of end, he thought. He looked into his father's eyes. It had been so long since he'd seen him, but that cold, stony hate still shone through.

"What next? You kill Crow? Then me? Your own son! It wasn't enough you left me to die once with nothing, now it has to be by your hand!" Isaac choked back tears. He didn't want to cry. He didn't want this man to witness the hurt in his heart. He thought of that moment. The moment he played over and over in his head. He'd tried to drink it away. To blot it out. His father locked him in that coop with nothing. To starve to death. To die. And now this. The hurt vanished and the anger took over. He glared at the monster before him.

Isaac's father crouched to his eye level. "I wouldn't kill you, boy, I was just waiting for Thad to be out the way. Now that's taken care of, what say you join us? We can try to be a family again, can't we?" He smiled but his eyes didn't crinkle. "I've changed."

Isaac could feel the tears welling. He wanted so desperately to believe him. "Then why didn't you come back for me?"

John shrugged. "I was a drunk. I didn't think you were alive. I'm better now, haven't touched a drop in years."

Isaac shook his head and looked to the ground. There was no way he didn't know he was alive. Everyone in Nassau knew him. This prick was lying, just like he used to. He hadn't changed.

"Untie him." John beckoned to the tall, hairy man who sauntered over and cut the rope on Isaac's wrists.

"Now can we go, Boss?" the hairy man asked and pointed to the castle.

"Of course. Come, Isaac." John held out his hand to Isaac. "Finish off the rest." He waved his hand in Joy and Crow's direction. "Then we raid that place!" He pointed in the direction of the thick stone walled castle and walked toward it.

Isaac scrambled to his feet. He couldn't feel his legs. He looked over to Crow who nodded and smiled.

"Don't worry about me, boy." Crow stared straight ahead and held his head high.

He couldn't even bear to look at Joy. He had to save them or at the very least try.

"Crow first but then make sure ya leave the beautiful Joy for me," Leon said and snatched up his blood-soaked club.

"Get the treasure, boy, for me and for Nelson!" Crow shouted as Leon raised his club.

Without wasting another second Isaac hurled himself between Leon and Crow, knocking them both to the ground. "The treasure! I have the map!" Isaac yelled and grabbed Crow by the arm. The pair scrambled to their feet.

417

"Ya fucker!" Leon reached out and grabbed Isaac by the leg, but Isaac kicked his hand away.

Click.

At least twenty barrels now pointed at them. "Don't shoot! I have the other half of the map! Molly wasn't lying, she didn't have it. I do," Isaac yelled and put his hands above his head. His heart raced. His father stopped in his tracks and turned to face him.

"I should have known you'd try something." John folded his arms. "No son of mine wouldn't." He gave a wicked smile.

"Let them go and you can have it," Isaac said.

"How about I have it and don't let them go? Besides, what says you're not lying to me?" John said.

"Why kill them? Thad's gone. They won't cause you any trouble. You have Nassau. And you have my word."

"A notorious captain and a bounty hunter? I'm sure they won't." John curled his lip in disdain. "You think I'm stupid?"

"No, what would that make me, Father?" Isaac tried to evoke some sort of emotion other than hate.

"Show it to me, the map," John said.

Isaac reached into his pocket. His hand brushed his flask which sparked an idea. He grabbed out the pewter vessel and searched for the map. His hand struck the folded tattered parchment. He took it out and waved it in the air. "See?"

Leon reached for it but Isaac snatched it away. A vile gleam flickered in John's eyes. Isaac remembered that look of insatiable greed well.

"Let them go and the location of Kidd's thirty thousand doubloons is yours." Isaac nodded. The eyes of every man around him lit up. "What do you say, Father?"

"There's not much stopping me from just taking that map and finishing the lot of you off," John said.

"Just shoot him!" Leon said.

"I'll make that call!" John shouted. "He's my son and I'm The Boss. Don't you forget it!"

Isaac recognized that face. His father was about to unleash his rage. Isaac took the flask and unscrewed the lid. "Might as well." He took a sip and swished the contents in his mouth.

"I'm sick of this! He's only important when it suits. Just shoot the fucker!" Leon yelled.

John stormed over to Leon and grabbed him by the throat. Isaac seized the opportunity to shred the map. He quickly tore at it, scrunched it up into pieces then stuffed them into his mouth and chewed. He wanted to gag. The foul, dry texture soaked up any moisture from his mouth. He took another sip of the rum.

"Boss!" the tall, hairy man shouted.

"What?" John yelled. He held Leon in his grasp and snapped his head to see. "What in the..." He dropped Leon.

Isaac stuffed another piece in and chewed. Then spat the gnawed contents on the ground. He coughed and spluttered. John grabbed Isaac by the scruff of the neck and shook him. His chest heaved with rage. His face turned red. He pressed a pistol barrel into Isaac's stomach.

"Now I'm the only one who knows the location, so you'd better listen to me," Isaac said.

"I should kill you now." His father's gaze didn't falter. He looked him hard in the eye and pressed the barrel deeper.

"But you want that treasure," Isaac said. He knew it was a risk, but he was out of options. He hoped somewhere deep down inside his own father couldn't actually kill him. "Take me with you but let them go."

John released his grip and took a long deep breath in. He swung around and looked at the faces of his men. A few sprinted off in the direction of the castle. They clearly couldn't wait anymore.

"Let's torture him, he'll speak up then," Leon said.

"I'll speak anyway, you just have to let them live. Why are you so intent on killing everyone?" Isaac yelled.

John paced, his eyes seemed to be searching for answers. Isaac didn't want to give him too much time.

"You have my word. I'll join your crew, lead you to the treasure but you have to let them live. All of them." Isaac waved his hand. "We'll be famous."

Isaac looked at Joy's beautiful, soft face. Blood trickled down her cheek. She stared at John with hard, unfaltering eyes. He looked to Crow. He'd kept his chest and head held high this whole time. A wry smile spread across his face. Death didn't frighten him. He was a brave man and more of a father to him than this prick ever would be. It was then he realized that, for the first time in his life, he cared about someone other than himself. These people were his friends, his family even, and he knew that to save them he would sacrifice the world. His world. "Father, what do you say?"

John walked toward Isaac. "My son, a Serpent of Death, who'd have thought?"

Leon threw down his club and spat.

John looked Isaac up and down. "You'll join my crew alright, but you'll never so much as even look in their direction again. They're dead as far as you're concerned! Hear me?"

Isaac nodded.

"Ya can't possibly believe him!" Leon shouted and shot John a glare.

"He'll help us find it, Leon. You mark my words, because if he doesn't, I'll hunt each of them down and strangle them to death myself." He pointed to Crow then Joy and turned to Isaac.

He grinned. Something in that smile unnerved Isaac, but he had no choice. "Now, lead the pillage of Thad's place and reserve the finest cell on the ship for this one." John pushed Isaac toward Leon.

"What?" Isaac said as two men grabbed his arms. "But I thought..."

"Thought what? You'd be roaming the ship free? You might be my son but I'm no idiot," John said and scowled at Isaac. "I'll keep up my end of the bargain for now, but you'll need to earn my trust."

Isaac's insides wrenched. "Still the bastard you always were," he uttered under his breath.

"We set sail tomorrow." John rubbed his hands. "Cut them loose." He waved in the direction of Crow and Joy and the others. "Now, run! Before I change my mind."

Crow and Joy scrambled to their feet and glanced in Isaac's direction.

"I said run! And don't cause me any trouble again!" He prodded Molly's broken, limp body with his foot. "I got what I wanted."

Isaac's feet dragged in the mud as two men pulled him away, and he watched his friends sprint off into the distance for the last time.

JOY LAFITTE

Joy took a sip from her rum-filled cup. Her eyes fixed on an intricate naval painting and moved across to the navy drapes which sheltered them from the searing sun.

Vella's house didn't quite match what Joy knew of Vella, but then again she hoped her house didn't match what people knew of her, just for very different reasons.

"So that's it? He's part of their crew now?" Popino asked and interrupted Joy's daydream. Her heart filled with sadness at the memory of Isaac being dragged away.

"They'll be going to Devil's Cay so hopefully we can rescue him there," Joy said and nodded as if trying to convince herself.

"We'll get him back," Slim said and kept his head down. He didn't move his eyes from the map as he busied himself plotting points. "Get me brother too."

Georgia poked her head around the door. "How's the patient?" she smiled at Popino.

"Getting there," Popino said and returned the smile though it didn't seem sincere.

He had moved from a makeshift bed to an armchair.

Joy noticed the way Georgia eyed him. She could tell her behavior made Popino feel uncomfortable and that amused her since he was usually so obsessed with women. Georgia shot Popino a wink and disappeared.

"I can't believe that man is Isaac's father. I don't even remember what he looks like. Did they mention Rose?" Popino wrung his hands together.

Joy shook her head. "Maybe Isaac will find her before we do." She forced a smile.

"Let's hope." Popino nodded. He shut his eyes and let out a sigh. "And where's Crow?"

"Gone to check on the ship," Joy said.

"Black Beauty. She's a delight. You wait until you see her." Slim stared off wistfully into the distance.

"I think I did." Joy put her cup aside and took off her hat. "It's not in great shape but those doubloons should help with that." She walked over to a polished copper pot which sat on a shelf. She had avoided checking her reflection up until now. The gash on her cheek still stung and though she'd cleaned it up, it wasn't pretty.

"It will fade," Popino said. Joy swung around and shrugged. She strode over to the seat next to Popino and sat down. She hated that she had a permanent reminder of Leon across her face. She bit her lip and tapped on her cup of rum.

"You know what there is in Devil's Cay, Miss Joy?" Slim said and rubbed his hands together.

Popino shook his head and leaned across to Joy. He spoke under his breath. "Do we really need him?"

"Melons!" Slim said.

Joy let out a huge, hearty laugh for the first time in a long time.

423

Slim was odd but he certainly lightened the mood. "You love those melons don't you, Slim?"

"Oh, Miss Joy, I long for another taste of that juicy fruit!" Slim licked his lips.

"Soon enough," Joy said. She welcomed the distraction.

Popino rolled his eyes. "Again with the melon talk!"

"You're just jealous," Slim replied and jigged in his seat.

Without warning, the door slammed open. Joy instinctively grabbed her blade, jumped to her feet and tensed, ready for action, only to see Crow standing there with his fists clenched.

"I can't." Crow stomped his way into the room. He switched between punching the air and rubbing at his head with his hands.

"Can't what?" Joy poured him a cup of rum and thrust it into his hand. He looked down and shook his head. "Whatever it is, this will make you feel better," Joy said.

Crow took a gulp and wiped at his mouth with the back of his hand.

"Is it... Isaac?" His name escaped her mouth, and instantly she wanted to take it back. She didn't want to hear what might have happened to him.

Crow shook his head. His eyes looked red as if he'd been crying.

"It's not the boy." Crow gulped the remainder of the rum down. "Top her up. I can't..." He shook his head.

"Just tell us!" Popino shouted. "Sorry, I just can't take much more. I don't think any of us can."

"It's Black Beauty. She's gone." Crow stared ahead dead-eyed.

"Gone? Stolen?" Joy asked.

"Burnt to a crisp. Woodman Jack too," Crow replied.

Joy's eyes grew wide. She looked at Popino whose face reflected her own.

"I liked Jack," Slim said. The corners of his mouth turned down.

"He was a creep, but he didn't deserve that. I'm guessing we know who's responsible?" Joy said. Her hands shook as she tried to keep calm. She was so close. They were so close. She swallowed the mounting lump in her throat. Crow handed her a piece of paper and took off his hat. She fumbled to open the note. Inside was a rough sketch of a human skull with three snakes slithering in and out of the eye holes and mouth. She read the words written underneath aloud, "Serpents of Death." She tossed the paper onto the nearby table. "Fuck them! I swear I'll hunt down those... those…"

Crow covered his face with his hat and screamed. Joy raised her brows and looked to the floor as the captain screamed again. He took away his hat and swiped the bottle of rum then tipped the contents into his mouth and slumped down against the wall.

The room fell silent.

"Those bastards." Slim sat back in his chair and folded his arms.

Joy paced back and forth across the room trying to muster a clear thought, but nothing came to mind other than fury. She looked to Crow who sat with his head between his knees.

"What are we going to do without a ship?" Popino put his hand to his chest.

Crow shook his head. His eyes looked glassy. "We're fucked!" he shouted.

Joy puffed out her cheeks and let the air escape slowly. She hadn't ever heard the captain sound so defeated.

She plonked herself down in the chair next to Popino and put her head in her hands.

"I've got an idea," Slim said and pushed the map aside.

"Please don't let it involve melons," Popino half joked.

Joy looked up. "What is it, Slim? Go on." She looked him in the eye and nodded in encouragement.

"You've got that coin, Miss Joy, the one from Jane." Slim sat forward and looked around as if checking for people listening. "We could borrow a ship with it." He sat back, his eyes shining with mischief. "How about The Fancy?"

Joy's brows dipped to a frown. "Jane's dead though. That coin's only good if people can call in a favor from her." Joy took out the small silver coin and placed the button-sized piece in her palm. She stared down and wondered what Jane would do.

"Why The Fancy? It's huge. Couldn't we get something that needs a smaller crew?" Popino said.

"It's Jane's ship." Slim crossed his arms and smiled.

Joy raised her brows in surprise. The rumor was The Fancy belonged to the governor. How had Jane come to acquire such a ship, she wondered. "I can't believe it's her ship," she said under her breath.

Slim nodded.

Joy shook off the surprise. "But they'll know, her people will know?" she said.

"Word won't have spread yet." Slim shook his head. "It will just be a rumor. She's just missing for now. We ask for one week, but then we steal it!" Slim pointed his bony finger into the air and grinned.

Joy's mouth fell open, stunned. "That's—"

"Genius!" Crow scrambled to his feet. "I don't know what this coin is but looks like we're going to Devil's Cay." He walked over and slapped Slim on the back.

"You think it will work, Slim?" Joy walked over to him.

"Oh yes, Miss Joy," Slim replied and grabbed the map. "I've plotted the route there, but it won't be an easy ride." He rolled up the parchment and clutched the scroll in his hand. "There will be foul sea beasts like nothing you've ever seen before. Waves so high they could engulf all of Nassau, but don't let that scare you." He grinned.

"Okay," Popino nodded, his face looked doubtful.

"I'm not scared. I'm sick of this life on land anyway." Crow gave Slim a nudge. "Right, I've got a crew to assemble!" Crow smacked his hands together and gave them a rub. "You'll be the second best crew I've ever had!"

Popino scrunched up his face. "Thanks?"

"We're back!" Crow slapped Slim across the back and laughed. Slim rocked forward with the force. "Meet me down at The Fancy in four hours, we'll leave right away!"

Joy took in a deep breath as she walked down the dock toward The Fancy. She'd never sailed before but the idea sparked a fire inside her. Though her heart pinched at the thought of leaving Raven for so long, at least Tom and Jim would keep a close eye on her, she reassured herself as she leapt over a hole in the timber jetty.

As she drew closer, she marveled at the magnificence of the vessel they were about to acquire. She squeezed the coin in her palm and jogged down the dock only to find Crow and Popino already loading up the ship.

"What's going on? How are you—"

"Nice of you to join us," Popino said. He clutched at his side with one hand and pushed items over to Crow with the other.

Crow turned to face Joy. "It's ours! Well, for now." He winked. "He needs to see the coin." Crow motioned to where a short, balding man stood holding his hat with both hands looking rather shaken.

"I told Richard you've the coin. I know him from working down here," Popino said.

Crow rolled his eyes and mocked Popino.

Joy shook her head at the pair and walked over to Richard.

"Miss Joy, I assume?" the balding man asked in a soft voice, his gaze fixed on the ground.

"Indeed I am." She smiled and tried to catch his eye which seemed to put him at ease.

"Please tell me you have the coin?" He looked around. "Popino told me you did but that man—"

"Of course!" Joy held out the silver in her outstretched palm.

"Sorry, just that man, he's erm… quite forceful. Threatened me then just started loading stuff on but Popino said you'd make it right. I know him from working down here, on the docks." Richard scratched at his arm.

Joy nodded.

"I've looked after her—the ship—for some time for Miss Hatch but never had the chance to speak with her." He looked to the floor. "I could use that favor. We… my family could," Richard said.

Joy's heart sank. She wanted to ask why, or what he needed, but by the same token she didn't want to know. She reminded herself the reason she was doing this—for Raven, for Rose, for all those other children, and now for Isaac too. She looked into Richard's eyes, all filled with hope at the prospect of having his moment with Jane.

"Hang on." She reached into her jacket and retrieved

her remaining coins, then took Richard's hand and pressed them into it along with the small piece of silver.

He opened up his hand and stared down. "What's these for?"

"For your troubles. Letting us borrow the ship. Putting up with him." She motioned with her head to Crow.

"Oh, it's really no problem, this is too much. My time with Miss Hatch is all I need." He held out the glinting, golden doubloons to Joy.

Joy put her hands up. "I insist, I'm not taking them back."

"Well, if you say so, Miss. Thank you." He bowed his head in respect.

Joy forced a smile and turned on her heel. She felt bad but hopefully that would soften the blow. Killing bad people for coin was one thing but stealing from regular townsfolk just didn't sit right.

Crow waved for Joy to hurry. "We're all ready!" In what short time she'd known him, she had never seen him so full of life.

"That didn't feel good," Joy said as Crow held out his hand to help her aboard. "Pff! Please." She swiped his hand away and rolled her eyes.

"Worth a try," Crow replied and stroked at his beard. "This way."

He walked toward the stern of the ship where the wheel was positioned. Joy followed closely. She recognized some of the crew as they scaled the nets and wound in ropes ready to set sail. A few gave her a nod, a few leered. "Down here." Crow ducked and headed through a door. He turned to her, "Captain's Quarters." She could tell he was proud. Joy followed him into quite a grand room. She hadn't expected anything like this on board a ship.

She saw a table that could easily seat ten people and around it she recognized familiar faces—Popino, Slim and...

"Grimm?" She cocked her head to the side.

"Miss Lafitte." Grimm raised his glass and gave her a nod. "You can have a seat next to me if you like?"

"You're no pirate!" Joy said.

"And neither are you." Grimm smiled and tapped the seat next to him. "Drink?"

"Sure." Joy took a seat opposite Grimm and looked around at several new faces.

Grimm poured two glasses of wine and handed one to Joy and one to Crow. "We start with the good stuff, save that god awful grog for when we no longer care."

Crow stood at the head of the table. "I'll make the introductions for our new crew." He nodded toward Joy then Popino.

Joy sat back in her seat and sipped at the fruity liquid.

Crow raised his glass. "We have Slim, our Sailingmaster. He knows these waters like no other and is a keen shot too." He spoke with such vigor that the liquid spilled from the cup with each sentence. "Next we have Grimm, our Master Gunner. We're a little light on weapons but you'll make good with what we've got." Crow took a sip of his drink. "Don't play cards with him though. You'll always lose." Crow laughed and spluttered a little as some of the liquid went down the wrong way.

Joy's brows dipped to a frown. "Master Gunner?" she mouthed then raised one of her lowered brows in Grimm's direction.

"Who's next?" Crow brushed the spilt wine from his

beard. "Ah, Grieves! It's been a while since we've had you to run the ship. If the rum runs out, we know who to come looking for."

Joy stared at the broad-shouldered man sitting opposite her. His arms were the size of two thighs. Only someone of Molly's stature compared. Joy felt a twinge at the thought of her. She hadn't deserved that ending.

Grieves gave Crow a nod and topped up his glass which his massive hand dwarfed. At the far end of the table, a woman with pale green eyes and long, black hair sat with her hands clasped in her lap. Joy marveled at her posture. She held herself with an air of calm, yet Joy could see a fire in her eyes. Next to her sat a slight man wearing a bright blue hat. He surely wasn't a pirate. Neither of these two were, Joy thought, though they were probably thinking the same of her.

The blue-hatted man put down the sketchbook he was holding and looked straight at Joy. His gaze was piercing. She wasn't sure where to look.

"Right..." Crow looked around. "Arnaud! This one won't be getting his hands dirty, but he's our thinker. Our spy. Them clothes are too nice to mess up anyway." Crow grinned.

"They certainly are," Arnaud said. He tipped his bright blue hat, crossed his legs and sat back. He still hadn't taken his gaze off of Joy but it didn't bother her. He didn't seem in the least bit threatening and in truth he was rather good looking.

Crow walked over to the woman with long, black hair and placed his hand on her shoulder. She didn't move. "Fiona, the first woman to ever become part of my crew. I took some flack for that one but I'm glad I did." Crow patted at her shoulder. Fiona didn't make any expression.

She kept a steely gaze. Crow scrunched up his face. "Where's—"

"Under the table," Fiona replied.

Crow lifted the tablecloth and motioned for who or whatever it was to come out.

A small woman crawled out and sprang to her feet.

"I know you!" Joy said. She hadn't meant to speak aloud but the surprise forced the words out.

"Nipper's like you with them blades." He nodded at Joy. "Our very own surgeon too. Hopefully that won't be needed though," Crow said and scratched at his beard. He looked to an empty seat next to him. His eyes glazed over as he reached into his pocket and retrieved a burgundy bandana. He gave it a shake and placed it on the chair then took off his hat and bowed his head.

"Finally, let us raise a glass to Nelson. Gone but not forgotten." Crow rushed the words. Joy could tell he was struggling to keep it together.

"He'll always be with us. He would've loved to get a taste of melon," Slim said.

Crow nodded. "He would."

Grieves cocked his head to the side.

"It's a big fruit," Joy said.

"Miss Joy tried some, didn't you?" Slim said.

Joy's cheeks flushed with embarrassment at the attention. She usually brimmed with confidence but for once she felt surrounded by people that might well be more skilled than her.

"Ah the beautiful Miss Joy, we welcome you. I'm sure you'll fit right in. Can kill a man in a heartbeat, so I wouldn't try anything." Crow raised his glass in her direction and took a sip.

Popino coughed. "Leaving the best till last?"

Joy rolled her eyes at Popino's confidence, though it did bring a smile to her face, as did Crow's introduction. She wasn't usually proud of what she did for a living.

"Oh, I haven't forgotten about you," Crow said and took a gulp of his wine. "I spent a lot of years hating you but luckily that friend of yours set things right."

Popino shifted in his seat.

"This one's a good thief, though I'm assured those ways have changed. Good at getting hurt too." Crow gave a chuckle.

"And handsome," Arnaud added.

"I'll say," Fiona said. She kept her icy gaze, but this time focused it on Popino. "Where's the friend?"

"Devil's Cay. My daughter too." Joy could see the light fade from Popino at the very mention.

"We'll get him back, the girl too. We wouldn't be on this ship if it weren't for the boy. Let's drink to him too. To Isaac!" Crow raised his glass and downed the contents.

"To Isaac," Joy said softly. She hadn't expected to miss him half as much as she did.

"To Isaac indeed!" a voice came from the doorway.

Joy sat bolt up-right in her seat. It couldn't be? She turned around to see a rather disheveled Isaac practically jump through the door with flagons in each hand.

"Isaac!" Joy yelled. She couldn't get out of her seat quick enough.

Popino and Joy both ran over and threw their arms around him.

"I've never been so happy to see you. My god you stink." Popino turned away and scrunched up his face.

"You weren't going to leave without me now, were you?" Isaac laughed. He squeezed Joy tighter than he ever had. She let go and looked at his face.

"Did you see her?" Joy asked.

Popino's eyes grew wide. "Isaac?"

Isaac shook his head. "Rose is already on her way to Devil's Cay, they sent her on another ship. I'm sorry, Pino," Isaac said.

Popino shut his eyes and nodded.

Joy returned to her seat. She needed to sit down. She couldn't believe he was here. She couldn't believe how she felt.

"Looks like Popino has competition," Fiona said under her breath and leaned into Arnaud.

Joy did her best not to react to the comment. It wasn't as if her and Isaac were even a thing anymore. She re-adjusted her jacket and tried not to seem ruffled.

"Grieves! I thought you died in the brothel!" Isaac said.

"Came close," Grieves replied. He had a much more jovial voice than Joy had expected.

"Arnaud! I wouldn't have expected to see you here." Isaac grinned. "I'm sorry about Margaret."

Arnaud nodded and rubbed a gold locket which sat around his neck.

Joy looked to Crow who hadn't said anything. He shook his head and combed his hand through his beard.

"You not pleased to see me, Crow?" Isaac joked.

Crow continued to shake his head. "How?" His eyes crinkled so much that they almost disappeared.

"Let's just say I used a trick I learned from a good friend." Isaac winked.

"Of course you did!" Crow grinned and strode over to Isaac. Joy could tell he was proud.

"He means me!" Popino said.

"I don't think so," Crow replied.

Isaac laughed. "You'd never believe it..." He pulled on

his shirt which was a bit too tight for him. He sniffed at the air. "What's that?"

His face dropped.

An older lady appeared. She walked with a stick and brought an air of musk and smoke with her.

"You!" Isaac said.

"Bonjour, mon cher," the lady spoke with a husky French accent. She grabbed Isaac's arm and squeezed then brushed her body up close to him and shuffled past.

"You were right!" Isaac said.

"Of course." She coughed and hobbled over to a seat in the corner.

"Those cards, the crow, the dog missing a leg, the biting snake!" Isaac blurted his words out faster than Joy had ever heard him speak. "Why didn't you tell me more?"

"That wouldn't be any fun now, would it?" She shot Isaac a wink.

Crow laughed. "Pont Neuf is always right, boy, and we never set sail without her. Glad you could make it at such short notice."

"I knew I'd be needed. I was ready." Pont Neuf caught her breath. Grieves rushed over to her with a drink. "Merci. We must cast off, Captain."

"Right you are!" Crow rubbed his hands together and made for the door.

Joy looked to Isaac. Something in his eyes seemed different. There was a light in them that hadn't been there in all the years she had known him.

"Who's ready for an adventure?" Isaac grinned. "Before you go... Captain." Isaac reached for Crow's arm and caught it. "Weren't we going to flip on that?"

Isaac pulled out a silver coin and held it up to Crow.

"In your dreams!" Crow replied.

435

"But you're a man of your word." Isaac put his hand to his chest and feigned shock.

Crow paused for a moment. A deep ridge set in between his brows. "Quartermaster?" His face softened and his eyes crinkled.

"Deal." Isaac smiled and followed Crow out. "I mean, I don't know what one does, but sure."

ABOUT THE AUTHORS

Together, Sophie and Chris Brousseau form Maple Lion Fiction; a husband and wife writing team with a passion for humorous storytelling and adventure.

Chris hails from Timmins in Northern Canada and Sophie from East Yorkshire in the UK. They met and lived for many years in sunny Melbourne, Australia but have recently relocated to London (the UK one, there's one in Canada too!).

If you're now wondering how on earth we write together, what we argue over (our most asked question) or who does what, head on over to www.maplelionfiction.com and sign up for our monthly newsletter where we share all.

Or come connect with us on your social media of choice @maplelionfiction and follow our progress as we write our next story.

AUTHORS' NOTE

It was the cold Canadian spring of 2011. Game of Thrones had just aired, and Chris' mind was swimming with ideas. You see, there was a distinct lack of pirate TV shows. He recalled how he loved the first Pirates of the Caribbean movie, how the pirate world was portrayed as a dark, savage yet humorous world, plus he'd always wanted to write a book. So, he decided to combine George R.R. Martin's style of writing multiple characters all with an intertwining story, write it in TV show like episodes and set it in a pirate world. He wrote around fifteen chapters worth and created a bunch of characters most of whom you've read in this book and then life took over...

Fast forward to 2014, Chris had relocated to Melbourne, Australia and those drafts were sat in his google drive where they remained for many more years.

Enter Sophie, a born adventurer with an overactive imagination who when they met had never tried her hand at writing fiction. After getting hitched they decided to work on a project together but didn't quite know what. When Chris mentioned the draft and the pirate world,

Sophie jumped at the chance to read it. She promptly killed off a couple of characters and together they created Molly. Chris finally finished that first draft and Sophie then got to writing a second draft, then a third... and the rest is what you read today.

We wanted the world to capture an 'old school' adventure. Something reminiscent of the eighties and early nineties adventure films we both loved growing up. Plus, there is something about pirates as characters that has always appealed to us. They can be kooky and cutthroat, unpredictably dangerous yet democratic, all great qualities for a rollercoaster of a story.

We hope you enjoyed your time on the *Isle of Chaos.*

Until the next adventure...